MODEL
BOYFRIEND

STUART REARDON
JANE HARVEY-BERRICK

DEDICATION

To Mum and Dad—for bringing me into this world.

Stu x

REVIEWS

We really hope that you enjoy this story. Reviews tell us that you've enjoyed the story, which is fantastic! But they also helps other people to make an informed decision before buying this book.

So we'd really appreciate if you took a few seconds to do just that when you've finished reading the final part of Nick and Anna's story. Thank you!

Stu x

MODEL
BOYFRIEND

ANNA'S PROLOGUE

HE'S SLIPPING AWAY FROM ME, I can feel it. But how do I hold onto a man like him, a man like Nick Renshaw? One of the most famous sportsmen in the world, a champion.

They say that if you love someone, you should set them free.

So that's what I'm doing—I'm letting him go, setting him free.

And praying that one day he comes back to me.

NICK'S PROLOGUE

I FEEL LOST. LIKE I DON'T KNOW WHO I am, like I don't know where I fit into this world. What's my purpose?

I'm 33, so it's about 30 years too early to start collecting my pension. Ha bloody ha.

I can't believe I'm actually here at this moment in my career, my last game.

My Testimonial.

Sixteen years, and it's gone by so fast, too fast. Sixteen amazing, testing years; teaching me, shaping me into the man I was destined to become, the man I was meant to be.

But what's next? What am I going to do now?

When I was just breaking into my first team, a fresh-faced kid of 18, I had a teammate named Scott Nadler, who was one of the senior players. He was a great guy who guided me and gave me some good advice (starting with not to hang my clothes on his peg—players are very territorial about their spot in the changing rooms so you've got to earn your place).

"Enjoy this," said Scott. "Try be present in every moment: in rugby, in sport, in life, because it can pass you by in a blink of an eye, if you let it. When your career is nearing the end, you'll wish you could do it all over again, only better, stronger, smarter … and injury free."

I didn't really know what to say so I laughed.

"Don't be daft, Scotty! You've got plenty of seasons left in the tank."

Of course he hadn't, and that turned out to be his last year of playing.

But his words stuck with me. But it was only when I was older and wiser that I really understood what he meant. All players worry about the game we just played; then we worry about the future and how we're going to play; instead of being conscious in the now, in the present moment with all our senses—just breathe, relax and enjoy being alive. Easy to say, hard to do. It's one of our biggest weaknesses.

It's funny how things work out. Advice given years earlier only makes sense when your experiences have made you wise enough to truly understand what it all meant. God, that makes me sound old! But these days 33 feels ancient.

Looking back, as a young player it seemed like the seniors would always moan about recovering more slowly as they got older, always hurt, the body just not being able to do what it used to do.

They would have a laugh with us young lads, "These kids don't know how good they have it! Take a long look, young whipper snapper, because you've got this to look forward to!"

Then they'd show all their ailments: bust up hands, broken noses, funny fingers that had healed crooked; always in first for physio and massages.

And now I'm one of them.

Rugby is a bloody tough game—the human body can only take so much impact, so much trauma, so much punishment, before it starts to scream *No More!* Even then, it's hard to handle because, as athletes, we won't accept it. Even when you know it's time, you refuse to believe that your body is broken. Your mind is strong, so you carry on for as many seasons as you can. You take painkillers to get you through the games: paracetamol, ibuprofen, tramadol, cortisone injections: any concoction the doctor can give. Post-game, we take sleeping tablets or diazepam in case the painkillers wear off during the night while we sleep and try recover.

With all the injuries I've had, I should be glad it's my last game, but deep down I'm not. I don't know what I'm going to do next—midlife crisis here I come. It's like leaving home again—I'm leaving the comfort of team sport, leaving the lads I've grown to call brothers, leaving the commitment, the comradery, the lifestyle, the sense of being a part of something bigger than myself. I feel empty.

Snap out of this! You knew this day would come, and there's more to life than playing rugby. I've got a life with Anna. Life off the field is good.

But what the hell am I going to do?

I need to relax. My testimonial board—the team of people organising this event—have done all the hard work for me. They have arranged everything right down to the post-game meal and celebrations. All I need to do is show up at these last two weeks of training sessions, put in the work with the boys, and enjoy this game. My team and the opposition team will be made up of friends, teammates and former teammates. It'll be amazing.

My last game. That sounds so weird.

I know it's natural to feel like this, because playing rugby is all I've ever known. I'm institutionalized. My whole adult life has been dedicated to this, to this lifestyle.

I keep trying to get out of my own head. Who needs critics when you wrestle with your own personality on a daily basis? I'm my own worst nightmare sometimes. I swear, playing this game makes us all crazy. Probably just too many knocks to the head. I'm joking. Maybe.

I'm sure Anna would analyze it all for me if I told her. But it seems too weak to share all this crap I have going around inside me. I need to focus on the here and now, not worry about everything else.

Only one fortnight of team practices to go.

I'm nervous but not in the usual way. The testimonial isn't about winning or losing—it's about respect and honour among brothers.

I've played in testimonial games for other players. Now I'm joining the retirement list.

There are no trophies, no anticipation of winning, no disappointment of losing—it's just about putting on a great performance.

Who am I kidding? I'm playing to win: I always do.

CHAPTER 1

THE TRAINING SESSIONS HAD BEEN going well all week. The lads for Nick's testimonial were enjoying being back with old teammates and rivals, back where they'd felt most alive. Some of them were still playing professionally, but the rest were already enjoying their retirement, if that was the right word. Fit, active men in their thirties—all retired. But the competitive spirit never left them, even when they left the game professionally.

Perhaps being a rugby player is a rite of passage where the sport becomes your identity, your skin, embedded in your heart and deep in your blood—so it never leaves you.

Nick felt it—that his whole identity was wrapped up in the sport that he'd loved for so long.

He shook his head to clear the rolling, twisting thoughts.

Enough! I'm getting sentimental in my old age, he thought with a sigh.

He glanced around the locker room with a feeling of pride and gratitude as friends, colleagues and former teammates changed into their shorts, shirts and boots, and … what the hell?

He did a double-take when he saw another face from his past: Kenny Johnson.

With a jet of fury that took his breath away, Nick was sent spinning back to the day when Kenny had destroyed their friendship and killed his trust; the day he'd seen Kenny screwing his ex-fiancée. The Best Man and the Bride-to-Be.

For a split second, the sense of betrayal was fresh and raw.

As Nick stared at his former friend, Kenny walked toward him, his expression unsure, as if Nick might lunge and beat the shit out of him—an act that had landed Nick in court five years ago, with a criminal record to match.

Kenny had broken the guy-code.

Nick stared at the other man's broken nose and worn, battered face, surprised to see remorse in Kenny's eyes. Nick thought about what it must have cost Kenny in pride, to come here today, into the lion's den.

The two men locked eyes, a thousand unsaid words roaring through the air, but then Nick blew out a long breath. Ultimately, Kenny had done Nick a favour by showing him that Molly was a liar and a cheat. It also meant that Nick had gone on to have a relationship with Anna, well, there was no comparison. He loved Anna with his whole being; Molly was nothing but a dark stain on his memory.

He hadn't seen either of them in years.

One of the other players saw Kenny and called out.

"Ken, you mad sort! What are you doing here?"

Kenny forced a grin.

"Hey up, lads, you're looking good out there. Some of you have still got it and some of you never had it, eh?"

"Piss off, Ken, you big pudding!" snorted Tufty, who was probably twenty pounds heavier since he'd retired. "I'll show you what I've got!"

"In your dreams, ya sausage!" Kenny turned away, his smile fading as he met Nick's frown. "You got time for a quick chat?"

Nick could see the hopeful expression on his face, the regret. He remembered that they'd been friends, mates, before Kenny had betrayed him. He decided that he wanted to hear what the man had to say.

So did everyone else in the locker room if the covert looks and sly glances were anything to go by. They all knew what had happened between Nick and Kenny.

Nick nodded.

"Sure, let's go for a walk." Then he turned to the other players. "Lads, top session! I'll catch up with you in the clubhouse. First pint on me."

Nick walked out of the room in silence followed by Kenny, and they headed to the Stands, staring out at the vast stadium, the rows of empty seats.

The silence grew uncomfortable as Nick waited for Kenny to speak.

"I never got to play here," said Kenny, hesitant, awed, and Nick could hear the wistfulness in his voice. "Not like you. You've had an amazing career—you were always the one, old golden balls," and he laughed sadly. "But that's not why I'm here." He sighed. "It's been a long time…"

Nick nodded, but didn't speak.

Kenny grimaced and stumbled on, his words coming slowly and awkwardly.

"I know I'm not your favourite person. I wouldn't blame you if you hated me. If it had been the other way around, well, I wouldn't have pissed in your ear if you'd been on fire."

Nick turned away.

"I'd never have done that to a friend," Nick said quietly but firmly. "Friendship means something to me, not just words."

Kenny dropped his eyes to the ground, shoving his hands in his pockets and shuffling his feet.

"I know. Believe me, I know," and he raised his eyes to meet Nick's stony stare. "But I just wanted to say I'm sorry for what happened. I should have known better, I should have been better. I'm not perfect, who is? But we all make mistakes—and that was the worst one of my whole life—I lost my best friend." He hunched his shoulders. "Anyway, so what I'm saying, the past is the past. And I can't change it, but I want to make things right, as much as I can. I'm so fucking sorry for what I did. I've regretted it every day since." He squared his shoulders. "I'm here because I want to play—I want to show my respect for your career by playing in your testimonial." He paused. "If you'll have me?"

Nick hesitated, seeing two roads ahead of him. He could carry on hating Kenny for what he did five years ago, or he could accept his apology and move on. It could never be the way it had been, but maybe it was time to let it go.

"Yeah," said Nick slowly. "It's been a long time, Ken. "We've known each other a lot of years. I'm not the type to hold a grudge, but what you did and what happened to me as a consequence of your actions—and my actions—can't be undone. We can't go back to how we were, the trust is gone."

Kenny lowered his head, shame colouring his roughened features.

Nick took a deep breath.

"I can't play alongside you again, we'll never be teammates, but I appreciate you stepping up and wanting to take part. I'm sure Coach will be happy to have you in the opposing side. I'll let him know you're available. I accept your apology."

Kenny swallowed as Nick held out his hand.

"Thanks, mate. That's … well, thank you."

"I'm in a good place now," said Nick quietly as they shook hands. "I think things happen for a reason."

AT THE END OF the following week, Brian Noble, the coach who'd volunteered to train the teams for the testimonial, gathered them all together. Including Kenny.

"That's the last session down. Well done, lads. It's been a pleasure working with you this fortnight. I'm impressed … and surprised how some of you got through the last few days of training."

He pointed at the group of older players who'd been retired a while, and they laughed, chucking towels at his head.

"Twickenham is a sell-out for our Nick, so if there's ever a place for ex-teammates to settle any beef between each other, it's on that field, in front of a sell-out crowd."

Kenny joined in the laughter, but Nick caught his faint grimace.

It had been a challenging week for him, and a few of Nick's teammates had given him a hard time, but he'd toughed it out.

"See you all on Saturday!"

NICK ARRIVED AT THE stadium over an hour before the other players. Anna had offered to come with him, but she also understood when he told her that he needed to do this for himself.

As he walked along those empty corridors, his footsteps echoed, surrounded with all the incredible memories—the crowds, the cheers, the electric atmosphere, the emotions, the sense of pride and achievement, winning the World Cup twice, the pinnacle of his career. And now, it was the last time that he'd play here. It didn't seem real.

The locker room smelled of pine-scented disinfectant. The team's shirts were already hanging in place. Nick walked around the room, touching them with a sense of awe, a tug of sadness. After today, he was on the outside. If he ever came back to visit, he'd be the one watching all the action, but no longer part of it. He was benched for the rest of his life.

When he reached the iconic number 17 shirt, his shirt, he sat down with heavy thoughts, memories filling his mind.

He forced himself to think about today's game. He was genuinely excited to play.

In theory, the game would be more relaxed than competition games, but he knew that as soon as the first bone-crushing tackle went in, as athletes, every one of them would want to win.

He picked up his kitbag and pulled out his lucky Speedos. They looked a bit threadbare these days because he'd worn them in every game since Anna had given them to him. He'd be wearing them today.

As he unfolded the Speedos, a note fluttered to the floor. He picked it up, brushing the crumpled paper flat, then reading the looping, handwritten words.

My darling Nick,
Enjoy today, my love. You deserve this. You've worked so hard to get here, on and off the field. Be yourself. Be amazing.
I love you,
A x

PS Don't get injured!

He smiled at the postscript. No, he definitely wasn't going to get injured today.

It was a small moment of peace, a few seconds of calm in what would be a crazy day.

The locker room began to fill up, first with the physios and then all the other players.

Over the next few hours before the game, Nick hardly had a moment to think. He had Press interviews, friends and former teammates to say hello to and reminisce for a few minutes, the joys and sorrows of shared experiences, a shared life.

The England manager Eddie Jones was there, along with Nick's friend from the Phoenixes, Jason Oduba, who should have been playing but had picked up a groin strain. Young Ben Richards was there, shy and quiet, a new signing for the Phoenixes. It seemed right to Nick to have a rookie playing—a way of passing the torch, perhaps.

He also had a meet and greet with the Chief Executive of West Bowing RFU, the amateur club he'd played in as a kid. He was donating £100,000 of the gate money to them.

The man pumped his hand vigorously, emotion shining in his kind old eyes.

"Thank you so much! This means a lot to us, that you've remembered us. All the youngsters we'll be able to help with this money—you don't know what it means!"

Nick nodded, embarrassed, because he did know what £100,000 meant to a small amateur club.

He was happy to donate the money but truthfully it was no skin off his nose. It was either donate it or let the taxman take it.

A player was allowed to keep a certain sum from the ticket sales at his retirement testimonial game, but above that, it was taxable. Nick preferred that the money went to his old club. But the rest of the gate money was his—and it had to last the rest of his life.

It seemed like half the world wanted to shake his hand that day: old teammates, a few celebrities, friends, rivals, and of course, Kenny.

The guy was still a dickhead, but Nick had forgiven him, and that felt good.

He smirked at Nick, then sauntered over to shake hands, grinning as he took out his two front teeth, the result of an injury from a long-ago game.

"Give my regards to Anna."

Nick raised an eyebrow as he shook Kenny's hand.

"You can give them yourself later, but I can't guarantee she won't punch you in the face. Mate."

Kenny laughed and went to get changed.

The noise level in the locker room gradually escalated as the excitement and anticipation built. When no one was looking, Nick popped a tramadol into his mouth and swallowed it down with water, massaging his aching shoulder. So many injuries, so many surgeries—he should be glad this was over.

Finally, the coach told everyone to be quiet.

"Well, lads, you all know why you're here. I'll hand you over to your Captain for the last time, Nick Renshaw."

A ribald cheer went up, and Nick grinned at the sea of faces, eyeing him expectantly.

"Thanks for playing today, lads. I really appreciate your support. I know you're not getting paid for this, but I am."

Everyone laughed.

"I know it's a friendly, but let's be honest, there's no such thing as a friendly rugby game." There were nods and smiles all around. Nick gave an evil grin. "And the first person to smash Kenny gets a thousand pounds."

The look on Kenny's face was priceless—well, worth a grand, at least.

"All joking aside, enjoy the game and let's put on a real show for the fans. Rah! By the way, nobody is allowed to tackle me!"

With a final laugh and slaps on the back, they left the locker room.

Nick walked out onto the field, hand in hand with two ten year-old mascots, kids from his old amateur club. The look of awe on their young faces was another reminder of everything he was saying goodbye to.

The noise on the field was louder than a train rushing towards him, louder than a tsunami thundering down. From the darkness of the tunnel, he watched the cheerleaders dancing to *Let's Get Ready to Rumble* and smiled. *God, I'll miss this.*

Then as the teams strode onto the field, the music changed to Bowie's *Heroes*, the Phoenixes' theme tune, Nick's team for the last four years. A massive roar from the crowd, a wall of noise, drowned out the music, and they started to chant—82,000 fans on their feet: "Ren-*shaw!* Ren-*shaw!* Ren-*shaw!*"

Emotion hit Nick in the centre of his chest.

They're here for me...

It didn't seem real. He waved to the crowd, and the roar became deafening.

It was overwhelming, completely staggering. Nick had played for sell-out games, for national games, for World Cups, but he'd never experienced this, *and I never will again.* The mix of emotions was hard to explain, even harder to deal with.

It was intense, his heart racing, and the pride of that moment would stay with him his whole life.

He glanced toward where Anna was sitting with his family, catching a glimpse of her waving crazily, jumping up and down, her mouth opening and closing as she sang along with the crowd.

Unable to take it in, his emotions overloaded, Nick jogged into position, anticipation racing through his blood. The referee blew the whistle, and he did what he was born to do.

Two hours later, Nick was dripping with sweat, his lungs heaving, staring up at the fans who were on their feet, clapping and cheering, all chanting his name one final time: Ren-*shaw!* Ren-*shaw!* Ren-*shaw!*

The compere waved him to the side and held the microphone between them, his voice echoing around the massive stadium.

"Great game today, Nick! What a way to finish! I bet you couldn't have written it any better, selling out Twickenham! How does it feel to finish your career here?"

Nick closed his eyes briefly, his emotions intense, confused, in turmoil. He forced himself to focus, to do what was expected of him.

"Thank you, Jim. Thanks for your kind words." He forced a smile. "First of all, I'd like to thank everyone who turned out today, the fans, the coaches, the players—it's been good to see some old faces out here, and some new ones. A massive thank you to all my Board, all the organisers who've made this happen. I'm not quite sure how I feel: this place, this ground. Coming here as a young boy, then coming here as an adult and winning two World Cups..."

The crowd erupted, and Nick had to wait until the cheers died down so he could continue.

"It's hard to believe I won't be back. I've had an amazing career and been very fortunate. It takes more than one person to win a game and I've had a great team supporting me, and not just the other players. I'd like to thank my manager, my family, my coach, Eddie Jones—there are too many to mention, but you know who you are. Thank you! Nick Renshaw signing off—peace out, Twickenham!"

Nick waved at the fans and the crowd shouted his name again, for the final time.

As Nick left the field, the other players were standing in front of the tunnel, clapping and thumping him on the back as he walked between them. The ones who'd been through this already knew how he felt; the younger players just enjoyed the post-game euphoria.

Nick wished he could have just five minutes of silence to get his head together, but that wouldn't happen.

He glanced up at the family and friends box and saw Anna with his sister and parents, all waving wildly. Even from this distance, he could see that Anna was crying as she blew him kisses.

He waved back tiredly, took one last look at the stadium that had been his second home, then headed for the locker rooms.

Time for a series of hot showers and ice baths, one after the other, to speed up the healing process of microtrauma in his muscles.

He didn't need a physio today since he hadn't been injured, thank God. Anna wouldn't have been impressed if he'd limped off the field.

Instead of changing into casual clothes, he wore a suit, white shirt and dark tie. His unwashed number 17 shirt was stuffed into his kitbag. He'd decide what to do with it later. Some players kept their kit; some auctioned it off for charity.

Then, with the rest of his teammates, he headed to the bar, but was stopped fifty times along the way by people who wanted to shake his hand or pat him on the back. His was smiling when he entered the bar.

The first person he saw was his ex-fiancée. A woman he despised.

"What the fuck?"

Molly McKinney smiled at him, her icy blue eyes as cold as her personality.

The name brought many memories with it, most of them bad. Nick's scheming, cheating ex-fiancée had effectively ended Anna's career as a sports psychologist by selling information about Anna's illicit relationship with Nick to the Press.

When Anna had worked for the Finchley Phoenixes at the same time as Nick, the club had no-fraternization clauses in their contracts. She was fired as soon as the relationship became public.

Anna had also spent a night in a police cell because of Molly's lies—an accusation of perjury in court. It was later proved false, but by then the damage had been done.

Molly strutted toward him, her breasts even bigger than last time he saw them, almost falling out of the electric blue dress she wore.

"Hey, Nicky! Great game! You was awesome!"

She swooped in to kiss him, but Nick stepped back, stunned, his lip curling with distaste. She was the last person he'd expected to see.

"Are you here for Kenny?" he asked.

It wasn't an unreasonable question, but Molly's face turned red and her eyes narrowed.

"Are you having a laugh? That loser! I came for you, Nicky. Old times sake and all that … we was good together."

Luckily, the cavalry in the shape of Anna and Brendan arrived before Molly could annoy Nick even further.

"Love what you've done with your new tits," snarked Brendan. "Don't let the door hit you on your Kim Kardashian on the way out."

"What's she doing here?" Anna whispered.

Nick shook his head, bewildered.

"I have no idea," Nick said truthfully.

"I'd be happy to have her scrawny arse chucked out," Brendan offered eagerly.

For a second, Nick was tempted, but then he shook his head.

"Nah, she'd probably love making a scene. Just ignore her—she knows she's not welcome."

He glanced over to see Molly being tugged into a corner by Kenny, who seemed even less pleased to see her, if that was possible. They started a heated conversation as she yanked her arm free and poked him in the chest.

"Rather him than me," he muttered.

Someone thrust a glass of champagne into his hand and Nick forgot about Molly. The drinks kept arriving at his table, and the couple of glasses of wine that he'd planned to have were long in the past as people kept buying him more drinks: shots, beers, more wine, another bottle of champagne.

He thanked everyone who bought him a drink, but passed them all to the other players and they disappeared fast enough.

He barely tasted the delicious three-course meal, and later he couldn't remember anything that was said to him.

But then the toasts started, and with all eyes on him, Nick drank first one glass, then another and another, long since passing his two-drink limit, until they all began to blur. He should stop, he knew he should, but he no longer cared.

It had been a long time since he'd drunk this much, and Anna watched him with worried eyes. She couldn't blame anyone for wanting to buy Nick a drink to celebrate with him, and there were very few people who knew that he'd had a serious drinking problem earlier in his career.

She didn't say anything, but she may, however, have kicked him in the shins. Nick just grinned, his smile loose and his eyes glazed.

The compere rounded up the speeches, thanking everyone, then ran through the highlights of Nick's career and presented him with car keys for a brand new Range Rover Sport, a gift from his sponsors.

In return, Nick said a few words and was able to hand over a cheque for £100k to his old amateur club.

"Adios, amigos!" he slurred. "Goodbye career. Hello retirement."

Anna took charge of the keys to the new car, then slid her arm around his waist.

"Well done, babe. I'm proud of you. Now put that drink down and get your sexy ass in the taxi. Oh boy, you'll be in a world of hurt tomorrow."

Her words rang with truth.

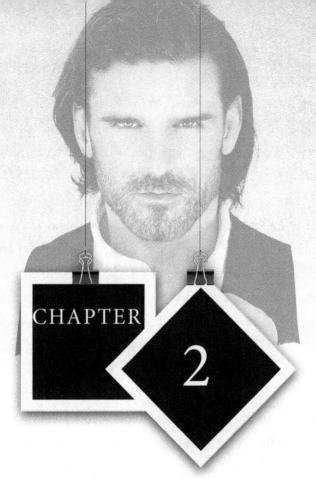

CHAPTER 2

Three months later...

ANNA STARED AT HER CELL PHONE for the fiftieth time. *Where is he? Where the hell is Nick?*

She was worried. In the months since his testimonial, he'd been quieter, growing more distant daily. Of course it was a massive change for him, saying goodbye to the sport where he'd had so much success and so many happy and fulfilling years. And he was saying goodbye to the support that had consumed all his adult years; most of his life, in fact.

She understood that he missed his teammates, that he missed being part of something bigger than himself. But it hurt to think that what they had together couldn't fill the gap in his life. She'd hoped ... but she'd been wrong.

I have to give him more time.

That had become her new mantra, as much for herself as for him. Perhaps if she gave him the time and space to rediscover his passion for … something, then they'd be able to move on. *Perhaps, perhaps, perhaps.*

They'd talked about this, they'd talked about life after rugby and at first he'd seemed so enthusiastic, so hungry for it. He'd said himself that rugby had been the main focus of his life for 24 years—since he was a child—and professionally for 16 years. But he'd been different lately, quieter, depressed, and she couldn't even remember the last time he'd picked up his guitar. The only thing he did was train, but with no end goal. And now he'd disappeared and she couldn't get in touch with him.

Nick had said that he was going out for a walk but he'd been gone for hours, and he hadn't replied to any of her texts or voicemails.

Where had he gone? What did the sudden disappearing act mean?

Anna stared at her cell phone, wondering who she could call. Was he just visiting with one of his old teammates and lost track of time? If Fetuao Tui was still in the country, she thought Nick would have gone to him, but he'd left to play for a team in New Zealand to be closer to his family, and was currently on the other side of the world. Gio Simone had gone home to Perugia in central Italy after ACL surgery, so there was no point asking if he'd seen Nick either.

In the end, she called Jason Oduba who was in the final year of his career at Finchley Phoenixes, the team where he and Nick had played together.

"Hey, Anna, great to hear from you! It's been a while. How's our boy doing? He said he'd come out and see us play, but I guess he's too busy enjoying being retired and not getting injured, huh?"

And he laughed.

Anna's stomach turned upside down, tying itself into a hard knot of doubt.

"He … he hasn't been out to see you play? Not even once? But he said that he had…"

Her words trailed off and there was an uncomfortable silence before Jason replied.

"No, darlin', none of us have seen him. We thought that you guys … we thought you were busy, so … well, maybe he watched from the Stands. I dunno. Sorry, Anna. I don't know what to tell you."

Anna's throat contracted as she felt his pity across the airwaves. Three times, Nick had told her that he was going to see his old team play, but now it seemed that he'd been nowhere near the Hangar Lane stadium. So where had he been? Why had he lied to her?

Anna realised that she was still clutching the phone in her hand.

"Oh, okay. Thank you, Jason. I hope it's all going well over there. We miss you guys."

"Yeah, yeah, you too, doc. Say hi to Nick for me. Tell him to come and to see us. Cheers, luv."

"Bye."

She paced up and down the kitchen of the home that she shared with Nick. *Where is he?*

Biting her lip, she decided to call Nick's sister, Trish. She'd always been there when Nick had needed her, and she'd become a great friend to Anna, as well.

She answered on the second ring.

"Hey! How's my favourite sister-in-law?!"

Anna gave a weak laugh. She'd been engaged to Nick for a while now, but they just hadn't gotten around to getting married.

"I'm the only one you've got as far as I know!"

"Meh, semantics! How are you? How's that great lout of a brother of mine?"

"Um, well, that's kind of what I wanted to talk to you about."

Trish sighed.

"What's the silly sod done now?"

Anna slumped down on the sofa in the cozy living room.

"It's probably nothing ... he went out hours ago and I haven't heard from him. He said he was going for a walk, but he's not replying to my texts or calls. I even called Jason, but he hasn't seen him in months, and Nick *told* me he was going to watch the Phoenixes play just last week. I don't know what to think, Trish."

Tears burned behind her eyes.

"A few hours isn't that much," Trish said gently.

"I know. I'm overreacting. I just ... he's been so different lately. Quiet and ... we both knew that retirement would be difficult for him—he's only 33, after all. I know he's having a hard time, but I'm worried about him."

Anna had trained as a sports psychologist: she knew all about the pressures professional athletes endured—the constant threat of career-ending injury, the difficult transition to retirement at an age when most people would still be working towards their peak, the lack of a tangible goal that faced him every morning. She knew all these things, but living with a man who was going through it was very different to scheduling weekly appointments with someone who didn't have the ability to trample on her heart.

"He's missing rugby," Trish said simply.

"I know. But I don't know how to help him anymore."

"You *are* helping him, Anna," Trish replied quickly. "I know it might not feel like it, but you are. He just needs time. Don't give up on him."

"Never!" Anna bit out.

Trish gave a gentle laugh.

"I know, luv. I know you won't give up on him. Just hang on in there."

Anna sighed.

"Okay, but if you hear from him…"

"I'll tell him to get his arse home."

Anna ended the call and stared unseeingly in front of her. Gradually, her gaze came into focus again, and she stood, determination in her expression. She'd had her wallow of self-pity, now she needed to do something.

She grabbed the dirty coffee cups from the side table and took them into the kitchen, dumping them in the sink. Then she strode into Nick's office, collecting two more cups. He seemed to leave a trail of them around the house. He drank far too many cups a day and…

Anna paused, staring at Nick's newly decorated office that had, until recently, been a spare bedroom. It had been one of the projects that they'd worked on together after he'd quit playing professional rugby.

The soft blue and pink wallpaper had been stripped away, and the old floral carpet had been torn up and thrown out. Now the walls were clean and fresh and white, and the double-bed had been replaced with simple, black, masculine office furniture. One wall held a set of framed photographs of Nick in action—his trophy wall, Anna called it. There were photographs of him meeting Princes William and Harry, and lifting the World Cup in front of eighty-two thousand fans at Twickenham. There were pictures of him flying through the air, scoring a try; photos of him leaping high, his hands outstretched, his beautiful, lean body sculpted and hard, his expression focussed, determined.

He's missing rugby…

With a sudden certainty, Anna knew exactly where she'd find

Nick. Well, she could think of two places he'd go, but Jason said he hadn't seen him so that narrowed it down.

Anna grabbed the car keys from the dish by the front door and hurried out. The sky was growing dark with angry purple clouds scudding across the sky, and the afternoon breeze had grown to a stiff wind that sliced through her thin clothes.

She shivered, but didn't take the extra minute to go and find a jacket. Instead, she jumped into Nick's Range Rover Sport, a vehicle far too big for most of the roads around London, in Anna's opinion, but a car that Nick loved. And besides, his sponsors had given it to him for free as a retirement gift.

She reversed carefully down the short driveway, even after all these years of living in the UK reminding herself to drive on the left.

In the distance, she could see the wide open space of Hampstead Heath, which was the main reason they'd bought this house. It was one of the more expensive parts of London, and they could have gotten a bigger place if they'd moved further out, but they'd both loved being close to the ancient 800 acre park, with its vast expanse and the thousand years of recorded history that went with it. At least it didn't have highwaymen lurking there anymore, demanding that unwary travellers 'stand and deliver!' their pocket watches and gold rings.

Each day, without fail, rain or shine, Nick went there for his morning run. And Anna loved it because she imagined picnics in the summer, two or maybe three children playing under those sprawling oak trees…

Forcing herself to focus on the road, she headed southwest across the city, cursing the heavy traffic which was the daily price of living in London.

It took nearly 40 minutes to drive 15 miles and Anna grit her teeth for at least 39 of those minutes.

Twickenham stadium loomed ahead, a dark monolith, absorbing the last, lingering light from the sky. Anna was used to seeing it on a game day, brightly lit, with cars thronging the roads around it and lines of people all heading inside.

But today the turnstiles were silent, and only a few security lights flared in the twilight.

Anna parked in the players parking lot and headed for the private entrance at the side, but it was locked and she couldn't see anyone on duty. Frustrated and feeling very alone in the gathering darkness, she made her way around the outside of the massive building toward the main entrance.

"Oi, who's out there!"

A scarily big security guard shone a flashlight into her face, making her blink.

"Mrs. Renshaw?"

Anna didn't bother to correct him about her marital status.

"Yes!"

"Sorry about that, luv," the guard said, lowering the bright beam of light. "We've had a bit of trouble with vandals lately. You looking for Nick?"

Anna's heart gave a gratified leap.

"Yes! Is he here?"

The guard gave her a strange look.

"Yeah, I let him in two hours ago. He's sitting in L33 in the South Stand. Is he alright?"

Anna gave an uneasy laugh.

"Oh yes! Just soaking up the memories, you know!"

The guard scratched his chin.

"Right-o, well, I s'pose you know your way around inside. I'll tell Bodie and Doyle to keep an eye out for you," and he tapped the radio mic attached to his uniform.

"Thank you," she said gratefully.

Anna's footsteps echoed loudly as she walked briskly along the empty corridor. She'd never been here by herself before; she'd always been with other people, always excited and nervous about a game or a presentation. Even Nick's amazing testimonial had been played here. But now the darkness and silence unnerved her, and the display of past players' photographs seemed to stare down at her, watching, judging. Seeing it like this, empty, haunted by memories, it was creepy. She found herself tiptoeing, as if she wasn't supposed to be there. And maybe she wasn't.

NICK WANTED TO be alone.

He sat in Twickenham's South Stand, the ground empty, flood lights dimmed. He closed his eyes, remembering being here as a young kid, watching his heroes play, dreaming of doing what they did, playing for England. He rubbed his tired eyes, despair weighing him down. It was all so long ago. But fast forward in time and here he was again, sitting in the same place.

He'd achieved what he set out to do—there should be no regrets. But it was so damn hard to let go, so hard to unplug.

Rugby lads were tough men, and Nick felt frustrated by his inability to suck it up and get a grip.

Ren-*shaw!* Ren-*shaw!* Ren-*shaw!*

He could still hear the fans cheer and sing. He could hear the studs from thirty pairs of boots echo through the tunnel as the players walked out to the field, the coach giving his pre-game speech, the victory song being sung after and drums thundering as the team celebrated.

All memories he'd never forget.

I'll never replace this. Rugby is under my skin, it's in my blood, it flows through my soul.

A place like Twickenham brought back so many emotions. He knew that every player went through the transition, wondering what was next, but that didn't make it any easier.

The underlying question had to be answered in his own mind: *if I'm not Nick Renshaw the Rugby star anymore, who am I? What's my purpose?*

If he was honest, not knowing who or what he was, it scared him. *I can't let Anna see me like this.*

But Nick was too late.

Anna didn't know what she'd find. She didn't know if Nick would want her there.

Making her way toward the South Stand, she saw him.

He was sitting in the shadows, elbows on his knees, staring out at the empty stadium, staring out at the silent turf. His gaze was distant, lost in the past, and Anna wondered what he was seeing, what he was hearing. Did the echoes of long gone games ring in his ears? Was the roar of a long lost crowd making his heart pound with ghostly reminders of past greatness? Was he seeing the moment that he stole the ball from the air and ran half the length of the field to score his most famous try? Was he reliving the moment when 82,000 fans leapt in the air, chanting his name?

For a moment, she studied his profile: the nose that had been broken twice, but still retained its fine outline; the strong chin, covered now with a neat beard; moonlight casting shadows across his sharp cheekbones.

His stillness frightened her and he seemed so lost, so very far away.

She walked toward him, her nerves jumping, and sat by him, stiff and silent. He knew she was there, she could tell by the gentle tilt of his head.

And then, without looking at her, he held out his hand toward her, and she took it, gratitude and relief filling her eyes with tears.

His skin was cool, as if he'd been sitting here in the dark for a very long time.

They continued in silence for several more minutes, simply sitting, their hands joined.

She waited for him to speak. And waited, and waited, her heart sinking a little more with each second that passed.

"I missed you," she said, at last.

Not just today. I've missed you so much for so long.

He squeezed her fingers gently, but still didn't speak.

His hair was longer than when he'd been playing, a mass of crazy curls that would have coiled untamed around his head if not for the woolen hat he wore, pulled down low. A single curl had escaped, drooping over his forehead. That small vulnerability, that softness on his hard face and harder body, it damn near broke her heart.

"Are you ready to go home?"

He turned his head toward her, his honey-coloured eyes full of shadows.

"Yeah," he said softly. "Let's go."

THE DRIVE HOME WAS QUIET. Anna stole quick glances at Nick who was gazing out of the window.

"Should we stop to pick up a takeaway?" she asked, even though she felt too tense to eat.

"Sure."

"Okay, great! What would you like? Thai or Indian? Or what about that French deli in the High Street? They do great salads."

"Yeah, whatever."

"You don't care?"

"No, whatever you'd like."

"Okay," she said flatly. "Great."

It wasn't that he was ignoring her, but he wasn't *with* her either. She didn't care about the damn food. She cared about *him*.

Frustrated, she zipped through Hampstead High Street without stopping, and drove to the empty expanse of the Heath instead.

Nick glanced at her curiously but didn't speak.

"Come on," she said, jumping out of the car. "Let's go for a walk."

"What? In the dark?"

"Yes," she said impatiently. "Now."

Nick raised his eyebrows but didn't argue. She wished he would. She wished he'd be animated by *something*. This shadowy version of Nick was hard to take.

Anna's anger and fear drove her up the steep side of the Heath, until she reached the top and stood panting, with London in all its night time glory glowing beneath her. The sky was filled with stars and she shivered.

"Anna, what's going on?"

Nick wasn't even out of breath as he stared at her, his forehead creasing with concern.

"Yes, that's what I want to know!" she gasped. "What's going on? I spoke to Jason today…"

She didn't have to finish her sentence—Nick knew exactly where she was going with that comment.

"Oh."

"Yes, Nick! *Oh!* You've been telling me that you've been going to see the Phoenixes play and all this time you've been lying to me! So what's going on?!"

"I didn't lie to you," he said gruffly, his arms folding defensively across his chest. "I didn't."

Anna simply waited.

"I did watch them play," Nick said again. "I just didn't go to Hangar Lane. I never said I did … you just assumed."

Anna gaped at him.

"*Of course* I assumed that you were going to the stadium. You played there for over four years—where else would you go to see them play a home-game?"

Nick grimaced and looked away.

"I found a pub that was showing the games and watched from there."

Anna blinked.

"But … why?"

Nick sighed and shoved his hands in his pockets.

"I didn't want to see the guys."

Awareness began to dawn inside Anna. She'd imagined a hundred different scenarios since Jason had told her he hadn't seen Nick, but this wasn't one of them. And yet, somehow she wasn't surprised either.

"Why didn't you want to see your friends?" she asked, her voice soft.

"It's going to sound stupid," he muttered.

"I just want to know."

"I'm not part of the team anymore," he spat out, his voice bitter with frustration. "I'm on the outside. I always used to hate people coming into the locker room before a game, retired players, sponsors, *well-wishers*. I wished they'd just fuck off because I needed to focus on my game-plan."

He ran his hands through his hair helplessly.

"I don't want to be one of those guys, harking after the glory days when there are other people still doing it, still out there, playing. I don't want to *watch* rugby if I can't *play* it." His frown deepened. "So I went to a pub I'd never been to before, wore my beanie and didn't speak to anyone. I didn't really want to see the game, but I couldn't *not* watch either." He glanced at her quickly. "And I knew you'd ask me about it."

Anna released the breath she'd been holding.

"Oh, Nick! I understand, I do. I just … I wish you'd told me." *It hurts that you didn't tell me.*

"Because it's pathetic!" he cried out, his voice full of resentment. "God, I know it's pathetic! I've got everything, *everything* I've ever wanted, and I can't help feeling like … like … like I have nothing."

Anna's heart shuddered as she felt the wounding weight of his words. She was crushed. *Am I nothing? Is what we have nothing?* Then she gave herself a mental shake: *this isn't about me. I just have to put on my psychologist hat and stop taking things so personally.* Which was easier said than done. She understood—hell, she'd written the book on it. But it still hurt.

She stayed silent, unwilling to speak, and Nick, now unburdened, couldn't stop.

"If I tried to say anything, I'd sound like an ungrateful prick. I've got a house that's damn near paid off, a brand new Range Rover Sport, a watch that costs more than my first flat, money in the bank, two investment properties in Lewisham, and a pension. A *fucking pension!* I'm 33, not 63! What am I supposed to do? Can you tell me, because I just don't know how to do nothing!"

"You have me," Anna said softly.

"What?"

"You have me, you have us."

Nick's face fell.

"Oh shit, Anna, luv! No, I didn't mean it like that! You, you're everything!"

But Anna had heard the words he'd said from his heart. He felt like he had nothing, but knew that wanting more sounded petulant, greedy. But she also knew a man like him needed a reason to get up in the morning—his own self-worth demanded it. She couldn't give him that.

She couldn't give him what he needed.

He wrapped his arms around her, those strong, muscled arms, and she leaned her head against his shoulder, her hands slipping around his waist naturally, the way they always did.

"I'm sorry," he said, his lips pressing against her hair. "I'm sorry."

"I'm glad you told me," she said, her voice barely a whisper. "I just wish you could have told me sooner."

He shrugged guiltily.

"I'm sorry."

So was Anna.

They drove home in silence, not touching, stopping only to pick up a salmon salad takeaway, although neither of them had much appetite.

Anna couldn't remember the last time he'd touched her, the last time his hands had reached for her in the solemn silence of the night.

NICK KNEW HE'D fucked up the second he'd sensed Anna next to him in the Stands at Twickenham. He felt even worse when he saw the seven missed calls, three unanswered texts, and two voicemails on his phone.

If you could call it 'feeling'.

Inside, he was empty, emotionless, as if the high water mark of his testimonial had seeped away when he wasn't paying attention. Nothing roused much interest from him: not working out, not going for nice meals, not being able to eat whatever he wanted, not even sex with Anna. Everything was muted. He knew the emotions were there, but they couldn't quite reach him—everything was at a distance. He was stranded in the ocean, and even though he could see the beach, he didn't know if he had the energy to swim back to shore. And he didn't know if he wanted to.

Depression settled over him like a blanket, thick and heavy and suffocating. He had no reason to feel this way. He had a beautiful fiancée; financial stability; adulation, too, if he wanted it.

"You're just bored, mate," Jason had said, last time they'd spoken, over a month ago.

He was still playing, but likely to retire at the end of the season. He planned to stay with rugby and had lined up a position as one of three assistant coaches at Bath RFU.

Jason was right—Nick was bored, but it was more than that.

At 33, Nick had already achieved everything. So what would the next 50 years of his life be?

But the question rolled around inside him, turbulent and painful: *What am I, who am I, now I no longer have rugby?*

Anna had every right to yell at him for being a selfish prick, but it was much worse that she sat at the kitchen table, picking at her takeaway without interest.

Nick chewed his food but didn't taste it, trying to think of something to say that would put a smile on her face. Something, anything other than this strained silence.

"I got an email from some photographer bloke yesterday," he began.

"Oh?" she said, glancing up and forcing a half-smile.

Seeing her work so hard to smile made him feel like a worm. He blundered on, hardly aware of what he was saying.

"Yeah. He said he wants to do a calendar with pictures of me and sell it for charity. Nudes! Ha ha, me, in the buff! I reckon one of the lads from the Phoenixes put him up to it."

But Anna wasn't laughing. Instead, she was staring at him with a thoughtful expression.

"Which one?"

"Which one what?"

"Which charity did he want to do the calendar for?"

Nick scratched his beard.

"Dunno. I deleted the email. I thought it was a joke."

Anna slapped her forehead.

"No! I read about this in the newspaper! Was it from Massimo Igashi, the famous photographer?"

Nick blinked at her excited expression.

"It was just a joke, luv. I thought you'd have a laugh."

Anna was on her feet, reaching for Nick's iPad and sliding it across the table to him.

"See if you can find the email."

"But…"

"Let me just see if it's the real thing."

She was excited. Nick wasn't. He thought the idea was barking mad, but if it made Anna happy…

He pulled up his deleted emails, found the one he was looking for and passed it to Anna to read.

Her eyes lit up as she scanned the email rapidly.

"Nick, I'm sure this is real! Oh, the charity is for testicular cancer—you did that Movember moustache for them two years ago. And I remember Bernard Dubois talking about this calendar—it's really big in France. You should do it, you should definitely do it! It's Massimo Igashi!"

"Never heard of him."

"Oh my God!" squeaked Anna, appalled. "He's the photographer who did Prince Harry and Meghan Markle's wedding photos! He's one of the top photographers in the world—his mother was Italian and his father Japanese. You *must* have heard of him! He shoots for *Vogue* and *GQ* and all the top magazines."

Nick stared at her, bemused. In all honesty, the only thing he ever read in the newspaper was the sports pages.

"Should I send an email back saying you're interested?" she asked.

Nick shook his head.

"Bloody hell, no! It said that he wanted me to pose naked. I've had enough dick shots in the Press already, and it wasn't even my dick!"

That was true.

Nick's teammate had once texted Anna a dick pic on Nick's phone, and a journalist had found it when their phones had been hacked. Hundreds of websites had published the picture of Gio Simone's penis, but with Nick's name attached to it. It had been a humiliating experience.

Anna cocked her head on one side.

"I don't think Massimo Igashi would do anything that wasn't tasteful—he's built his reputation on beautiful but erotic images. And anyway, if there was anything even slightly concerning about him, he wouldn't have been picked to do the Royal photos."

Nick appreciated Anna's willingness to think the best of people, but that didn't necessarily mean she was right.

"You sure? Mario Testino did all those pictures of Princess Diana, and now they're saying he sexually exploited models."

Anna's face fell.

"Oh, you're right. I'd forgotten about that." She paused. "But you could still talk to Massimo Igashi, couldn't you?"

Nick gritted his teeth.

"Why are you so excited for a bunch of strangers to see my tackle?"

Anna's smile vanished.

"I'm not … it's not that. It's just … it's different." She bit her lip. "It sounds … fun."

No, it doesn't.

"It's kind of funny, right?" she added lamely. "What do you think? Will you find out more?"

"Yeah, if you like."

Anna frowned at him.

"If *I* like? It's *you* they're asking, not me."

Nick was caught between a rock and Anna's hard stare. He gave her a quick, insincere smile.

"Yeah, why not."

Anna grabbed the iPad and flung herself on the sofa, jabbing the screen hurriedly as if she was afraid that Nick would change his mind.

If he could have crossed his fingers and hoped that he never heard about the calendar again, he would have, but his fingers had been bent and broken so many times, they'd didn't always behave the way he wanted them to.

He sighed and slumped in his chair.

Ah well, if it made Anna this happy, it was fine by him.

Or it could all go horribly wrong.

ANNA WAS GRABBING at straws. Why the hell had she pressured him into this calendar idea when he was clearly uncomfortable about it? She had no idea if this was a good idea or not, but it was something different, something to break the stalemate, something to break through the glass wall that Nick was locked behind—and they desperately needed that, both of them.

He'd refused point blank to celebrate his upcoming birthday or even talk about it. Any cards he'd received had gone in the trash unopened.

She'd already tried everything that she could think of, used every technique at her disposal, and he'd remained aloof, unconnected. It scared her.

Maybe desperation was making her reckless, but Anna had heard about the calendar project before. In the past, it had been focussed on a French rugby club in Paris, *Stade Français*, and the calendar had featured only their players—*Dieux du Stade*—Gods of Stade. Massimo had announced his intention to photograph different athletes, portraying them as Greek sculptures, with their musculature on display. Tasteful, suggestive of nudity rather than explicit.

Every year, the calendar raised money for cancer research, particularly testicular cancer—but one unexpected benefit had been that it significantly raised the profile of the Parisian team, as well as popularising rugby in France.

She wanted to trust Massimo Igashi—she desperately hoped this wasn't going to backfire.

It would be a great opportunity for Nick, something for him to focus on. Not that he was out of shape, far from it. He'd kept up his daily training almost as intensively as when he was still playing for the Phoenixes. Perhaps he'd lost a little muscle tone after recovering from the last operation on his shoulder to repair a torn rotator cuff, but as far as Anna was concerned, Nick's body was already a work of art.

She completely failed to consider how she'd feel with thousands of women—and men—seeing her husband-to-be in all his glory. It simply didn't occur to her.

All she wanted was a project for Nick. Was that so selfish?

CHAPTER 4

Nick assumed that the calendar photoshoot would be simple: one day out of his life, then finished. He'd been involved with team photos before and he'd even let his tattoo artist take some shots to display in his studio. Those had ended up in the newspapers and on websites everywhere. Not that he cared or could have done anything about it if he did. Besides, his body was simply a tool with which to do his job—when he'd had a job.

The next day, however, clued him in that this wasn't going to be your ordinary photoshoot.

He'd been out for his morning run, as usual, when Anna waved the iPad at him excitedly on his return.

"You've had an email from Massimo. It's been killing me not to read it!"

Rubbing the sweat from his eyes with a towel, Nick frowned as he scanned the email, the furrows in his forehead deepening.

"Well?" Anna asked impatiently.

"They want to do the shoot in Cannes."

He shrugged, tossing the iPad on the kitchen table.

"The south of France? Wow!"

Anna was excited, but Nick didn't seem impressed.

"Just think of all the money the calendar will make for charity," she said half hopefully.

Nick raised an eyebrow.

"It's a few days out of your life," she pleaded, unsure why she was still peddling the idea to him. She sighed. "Look, if you don't want to, it's fine. Your body, your choice, right? Forget I suggested it." She hesitated then forced a smile. "Maybe you could help me round up some of your old teammates so I can interview them for my book?"

Nick winced, his gut twisting at the reminder of the empty days stretching in front of him.

"Yeah, sure," he muttered as he drew in a deep breath. "And I'll do the calendar thing. Probably won't sell any with my mug on it."

Then he stomped out of the room.

Anna's shoulders sagged, exhausted from tiptoeing around him. She read the email again. Apart from the fact that Nick was required to fly out to Massimo's studio in Cannes, a few miles southwest of Nice, for three days—one day of prep and then the two-day shoot—Nick had been sent a strict exercise and diet sheet. The diet sheet wasn't very different from the ones Nick had used at his rugby club, although this was considerably lower in carbs, but even so, it seemed a lot of effort and Anna was slightly appalled when she read it in detail...

Massimo Dieux Du Sport Calendar

One month before, the model will start to lower their intake of carbohydrates and increase their training to create a deficit that will lead to a leaner, more sculpted physique, suitable for this project.

Week 1
Monday
Morning: Back and chest
Afternoon: cardio run, High Intensity Interval Training or circuit training

Tuesday
Morning: shoulder and abs
Afternoon: cardio, run, hiit or circuit

Wednesday
Morning: legs
Afternoon: cardio, run, hiit or circuit

Thursday
Morning: Arms and abs
Afternoon: cardio, run, hiit or circuit

Friday
rest

Saturday
Morning: full body weights circuit
Afternoon: cardio

Sunday
rest

The model should be exercising twice a day, 4-5 days a week, with the emphasis on weights in the morning and cardio later on in the day; a split routine, shoulders and abs, back and chest, arms and abs, legs and mobility.

As Anna scanned down the weeks 2 to 4, her eyes widened. This was a workout very similar to the preparation for a big game day. The main difference was the reduced carbohydrates—the distinct lack of rice, pasta or sweet potatoes.

Suggested menu options

Breakfast: Eggs or omelette with fresh vegetables, kale, spinach, nuts.
Mid-morning: protein shake.

Dinner: chicken breast with steamed vegetables, salad, fruit for dessert.
Mid-afternoon snack: protein shake, chicken salad.

Dinner: salmon fillet with steamed vegetables.
Snack: protein bar.

Avoid caffeine and processed sugar.
Suggested alternatives: green tea, water, herbal infusions.

Preparing for the Photoshoot

For the last three days before the shoot, reduce water intake to a level of moderate dehydration.

Anna grimaced. That was certainly not an instruction that a healthy athlete would follow—hydration was key. But she also knew that a dehydrated body emphasized the muscles and sinews, leading to a super-ripped physique that photographed well.

But it wasn't healthy.

On the morning of the shoot, the model should go for a run or complete a cardio-based workout.

No food or water, but black coffee is permitted.

Anna gritted her teeth. She'd practically demanded that Nick sign up for this.

What the hell was I thinking?

She could cope with most of it, but the suggestion that he should deliberately dehydrate himself made the corner of her eye twitch.

There was a contract attached to the email, which Anna immediately forwarded to Nick's former manager. If there was any cause for concern, Mark Lipman would spot it in a nanosecond. Even though Nick was no longer playing professional rugby, and Mark was retired, he'd stayed in touch, earning Anna's undying gratitude for his kindness and support.

Wondering if she was doing the right thing by forcing Nick into this, she finished dressing, ready for the twice-weekly meeting with her P.A., Brendan.

Ten minutes later, there was a knock at the front door and Anna smiled, seeing her friend and assistant on the doorstep.

"Annie, darling! Gorgeous as ever. Almost as gorgeous as myself," he said, bustling inside. "What's wrong with his nibs? He looks like that grumpy cat meme that everyone thinks is so hilarious."

Anna pulled a face.

"Yeah, um, that might be my fault."

"I've told you before, Anna," Brendan grinned slyly, "withholding sex is a great incentive to get your own way. Just hang on in there. Although," and he fanned his face, "I'd never turn down your delish diva of a boyfriend—excuse me, fiancé."

"Bren! I don't ... I wouldn't..." she huffed, while Brendan grinned and helped himself to a cup of coffee. Then she lowered her voice. "Nick's been asked to do a photoshoot for a calendar—with Massimo Igashi!"

Brendan slammed his coffee cup down so hard that hot, brown liquid spilled onto the table.

Anna threw him an aggrieved look as she wiped it up.

"Stop the press!" he shrieked. "Why am I only hearing about this now? I'm only your best friend! I'm only the best personal assistant you've ever had your hot little hands on!"

"Don't be such a drama queen, Bren."

"Can't help it," he sang. "It's genetic. Now come on, spill the beans."

Anna told him everything that had happened, starting with finding Nick at Twickenham the night before.

Brendan looked at her thoughtfully.

"So, basically you've bullied Nick into doing a nudie calendar, when he'd instantly dismissed the idea and deleted the aforementioned email from his inbox."

Anna frowned.

"It wasn't like that!" Then she groaned and dropped her head to the kitchen table. "It was exactly like that!" she mumbled, then sat up. "But Bren, what was I supposed to do? He's drifting, lost, and I don't know how to reach him!"

Brendan sat astride a kitchen chair, his long limbs folding underneath him as he adjusted his glasses, tortoiseshell today, that gave him a hot librarian look as he listened intently.

"All those years he was with different clubs—it's been nothing but rugby since he was a child," she tried to explain. "In a way, he's been institutionalized. He had a whole team behind him: doctors, physios, managers, coaches, agents, publicists, other players—his friends. Now … he just has me." She shook her head. "I've seen this so many times before, but being so close to it—it's hard."

Brendan nodded.

"I know. I read in the paper about that retired rugby player Scott Moore…"

Anna shuddered.

"Oh, that was just terrible! That poor guy!"

"He got sentenced to 23 months," Brendan said. "He was driving at 150mph and police chased him for fifty minutes."

"He could have killed someone."

"Yeah, but when they caught him, they had to taser him like five times or something before they brought him down. He just kept on getting up. They make rugby players tough—even ex-rugby players."

Anna grimaced.

"It's the kind of story that makes it into all the sports psychology magazines as a case study of how not to handle a career or retirement. Apparently, he was the youngest ever rugby Super League player at sixteen, although he was disciplined many times during his playing years. But prison! What a way to end a career when you've played for your country."

"At least he didn't rob a KFC like that other ex-player, Malcolm something," said Brendan.

They sat in silence, staring into their coffee cups.

"Nick's doing pretty well by comparison," Brendan said, at last.

Anna gave a short, disbelieving laugh, and Brendan looked up sharply.

"Comparing him to two ex-players who are currently in prison? Yeah, definitely better than that!"

Brendan raised an eyebrow, a sure sign that he was coming back swinging.

"How long did it take you to go from being a sports psychologist to an Agony Aunt?"

Anna bristled.

"I'm an advice columnist," she said indignantly.

"It took you … what, six, seven months?"

Anna paled.

"My father had just died. And then all the Press intrusion—I lost my job! I was fired! Publically vilified and humiliated! It was a little different."

"I know," Brendan said calmly, reaching across the table and squeezing her hand. "All I'm saying is that any major adjustment in your life takes time to get used to. It's only been three months for Nick."

"Four."

"Okay, four months since his testimonial. That's not very long in the course of a lifetime." He levelled her with a look. "I'm not telling you anything you don't know, Dr. Scott."

Anna squirmed. She loved and hated that Brendan didn't let her get away with anything. Even though she was his employer, he'd never paid much attention to those sorts of boundaries—it was part of what made him a fantastic assistant and true friend.

"Am I pushing too hard?" she said quietly, staring down at their joined hands.

Brendan pulled a face and pushed her coffee cup toward her.

"Yes, no, maybe. Does Nick think you're pushing too hard?"

Anna matched his expression.

"Probably."

Brendan gave her a sympathizing smile.

"It doesn't mean that the nudie calendar is a bad idea. I've always said that Nick was hotter than lava. I'd definitely buy a sexy calendar of Naughty Nick."

Anna groaned. She hated the nickname that the media had come up with, or worse, 'Nasty Nick'—it bore no resemblance to the quiet, sincere man she knew.

Brendan's grin grew wider.

"Of course, I'd expect mine to be signed, 'To the incredible and unbelievably gorgeous Brendan Massey, with love.' You know: something simple, heartfelt."

"You're nuts!"

"You're crackers. Now, when is this photoshoot happening and can I be your on-site P.A.? Don't even think about saying no."

"Um, well, it's in Cannes next month. I wasn't going to go…"

Brendan gaped at her.

"Why wouldn't you?"

"Because this is for Nick—something for him. I don't want it to be about me."

Brendan stood up and put his arm around her.

"You're being a little wuss, Anna-banana. *Of course* we're all going. I'll book the flights and hotel now."

He pulled his laptop out of his bag and settled at the table.

"Besides, if anyone is going to drool over your hot boyfriend— sorry, hot fiancé—I should definitely be there to see it. And take notes. Possibly some pictures on my phone."

"What about me?" Anna huffed with a smile on her face.

Brendan waved a hand dismissively.

"You see his Holy Hotness all the time. Give someone else a chance, girlfriend."

CHAPTER 5

Nick was hungry.

Being hungry made him grumpy.

Being grumpy made Anna anxious, and he hated that.

Besides, it was a beautiful morning in Cannes, the sea sparkling in the sunshine.

Nick sighed as his stomach growled. A cup of black coffee with no breakfast was *not* his preferred way to start the day. If this had been a game day, he'd be tucking into oats with fruit, scrambled eggs and avocado on toast, plus a large mug of tea. He'd be loading on carbs, not thinking of pasta with fond memories of the long ago.

The red wine from the night before had left him slightly dehydrated, so today, Paracetamol was his friend.

Ignoring the guilty expression on Anna's face as she tried to hide the fact that she'd ordered a *brioche* with jam, and something that looked suspiciously like *pain au chocolat* to have with her morning coffee, Nick headed to the shower.

He gazed into the mirror. His reflection stared back.

Who are you? I don't know. A rugby player?

Who are you now? No one.

Angry at himself, he ducked beneath the hot water pouring from the shower and tried to wash away his tangled feelings under the powerful jets.

He'd been intending to do a cardio workout in the hotel's fitness room but had been lured outside by the jewel-bright sunshine. Instead of a sterile gym, he'd gone for a long run along the Boulevard that fringed the glittering dark blue of the Mediterranean Sea.

A cool breeze had brought with it the scent of pine, spicy herbs and sweet flowers, and Nick had felt the freedom of being away from the weight of his problems in London.

As he walked through the opulent hotel room, he side-eyed Anna, who was avoiding his gaze. She'd obviously decided to take advantage of his absence by filling up with those freshly baked pastries that looked and smelled amazing. And the worst of it was he'd be on short rations for the entire length of the two-day shoot. He couldn't wait for it to be over.

And yet…

He was curious to see what would happen.

Day one was in Massimo's studio, and day two was at a beach a few miles from the town of Cannes.

He turned off the shower, the pressure having felt wonderful against his tired muscles. His skin had been polished and buffed into perfection the day before, when Massimo's assistant, an energetic woman named Elisa Wang, had booked him into Cannes's top spa for a seaweed wrap and some kind of hot mud that was supposed to be cleansing. That was after shaving his chest, although he wasn't particularly hairy. Thankfully, he hadn't been required to wax his chest because that left his skin red and irritated for several hours, sometimes days. Waxing and shaving wasn't a process that was completely new to him—like many professional rugby players, he'd kept body hair short to avoid having his chest or leg hair pulled, twisted or yanked in the scrum by an opponent. He'd seen it done, and even when it happened to someone else, it made his eyes water.

The wrap and hot mud had been surprisingly enjoyable and a new experience that he wouldn't mind revisiting with Anna. Then he'd had his eyebrows threaded to shape them; extraneous nose hair and ear hairs trimmed, which was embarrassing because he hadn't known that he had any. He'd agreed to some gentle manscaping but had turned down the offer to have his ball sack and arsehole waxed. That did *not* sound like fun. But it gave him a new respect for women who underwent a Brazilian wax job.

He was also anxious that the meat and two veg weren't going to be photographed for publication: he hadn't signed up for *that* sort of calendar. At least, he didn't think he had. Surely his manager, Mark, would have warned him?

He'd also tolerated a spray tan two days ago in London, that had transformed his pale, winter skin into something subtly tanned, more gold than anything else, and the colour he'd be naturally after playing a summer season on tour in South Africa or the Pacific Islands.

He tried to see himself the way the photographer would, but couldn't.

Elisa had also kindly informed him that a hairdresser, makeup artist and stylist would be at the shoot. And on hearing his surprise, promised that it was only because the lights in a studio shoot tended to make everyone look washed out, even with a spray tan.

"Why do you need a stylist?" Anna had asked.

Nick couldn't answer and Elisa only vaguely mentioned something about 'props'. The only props Nick knew weighed 20 stone and were the first line of defence in a rugby team.

Despite all the strangeness of this new world, Nick was intrigued; and despite Anna's increasing unease with the nudity element, that part hardly bothered Nick. He'd been in a thousand locker rooms where the team changed, showered and dressed together.

A loud knock at the door announced Brendan's arrival.

"*Bonjour*, beautiful people! The car will be here in 15 minutes. Ooh! Pastries!"

"Hey, Bren," Anna said, thrusting a *brioche* at him quickly.

Brendan stuffed half the pastry in his mouth and groaned with appreciation, then realized that both Nick and Anna were staring at him.

"Wha'?" he mumbled over a mouthful of crumbs.

Nick stomped off to the bedroom as Anna shook her head.

"What's up with, Mr. Gorgeous-but-Grumpy-arse?" Brendan asked.

"He's not allowed to eat this morning. Or most of the day."

Brendan's eyes widened.

"And you were eating these in front of him, you little minx!"

Anna gave a guilty smile.

"I thought I'd eat them while he was out for his run, but he came back early and caught me."

"Bad, bad fiancée!" Brendan scolded. "*Nil points* for you!"

Anna giggled.

"I know, I'm bad to the bone." She paused. "Good, aren't they?"

Brendan licked crumbs from his lips and nodded.

"Divine!"

Nick walked out of the bedroom wearing an old Phoenixes t-shirt, cotton shorts and flip flops. The instructions he'd received were to wear loose clothing.

"Good boy," said Brendan approvingly. "No sock marks."

Nick grinned wolfishly.

"No underwear either. I'm free-balling."

Brendan's mouth dropped open and then he pouted.

"You're such a tease, Nick."

"Then stop flirting, Bren," Anna smiled, shaking her head.

"I can't. It's my default setting. I think it must be because I'm a glass-half-full man. Optimism that hot guys will fancy me is like breathing: I don't even know I'm doing it. *Do not command the seas to retreat!*" he said in a mock Shakespearean voice.

Then his phone buzzed and he was immediately in P.A. mode.

"The car is out front. Everyone ready?"

Brendan led the way, with Nick and Anna following behind holding hands.

The car was what the French limo service described as a business car, to Anna it was as minivan, and to Nick and Brendan, a people carrier. It was large, black, had heavily tinted windows, and the driver wore a shirt and tie.

Brendan surprised them all by rattling instructions to the driver in rapid French.

"I didn't know you spoke French," Anna said, with envy in her voice.

Brendan raised an eyebrow.

"Never underestimate the little people, Annie."

"I'm sorry. I didn't mean…"

He waved a hand then asked the driver a question, listening intently to what seemed like a very long explanation.

"He says that Monsieur Igashi's studio is in *Le Suquet*, which is the medieval part of the town. Apparently the views are to die for and there's a great place to have a lazy lunch by the citadel with delish *Provençal* seafood. They say the lobster is heavenly. Sorry, Nick."

Nick threw him an aggrieved look and Brendan giggled guiltily.

"Anyhoo, it sounds fabulous. Oooh! Cobbled roads—just like home."

The van wound its way upwards through streets that grew narrower and the buildings older, until it stopped outside a large, square house of sun-drenched yellow stone and terracotta roof tiles.

The driver opened Anna's door and nodded politely at her, then discreetly accepted a ten Euro note that Nick slipped into his hand.

"Smooth moves," Brendan whispered. "I'll have to practise that. Although as a mere Personal Assistant, I don't earn enough to tip ten Euros at a time."

"Ask your boss for a raise," said Nick with a smirk.

"I would, but she's mean. She hurts me."

"I heard that!" scoffed Anna. "Don't make me embarrass you in front of Mr. Igashi!"

"See what I mean?" Brendan hissed.

Anna and Brendan were still squabbling when the studio's heavy door swung open on silent hinges.

It was an imposing entrance, massive, ancient, and arched like a church door, the thick oak studded with iron. A young, elegant woman stood in front of them with a welcoming smile.

She was tall, slender with a pretty face framed by shoulder length black hair.

Anna took in the woman's skinny jeans and long-sleeved silk t-shirt, the stylish outfit topped with a Hermes scarf.

"*Bonjour!* I'm Elisa. Welcome! It's very nice to meet you at last. Please, come in."

She waved them inside to an enormous cathedral of light, framed by metal gantries that bristled with a range of different spotlights, similar to those in a theatre.

They all shook hands and then Elisa led them to meet the famous photographer.

Massimo Igashi was short and neat with thick iron-grey hair, and a boyish face remarkably unlined for a man who had passed his seventieth year. His hazel eyes were framed by wide, black, rectangular glasses, and his clothes were worn with the aplomb of a man who spent half his life at Europe's top catwalk collections.

His gaze skipped over Anna and Brendan, nodding politely, and then he fixed his eyes on Nick.

It was an unnerving experience as the photographer's eyes roamed over Nick's face and body, studying everything, missing nothing.

Then he grinned and laughed so loudly, Anna jumped.

The maestro rattled off something in French that made Brendan smile broadly.

"He says you have a beautiful face and he is hopeful that the rest of you is as beautiful," Elisa translated.

A dull flush reddened Nick's cheeks. Perhaps something had been lost in translation. Had the photographer really called him 'beautiful'?

He smiled uncertainly as Monsieur Igashi pumped his hand firmly.

Then another woman appeared, almost identical in looks to Elisa, but this woman was spiky where Elisa was smooth, and dressed like a Goth with matching black lipstick. She barely gave them a glance before she was climbing the scaffolding like a ninja.

"That's my sister, Ning Yu," smiled Elisa, unperturbed by her sister's abrasive demeanour. "She is a magician with the lighting—even the Maestro says so. She will make you look even more beautiful," she nodded again at Nick.

The photographer bowed and moved back to the tripod situated in the middle of the room, muttering to himself.

"Does Monsieur Igashi speak English?" Nick asked.

"Yes, of course," replied Elisa with a smile. "When he works, he speaks French, Italian or English, but when he edits his work, it is always with Japanese on his lips."

Nick raised his eyebrows.

"That must make it difficult for you."

"Not really. My Japanese is not quite as fluent as my other languages, but I am learning. Now, if you will follow me, I'll show you where you may find coffee and croissants."

Nick started to follow her, but with a smile, she pointed to a door at the side.

"Your changing room is through there," she said. "I've put a robe out for you in case you didn't have one."

Nick flushed. He hadn't even thought about bringing a dressing gown.

He nodded at her and walked into the room.

The walls were painted white, but there were blue accents throughout the room that gave it a nautical air as if he was in a ship's cabin.

A large mirror with lightbulbs around it filled one corner of the room, and there was a small, but comfortable-looking sofa with a cotton robe in dark blue draped across it. Nick also spotted a carafe of hot coffee. He looked at it longingly then broke, poured a small cup and took several sips before he forced himself to stop.

He changed out of his clothes quickly and pulled on the robe which reached his knees. Then he sat on the sofa, feeling self-conscious, waiting for instructions.

A few minutes later, there was a light tap on the door.

"Come in! Um, *Entrez!*"

Another woman, this time with two blonde pigtails tied into little puffballs smiled at him. She seemed to be about 20 and carried a large bag with her. Giving Nick a dazzling smile, she patted her chest.

"Fabienne!"

"Hi," said Nick shaking hands. "I'm Nick."

"*D'accord.*"

Then she pointed at the chair in front of the mirror.

"Please," she said, the 's' soft and sibilant.

"Um, okay."

Nick quickly worked out that Fabienne was the makeup artist.

She stared at his face critically, her eyes catching on the slight bump on his nose where he'd broken it—twice—travelled over his cheekbones, critically assessed his chin and forehead, then laid out her equipment like a surgeon about to perform an operation.

She began by moisturizing his face, massaging lightly. Nick closed his eyes, determined to enjoy the new sensation. He only glanced up when she stopped and dabbed on something else, a clear liquid. He had no idea what that did.

Then she picked up several different tubes of various skin tone colours, mixing them together like an artist's palette, and applying it to his skin with a small sponge.

Nick had expected the makeup to make his skin feel dry or masklike, and he was surprised when it didn't.

More colour was expertly added below his eyes, to his forehead, cheeks, nose, and then to his surprise, she pulled out a black eye pencil and brushed it along his lower lashes and eyebrows, before adding a little mascara.

Fabienne hummed to herself as she worked, completely absorbed, tutting softly when the sponge caught on Nick's beard.

After twenty minutes where Nick was drifting off to sleep and trying to ignore the gnawing sensation in his belly, she dabbed some lightly tinted gloss on his lips and spoke again.

"*C'est finis! Ciao*, Nick!"

He smiled and thanked her, and she gave him a saucy wink as she walked out.

He was somewhat shocked when he looked in the mirror. It was like seeing an airbrushed version of himself. He frowned at the mirror and his reflection frowned back. Yep, airbrushed—that was exactly what it was.

He stood up and stretched, but as soon as he was out of the chair, yet another woman hustled in and pushed him back, gripping his hair tightly with both hands and muttering to herself.

This must be the hair stylist, although she didn't introduce herself. Her mood indicated that he was the raw material that somehow she had to fashion into a model—and her job was impossibly difficult.

When she'd finished brushing and gelling and spraying, Nick's hair was a wild mess of curls and it looked as though he'd just tumbled out of bed.

"Fifteen minutes to do that," he grumbled to himself when the woman left. "I could have saved them the money."

Elisa peeked around the door.

"Maestro is ready for you, Nick."

"Sure, right, okay."

Nick felt his skin prickle—with nerves or just awareness, he wasn't sure. The ancient stone floors felt warm under his bare feet, as if the sun had soaked into them over the centuries. The studio itself was several degrees warmer than the changing room, but instead of being full of sunshine, the heavy shades had been pulled, and it was spot-lit with a pool of light at one end and darkness everywhere else. Nick couldn't even see where Brendan and Anna were sitting.

Maybe it was better like that, then he wouldn't have to see their reactions or worry about what Anna was thinking.

Monsieur Igashi was surrounded by his harem of assistants:

Elisa, Ning Yu, Fabienne and the surly hair stylist whose name he'd never learned.

It was slightly disconcerting to see so many women on the set. But Nick was body-confident if nothing else. He'd spent too many years in locker rooms being naked or half-naked, surrounded by other players, managers, physios, doctors, PR people to be embarrassed. Being at ease with nudity was almost second nature.

Except that here, everyone would be focussed on him.

The photographer seemed deep in thought, contemplating his camera in silence. Then he smiled and beckoned Nick forwards.

"My vision is that you are warrior," he said, in near perfect English. "I will show you as *Atleta di Fano*, or the *Artemision Bronze*—famous Greek statues. Nick, do you know what the word 'photography' means?"

"Um, well, yeah?"

Nick was puzzled by the question, but the photographer smiled.

"I mean the Greek origin of this word: *phōtos* is 'light' and *graphé* means 'lines' or 'drawing'. So you see, photography means 'painting with light'. And this is the miracle we shall produce today."

Nick was fascinated. He'd never thought of it like that and was now intrigued to see how this was going to work.

Massimo bowed and pointed to a chair in the corner.

"Please, to undress. You may put your robe over there."

Nick strode over to the chair and slid the robe from his shoulders.

This felt awkward. It was completely different from being in the locker room with thirty other lads, all naked: here he was the only one.

He felt seven sets of eyes burning into his back and bare arse. Even walking felt unnatural, and then he had had to turn around.

He peered into the gloom when he heard a sudden noise.

At the back of the room, Anna clamped her hand over Brendan's mouth, ending the gasp he'd let out when Nick had dropped his robe, his eyes locked below Nick's waist.

"Not a word," she hissed.

Brendan's wide eyes slid to hers and he shook his head, then mimed zipping his mouth.

Eyes narrowed, Anna glared at Brendan until he gave her a sheepish smile.

It was harder than she'd imagined—so much harder—seeing Nick surrounded by beautiful young women while he stood proudly naked in front of them. Much harder.

I'm just being silly and jealous, she told herself sternly. *Completely irrational. And I am the idiot who encouraged this.*

Her heart was hammering so loudly, her pulse racing so crazily, she had to force herself to take several deep breaths or risk passing out.

But it was more than raw jealousy; it was the feeling that he belonged here and she didn't. It was as if their relationship had slid into something unequal. And while she didn't think of herself as ugly, she knew that Nick was in a different class. She'd always known that, even if he hadn't.

The pretty young makeup artist smiled up at Nick, and when he smiled back, Anna's heart clenched painfully.

Then the girl sprayed him all over with a product that made his skin glisten the way it did after a workout or shower.

"You doing okay over there, Annie?" Brendan asked quietly, his voice loaded with sympathy.

Anna nodded, because she couldn't find the words to speak. This whole experience was so much more intense than she'd expected.

Brendan reached out and squeezed her hand, but didn't speak again.

"This is a very strong look, Nick," said Massimo seriously. "Let's try this pose that we talked about earlier."

With something to focus on, Nick's nerves began to dissipate.

He suspected that the first dozen shots Massimo took would show a guy who looked like a deer in the headlights facing a double-decker bus on a motorway.

But after that, everything started to improve. Massimo called him over and showed him on the camera's screen some of the shots he'd taken. He certainly looked less startled in the later pictures.

"Look, Nick, this is a good angle for you—you have very strong profile." Then Massimo smiled. "Most people look better in profile. We must capture your best angle. Now we will change the lighting: this one higher, this one lower, to create the shadows on your abdominals and on your pectoral muscles. Too much light coming forward flattens the image. We must show this magical physique."

Nick nodded his understanding. He saw what the photographer meant about painting with light and shadows, and he wasn't bothered by the nudity—the pictures were beautiful. Even he thought so.

He shot a smile toward where he assumed Anna was sitting, then went back to focusing on giving the photographer the angles and poses that he wanted.

Anna caught his smile and returned it weakly, even though she knew he couldn't see it.

For the next two hours, she watched Monsieur Igashi snap hundreds of photographs, stop, talk to Nick, choose a new pose, rearrange his long limbs, contour the lighting around him; sometimes coming in close to focus on Nick's eyes or chest or thighs or calves, sometimes from the back of the room, but always moving, never still.

He encouraged Nick constantly, and the slightly startled expression that Nick had worn in the first five minutes had completely vanished.

Instead, his intense focus spoke to the camera, that depth of emotion that Anna thought was hers alone, was on display.

Anna realized with a pang that he was at home in front of the camera. So why did that bother her? She'd pushed hard for this project, and it was going even better than she'd imagined. But now…

The pretty makeup artist retouched Nick's face with a brush, and Anna watched as he closed his eyes so she could work. The woman was standing so close to Nick, yes, utterly focused on her work, but so close. Too close, her chest almost touching Nick's, her thighs close to Nick's splendid cock.

Red hot jealousy flared through Anna, even as she told herself that she was being ridiculous. But she couldn't watch this any longer.

She turned to Brendan and whispered.

"I'm going to get some air."

"I'll stay here and keep my eye on Baby Spice," he whispered back, his eyes narrowed on the pretty makeup artist who'd said something to make Nick laugh.

Anna fled.

CHAPTER 6

A NNA STRODE ALONG THE EXQUISITE, cobbled street, arguing furiously with herself. She hadn't been able to sit there a second longer and watch another woman touch Nick like that. Although, seriously, what could have possibly happened with everyone watching? Nothing. Nothing had happened, nothing *would* happen. Nick hadn't encouraged her, and the girl had even particularly been flirting with him—they were all doing their jobs.

"Ridiculous!" she snorted loud enough to startle a couple of tourists.

Panting from the steep climb, she realized that she'd reached the summit of the Old Quarter. She stared down the long, twisting streets, taking in the ancient stone buildings, and squinting into the sun that danced and glimmered on the distant sea.

Her body began to relax and she could almost laugh at herself.

Almost. She allowed herself to remember that her feelings were completely natural. In no other environment other than modelling, or perhaps a medical facility, would Nick's naked body be scrutinized at close quarters by so many strangers.

It was modelling that was unnatural, not her feelings.

The realization made Anna feel a hundred times better. It didn't completely soothe the hurt in her heart when Nick had smiled at the young makeup artist, but she could persuade herself that it was meaningless.

She realized, several hours too late, that there was a reason why nude photoshoots were usually closed sets. She also remembered reading an article about sex scenes in movies, and why significant others didn't attending the filming—precisely because it was awkward and stirred difficult emotions.

She strolled through the maze of narrow streets, taking time to enjoy the scenic old town, before finding a coffee shop where she indulged in a delicious lobster salad, a local wine, sweet and cool, followed by wonderful rich coffee, and a cheeky dessert of *petit fours*.

And treating herself to a glass of wine and sugary goodness denied to Nick, gave her the tiniest little smug smile.

She texted Brendan to let him know where she was and that she was fine after having a good wallow. He messaged back that the shoot was wrapping up so it was safe to return.

At that moment, Anna appreciated him even more as a friend than as her wonderful assistant. Brendan was her best friend—he understood her, protected her when she needed it, then kicked her ass when she deserved it.

She slid her sunglasses into place and made her slow way down the winding alleys, pausing every now and then to examine a curio or admire a display in a shop window.

Feeling more like herself, she reached Massimo's studio and used the huge iron knocker to let them know she'd returned.

Elisa opened the door with a smile.

"How was your walk, Anna? *Le Suquet* is beautiful, no?"

"Very! I had a lovely time, thank you. Is Massimo pleased with the shoot?"

Elisa beamed.

"Maestro is satisfied. He says Nick is very compelling." Elisa touched Anna's arm lightly as if to emphasize her point. "This is a great compliment."

"Well, thank you!" Anna laughed. "But it's all Nick's work—well, him and his parents! It's got nothing to do with me!"

Elisa smiled as if she knew a great secret, and leaned forward to whisper.

"Maestro confides he cannot photograph happiness if it does not exist."

Anna was flummoxed.

"He said that?"

"Yes. You are surprised?"

Anna paused, not sure how to answer. But then she heard Nick's voice and peered over Elisa's shoulder.

He was dressed now, wearing the shorts and t-shirt that he'd arrived in, leaning over Massimo, dwarfing the older man. They were both bent over Massimo's camera while the Maestro explained some of the technical aspects.

Even Ning Yu joined in the conversation, her face surprisingly animated as she explained the lighting effects she'd used, and why she'd selected the different diffusing lights. She showed how she'd lowered the lights and added a spotlight to create drama for the black and white photographs.

Nick was frowning slightly, as if deep in thought or concentrating very hard, nodding every now and again to show that he understood.

The residual tightness inside Anna dissolved. Nick was completely engaged in the project, totally focused. He *was* happy.

Perhaps this was the interest that Nick would find outside their relationship. Much as she would like to be everything to him, Anna knew that wasn't possible—it wasn't even healthy. She was fair enough to know that her own work as an advice columnist and self-help author was something that she valued. Nick needed the same stimulus, he needed goals.

She walked further into the studio.

"How's it going?"

Nick glanced up, his eyes bright with interest.

"Hey, luv! I missed you. Did you have a good time? Brendan said you'd gone to find something to eat," and he raised his eyebrows, clearly amused and just a little envious.

Anna blushed and crossed her fingers as she lied.

"Just coffee. But tell me about the rest of the shoot? I saw the first half…"

Nick gave an embarrassed groan.

"I was pretty rubbish at the start. Standing around posing isn't as easy as it looks. I've been holding so many positions and trying to flex at the same time, I'm knackered! I never knew that modelling was so tough."

His eyes slid away as if he was rifling through the overload of experiences from the morning.

"It felt a bit weird to have everything flapping around in the breeze, but all the guys were really cool about it, so that helped."

All the guys? Try four beautiful women and two gay men, Anna thought to herself cattily. She managed to keep a smile on her face, and Nick grinned at her.

"Massimo promised that there won't be any dick shots. Been there, done that!"

This time, Anna laughed.

"Well, that's a relief," she smiled. "But you looked amazing out there." She leaned closer and whispered in his ear. "Got me all worked up seeing you like that."

Nick shot her a surprised look, then pressed a quick kiss to her forehead and a lingering kiss on her lips. Her arms circled his waist and she rested her head against the solid warmth of his chest, breathing in the scent of laundry soap and Nick's faint cologne.

After a moment, he stood up straight and stared at her seriously.

"You know it didn't turn me on, right? You could see that. You're the only woman who gets me hard, Anna."

Her cheeks heated with gratitude and desire.

"I do know that," she whispered.

And this time she meant it.

Nick's intensity lasted all the way back and he didn't let go of her hand in the car. Brendan sat with the driver and chatted in French while texting on his phone.

As they sat in the back seat, Nick brought her hand to his lap and let her feel the hardness under his shorts.

Anna's breath stuttered as she saw the heat and desire in his eyes.

She tried to pull her hand free, but Nick pressed it more firmly to his straining erection, a challenge in the sly smile on his face.

"We can't!" she hissed, throwing a quick glance at Brendan and the driver.

Nick raised an eyebrow.

"We can't," Anna said again, more weakly.

He clamped his large hand over her smaller one and moved her fingers up and down his length with firm strokes. He leaned his head back against the seat, his eyes closing and his mouth falling open.

His hand relaxed as Anna gripped him more firmly, still casting nervous glances at the front seat.

She moved faster, feeling the tension in his thighs as she increased the pressure. She squirmed in her seat, the erotic charge electrifying between them as her panties grew damp, and her own need became unbearable.

Sensing her distress, Nick's hand slid across to her lap and his long fingers crept beneath her skirt, then inching upwards, until he hooked two fingers inside her.

Anna shuddered, coming immediately as he pressed his thumb to her clit, sending her rocketing skywards.

Nick moved his free hand back to his lap where Anna's hand had stilled, setting up a fast, rough pace, but leaving two fingers inside her, moving them to the same rhythm.

Anna whimpered and nearly swallowed her tongue, clenching her thighs to make this stop. But he didn't. The rhythm was relentless and she felt herself building again.

Suddenly, Nick released her hand and plunged his into his shorts, coming in short, thick jets over his fist.

His eyes opened slowly as his breathing evened out and a relaxed, pleased smile spread across his face.

Wordlessly, Anna searched in her purse for a tissue and passed it to him.

Nick grinned as he calmly cleaned himself up.

Anna was in shock. She'd never … not in public … not with two people, and one of them a stranger sitting just a few feet away!

Heat poured from her whole body.

She pushed the button to open the window, fanning herself.

"Feeling hot, luv?" Nick asked, leaning toward her and kissing her neck softly.

"Just a little," she lied.

"It's definitely hotter in the back seat," Brendan quipped, pointedly staring out of the window.

Anna's cheeks blazed red as Nick let out a low laugh.

At the hotel, he dragged her into their room.

"I can't believe you … that I…" she huffed, still stunned by her own rash behavior.

"Didn't you know they call me Naughty Nick?" he laughed.

Then he pulled her into the shower and didn't wait for her to undress as the water poured over their bodies.

"Nick! My clothes!"

But Nick was a man on a mission.

"Forget about your clothes, baby," he whispered in her ear, kissing her neck and not so gently tugging her hair.

She moaned, half appalled when he tore open her shirt, ripping it from top to bottom, revealing her breasts.

Her bra disappeared with one swift movement.

Nick was impatient, aroused by Anna's words, the car ride, horny as hell, and shower sex had always been a real turn on for him.

He stared, mesmerized by the water spraying and bouncing off Anna's breasts. Her own excitement built as she caressed and squeezed his muscles, kissing and biting his chest.

"I love you, naughty Nick," she whispered with a smile. "Show me what you've got!"

Her words were a spur and he shrugged out of his wet clothes, kissing every part of her body.

"You make that look so easy," she breathed out. "Very James Bond, the name's Renshaw, Nick Renshaw, 007 license for shower sex!"

She felt the rumble of Nick's laugh against her bare skin, but there was nothing amusing about his rigid cock, throbbing and pulsating against Anna's wet body.

All humour gone, she was grinding up and down on him, digging her nails deep into his chest and abs.

He slipped one hand up Anna's wet skirt and ripped down her knickers.

"Naughty Nick is so rough today," she groaned.

Yes, the beast had been let out to play. The hours of standing around naked and being told what to do, his hunger and frustration rolled out of him as he rubbed her clit in a circular motion, moving with her as she pressed up hard against his hand, her moans and groans guiding his fingers.

"I need you to fuck me hard," she hissed.

Lust flared in his eyes and he picked her up easily, lowering her onto him roughly and she gasped as he pressed her against the shower tiles.

He thrust deep inside her again and again, the hot water pouring down with every movement, Anna's moans increasing to breathless screams as she climaxed.

Nick kept thrusting harder, faster, slamming into her as Anna cried out again, half pleasure, half pain, and then he exploded inside her, his body tightening, the cords on his neck standing out, the muscles in his arms and thick thighs rigid.

Anna gasped for air, and Nick slowly relaxed, allowing her to slide down his body, her soaked skirt catching on him as they kissed, softly now.

THAT EVENING, LIMBLESS and satiated, Anna dressed for dinner.

Brendan had cried off, saying he wanted to find a club where he could 'dance till dawn', his words. In reality, it probably meant finding a guy to hook up with then gossip about the next day.

Anna was happy to have Nick to herself. Sex with Nick was always hot and steamy, but there was something about the wantonness of their behavior, the chance of being caught, then shower sex with the rush of water over their bodies, Nick's solid heat, the cooler tiles, the ruggedness of it as he'd held her up and slammed into her, his beard reddening her skin as he panted into her neck.

Just thinking about it made her cheeks glow and her mouth dry. It had been so long since he'd wanted her this badly.

Nick seemed distracted by the number of restaurants they could see as they strolled through Cannes. He hadn't eaten all day but had drunk a liter of water straight down once the shoot was over.

Elisa had gently instructed him that he could have seafood or chicken and salad tonight. Still no carbs since there was another day of shooting yet, this time on location at a private beach.

Anna wasn't relishing going through it all again, but at least this time they wouldn't be stuck in the confines of a stuffy studio, and if she needed to go for a walk, the beach would be perfect.

Nick watched as Anna pointed at the menu, choosing a shrimp paella, then placed his own order for seafood salad. He promised himself that he'd have one of everything on the menu tomorrow night.

Anna had been quieter than usual at the shoot and Nick was astute enough to see that she was feeling excluded, maybe even slightly threatened. At first, he'd concentrated on trying to relax while posing naked, but as the morning had gone on and his confidence had returned, he'd gradually become more and more involved in the process of modelling and the way Massimo worked.

He didn't always understand the reason for the slight changes to his position or to the lighting that Massimo asked for, but he tried to work out the reasoning. In other words, he soaked up everything he could about the experience, finding it far more complex and interesting than he'd expected.

When they'd taken a break and Brendan had told him that Anna had gone out, he'd been disappointed not to be able to discuss it all with her. But something about the *way* Brendan said it made him wonder how Anna was feeling about the shoot.

He put himself in her shoes and knew instantly that he'd be mad as hell if she was posing nude in front of a bunch of strangers, in front of men.

But then again, she had talked him into this gig. Although he was well aware of her reasons.

It was hard to put into words how he felt: drifting was the word that came closest to how he'd been feeling.

And bored. That was the other word.

He'd been looking forward eagerly to a life where he didn't get injured all the time, but he missed the rush of adrenaline that came from scoring a great try or leading his team to victory. He missed being part of a team.

Get over it, a voice inside told him, and maybe that voice had an American accent a lot like Anna's.

His smile was wistful. Yes, he had to find a way to move on with his life. Drifting was no way for a man to live.

When the seafood salad arrived, he ate slowly, forcing himself to enjoy the good food, the beautiful views along the boulevard full of luxury boutiques and out across the yacht harbour, and here, with the woman who always stood by him.

CHAPTER 7

THE NEXT DAY, THE CAR SERVICE took Nick, Anna and Brendan to the harbour where Elisa met them with several bags of camera equipment and a warm smile.

Dawn hovered nearby and the sky was awash with spectacular pinks and purples, a hint of orange on the horizon.

Anna yawned and shivered, glad that she'd brought a jacket and wrap with her.

"I thought we were going to a private beach?" Nick asked Elisa, hoping the venue hadn't been changed to somewhere as public as the harbour.

"Yes, of course. We are taking the Maestro's boat to Île Sainte-Marguerite, it is the largest of the four islands you can see over there. Only fifteen minutes."

Nick was beyond happy not to have to spend another day indoors, and Anna was more relaxed, too.

He'd had his doubts about this whole trip, but it had been a good thing for them; good to leave the doubt and indecision behind in London, and enjoy the simple pleasure of spending time together.

Massimo appeared a few minutes later, accompanied by Ning Yu who was shouldering more equipment. Nick stepped forward to help her, earning both a scowl and a curt nod.

The Maestro's yacht was a dainty 37 footer with two masts, fore and aft, white with a bright blue trim. It bobbed in the water, small but perfectly formed, surrounded by larger yachts and motor cruisers that dwarfed it.

The yacht was named *La Belle* and it certainly seemed to fit.

The Captain, the man who would sail them across the open water of the *Golfe de la Napoule*, leapt down from the deck, greeting Massimo in strangely accented French. He was weathered, with craggy, sun-blasted skin, of indeterminate age and spoke no English.

"I think that's the Provençal dialect," Brendan whispered. "I picked up a few words last night at the same time as picking up a delicious sailor called Ciprian. He certainly lived up to his name, the old goat."

Nick shook his head, amused, but Anna frowned.

"I hope you were careful."

"Annie, darling, a little danger is part of the fun."

Brendan was delighted by the yacht trip and had dressed the part, looking something like Tadzio in *Death in Venice*, wearing an old-fashioned one-piece bathing costume with blue and white stripes. Even though the air had a slight chill to it, he behaved as if it was the height of summer.

Massimo patted Brendan's hand and took several photographs

of him leaning against the side of the yacht, staring toward the far horizon.

"Gorgeous as I am," he sighed, "the years march on. I'll be able to look back on the Maestro's photographs and think, 'I was adored once, too'."

Anna rolled her eyes.

"I'll always adore you."

"Of course you will," snorted Brendan. "That's in the BFF code. I'm talking about showing pretty little things of the future what they missed out on when Uncle Brendan was in his prime."

His words were said with humour, but Anna detected an undercurrent of sadness. In all the years she'd known Brendan, he'd never dated anyone longer than a week. He said he had no interest in settling when fishing was one of his favourite hobbies in a sea full of hotties, his words. But Anna wondered.

The Captain untied the heavy rope knots so the yacht could slip its moorings, a Gitane cigarette drooping from his lips, then stepped aboard the little yacht with the speed and grace of a man half his age.

Once they reached the open sea, the Captain shut off the small motor and unfurled one of the sails. The stiff breeze whipped the canvas taut as the yacht cut through the water, kicking up a fine mist of spray from the prow.

It was chilly out on the open sea, and Anna was pleased when Nick wrapped his warm body around her, leaning his chin on the top of her head.

"Having fun?" he asked quietly.

Anna craned her neck up, smiling.

Her hair, usually carefully combed, was windblown and tangled on the short trip, and yesterday's sun had scattered freckles across her nose and cheeks, making her look happy and carefree.

"You're really…" he said, his words caught by the wind and tossed away. "I'm sorry I've been so … so…"

Anna touched his arm lightly, her chocolate eyes warm with love. "I know. It's okay. We'll be okay."

She wished he'd tell her that he loved her, but he didn't.

As they neared the island, the waters of the Mediterranean turned from the deep navy of early dawn to a brighter turquoise that glittered in the morning sun. Anna raised her hand against the glare, admiring the beaches of white sand punctuated by rocky inlets.

They finally anchored at a tiny, secluded cove, fringed by palm trees leading up to a beautiful whitewashed house that made Anna think of Jay Gatsby or Agatha Christie novels set in exotic locations.

"Wow, this is so beautiful," Anna breathed. "Who lives here?"

"It belongs to a friend of the Maestro," said Elisa. "I love coming here."

The Captain dropped the anchor over the side then lowered a small, rubber dinghy and helped them all climb aboard.

Massimo had his camera in his hand and leaned out dangerously far to capture shot after shot of the glittering, shifting light and the spectacular backdrop of cliffs and brilliant white sand.

Once ashore, Massimo was in a hurry, wanting to capture the long, slanting shadows of the photographer's golden hour, a magical moment when the sun was low in the sky, the light redder and softer.

There was no makeup today but Elisa had double duties as hair stylist and the Maestro's gopher.

She combed and gelled Nick's hair with Massimo barking orders to Ning Yu.

Within a few minutes, they were ready, and Nick was stripping off his clothes.

Anna never got tired of seeing that—his beautiful body and smooth skin, his glistening ink and perfect musculature. She also knew where to find the fine web of scars that spoke of his many surgeries, all from rugby.

His thick thighs and quads, the dips and valleys of his abs, the wide shoulders and prominent pectoral muscles, all aligned with a face of symmetrical beauty, and those expressive, honey-coloured eyes—no wonder Massimo had wanted to photograph him.

The Maestro worked quickly, one eye on Nick, one eye on the rising sun.

By 11AM, they had to take a break. The direct sunlight was making Nick squint, and the higher the sun climbed, the more hooded his eyes appeared, the shadows hiding all expression.

"It would be better," Elisa whispered to Anna, "to have high cloud, so the light is good, but not so harsh."

Nick was stoic, but Anna could tell that his patience had worn a little thin after more than three hours of working to hold unnatural positions. The temperature was rising, too, and twice she'd sprayed him with sunscreen, and he'd had to keep moisturizing the skin on his legs because of the salty water.

They were all happy to take a break.

"How you doing?" she whispered to him as he sipped at a bottle of water.

"Great," he said, deadpan. "I've had sand in my eyes, sand in my arse-crack … and elsewhere. I'm hot and sticky."

He gave her a big grin and winked at her.

"But I don't have an eighteen stone prop trying to pulverize me in a scrum either. I'm good."

She laughed.

"Always an upside then!"

The sun continued to climb, boiling away the wispy white clouds, and leaving the sky a scorching blue.

They all retired to the sun umbrellas and sat in the shade, sipping cold drinks and eating fresh fruit salad, tiny sandwiches, miniature croissants and quiches, all delivered by a cheerful islander driving a golf cart.

Nick had a small piece of fruit, then set off to explore the island.

"He can't bear to see all this delicious food," mumbled Brendan, stuffing another shrimp *vol au vent* in his mouth.

"I know, I feel so guilty," agreed Anna, spreading a delicious garlic and herb cream cheese over a croissant.

They exchanged a glance and both started giggling.

"Poor Nick."

"He's so grumpy when he's hungry," said Anna.

"Maybe he's off exploring a sandwich shop," Brendan suggested.

Anna shook her head.

"Seriously? No. He's far too iron-willed for that. He knows he has another two or three hours of shooting yet. But wait until tonight—he'll be eating everything in sight, especially chocolate."

"Ah, so the man of iron has a weak spot!" Brendan crowed. "And it's not just you!"

Conversation gradually fell away, and they napped through the drowsy afternoon, the sound of the waves lapping at the beach leaving them limp and languid.

When Anna opened her eyes hours later, Nick was back, stretched out on a sunbed, his skin bronzed and maybe even a little pink in places.

She thought he was asleep because his eyes were hidden behind sunglasses, but then he turned his head toward her, and gave his trademark grin.

She started to speak, but he held his finger to his lips and silently stood up from the recliner, holding out his other hand in an invitation.

Again, Anna started to speak, but he shook his head, that slow, sexy smile curving his full lips upwards.

As she took his hand, the palm felt warm and slightly rough, and he wrapped his fingers around her, tugging gently.

Slipping slightly in her flip-flops, she followed him toward the sea.

He bent down and slid off her footwear, tossing them over his shoulder. Then they paddled through the clear, shallow water until the sea reached mid-thigh. The current tugged gently, feeling cool and delicious against Anna's sun-heated skin.

As they cleared the rocky promontory, she found herself in a tiny, hidden cove; somewhere that could have been a smugglers' cave in earlier times.

Nick pulled her against him, kissing her lips, her cheeks, her nose, her forehead; licking up the side of her neck, and tugging on her earlobes with his teeth.

His bare skin was hot under her searching hands, and then she felt his hard length straining against the shiny material of his lucky Speedos.

She paused.

She'd given him those swimming trunks, and he'd worn them for every game including his testimonial.

"These have a lot history," she whispered against his throat.

Nick smiled wickedly but didn't speak. His silence was tantalizing, drawing her into his game.

Anna let out a long breath that ended in a sigh.

Maybe he was right. Maybe they'd talked enough for now. Although in recent months there had been too many shadowed silences, too many things unsaid. Maybe now, connecting without words was something they both needed.

She silenced her busy mind and gave in to her body's demands.

Anna gripped the thin material of Nick's Speedos and pushed them over the firm globes of his ass. The material caught at the front on his thick cock and he groaned softly, sliding the material down the heavy muscles of his thighs and calves.

He gripped her waist pulling her towards him as he kissed her chest, nuzzling her breasts and biting her nipples through her bikini top.

She felt rather than saw him undo the twin bows that held her bikini together at her shoulders, not knowing where he threw it, not caring.

He didn't bother to remove the bikini bottoms, simply nudging the material aside and lifting her up quickly.

Anna gasped, then wrapped her legs around him, sinking down, sliding shaft to root.

He used his incredible strength to lift her up and down—slow, deep strokes that she felt to her core. The sun beat down on her head, on her back, on her arms, and the heat built up inside her, the movement becoming rougher and more uneven.

The coil of desire tightened inside her, threatening to spring loose at any second, at any moment, at any…

Anna shrieked as her orgasm struck, and she quivered and shook in Nick's arms. He swore quietly as he exploded inside her and slowly sank to his knees, the hot sand coating Anna's sweat-slick back.

They lay together on the baking sand, hot and sweaty and sticky, their mouths open, their eyes closed.

Nick pulled out and rolled off her, but left his hand resting on her stomach as her breathing eased gradually.

"Yoohoo! Where are you, little lovebirds?"

Brendan's voice echoed around the cove, and Anna saw him splashing through the shallows.

"Bren!" she squeaked, sitting up and clamping her hands over her breasts. "Give us a minute!"

He halted his approach and threw a hand over his face theatrically.

"My eyes! They burn! I shouldn't have to see my boss in the nuddy nud! Isn't there a law about that? Sexual harassment? I'm harassed because I'm not having sex in my tea break but my boss is?" He pulled his hand from his face and glared at Anna. "I'm traumatized!"

"Go away, Brendan!"

"Charming," he snorted, turning on his heel and disappearing the way he came. "The Maestro requires his nibs back at work. Speedos optional."

Nick started laughing and Anna threw him a dirty look—and then couldn't stop giggling.

"Oh my God! Maybe we've scarred him for life! He could sue me for workplace stress."

"Yeah, probably. But I think it was your boobs that stressed him out—he's already seen my knob."

They walked down to the water, washing the sand from all the interesting places that sand should never go.

Anna winced—her poor vag felt like it had been sandpapered, and Nick looked a little uncomfortable as he pulled his wet Speedos back on.

Note to self—beach sex is sexier in books.

Nick finished the shoot, ignoring the damp heat hanging in the air between them, then insisted on swimming back to the boat.

Anna watched him cut through the deep blue waters, his sun-kissed skin gleaming like some ancient sea god, his tattoos lending an otherworldly quality.

Massimo snapped the last shots of the day, catching Nick in motion as his arms cut through the waves, then settled onto the bench seat of his yacht with a satisfied grunt.

They were all tired; weary from the early start and long day, from the heat, from the lazy lunch and wine in the afternoon, and with the quiet satisfaction of a job well done.

Nick pulled himself onto the yacht, seawater pouring from his body as he tipped his head back and drank a litre of mineral water straight down. His eyes widened as Anna laid out the sandwiches and quiches that she'd saved for him, inhaling them lustily. And then satiated for now, he sat next to Anna, his damp skin cool to the touch and smelling of the sea. Anna felt the slow tug of desire. *This man, this beautiful man.*

She leaned against him, her eyes closing in the early evening sun, and felt at peace.

Their post-shoot party was held at a small restaurant not far from the studio. Nick didn't speak for the first half-hour, eating everything in sight, all the treats that he'd been missing.

They talked about the shoot and how pleased Massimo was with it; they laughed at the silly jokes of shared experience, and even Ning Yu managed a quick smile.

Then with full stomachs and heavy heads, they all went their separate ways with promises to keep in touch.

The holiday was over.

CHAPTER 8

Lᴏɴᴅᴏɴ ᴡᴀs ᴄᴀᴜɢʜᴛ ɪɴ ᴀ ʙɪᴛᴛᴇʀ ʙʟᴀsᴛ of winter. The weather was as rare as its citizens were unprepared. Winds of arctic temperatures roared from the Russian Steppes and the 'beast from the East' as the Press named the harsh conditions held the city in an icy grip.

Anna shivered, pulling her thick cardigan around herself more tightly and felt ridiculously grateful for the furry panda slippers that Trish had given her the previous Christmas.

Nick was downstairs in the basement, and Anna could hear the faint sounds of his pounding feet on the treadmill. She wished that some engineer could come up with a way of turning all that energy into heating for the old house. The high ceilings and large rooms that had caught her eye when they'd been house hunting, had needed a lot of wall insulation and new double-glazing to make them bearable in winter, and because she felt the cold keenly, Nick had also splurged out on underfloor heating downstairs. An indulgent luxury that she was thankful for every day, especially now.

Soft flakes drifted past her window, the panes frosted with ice at the corners. Outside, the world was white and almost silent. The roads had been salted and gritted the day before, but snow ploughs seemed to be few and far between in London, except for the main arterial roads, and only compacted ice lay dangerously beyond their driveway.

Anna turned her attention away from the Christmassy scene and back to her laptop, soon becoming absorbed in her work. Ninety minutes later, a damp and sweaty Nick appeared from the basement, radiating heat like a furnace. Anna didn't know whether to hug him or toss him in the shower. Not that she could toss 180 pounds of muscled man anywhere.

"How's the writing going?" Nick asked.

"Good. Flowing a little more today. What are you going to do now?"

Nick shrugged.

"I could make something for lunch."

"It's only eleven o'clock, babe."

"Oh, right." He glanced out of the window. "I think I'll go for a walk."

"It's about twenty degrees out there and it's snowing—it's practically a blizzard!"

Nick gave her a half smile.

"Yeah, but I thought I'd walk across the Heath, maybe take some photographs. This is the first time it's snowed this much since I've been in London."

He strode out of the room and Anna heard him running up the stairs then rummaging around in one of the closets. She was glad to see him enthusiastic about something: not much had caught his interest since he'd been back in London. He hadn't even been that interested in her, it seemed. After the amazing, outdoor sex that they'd had in France, they hit a dry patch. In fact, they'd hardly made love since they'd been home, maybe once a week if she initiated it—not like the twice a day it used to be. Twice a day at the least. Nick's continuing lack of interest battered her confidence daily.

If she'd hoped that the photoshoot with Massimo would change everything for the better, she'd been disappointed.

Anna sighed and went back to work. With Nick's absence, the temperature in the room seemed to drop.

Minutes later, he reappeared dressed in walking boots, a fleece-lined waterproof coat, black beanie and thick gloves, and with a camera bag slung over his shoulder. He seemed more animated than usual and gave her a lingering kiss on her lips, then winked at her as he walked out of the room.

"Wait! You have a real camera? How come I've never seen that before?"

His head appeared around the door, his expression surprised.

"Haven't you?"

"No, never."

He shrugged.

"I used to like to do a bit of photography. I just got busy, you know. Seeing Massimo at work reminded me that I haven't done any in a while."

Jeez, thought Anna, *we've been together nearly five years—that's a long while!* But she didn't say that.

"Wow, that's pretty cool!"

"I just thought I'd mess around with it," he shrugged.

"Well … have fun," she called after him. "If you see Santa, get a selfie!"

She smiled when she heard his laughter echoing down the hallway. Then her smile faded—his laughter seemed rarer these days, too.

Forcing herself to get back to work, she turned her gaze to her laptop, but her thoughts drifted to Nick like the snow falling past her window.

Two hours later he returned, his eyes bright and his cheeks red from the cold. His boots were heavy with snow and the bottom of his pants were white. He stamped his feet on the doorstep, then bent to unlace his boots.

"It's amazing out there," he said, shaking flakes of snow from the hair that escaped his beanie. "I got some great shots. I wish I had a better lens."

Using the viewfinder, he scrolled through the photographs of Hampstead Heath in the snow, the landscape stark and unfamiliar.

"These are really good," Anna said, surprised and pleased. "What kind of camera is this?"

Nick lifted a shoulder.

"It's a Nikon D6-10, a digital SLR."

That didn't mean anything to Anna, but she thought the pictures were really wonderful.

"You could get some of them printed out and framed for your office," she suggested.

"Yeah, I might do that," he said thoughtfully. "I'm going to download them and edit them."

Her smile vanished as Nick left the room. The warmth and connection they'd found in France had disappeared into short conversations and deeper silence. He seemed further away than ever.

An hour later, and Anna's stomach was growling with hunger. Nick hadn't appeared from his office, so she went to find him there.

He was still at his laptop, absorbed in editing the snowy scenes he'd just taken.

"Stunning," Anna breathed, admiring his photographs. "They look even more amazing seeing them that size. You're talented, Nick."

Nick blinked, surprised he hadn't heard her coming in.

"Thanks, they came out pretty good."

"Can I look?"

Nick rolled his chair away from the computer so Anna could flick through them.

"You should frame that one and … wait, what are these?"

She saw a series of photographs from France, pictures that she hadn't even been aware Nick was taking.

"Did you use for phone for these?"

"Yeah."

There were scenes from their hotel including one of her sleeping that took her breath away. She looked so peaceful—and the soft lighting of early morning was flattering.

"You look beautiful," Nick said quietly.

"Thank you. I … wow, I had no idea you'd taken all these."

She scrolled through a series of shots taken behind the scenes at Massimo's shoot in the studio and from the island. It was fascinating seeing the Maestro and his team at work, seeing the way Nick had seen them.

"Oh, by the way, you got a package from Massimo. It must be a copy of the calendar. I didn't open it, but only because I have an iron will," she teased.

Nick cringed.

"Oh crap, I'm not sure I want to see it."

"Well, I do! Hurry up and open it! I want to see if you're Mr. December."

Nick threw her a look, but opened up the package that she handed to him, pulling out a shrink-wrapped calendar. His eyebrows shot up.

"What? What is it?"

"Eh, they've put me on the front," Nick said, sounding surprised.

The cover was a beach shot, one of the last of the day, showing Nick striding from the sea, water pouring from his shoulders and chest, his hair slicked back. In the photograph, backlit by the setting sun, he looked beautiful and athletic, but it was suggestive too, and you couldn't tell that Nick was naked.

"Oh my God! You look amazing! I wonder if Massimo would give me a print because I'd frame that."

"Yeah, and we can stick it in the bog," Nick muttered.

"Shut up! I love it! Ooh, I wonder if he's used any other pictures of you."

Anna peeled off the cellophane while Nick hovered over her shoulder, not sure if he wanted to see anymore pictures or not. He hoped none of the lads would hear about his nude modelling photoshoot before he saw them on Saturday, because he was pretty certain he'd get the piss ripped out of him.

In fact, there were two more photographs of Nick inside, both from the studio shots where he had been obviously naked.

It was strange seeing himself there in black and white. He could see it was him, but it was separate from who he was, maybe like being an actor. He could see the concentration and that he'd been in the moment, but it was weird viewing himself like that.

"These are so beautiful, Nick, really artistic. And hot!" Anna gave a quick laugh and fanned herself. "How does it feel?"

He shrugged.

"Hopefully they'll raise a lot of money for charity."

"I'd say that's a given," Anna agreed, staring at the erotic images of her fiancé.

"I'm going to make lunch," he mumbled, leaving Anna to look at the other athletes in the calendar.

Soon, the delicious aromas emanating from the kitchen pulled

Anna from her reveries. Nick's stir-fried Asian vegetables were to die for and so darn healthy she could practically feel her body soaking up the minerals and vitamins. It was a good thing she'd hidden some cupcakes in her office. A balanced diet was so important.

"I'm going to see the Phoenixes play on Saturday," Nick announced, as he sipped a glass of some suspiciously green juice.

"Oh, that's great!" she said, too brightly. "Did Jason get in touch?"

"Yep. His last home game."

Anna was pleased . They'd all been friends since Nick had arrived in London, and Jason didn't have many games left with the top league team: he used that fact to extract Nick's promise that he'd go.

"Don't you want to see the Phoenixes play?" Anna asked, puzzled by his lack of interest in the team that had been his home for four years.

Nick frowned.

"Yes, no, not really," he said quietly.

Anna had an idea about his ambivalence but she wanted him to spell it out for her. One of her dad's favourite sayings was that 'to assume makes an **ass** out of **u** and **me**'. And second-guessing Nick wasn't getting her far these days.

"Yeah, I'll go to see Jason and support the lads," he said. "But it's different, being in the Stands. I'll still want to get out there on the field, I know that much, but at the same time, I've made a clean break from rugby."

Anna raised her eyebrows, but as she thought about it, he was telling the truth. Even when the Six Nations had been on TV, an international series of games between the three countries of the UK, plus Ireland, France and Italy, he'd only glanced, watching just a few minutes of each game.

She'd guessed at his mixed emotions, but hadn't realized how important the clean break was to him.

This would be the first time that he'd gone to see some of his rugby friends and attended a home game.

Anna nodded slowly.

"Yes, I saw that back home in the States with some of the football players I worked with. You'd think players would be fans, but that's not always the case. Some love to watch it and go to the games— others, not so much. It's understandable."

Nick rubbed his face.

"I used to like going back to the amateur clubs I played for when I was growing up, just to watch. It's different, you know? The ties to the club as a kid. But with a professional club that you used to play for, being in the Stands can be hard. I'll go and see Jason because he'll give me a bollocking if I don't, but yeah, I'd rather play than watch."

"Want me to come with you?" Anna offered.

Nick gave her a quick smile.

"Nah, that's okay. It'll be freezing cold on Saturday. And anyway, Jason will want to have a few drinks afterwards."

Anna smiled to herself. She knew that was code for the whole team going to get blitzed, even though Nick wasn't much of a drinker himself. Not anymore.

"Fair enough—a guys' night out then."

Nick looked as though he wasn't sure he wanted to go, but Anna thought it would make a change for him. He'd hardly seen any of his friends since returning from France or since his testimonial, in fact.

Over the next couple of days, Anna's mind drifted back to the photoshoot, but it wasn't Massimo's images that drew her attention, but the photographs Nick had taken. Maybe she was clutching at those proverbial straws again, but his interest in photography was fresh. He didn't really have any hobbies—he'd always been too busy before. The occasional poker night with his teammates hardly counted, especially since he didn't even do that anymore.

On impulse, Anna sent an email to Massimo, attaching Nick's snowy landscapes and behind-the-scenes photos from the shoot, and asking his advice about additional lenses for Nick's camera.

He replied that evening with encouraging comments. She was slightly taken aback when he suggested that she buy two new lenses, one 50 ml and one 85 ml, and a tripod for Nick, purchases totalling over £1,000. Nevertheless, she placed the order online and crossed her fingers.

NICK'S HOPE THAT the calendar shoot would stay under the radar for a few more days was blown to smithereens the next day. It seemed that Massimo, or the charity's marketing people, had also sent copies of the calendar to the British Press.

Nick was notorious once again. The headlines ranged from fairly restrained:

Rugby Rocket Turns Top Model
Renshaw's Calendar Debut

to the more excitable tabloid Press, screaming their headlines in three inch high capital letters:

Rugby Ace Gets Raunchy
Naughty Nick in the Nude
Nick Strips Off.

But the first Nick and Anna knew about it was when the phone wouldn't stop ringing with journalists wanting quotes. Anna put

Brendan to work answering all their calls, and sending out a hastily cobbled together press release that explained the charity's aims, with a brief quote from Nick simply saying that he'd enjoyed working with Massimo.

But when Nick arrived at the Phoenixes' stadium on Saturday afternoon, he walked into a locker room that had been papered with photocopies of his calendar shoot, all with the additions of moustaches, DD-breasts, three nipples, giant dicks, and various other graffiti.

"Naughty Nick, will you sign my boobies?" Jason screeched when he saw him.

"Fuck off," he replied mildly, having both dreaded and expected this.

The team razzed him for the next ten minutes until Sim Andrews, the head coach, rescued him by telling the team to focus on the coming game.

They shook hands, and Nick's former boss gave him a wry smile.

"Good to see you, Nick, but you picked your moment to come for a visit."

"It didn't seem like a bad idea at the time!" Nick groaned.

Sim laughed.

"I think you've played a blinder, mate. You'll have other photographers lining up to take a picture of your ugly mug."

Nick blinked.

"You think so?"

"Yeah, I reckon. And publishers wanting to write your autobiography for you."

Nick shook his head.

"I've already had some of those after my testimonial. And I'm only 34—that's a bit young for an autobiography, I think."

Sim shrugged.

"Dunno, mate. It seems to be that some of these popstars have books about them before they've hit puberty. But what do I know? I'm just an old fuddy-duddy. Right, better get this lot in shape. You gonna be in the Stands or the Box with the bigwigs?"

"I'll be line-side," said Nick, earning an approving shoulder thump from Sim.

"See you down there, lad."

Nick stared around the locker room, taking in the organized chaos as the fifteen players littered the place with clothes and rugby uniforms; physios applied support bandages and the room was filled with the scent of Tiger Balm, Vic and Deep Heat.

He missed it with a pain that nearly crushed him. He wanted to walk out and never come back, but he couldn't: he'd made promises. Instead, he headed line-side and chatted with the fans and supporters he met.

The air was cold and crisp, but at least the snow had disappeared. It rarely stayed long in the soft South of England.

As the game progressed to the second half, Nick felt the tension build in his body, the unused adrenaline coursing through him as he watched the plays and found himself mentally playing the game with the lads, cheering when they did well, throwing his hands in the air when they made a mistake or fumbled the ball. It felt like torture because his body and mind were telling him he should be out there with them, leading his team.

But there was another part of him that wanted to get the hell out of there—even though he stamped his feet and jumped up and down, the cold seeped into his body, setting off an ache in his shoulder that reminded him of his most recent surgery, less than a year ago, followed by a birthday the previous October that took him into his mid-thirties.

He had to face it: 34 was too old for a rough game.

Just one more match, begged his heart.

Too old, mate, his head replied.

Nick would have left at the end of the game if he hadn't promised Jason that he'd go for a drink with him and the lads from the team.

The younger players were gratifyingly in awe of him—after all, Nick was the Captain who'd led the Phoenixes to more wins than any other before him, and had taken England to two World Cup victories.

But he was part of their history, not their present, not their future.

He would have given a lot to be able to lose himself in a haze of alcohol, but an early brush with alcoholism had left him wary of boozing it up with the lads. Instead, he had one lager, then stuck to water.

"We wuz the best, weren't we, mate?" Jason announced, draping a huge arm around Nick's shoulders. "Best Backs a team ever had. We were legends, mate, legends." Then he turned to look at him. "How do you do it? How do you retire? 'Cos I fuckin' 'aven't got a clue. I tell ya, Nick, I'm dreading it. I'll feel like me todger dropped off." He gave a cynical laugh. "Maybe I'll do what you do and get me knob out for money. You fink I could be a calendar model?"

Ben Richards, one of the new players, grabbed Jason around the neck and rapped his knuckles on his head.

"Nah, mate. Yer too ugly, but I fancy ya anyway!" and then gave him a loud, squelchy kiss on the cheek.

Jason bellowed his indignation, and there was a brief tussle before they gave up and Jason leaned on the bar to order another round of drinks, effectively blocking out any answer Nick could have given him. Not that he had one.

He wished he did. His teammates all thought he was waving, when really he was drowning.

He couldn't talk to them, couldn't tell them how he really felt.

Later on that evening, when Nick was propping Jason up to stop him slipping from his barstool to the floor, he felt his phone vibrate with an incoming call, but when he saw it was an unlisted number, he let it go to voicemail.

Finally, the barman called last orders, the drinking up time, and the pub closed. The rest of the Phoenixes decided to go on to a club and make a night of it. Nick shook his head and said he was going home to Anna.

There were a number of ribald suggestions called out when he said that, several of which were anatomically impossible. Nick couldn't wait to leave the stuffy pub and rid himself of clothes that stunk of spilled beer.

It wasn't until he was on the Tube heading home, that he listened to the message he'd received earlier.

Hi Nick, my name is Adrienne Catalano. I have a modelling agency in Manhattan. Massimo Igashi sent me the shots from the calendar you did with him. You've got a look that we think is really great and we want to represent you in New York. I don't know if you've considered a career in modelling, but why not come out for a month and see how it works? Give me a call and we'll talk some more.

Nick listened to the message twice, then Googled Adrienne Catalano. He was almost more surprised when he found that she ran a legitimate modelling agency in New York.

Nick's immediate instinct was to tell her that he wasn't interested, but then he wondered … he had to do something with his life. He couldn't keep living off his savings, and there was no way he'd live off Anna, despite her assurances that everything was shared—he couldn't keep on disappointing her.

When he got home, the house was silent, but she'd left a light on for him in the hallway, a note on the kitchen table, and a glass of milk with a cookie on a plate. Nick smiled to himself as pulled out a chair and sat down heavily to read her note.

Hope you had a good evening and that Jason behaved himself (mostly). The milk is in case you had one of those kebabs on the way home, and the cookie is homemade because I love you.
Anna x

Nick sat at the table, eating the chocolate chip biscuit and drinking the milk, thinking about what he wanted his future to look like. He sat for a long time.

Then he climbed the stairs, shedding his clothes as he went, and slid between the soft sheets, warmed by Anna's body.

"Hey," she said, her voice husky with sleep as her eyelids fluttered. "How was your evening? Did Jason…?"

Nick silenced her questions with a kiss, slowly emptying his mind as his body took over, making love to the woman beneath him, all words lost.

THE NEXT MORNING, ANNA WAS STILL in bed when Nick told her about the modelling agent's email.

He'd clearly been awake for hours, although she hadn't heard him get up. But that was nothing new. He was often up and away for his morning run before she'd crawled to the shower and had drunk two cups of coffee to make herself feel human.

The scrambled eggs on toast that he'd brought her grew cold as she listened to the agent's message.

She looked up, wondering what sort of reaction Nick expected from her, but his face was a blank sheet, and she couldn't read him.

"Wow!" she said quietly, staring at him. "This is … wow!"

Nick raised an eyebrow.

"Yeah, crazy, isn't it?"

"I wouldn't say that. The pictures Massimo did turned out amazing. I guess we should have thought that you'd have gotten an offer like this. What do you think?"

Nick shrugged.

"Dunno. She seems legit. I've only been to New York once when…"

His voice trailed off and they were both silent. The only time Nick had been to New York was for the funeral of Anna's father. That had been a bad day, a difficult time in their lives. Neither of them liked to think about it.

"So, do you want to try it?"

Nick settled back on the bed, leaning against the headboard.

"Your eggs are going cold."

Anna didn't want eggs, but he'd made them for her, so she picked up her fork and began to eat.

"Want to share?"

He shook his head.

"I had mine an hour ago. I've been waiting for you to wake up."

Anna wasn't sure, but had she heard a note of enthusiasm in his voice? She forced herself to wake up more fully and willed her brain to make the connections.

"It wouldn't hurt to give this woman a call, find out a little more."

"Yeah, okay. I'll phone her on Monday."

Anna smiled.

"Babe, that's something you'll have to learn—New Yorkers are *always* on. I bet if you called her now, she'd answer."

Nick looked scandalized.

"It's only, what, three, four in the morning over there!"

Anna grinned at him.

"Hmm, maybe it's a little early," she teased.

Nick gave her a look as if she was the crazy one, but Anna had lived in New York for years, even gone to college there—she knew how full-on it could be. It truly was the city that never sleeps.

She was about to take another bite of her cooling eggs when she realized that Nick was staring at her with hungry eyes. She was so surprised, she almost dropped her fork. Last night had been the first time in a while and now he wanted her again?

Anna's heart gave a hopeful leap as Nick took her plate and placed it on the floor, his heavy frame looming over hers, pressing her into the mattress.

"SO WHAT DID the agent say when Nick phoned her?" Brendan asked eagerly, adding a third spoonful of sugar to his coffee on Monday morning.

Anna smiled.

"Basically, she told him to haul ass over there, go to some casting calls and see what happens. No guarantees, but she thought she'd be able to get him work as a model."

"Oh, it's like a fairytale," Brendan sighed, hugging his coffee to his chest and blowing into it. "It's like a glass slipper or lucky Speedos."

Anna narrowed her eyes.

"I'm regretting telling you about the lucky Speedos."

Brendan grinned at her.

"I think it's romantic. Maybe some gorgeous hunk will give me a pair of lucky Speedos one day—preferably his own."

"Oh my God! Do you ever stop?"

Brendan shook his head.

"Nope. I am a verified sex machine. How about you, Anna-banana? How's your sexy life these days, because you definitely have that post-orgasmic glow this morning."

Anna was well used to Brendan's lack of anything resembling boundaries and forced herself not to blush.

"None of your business."

"Oh, you so did, you little minx!" he cooed, pretending to swoon. "A good rogering by the rugby Romeo. I'm totes jelly."

Anna tried to ignore him.

"We have work to do, just in case you were wondering."

"Oooh, Mrs. Spiky is in the room. I thought getting laid was supposed to make you laidback."

"Brendan!"

"Fine, fine. So, I spoke to your publisher and gave them the list of images that need to be sourced, and I've booked your appearance on *Loose Women* for the seventeenth. David Beckham's management declined your request for an interview—boo! But both Jonnie Peacock (God, I love his name) and Jonny Wilkinson said yes, dates to be confirmed. I've sorted through your email correspondence, ignored the loonies, forwarded the ones you need to look at personally, and replied to the rest. Oh, and Nick has had 1,753 orders for the calendar from his website, which I've passed on to the *Dieux du Stade* team."

Anna's head shot up.

"How many?"

"I know, and that's in just five days! It's like dating a Bond girl, you know, you dating Mr. February, Mr. June and Mr. August. Nick can be my Valentine any day of the year, you lucky cow."

Anna pursed her lips but didn't reply.

In hundreds of ways it was great dating Nick, but seeing other women ogle him had gotten old the first year they were together, and that had intensified since the calendar came out. She could only imagine what it would be like if the modelling took off. What if he became as well-known as Jamie Dornan or David Gandy? How would it feel then? It was one thing to be famous as a sportsman, but Anna wasn't naïve: modelling was about selling sex.

"Anna, what's going through your mind? You look constipated."

"God, Bren!"

But Anna laughed anyway. Brendan could get away with anything. He knew it and used the fact shamelessly.

"It just gets a bit tedious seeing other people, women, staring and whispering. Three of them came across to get selfies while we were having lunch at that pub by the Heath yesterday."

"Ooh, I love it there—very romantic. I adore their food and that corner nook with the enormous fireplace."

"Well, it was romantic until they barged in. Nick was polite, as always, but it just spoiled it."

Brendan shook his head.

"Green is not a good colour on you. You gotta do what Swifty says and shake it off."

"Easy for you to say—you're not engaged to Mr. February."

Anna's voice was wry as Brendan grinned at her.

Pleased that he'd made her smile, he pulled out his iPad and brought up the calendar feature.

"Now, when is Nick thinking of going to New York? I need to make sure that the schedules don't clash if you're going to be away for a month and…"

"Bren," Anna laid her hand on his arm. "I'm not going to New York; Nick's going by himself."

For once, Brendan was silenced, his mouth hanging open in surprise. Then he gave her a severe look.

"Would you like to explain that to me, Dr. Scott? Because I don't see anything in your schedule that would prevent you from going."

Anna bit her lip and shook her head.

"I just think he needs to do this by himself."

Brendan tapped his finger against his chin.

"And you think that because?"

Anna sighed.

"Bren, you've seen what he's been like since the testimonial. Going to France was the first time I've seen a spark in him since he retired. He needs to find his way on his own without me holding him back all of the time."

Brendan's eyes widened.

"You think you hold him back?"

"Not in so many words but … okay, yes, I do think that sometimes."

"Uh huh, and what is it that you think he'd be doing if you weren't here?"

Anna swallowed.

"I don't know. I'm not even sure he'd stay in London. He'd probably go back to Yorkshire to be near his family."

Brendan raised his eyes to the ceiling as if seeking divine intervention, then pinned Anna with a look.

"Anna, you're talking crap. Nick doesn't know what he wants to do. And as you've told me a thousand times, that's completely normal for a former athlete. He's quite clear that he doesn't want to coach and that he's made a clean break from rugby, but he doesn't know what's next for him. So why you think *you* should know is a complete mystery to me. I mean I'm 29 and I don't know what I want to be when I grow up."

"Bren, you were 31 last birthday."

"Ssh! Walls have ears!" he said dramatically. "And don't change the subject. Why aren't you going to New York? The truth now."

Anna leaned back in her chair.

"Like I said: he needs to do this on his own. I don't know if it's what he wants and neither does he, but having me hanging around his neck isn't helping. *I'm not helping.* Honestly, Bren, I think I make it worse for him, like he feels guilty because he sees me working all hours and he doesn't have anything to focus on. I don't want him to feel guilty. I want him to find something that he wants to do. Maybe it's modelling, maybe it's not, but it's got to be because it interests him, not because he thinks that I want him to do it."

Brendan squinted at her.

"Hmm, that makes a sort of twisted sense. What did Nick say when you told him that?"

Anna cringed.

"What did you do?" Brendan cried out.

Anna sank lower in her seat.

"I lied," she mumbled.

"What?"

"I lied! I told him I was too busy to go to New York."

Brendan slapped his forehead.

"Annie!"

"I know! I know! Don't yell at me." She took a deep breath. "I'm going to miss him so much. But I'm setting him free."

CHAPTER

10

NEW YORK CITY.
Nick felt a surge of excitement rippling through the wave of tiredness from the transatlantic flight.

And a sense of liberation. Although maybe leaving London on 1st April—April Fool's Day—could be an omen. He hoped not.

A clean sheet.

And with that came the now familiar pinch of guilt. He missed Anna, but it was a relief to be away from her disappointment, her sadness.

She'd been so excited by the offer from the modelling agency, and encouraged him to talk to Adrienne and seriously consider modelling as a career. Anna had said all the right things, been supportive, but deep down Nick knew that she'd have said that about anything he showed the slightest interest in.

He knew that he'd been drifting since he'd retired from rugby. He missed it like hell. He missed the team, he missed the training, and God, he missed game days—the high from a big win—there was nothing like it.

He didn't miss getting injured and he didn't miss the pummeling his body took every weekend.

But rugby was in the past and he had to find a way to live in the present; he had to think about the future.

Maybe the modelling gig would be something. Nick hardly cared because it was so foreign compared to everything he'd ever done before—he'd never thought about his looks, never thought about the way his body was sculpted except in so far as how he could perform on the rugby field. But if a world renowned photographer like Massimo Igashi said he had what it took, he'd be a fool to ignore it.

Besides, he couldn't stand seeing the way Anna watched him constantly, as if he was going to break apart or maybe just vanish if she took her eyes off him. She smiled, but beneath the surface, he felt her doubt, her uncertainty. Did she doubt him, or their engagement? He wasn't sure.

But he did know that he had to find something outside their relationship; it wasn't fair for all the responsibility of his life to weigh on Anna. He was a man and he needed to act like one. He needed to do this on his own terms.

So he'd been relieved that the main core of the agent's contacts extended across the US, but not so much in Europe. In the UK, France, Germany and Italy, he was Nick Renshaw, Rugby World Cup champion; in America, he was an unknown—and that suited him. If he was going to make it as a model, then it would be on its own merit. He never, ever wanted to hear someone say, *Didn't he used to be somebody?*

Striding across the arrivals hall at JFK, he swung his heavy backpack onto his shoulder and found the line for his pre-booked taxi along with a group of German tourists. As they drove through the darkening streets of Queens, he stared out of the window as the minivan crossed the East River into Manhattan, waiting patiently as the taxi dropped off the tourists at several hotels and then stopped at a Midtown address.

Nick thanked the driver, gathered his bags and jogged up the short flight of steps to a glass door. A receptionist peered at him then buzzed the door open.

He smiled at her politely.

"Hi, I'm Nick Renshaw. I have an appointment with Adrienne."

"Excuse me?"

Nick repeated himself, then watched with bemusement while she wrote down his name incorrectly three times before she got it right.

"Oh! Nick, Ren-*shuer*!" she said as if the light had just dawned. "It's your accent. Are you Scottish?"

"No, from Yorkshire."

"Is that in Scotland?"

"No, England. Northern England."

"Oh wow, you don't sound English. Okay, that's cool. I'll let Adrienne know that you're here. Do you have your book?"

"My book?"

The woman gave him a surprised look.

"Jeez, your *book!* Photographs of you modelling."

"Oh, my portfolio, yeah, right," Nick nodded.

Elisa had sent him a selection of photographs from Massimo's shoot: the requisite full body, half-body (waist up), and full face pictures that every potential model needed, apparently. Nick had also brought some shots of him in action playing rugby, but he was on the fence about whether or not to include them in his portfolio. Maybe someone would advise him on that.

His new agent, Adrienne Catalano, was a contact of Massimo's. On the basis of the photographs from the calendar shoot, she'd agreed to sign Nick, but this first meeting face to face was still important to establish a good working relationship.

As he was waiting, he glanced around at his surroundings. The walls were stark white, decorated with stylish monochrome photographs of beautiful women, as well as some who looked homeless or as if they'd been dosing up on meth. Nick had never understood the appeal of heroin-chic as a look. He preferred a woman who was a healthy weight, who looked like she enjoyed her food—someone like Anna.

There were only a few pictures of guys, and none who were built like Nick. These men were all super slim fashion models, and although they had defined muscles, they weren't ripped like he was. Several of them were downright skinny.

Nick already knew how difficult it was for him to find clothes that fit. His quads were far bigger than average and getting jeans to fit over his thighs that didn't also hang off his waist was a challenge. Thank God for stretch denim.

"Adrienne will see you now."

Nick followed the receptionist down a narrow hallway decorated with more framed photographs, these all from magazine covers and in colour, and into Adrienne's office.

Sitting behind a heavy desk was a short, fierce-looking woman, dressed entirely in black. Her dark brown eyes were framed by thick glasses and topped by a blunt fringe.

As she reached out to shake hands, her wrists jangled with dozens of silver bangles and bracelets.

"Hey, Nick! It's nice to meet you! How are you? How was the flight? Did you bring your book? Great. Have you checked into your hotel yet?"

Nick blinked, bombarded with questions and still on London time, which by now was about midnight.

He pulled out his portfolio and placed into Adrienne's waiting hand.

"Yeah, not too bad thanks," he replied. "I thought I'd check into the hotel after this."

Adrienne scanned through the photographs quickly, muttering under her breath, then slid them into a pile and clasped her heavily ringed hands on top.

"So, Nick, here's the thing: we only have two other fitness models on our books and that's something I want to change since it's a growing market. In the past, we've focused on fashion models, which is a very different business. With your build, you wouldn't fit into that spec, although that's changing, too. Okay, take your shirt off, please."

"Now?"

She smiled at him in amusement.

"Gotta see the goods. Photos can be touched up."

Feeling slightly more self-conscious than he had with Massimo's team, Nick removed his leather jacket and t-shirt, standing topless in front of Adrienne as she scrutinized him across her desk.

"Nice ink. Turn around."

Nick followed her instructions, feeling her gaze burning across his back.

"Okay, you can get dressed now."

Nick picked up his t-shirt and yanked it over his head.

"So, the thing is, with that amount of ink, half the mean's health magazines won't want you. Sure, everything can be photoshopped, but that takes time, and time is money."

Nick deflated. He was proud of his ink—every piece meant something important to him and he didn't regret a single hour spent in his tattooist's chair. Had he come all this way for nothing?

Adrienne appraised him critically.

"But there are some niche markets that like that sort of work. I'll be honest: I have no idea how well castings will go for you. But Massimo's name will go a long way to get you in the door. In this business, there are people who have the stamina to keep bouncing back, and there are people who are damn quick to complain when things don't go as they plan. I've been in the industry 27 years. Some models spend years submitting and attending open calls. Well, you're only as good as your last picture. If you're not being asked in after they've seen your book and comp card, you're not right for the client right now. It doesn't mean that you won't be right for them in the future. There's only a certain amount of hours for them to see twenty or thirty different models. So you'd better be ready to be rejected. But you don't quit: you submit and resubmit your book. The industry changes like the wind. You're in good shape—I say, let's go for it. Are you ready to work, Nick?"

He grinned at her.

"I'm ready."

Adrienne hid a smile.

"Like a lamb to the slaughter," she sighed, amused by his enthusiasm, and handed him a piece of paper. "These are the addresses for seven castings that I'm sending you to tomorrow."

"Seven? Wow."

Adrienne raised an eyebrow.

"You could be doing as many as twenty castings in a day. That's quite common, but I thought I'd start you off gently. I'm sending one of my other models, Orion, as well. And this is your comp card."

"My what?"

Adrienne clicked her tongue.

"Gotta learn the lingo, Nick. Your comp card is your modelling résumé. Here…" and she handed him several stiff pieces of paper with one of Massimo's headshots on the cover. Nick flipped it over to find that the back had thumbnail pictures from the shoot, with Nick's vital statistics: height, weight, chest, waist, shoe size, eye and hair colour, nationality, and Adrienne's agency details. There were no rugby photos on it: not a single one.

Nick frowned and opened his mouth to speak, but Adrienne was already finishing up and checking the emails on her laptop.

"Now, the other way to get known is to see and be seen, which means I'll be telling you about parties where you can make important contacts. Go, be friendly but not too friendly," and she fixed him with a fierce stare.

Nick gave a small frown.

"I'm engaged."

"Hmm. Be polite, schmooze, but don't drink too much. Be professional at all times. Capiche?"

Nick nodded and Adrienne gave him a sharp look.

"Okay, so tomorrow, the first one on the list isn't an open call, so you'll probably be there about twenty minutes—could be less. Same with the others. Oh wait, number six is open so you could be there longer. Good luck, Nick. Call me when you're done. And when I find a party for you, I'll text you the details."

Nick left Adrienne's office a little stunned. He hadn't expected to be sent to a casting so quickly—certainly not seven in one day—but maybe this was how things were done in New York. He was more than happy to be busy.

All he needed to do now was eat and sleep. But not eat too much.

Yeah, that was the one part of modelling he wasn't going to enjoy.

Bringing up his hotel's address on his phone, he navigated his way through the evening streets, shivering slightly. New York was colder than it had been in London and he was regretting not bringing a heavier coat. Nick hadn't brought many clothes with him because he was only staying a month.

The hotel was one of the cheaper chains. Anna had wanted him to get something more upmarket, but Nick didn't need much to be comfortable. At least he didn't have to share with a teammate who snored his head off—take a bow, Jason Oduba.

Dumping his bags on the bed, Nick tested the mattress while he called Anna. She answered on the first ring.

"Nick! How are you?"

She sounded tired and he knew that it was nearly two in the morning. That ever-present guilt pinched a little harder.

"How was the flight?"

"Yeah, okay. The usual."

"No problems at immigration?"

"Nope—I had all the right paperwork and the queues weren't that long."

He heard the tension leave her voice.

"Did you meet with your agent yet?"

"Yep, Adrienne seems nice. I've got a casting call in the morning. Well, seven of them."

"Wait, did you say *seven?*"

"Yep! Crazy, isn't it? The first one is at 8.30AM."

"So early? And really, *seven?*"

He heard the surprise in her voice.

"Adrienne says that twenty in one day is normal."

"Wow! That sounds … full on, but I know you'll be great."

The warmth in her voice reached through the phone line to Nick. Why had it seemed a good idea to fly 3,000 miles away from her? But he knew that he'd always regret it if he didn't try this.

He decided not to tell her that he was supposed to attend parties as a way of getting noticed. He already knew that she was anxious about him being away from home—he didn't want her to worry even more.

They talked for a few more minutes before the time difference caught up with both of them and Anna started yawning.

Nick promised to call her the following day as soon as he'd been to the casting calls.

He sat on the bed and opened his suitcase, pulling out clothes and something to wear for the next day. At the bottom, he was surprised to find his camera bag, because he knew he hadn't packed it, along with two more small boxes containing new lenses. The first one had a note tucked inside.

My love,
I sent your photographs of Hampstead in the snow to Massimo. He thought they were beautiful, and recommended that you have these two extra lenses. I have no idea what they do, but I hope you find some use for them in the city.
Be yourself. Be amazing.
I love you.
A x

He unpacked the lenses, the possibilities running through his mind, then with a smile on his face and his camera bag over his shoulder, he headed out to find a light supper. When he finally got back to the hotel, he passed out for seven solid hours.

THE NEXT MORNING, Nick reached out for Anna, but his hand slid across cool, empty sheets and he remembered where he was.

New York City, baby! And he was here to kick arse, English-style. Well, Yorkshire-style.

He drew back the curtains, staring out at a concrete wall just a few feet from the window. Squinting upwards, the sky was the colour of charcoal, ominous with dark, heavy clouds.

Nick didn't care.

He stretched out his muscles, loosening everything and chasing away the usual aches and pains he felt on waking. After warming up, he sipped a few precious drops of water, then pulled on his sweats and running shoes, and did a quick three-mile circuit of Midtown, before going back to the hotel for a cup of coffee.

He was hungry but tried to ignore his stomach's complaints.

It'll be worth it if I get a job, he told himself.

And even if he didn't, it would be good experience.

He took a short shower, trimmed his beard and tied his hair back so it didn't hang in his eyes. He wore jeans and a plain grey t-shirt that clung to his shoulders and chest. If the casting calls were anything like yesterday, he wouldn't be wearing it for long. Nick shook his head in amusement: some people had damn strange jobs.

He opened a new pack of ibuprofen, stared at it for a moment, then swapped it for tramadol and popped two into his mouth, throwing his head back as he swallowed them. His shoulder was aching from sleeping on an unfamiliar mattress, and he wanted to feel his best for the interviews or whatever they were.

That's what he told himself.

CHAPTER 11

S INCE THE FIRST CASTING CALL WAS AT offices on the Upper East Side, only a couple of miles away, Nick decided to walk. Besides, he'd spent the whole of yesterday cooped up in a flying tin can.

With his portfolio and comp cards in a messenger bag, he strode through the streets, ignoring the light misting of rain that fogged the windows of numerous diners and coffee shops.

Everyone moved fast, everyone was in a hurry, and Nick felt the energy of the city rush through him. He felt excited, and he hadn't felt that for a long time.

At the last minute, he'd decided to take his camera with him. He probably wouldn't have time to do anything, but it would be good to take some test shots and work out conditions for the new lenses, if he had the chance. He still couldn't quite believe that Anna had done that for him, even going to the trouble of contacting Massimo.

He was damn lucky to have her in his life. The thought brought mixed feelings, because every day since he'd retired, he felt like he was letting her down in some subtle way. Not knowing how he'd spend the next fifty years was weighing on them both. He couldn't take another day of her relentless encouragement.

When he reached the address for the casting, he found a warehouse building that was accessed by a metal staircase attached to the outside wall. He was disappointed to find twenty other guys already there for the audition. All were a minimum of six foot and athletic, aged between 20 and 35; all carried comp cards and portfolios. But there the similarities ended. There were guys with long hair, short hair, blond hair, black hair, red hair, dyed hair, no hair; clean shaven, bearded, moustached, designer stubbled; black skin, white skin, and every color in between, from a guy whose skin shone in ebony glory, to a guy with the reddish-bronze tones of a man who could be Native American, to the olive tones of several men who appeared to be Hispanic, and two pale-skinned Slavic types with cheekbones that you could use to chisel granite.

Apparently, a shoot for *Men's Health* magazine was pretty random in the look that they were searching for.

He didn't want to unpick the irony that models had to be in amazing shape 365 days of the year, but got paid the most for wearing clothes.

He pulled out his camera and snapped a couple of quick shots—something to show Anna later.

He approached a bored woman at the reception desk and handed her his comp card.

"Name?"

"Nick Renshaw."

"Twenty-three. Take a seat."

There weren't any seats. Several guys were sitting on the floor, ear-buds in, heads nodding to music. Most of the rest were looking at their phones, and one guy seemed to be asleep.

Nick leaned against the wall, angling himself so he could look out of the window. People-watching was endlessly fascinating in New York, and from here he could keep an eye on proceedings at the casting, as well.

One of the models stood up from his position near the front of the line and strolled over.

"Nick, right? I'm Orion Lucas—Adrienne Catalano said I'd be seeing you here."

They shook hands, sizing each other up.

"How you liking New York?"

"Yeah, good so far. I only got in last night so I haven't seen much yet."

"You never been before?"

"Not really, but my fiancée is from upstate so she's told me some places that I have to visit."

"She with you?"

Nick shook his head.

"No, she had to work."

"Tough break. So what's your method?"

Nick was puzzled.

"My method for what?"

"You know, training and dieting for a casting call."

"Oh, right. Low carbs, high protein; cardio in the morning, weights in the afternoon; dehydrate for the shoot day."

"Man, I hate that part," said another model, listening to the conversation. "I get so thirsty I'd cut a motha for a soda, yeah? Makes me crazy."

Another model joined in, complaining bitterly about having to give up beer, even over New Years.

Nick was aware that if he was going to make it in this business, he had to be in the best shape of his life every single day, but having trained as a professional athlete, he was used to it; he was used to the discipline, enjoyed it even. The only difference now was that he was 15 pounds lighter than when he'd been playing.

The guys droned on about their protein shakes, diets, and workouts in tedious detail. Most of them seemed to know each other, having met at other castings, and Nick was surprised by how small the pool of models seemed to be. There was camaraderie combined with competitiveness that made for an air of bored tension and frustration, and several of them bitched about the wait.

Two were Instagram models who got called to castings even though they didn't have agents. The business was changing, they said. Nick knew that he had a lot to learn.

"You dating?"

Nick glanced over and saw that Orion was talking to him again.

"Yep, she's back home."

"Oh yeah, you said. My bad. So, how long you been together?"

"Nearly five years now."

"Wow, that's like a really long time!" said Orion. "I didn't have a girlfriend until I was 19. I was short and skinny at high school—crazy, I know. And I took a virginity pledge."

Nick frowned.

"What's that?"

"Wait, you don't have that in the UK? Man! In my church, they encouraged us to save ourselves for marriage, you know?"

Nick could see that Orion was serious.

"What happened?"

"I grew to 6' 1" and began working out. Then I started getting hit on." He shrugged. "But once you start having sex, it's kind of hard to stop. And I know it sounds shallow, but once I went to this girl's house just to have sex. She made me wait outside because she didn't have her makeup on. I mean really, we were going to have sex for 20 minutes—it wasn't a date."

For some reason, Orion's words reminded Nick of Molly. That was exactly the kind of thing she'd do. He didn't like thinking about his ex-. Ever.

He caught a few words of the conversation that Orion was having with the model standing next to him as the guy held his two thumbs together.

"My dick is wider than that."

"Mine isn't," said the other model sadly.

Nick glanced at Orion and he shrugged.

"Steroids. It makes your dick small and your hair fall out. See that bald guy?"

Nick followed his gaze. The model's biceps were bigger than Anna's thighs.

Nick wasn't naïve. He'd seen athletes fall to temptation in the bid to get bigger and stronger, or recover from injury more quickly. But the repercussions of being caught were serious. Nick had never taken steroids—it put too much strain on the heart; all his physique had been gained the hard way.

He thought about the tramadol he'd taken that morning.

"He won't get the job," Orion continued to whisper. "I don't know why his agent keeps sending him. Plus he's really *old*, like thirty or something."

Nick tuned out the rest of the conversation.

When Nick's number was called, he walked into the room where a panel of three men and two women were sitting behind a long table.

"Nick, if you could change into your underwear behind the screen and stand over there."

Nick did as he was told, wearing his lucky Speedos, but before he'd even turned around, one of the women said, "God, no, too many tats. Didn't we put that in the spec?"

"Guess not," said another.

"Where are you from, Nick?"

"The UK."

"Uh-huh. And how long have you been in the Big Apple?"

"I arrived yesterday."

"Uh-huh. Have you modeled before?"

"Just once. I did a calendar shoot for Massimo Igashi."

The man stopped writing notes and looked up.

"You did a shoot with Massimo?"

"Yes, the photographs are in my portf— book," and he pointed to a couple of images.

"And you're a ... rugby player?"

"Uh, yeah ... I'm ... on a break," Nick said, not wanting to admit that he was officially retired.

That just sounded so *old*.

The interviewers exchanged looks with each other and made some more notes.

"Well, thank you for stopping by."

Nick dragged his clothes back on, picked up his portfolio, and walked out of the room.

Orion was waiting for him.

"You strike out, too?"

"Yep. I was in there less than a minute."

Orion laughed ruefully.

"Pretty brutal, huh? Welcome to the Big Apple. Better head to the next one."

At the second call, Nick was in for nearly five minutes and thought he might have a chance, but when they asked him to put on the clothes that they'd laid out and he couldn't even get the trousers over his quads, he knew that he wouldn't be hearing back from them.

When he looked at the models he was competing with, although they were athletic, they weren't as muscled as him. So even though he was pounds lighter than his playing days, he was still b-i-g.

The third casting went the same way. The fourth one decided that he had too many tattoos. The fifth one was cancelled with no notice, but the sixth one was an open casting with over a hundred guys lined up through the hallway and down the stairs. One young lad had flown in from Ohio and was devastated when he'd been shown the door in less than three minutes.

Nick felt for him, but there was no advice he could offer.

Orion had had a similarly luckless day.

"You wanna go get a beer?"

"I wouldn't say no," Nick agreed tiredly.

They sat and drank for a couple of hours and Orion admitted that his real name was 'Ryan' but that he used a stage name for his modelling career.

"So you haven't really done much modelling, brah," Orion surmised.

"Nope. Just gonna see how the cards fall."

Orion finished his third beer and ordered a fourth.

"Well, lookout for the sleazoid photographers—there are plenty of those around."

Nick frowned.

"What do you mean?"

"Do you do nudes, brah?"

Nick shook his head.

"No, I told Adrienne that I wouldn't do that."

It was true and she hadn't been happy about it. But Nick knew that if those types of photographs got into the British tabloid press, the media storm wouldn't be pleasant, for him or Anna. It had been hard for him to trust Massimo Igashi, but seeing the results of the shoot in the calendar hadn't been too bad, and no dick pics had reached the newspapers or websites.

"Smart move, brah," Orion said, nodding thoughtfully. "Some just want to see you naked. Some photographers make it a requirement if you shoot with them, you have to shoot nudes which they can keep or sell to private collectors. It's the same with girls, I'd guess."

"Private collectors?"

He definitely didn't like the sound of that.

"Yeah, and even the ones who don't do nudes can be just as bad—they sleaze all over you." Orion waved his bottle around. "You'll see."

THE REST OF the week passed the same way. At each casting call, there was something wrong with him and the rejections kept on coming. Everyone assured him it was normal, but it was hard to take.

Nick realized that it really wasn't unusual to do as many as twenty castings in a day, every day, for a whole week. Hell, it wouldn't be easy to stay positive when you were rejected that many times in a day. By the end of the week, yeah, he was so over it.

But at least he was getting to see New York. He loved that there was a Starbucks on every corner and that he could walk everywhere in Manhattan. He was also learning his way around the Subway system.

He was used to the fast pace of London life, but this was even more frenetic. By the end of two weeks, he was striding along the streets as fast as a native. He even found a few spare hours to visit

Times Square, went to the movies—twice—and checked out all the Thai food in the area, a guilty pleasure.

He missed Anna and Facetimed her every night, trying to talk positively about yet another round of rejections. She was remorselessly upbeat, certain that he'd get work soon. He didn't like to disabuse her ideas and point out that at each casting there were younger, better-looking, more eager guys. And most of them could wear normal jeans over their quads.

That evening, Adrienne gave him details of a party in Lower Manhattan that he needed to attend, dressed 'smart casual', whatever the hell that meant. Nick preferred either jeans and a t-shirt, or a three piece suit. He disliked trying to do something in between.

In the end, he wore his favourite black jeans, with a plain white shirt. He glanced at himself in the mirror. *Good enough.*

It felt odd turning up at a party where he didn't know the hosts or any of the people going, but when he rang the buzzer to the penthouse suite in a large apartment building, he was ushered in with no questions asked.

The room was full to bursting, with dozens of people spilling out onto the wraparound balcony that gave a stunning view across the East River and toward Brooklyn.

Nick was happy to stand outside, leaning on the balcony with a cold beer in his hand. For one thing, the room was thick with cigarette smoke, and Nick valued his lungs too much to stay inside.

He glanced down as a woman came to stand beside him.

"Quite a view, huh?"

"Yeah, it's beautiful," he said.

"Oh my God! I just love your accent! Scotland, right?"

Nick shook his head bemused. She was the second person who'd thought he was from north of the border.

"No, Yorkshire. But I guess I have quite a strong accent," he chuckled.

The woman eyed his broad shoulders and narrow waist.

"What brought you to the Big Apple?"

He answered slightly self-consciously.

"I've signed with a modelling agency, so I'm just seeing how it goes for a while."

She smiled broadly.

"I shoulda guessed," and she held out her hand. "I'm Kirsten."

"Nick. Pleased to meet you."

"The pleasure's all mine," she purred, shaking out her hair of thick, honey-coloured curls and smiling seductively.

Nick couldn't help noticing that she had an impressive chest. Unfortunately, she caught him glancing down and immediately got the wrong impression.

"Well, that's a little premature, Nick, but maybe if you bring me another drink..."

Nick's eyes widened as he shook his head.

"Sorry, um, sorry! I ... uh ... no offence, but I'm engaged."

Kirsten laughed loudly at his panicked expression.

"Oh well, in that case, maybe we can have an old fashioned conversation?"

Nick smiled with relief.

"That would be great."

They chatted for another hour and Nick did absolutely no networking whatsoever. Then they decided to leave the party to find somewhere to get some food.

As they left the apartment, Nick opened the door for Kirsten, who smiled up at him appreciatively.

Suddenly, Nick was blinded by a flash as a reporter snapped a picture.

"Bloody hell, mate!" Nick protested.

The man ignored him, snapped another couple of pictures then turned to his colleague who hadn't even raised his camera.

"You know the dude?"

"Nah, man. He's no one."

Nick knew that it was better that no one over here recognized him, but the insult stung.

"Couple of charmers, huh?" said Kirsten, shaking her head.

Still irritated, Nick escorted her to dinner at a nearby Italian restaurant where they enjoyed each other's company, before Kirsten called a cab and kissed Nick on the cheek when she left.

THE NEXT DAY, Nick got his first 'yes'.

The casting had gone well, and the clients had seemed genuinely interested in his rugby career. They asked a lot of questions about the sport and how long he'd played, and then told him they wanted him for some sportswear ads that they'd be doing for a well-known company.

Feeling good, Nick considered blowing off the final casting of the day, but decided that since his luck was changing, he'd make the effort.

Orion was already there and came right over to Nick.

"Man! I heard you got the Walmart job! Nice one!"

Nick raised his eyebrows.

"How do you know it's for Walmart? Even *I* don't know that."

Orion grinned.

"Word gets around, but one of my buddies recognized the marketing woman who interviewed you because she saw him last year for a different campaign." He shrugged. "Like I said, word gets around." Then he side-eyed Nick. "I heard that Bruce Waters is the photographer on that."

"I don't know, they didn't say."

"Walmart use him sometimes. Just … look out for him."

"What?"

Orion pulled a face.

"He's kind of sleazy."

Nick's face hardened.

A COUPLE OF days later, a car arrived at Nick's hotel to take him to the shoot. He'd been keyed up about it ever since Orion's cryptic comment. He'd Googled the photographer's name, but nothing of concern had shown up. Anna had said he shouldn't take the job if he had doubts, so Nick decided to play it by ear.

He felt better when he saw that the shoot was at a gym that was part of a well-known fitness chain. Nothing sleazy about that.

He was met at the door by a fresh-faced, smiling woman of about 23, who immediately offered him coffee, water and bagels.

"Eh, sorry," he smiled. "No food for me until the shoot's over, but I'll take a black coffee."

She blushed bright red.

"Oh em gee! I'm so sorry! I completely forgot! I'm an intern— this is the first shoot I've done. I'll get you that coffee. And, oh wow, I'm real sorry."

"I'll take over from here, Laura," said a short, whip-thin man with a shaved head and a Frank Zappa beard and moustache.

"It's Alana," muttered the girl as she scurried away.

"I'm Bruce," the man said, holding Nick's hand for just half a second too long. "My goodness, Mike, you're even more imposing in person than in print."

"It's Nick."

The man didn't appear to hear him, too busy examining Nick's body, his lips wet and his eyes moist.

"Now, Mike, I'd just like to have a word with you in private—discuss what we'll be doing today."

Assuming a blank expression, Nick followed him.

"We have the gym's studio booked all day," said Bruce. "So I thought it might be fun to do some work that's a little more expressive, more creative, once the bread and butter shots are finished. What do you say? I think we could create something wonderful together."

"What did you have in mind?" Nick asked, folding his arms over his chest, definitely not feeling relaxed.

"Call me Bruce," he said, touching Nick's shoulder, then patting his arm. "And of course there's more money, as a little sweetener. You have a beautiful face," and he ran a finger along Nick's jaw before he could step back. "But let's chat later."

Nick had a pretty shrewd idea what the after-shoot would involve, thanks to Orion's heads-up. But it wasn't hard to pick up the sleazy vibe either.

But if Nick thought the man would be easy to deflect, he was dead wrong.

Bruce was too touchy-feely, invading Nick's personal space at every possible opportunity. He criticized the hair stylist to the point of making her cry, and then insisted on running his hands through Nick's hair and massaging his scalp. Then the makeup artist was also declared incompetent, according to Bruce, and he had to take over brushing powder over Nick's face, stroking the brush along his cheekbones repeatedly.

The final straw for Nick was when Bruce shimmied across with a bottle of baby oil with the clear intention of rubbing it over him personally.

"Thanks," said Nick, grabbing the bottle. "I can do that."

There was silence in the studio as all the assistants pretended not to see the tense standoff.

Bruce walked away with an annoyed huff as Nick applied oil to his chest, arms, legs and back.

After that, the shoot went more smoothly. Bruce's instructions were terse, but if there was one thing Nick knew, it was how to look the part in sportswear.

But at the end of the shoot, Bruce packed up his equipment without speaking to anyone, except to yell at Alana to call him a cab.

He heard later that Bruce had called Adrienne to complain about Nick's 'unprofessional attitude'.

To make things worse, Nick's innocent encounter with Kirsten had been published in the British press with a suggestive headline:

Naughty Nick—up to his old tricks in New York

The photograph showed him smiling warmly at Kirsten. Her low-cut dress showcased the chest that had caught Nick's eye, and the two of them looked very cosy together.

The story was two days old—which meant that Anna must have been aware of it for two days, but hadn't said a word.

Nick phoned her immediately.

"I just saw what they're saying about me in the tabloids," he began. "You know it's just rubbish, don't you?"

There was a long pause and Anna sighed.

"Yeah, I figured that. But when you didn't say anything…"

Nick rubbed his forehead.

"I didn't know there was anything to say! I met her weeks ago…"

At Anna's sharp intake of breath, Nick knew that he'd said the wrong thing and backtracked hurriedly.

"She was just someone I met at a party. We talked for a while and then went to grab dinner. I haven't seen her since. That's it."

Anna's voice sounded very small.

"That happened weeks ago but you never said a word?"

Nick grimaced.

"I didn't want you to worry. God, I've made it worse, but I swear! Nothing happened! You believe me, don't you?"

"Yes," Anna said softly. "Of course I do, but Nick, don't let me read about it in the newspapers next time; don't let me be the last to know. You have no idea how much that hurt." Her voice dropped to a whisper. "I had journalists outside the door asking how I felt about your new girlfriend."

Nick felt like the biggest shit ever.

"I'm sorry, Anna. I love you. I'd never hurt you—not knowingly."

"I know."

Nick's heart cracked at the sadness in her voice, and he promised himself that he'd never keep anything from her again, no matter how seemingly insignificant.

NICK'S EXPERIENCE WITH the sleazy photographer was nothing new, according to Orion. And all the models he met at other castings had similar stories. It seemed to be accepted as part of the industry, unpleasant, but inevitable.

Some of the models said they would have taken the extra bucks, and a twenty-something guy named Eduardo summed up that attitude:

"If he wants to jerk off to photos of me with my dick out, why should I care? At least I've gotten a better chance of getting picked for another campaign in the future."

Nick wasn't so sure. He couldn't see a family-oriented company like Walmart wanting models who could end up on porn sites, but he kept his opinions to himself.

He realized how amazingly lucky he'd been to work with a genuine artist like Massimo.

When he told Anna, she was appalled.

"I can't believe that photographer gets away with it! What did Adrienne say?"

Nick settled back on his hotel bed during their nightly Facetime.

"She said that she knew, but he hadn't crossed any boundaries and that's how he gets away with it. Because I made it clear I wasn't interested, he didn't go any further."

Anna looked furious.

"Yes, but imagine if you're 19 and alone in New York and trying to make it as a model, getting deeper and deeper into debt, believing someone like that when they tell you all the models do it. You'd have no one to talk to, nowhere to turn. Ugh, it makes me sick!"

Nick had to agree. The whole encounter had left him feeling unclean. But there was no doubt that the work had dried up.

Now, he was bored and feeling stir crazy.

In the past two weeks, he'd only been to three castings and hadn't received a single call back.

That evening, he'd picked up and discarded his iPad a dozen times, checked out at least fifty of the hotel's free TV channels before he got bored of that, too. He even wished he'd brought his guitar, although it had been months since he'd picked it up and played it.

He didn't like feeling bored, it seemed such a waste of life. But he'd already been for a six mile run and a two-hour workout. He missed Anna more each day, the loneliness and sense of failure adding another brick to the weight pressing down on him. Back in London, their quiet evenings while they cooked dinner together were special. Sometimes they went to the cinema or a sport fundraiser. Nick liked his home and he missed it.

But he was also smart enough to know that if he was at home now, that sense of dissatisfaction, the failure that he carried with him would be just the same. Being in New York proved the point that wherever you go, you take your problems with you.

He hadn't expected it to be easy, so he just kept going: another day, another dollar. He was here, so he was going to make the most of it.

He'd also done a lot of sightseeing, capturing his experiences on film, and enjoyed sharing them with Anna when they Facetimed each evening.

There were times that he wished she was with him, but she was busy at home with work and her own life; there were also times when Nick enjoyed doing something for himself and by himself. He'd been part of team life since he was a kid—it was refreshing to make a go of things on his own.

He walked everywhere, believing it was the best way to get to know a new area. He'd done that when they first moved to London, and still enjoyed exploring new parts of the city.

One thing that had surprised him about New Yorkers was how upfront they were. Both men and women hit on him when he was out, even joining him at a restaurant table while he enjoyed a meal alone.

At first, he'd simply told the truth and would say that he was travelling by himself, but he was engaged. That didn't seem to put off anyone; in fact some women had taken that as a come-on, and twice women had simply sat down at his table and started talking to him.

No matter how politely he tried to tell them that he wasn't interested, they just wouldn't take no for an answer until he'd actually stood up and walked out.

So many times, in fact, that he'd started telling people that he was rushing to catch a flight, and then he'd end up bolting his meal and getting indigestion. He didn't know what it was, but New Yorkers were a lot harder to blow off than the British.

Occasionally, he bought a boxed salad or deli meal and took it back to the hotel to eat in peace; but just recently he'd found a diner that had a counter you could sit at, and since he started getting to know the staff, they intervened if they found him stuck with another admirer.

"You're too nice," the owner, Franco, had told him. "Just tell 'em to take a hike."

Nick shook his head.

"I couldn't do that."

"Well, imagine that your girlfriend was the one being hit on. What would ya say then?"

Nick glowered, his eyes narrowing.

Franco laughed.

"Give 'em that look, buddy!"

But that evening, since Nick had already eaten and had a light beer on his way back to the hotel, he didn't even have the excuse to go out to get some food.

Just as he'd decided to go back to the gym for another workout, his cellphone rang and Orion's name flashed up.

Normally, Nick would have let it go to voicemail, but tonight he was bored enough to answer.

"Nick, buddy! How ya doin'?"

"Not bad. How are you?"

"Yeah, I'm good, great! Adrienne is sending me for another casting with a top clothing company next week. She's really excited about it—she says it could be the big one."

Nick didn't bother to reply. He'd had the same conversation with Orion a dozen times before. The guy was always convinced that the next call would be from Giorgio Armani in person, offering him a six-figure contract. Either he really believed that or he'd read in a self-help book that portraying a positive image would bring its own rewards. He certainly didn't believe in downplaying his assets, which meant that he and Nick had almost nothing in common—other than their agent.

But Nick had no friends in New York, so Orion was it.

"You busy tonight?"

Nick was cautious.

"Got a few things I was going to take care of…"

"Can them, brah. I've been invited to this party tonight and I was told to bring some friends. Word is, it's going to be amazing. Everyone will be there—great place to get noticed. You in?"

Nick had done the club scene in his twenties—it was mostly about drinking and hooking up, neither of which he was interested in doing. He also wasn't interested in repeating the Kirsten fiasco.

Orion sensed his hesitation.

"Ah, come on, man! It's kind of a big deal—a lot of scouts and agents will be there—see and be seen, right?"

Nick weighed up the choices: another night in by himself, or hang out with Orion and his friends for a few hours.

In the end, Nick found himself agreeing to meet Orion in Greenwich Village at a bar they'd gone to once before.

Orion was sitting with three other guys in their mid to late twenties who were all trying to make it in the modelling biz. Nick recognized the quick appraisal they gave him, the look that he saw at every casting as the other models assessed the competition.

He shook hands with them, then sat down on a barstool while Orion went to the bathroom and then to get the drinks. Nick had asked for a bottle of Heineken, but Orion reappeared with a tray of tequila shots.

They downed two each in quick succession, then Brodie, who seemed to be the one with the connections, announced it was time to leave. Orion was almost leaping out of his seat, so antsy to leave. From the way his pupils had shrunk to pinpricks, Nick guessed that more than a bathroom break had taken place.

He didn't like being around drugs—it reminded him of how out of control he'd been when he was drinking during a really low point in his life. He promised himself that whatever went down at the party, he'd only drink water.

Brodie led them down a side alley, stopped at a heavy steel door and knocked twice.

An enormous doorman waved them in, then signaled his equally vast colleague to pat them down. He found Orion's stash of … whatever it was, probably speed … but handed the packet back to him. But the phones were confiscated.

Nick gripped his phone in his hand and narrowed his eyes at Orion who shrugged.

"Lot of powerful people here, brah, like I said. You gotta go with the flow."

Reluctantly, Nick handed over his phone, then they were allowed to enter.

The narrow staircase opened out into an enormous warehouse apartment, with runway lighting turned down low, and the music turned up.

Everywhere Nick looked, people were dancing and drinking.

The smell of weed was thick in the heated air, and Nick felt sweat breaking out across his body. Orion pushed a bottle of beer into his hand and yelled something in his ear that sounded like 'rabid arty' or possibly something about rabbits. Oh, wait, 'rad party'. Was it 1990 again?

Nick thought it was more naff than rad, or 'lame' as Orion might have said if he wasn't so jacked on speed. He'd rather have a beer with his mates down the pub than stand around watching strangers getting stoned. Any athlete who took drugs risked his career: urine tests were random, four picked from the team sheet or training sheet—and mandatory.

A representative from the drug testing company would watch you piss into a tube, two samples, and a positive result for a banned substance would result in a ban: six months for amphetamines, and up to two years for steroids.

Even common cold remedies could contain banned substances.

"Let's get our party on!" yelled Orion, ripping off his shirt.

He wasn't the only one. Anyone who was young and hot was showing a lot of skin. Several of the girls were wearing bikinis, although Nick hadn't seen a pool. The older party guests exuded wealth and power, and wore designer clothes and expensive jewellery.

Nick grimaced and turned in the other direction, pushing his way through the crowds. Men and women were openly snorting coke, their eyes too bright, their laughter too loud, acting like they were having the best time on earth.

It was pretty obvious that a number of the partiers were underage: definitely under 21, probably still in their teens. Nick winced as a girl who looked like she should still be at school, smoked something that wasn't a cigarette or a spliff, her eyes glazing over and rolling back in her head. The surrounding people laughed as a guy caught her when her knees gave way and carried her from the room.

And it wasn't just girls. Young, thin, pretty boys who looked as though they were enjoying a growth spurt strutted around the room in muscle vests and skinny jeans, hanging off the arms of the rich and powerful, hoping that some of the shine would come their way.

It was as if the *#MeToo* campaign had never happened.

Nick recognized the sleazy photographer from the week before, the short guy with the roving hands.

"The bad boy brooding look really works on you, sugar."

Nick frowned down at a woman who'd been hiding her age behind Botox for at least three decades.

"I'm gonna take a guess and say … you're a model. Am I right?"

Nick nodded, his stance wary.

"Come sit with me a little bit. I have friends who could use a guy like you. All you need is the right connections and you're golden."

She patted the sofa and crossed her legs, letting the thigh high split in her dress reveal her lack of underwear.

"No, thanks," Nick said, his lip curling as he backed away.

"You're quite a prude, aren't you?"

Nick's eyes darkened with anger. As a rule, he wasn't prone to losing his temper anymore, but he'd been on edge since he arrived.

"If you think using these kids is prudish, then yeah. If you think telling them that they're going to get rich and famous by sleeping with people old enough to be their grandparents is prudish, definitely."

She laughed in his face.

"How long you been in the Big Apple, sugar?"

"Too bloody long," Nick muttered as he walked away.

He dumped the rest of his beer and headed for the stairs. Orion had disappeared and Nick had no intention of looking for him or the other models he'd arrived with.

He passed two girls making out, half naked, ringed by a group of much older men cheering them on, one of them filming the whole scene. *How the hell had he been allowed to keep his phone?*

As he passed back along the corridor, the party had ramped up and couples or groups were making use of the bedrooms, fucking and being fucked. It wasn't the sex that bothered him but the feeling that this was about people being used: young, desperate models, actors and actresses, prepared to do anything to work their way to the top, when instead, they were being sucked into the gutter.

Nick felt dirty by association and wondered if the police would be interested in this so-called party: underage drinking, probably underage sex too, maybe people being paid for sex, he wasn't sure. There were definitely drugs available.

He jogged down the stairs and demanded his phone back from the stony-eyed doorman. Nick's breathing was fast as his anger rose. He stood almost nose to nose with the 250 pound man, matching his cold stare until his phone was returned, then he was out in the street.

He filled his lungs with the night air, breathing in the stink of car fumes, which was preferable to the stench of money, privilege and predators in the building behind him.

And suddenly a memory came back to him, an assistant coach from one of the under-15s teams he'd played for: a creepy guy who was always around when the boys showered after practice. Nick hadn't thought of him in years.

He pulled out his phone to call the police and then paused. He'd been present at the party—any number of people could identify him. If he called the police that would be a short hop to them finding out that he had a criminal record. And then, no one would believe a word he said.

Anna would do the right thing.

Those were the words that echoed through his mind. In the end, he bought a cheap pay-as-you-go phone, considering the $37 well spent when he dialled 911 and told them what he'd seen, doing his best to disguise his voice.

Then he binned the phone and headed back to his hotel, sick at heart.

"You did the right thing," Anna whispered as Nick lay in bed.

Her day was just starting but Nick hadn't slept yet.

"Did I? I could have done more."

Anna sighed.

"In an ideal world, yes, you could have called the police and waited for them to arrive, then point out the perpetrators. But it's not an ideal world and you'd have been putting yourself at risk."

Nick closed his eyes. He'd needed to hear her words, needed to hear her voice, needed her to tell him that he wasn't a complete shit and a coward.

"What you saw goes on in every industry, everyone knows it. With all the publicity from Weinstein onwards, more has come into the light, but there's just as much hiding in dark corners. You can't be everyone's hero, Nick." She paused. "But you are mine."

Nick gave a quiet huff of laughter.

"How do you always know the right things to say?"

This time the pause was even longer and her voice was serious.

"Because we've both been through the fire, and we both know that black and white are just colours on a page."

Nick held the phone tightly, concentrating on her voice.

The next day, Nick scanned all the news sites to see if there was anything about the party, but he couldn't find a single mention. And when his curiosity couldn't take it anymore, he texted Orion, but the only response he got was a winking emoji.

The party was never mentioned again.

CHAPTER 12

Nick's month had passed several weeks ago and summer was around the corner, but he wasn't ready to admit defeat and go home. He missed Anna with a physical ache in the centre of his chest. He found himself rubbing the spot at random moments.

He'd moved to a cheap room to save money, but the thought of failing at this left a bitter taste in his mouth. Just one shot, one chance, one good shoot and he'd feel less of a failure.

Anna told him to take his time and that she'd support him whatever he decided. In some ways, he wished she wasn't so upbeat about his so-called modelling career. It would have been nice to hear that she missed him and wanted him home. But she was resolutely positive that this would work out, so he had no choice but to keep trying—for a while, at least.

On the way back from his workout, Nick saw that he'd had a

message from Adrienne's assistant to call her. As the gym was quite close to the agency, he decided to drop by instead.

"Hey, Nick," said Adrienne's PA when she saw him. "How ya' doin'?"

"Yeah, alright thanks, Shonda. How are you?"

She closed her eyes dreamily.

"Oh wow, I just love your accent! Let me see if Adrienne can see you."

After a short conversation, she told him to go on in.

"Nick, have a seat. I might have something for you."

"Wow, really? That would make a nice change."

Adrienne threw him a look.

"I told you at the start, you've gotta be tough in this game."

Nick felt duly chastised.

"So, how do you feel about romance?"

Nick blinked.

"Um, Anna says I can be romantic."

Adrienne cackled loudly.

"I'm sure, honey! I meant, how do you feel about doing a photo shoot for a romance book cover? Small shoot, established photographer who's looking for someone just like you. Hmm, let me see … yes, his name is Golden Czermak, nice guy, well known in his field. Prefers fitness models and I think he does some modelling himself. He's in NYC for a couple of days and wants to fit in a shoot tomorrow at his hotel room. Legit guy. Interested?"

"Has he seen any pictures of me?"

Nick was cautious. He'd lost so many gigs because they didn't like his size or his tattoos—he really wasn't interested in wasting more time.

"Yep, and he likes your look," Adrienne said immediately. "He's got plenty of ink himself, so that won't be an issue."

Nick nodded.

"Sure, I'll give it a go."

"Excellent! Here are the details."

Nick was slightly dubious since the shoot was at this guy's hotel, but he figured if he didn't like it, he could just walk out. Although checking over the photographer's Facebook page, he seemed on the level.

So the next morning, Nick turned up at the hotel room in Midtown and knocked on the door.

It was yanked open by a small, energetic woman with cropped black hair and a wide-eyed, windswept expression.

Several more women were giggling and laughing behind her, and when Nick heard the sound of a champagne cork popping, he thought he'd walked into a hen party—a bachelorette party, as they called them over here. Either way, he was in the wrong room and he started to apologize. But the woman grabbed his arm and dragged him into her lair.

"Hi! You must be Nick! Of course you're Nick! Here for Golden's shoot, right? Come on in. I'm Elaine. I'm the tattoo artist."

Nick raised his eyebrows and Elaine laughed shrilly.

"Oh, not like that! They want a specific tattoo for the shoot so I have to paint it on. It'll wash off in the shower so don't worry."

"I already have a fair bit of ink," he warned her.

"Oh my God! I love hearing you talk! Your voice is amazing. Are you Irish?"

"No, English."

"You're kidding me?"

"No."

"Oh, okay. Hey, this is Meagan," and she introduced Nick to a thickset woman with short purple hair and colourful tattoos decorating her arms. "She's the author. It's her books that you'll be on the cover of."

"Hi, Nick. It's nice to meet you."

"You, too."

Then Nick was introduced to the photographer. Golden, was a quiet, handsome man, with some serious muscles and almost as many tattoos as Nick. He shook hands and motioned to a petite woman with mousy-brown hair to come over.

"This is Shelly—she's your co-model for this shoot."

Nick was taken aback. He hadn't anticipated doing a shoot with another woman. Although he had been warned it was for a romance cover, but still, Adrienne should have told him…

"Um, Golden, my agent didn't say anything about it being a couple's shoot."

"Is it a problem?"

"I've never done it before and, well, I'm engaged."

Golden gave him a relaxed smile.

"Okay, we can work around that. The shoot will be hot, a little sexy, but these covers have to pass the Amazon judge and jury, so there'll be nothing too erotic. You be okay with that?"

Nick nodded, deciding to trust the photographer, for now, at least.

Then he was introduced to three more women: the author's agent, the makeup artist, and another woman named Janice, but he never did find out what her role was in all of the chaos.

There were a lot of people crowded in that hotel room.

As the noise level rose, Golden calmly continued to discuss the plans for the shoot.

Nick liked him immediately: he was easy to talk to and straight to the point. And somehow, he managed to tune out the women behind him who seemed to be enjoying the party.

For now, most of the attention was on Shelly as she was poured into a leather skirt and bustier, and given a waist-length wig that looked about as natural as horns on a camel.

Golden remained impassive as the volume increased behind him, but the stiffness in his body gave him away.

Nick was relieved to have an ally to help him endure this.

Elaine walked over, a large makeup bag in her hands.

"Nick, can I get you a drink or some water? I need to work on your tattoo, and it could take a while."

"Just water, thanks."

She handed him a bottle and pointed to a desk chair.

"If you could take off your t-shirt and lean forward…"

Nick whipped his t-shirt over his head, but looked up, startled, when the other women shrieked with approval.

"They're a little excited," Elaine explained breezily. "It's going to be an awesome shoot."

"Okay…"

Nick leaned forward while Elaine studied the existing ink on his back.

"Hey, Meagan, can I borrow you a moment?"

The author glanced up, slightly pink in the face, either from the champagne or from all the naked man-flesh in front of her. Probably both.

"Sure!"

"Okay, so I can match the new tat to this style, which would probably look more realistic, or go for the death metal typography that you had in mind."

Death metal?

"Oh, wow, okay. I don't know. What do you think, Isabel?"

The agent strode over confidently.

"Yeah, go with Elaine's idea. I love that." And she leaned on Nick, patting his shoulder. "That okay with you?"

"Sure, whatever."

"Okay, cool!"

Elaine dabbed some liquid on his back, wiping a piece of cotton wool over his skin. Then he felt the soft sweep of a paintbrush as she worked on the fake tattoo.

After fifteen minutes, Elaine was finished, and the harem gathered around, cooing over the work.

Then the makeup artist who doubled as a hair stylist slicked some gel in Nick's hair, tied it into a short ponytail, sponged foundation onto his cheeks and nose, then brushed some powder over the top.

Golden unfolded his arms and gave Nick a brief smile that seemed to say, *Let's get this over with as quickly as possible*, then he switched on the two portable lights he'd set up.

"I'll start with a couple of close-ups of your ink and the fake tattoo, okay?"

"Sure."

Nick followed Golden's direction, pleased to find that he understood more quickly now what sort of poses a photographer wanted from him, how to move his body and tense his muscles for the most defined look.

Then Shelly was brought into the frame, and Nick had to gaze in her eyes.

"Nick, you're looking kinda angry, buddy," Golden advised. "Imagine that she's your woman."

Nick closed his eyes for a second and thought of Anna. Then he looked down at Shelly, trailing a finger down her cheek.

The women screeched again, which put Nick off, but he tried to keep Anna's face in the front of his mind. He imagined the look on her face when he kissed her, when he touched her ... he had to shake the thought away.

Then he was asked to pick Shelly up and push her against the wall as if they were having sex. She was much lighter than Anna, and she almost flew backwards, thudding slightly against the thin plasterboard.

"Sorry," Nick murmured, but Shelly just nodded, surprised and breathless.

Behind them, the chorus oohed and aahed loudly.

They worked for several minutes before Golden stood upright and stretched, then turned to the author who was nominally in charge of the shoot.

The women squealed, although Nick wasn't sure what that was about—Golden exchanged a tired look with him. It was the strangest photoshoot Nick had ever been on—not that he'd been on many, but still...

Golden shrugged and then he went back to checking the light meter on his camera.

"Oh my God! Oh my God! We should totally do the leather jacket!" shouted one of the women.

She might have been the editor or the publisher, maybe the agent, Nick wasn't sure anymore. She hadn't been looking at his face when they met; instead her eyes were crawling all over his body. Just because he was starting to get used to it, didn't mean he liked it.

"I'm going to be sweating in a leather jacket," Nick pointed out mildly. "And that'll smudge the fake tattoo."

"Yeah, but we totally need that shot. If we're quick..."

Nick nodded and did as he was asked, carefully sliding the leather jacket over his broad shoulders.

Golden took some more photographs with Nick staring intensely into the camera lens, then they referred back to the author.

"Okay, Meagan, so what's the story? What are we saying in this scene? Do you want to have Nick on the bed?"

Probably the wrong thing to say.

The women went into a huddle, glancing over their shoulders at Nick and giggling. God, that was annoying. Then the publisher spoke to Golden.

"Can you ask him to take his pants off?"

Golden glanced at Nick, his eyebrows raised.

"You okay with that, Nick?"

"Sure."

Nick kicked off his boots and slid his jeans over his hips, ignoring the excitement from his audience.

"Oh my God, look at his butt!"

"Cutest bubble butt ever!"

Nick felt like reminding them that he was a person, not just a piece of meat, but decided the quicker it was over, the better.

Then he lay on the bed, his heated gaze turning up the temperature in the room as Golden caught every expressive movement of his face and body.

When Shelly joined him, wearing just a bra and panties, laying on top of him, their legs twined, Nick tried to keep his mind on Anna. But that felt wrong, too.

When he had to pin Shelly underneath him and pretend to kiss her, he winced internally. This wasn't fair to Anna. It wasn't even fair to himself.

Finally, the shoot was done and Golden turned off the bright lights. His face was smooth but Nick saw the relief in his eyes that this job was finally finished.

"Want to go get a beer?" he muttered to Nick.

"Sounds good."

Nick dressed, shook hands with the author, got kissed by all of the other women, and a few minutes later, he and Golden wandered down to the hotel's bar.

"That was…different," said Nick with considerable understatement.

Golden sighed and rubbed his temples.

"I'm used to working by myself—that was…"

He didn't have the words, but Nick nodded anyway.

"It's not always like that," Golden said at last. "Well, I've never known it like that before. It's usually really professional. I hope you didn't feel too uncomfortable?"

Nick took a long drink of beer and rested the cold glass against his forehead. The truth was he'd already decided no more couples' shoots. It felt disrespectful to Anna, to what their relationship meant to him. He didn't want to look like he was screwing other women, even if was just make-believe.

"Nah, I was just glad you were there, mate. Safety in numbers."

Golden laughed.

"You called that one right, buddy! So, what do you think of the world of modelling for romance novels?"

"Harder than I was expecting, and a lot more waiting around. How long have you been a photographer?"

Golden smiled, his eyes crinkling with pleasure.

"Since I was a kid, I guess. I've always enjoyed taking pictures. I prefer shooting out on location. I get to see some magnificent places. It's hard to explain, but even if it's just an alleyway, there's a vibe that you pick up on, and the model can play off, for us to get the shot. Locations make wonderful backgrounds and textures." He rubbed his chin thoughtfully. "Although studio shoots do have more control over light."

Nick remembered that from his experience with Massimo.

"Do you think you'll stay in the modelling business?" Golden asked.

"Maybe. I'll definitely give it a go while I'm here, but long term…"

"I think you could do really well," Golden said thoughtfully. "Confidence is important—one of the most important things, in my opinion. And I don't mean ego or douchiness," and he laughed. "I think that confidence leads the rest—your looks, your form, and so on—to create great shots. Physically, models that are fitter tend to do well in the romance industry. You know, with the target demographic and 'fantasy' element." He shrugged, "But too shredded and you cross into bodybuilding territory which is a more difficult sell, although appealing in its own right—or not, depending on how many veins you like to see." He raised an eyebrows. "But overall though, all elements should work in unison, and confidence should shine through in the final shot." He gave Nick a long look. "I know you only started doing this recently; I was surprised how quickly you were able to get into poses and routines. And that gorgeous face helps!"

Nick laughed a little uncomfortably. He still wasn't used to his looks being more important than how good his game-play had been on any given day.

"What sort of camera do you use?" Nick asked, wanting to change the subject, but also to understand and learn.

"I use a Nikon D800, typically with an f2.8 24-70mm lens."

Nick leaned forward, his interest piqued.

"And that works well indoors and out?"

For a while, they talked technique, lighting, lenses, and the golden hour that was the favourite time of day for photographers to shoot.

And then Nick asked the question that he'd been wondering about all day.

"Tell me how you got into the romance book business?"

Golden gave him a slow, sly smile.

"Now that is a very interesting story. But we're going to need more beer…"

CHAPTER 13

"**A**RE YOU SERIOUS? SHE LOOKS LIKE a kid.**"

Nick hadn't been at all keen to do another couples shoot after his experience with Shelly—he had nothing against her—but getting in intimate positions with another woman, even when there seven other people in the room, felt like cheating on Anna, and he was *not* okay with that.

Adrienne had talked him into it, saying that this was going to be a big shoot, an important client, and that he'd be a fool to turn it down. She'd gone on to point out that there were a hundred other guys who'd jump at the chance, and on and on.

In the end, he'd agreed to do it provided there was no nudity on either side.

He thought he knew what he was letting himself in for…

But this *girl?*

Nick was appalled. He was supposed to do a sexy photoshoot with a *child?*

The client liaison manager threw him an impatient look.

"Are you saying you don't recognize her? Cee Cee Eloy the next supermodel, buddy. She's been on more covers this year than Gigi Hadid. She's doing you a favour by shooting with an unknown."

Nick ignored the dig.

"How old is she?" Nick persisted.

"Fifteen."

The girl strutted over, careful makeup accentuating her porcelain skin and wide, doll-like eyes. She yawned.

"I'm 13. I had to suck a lot of dicks to get where I am."

Nick's mouth dropped open. *She's joking. Dear God, I hope she's joking.* But maybe she wasn't.

He hadn't seen anyone quite as young as her at the party Orion had dragged him to, but that didn't mean it didn't happen. Nick wasn't naïve—it just wasn't something he liked to think about.

He'd been warned that the industry was tough, that it idolized youth, that it preyed on innocence. Seeing it … seeing her in the flesh was slightly horrifying.

"Where are your parents?"

The girl rolled her eyes and yawned again.

"I'm legally emancipated."

"Look, buddy…" the liaison guy began.

"My name's Nick."

"Whatever, Nick! Look, you were booked for the shoot—you walk out now, you'll have cost the client thousands. Cee Cee gets $10K an hour, you hear me? Whatever you're earning on this little number, she's getting twenty times more. *She* calls the shots. You and me, we just work here. You walk, the perfume company will sue your ass for the cost of today, for the delay, their legal fees, loss of potential earnings from the ad, the sponsors, the magazine the shoot is booked with. And that's just to start. You'll be finished in this town, buddy. You want that?"

Nick's nostrils flared.

"But she's a child! And I'm supposed to…

"…seduce her. Yeah, we know. You're the serpent in the Garden of Eden; she's Eve, represents innocence, yadda yadda yadda. It's a big campaign. So get on set, do your job, and stop fucking this up for everyone else."

Nick ignored the man and stomped off to the room where he'd left his clothes.

He called the one person who'd understand. And it wasn't his agent.

The phone rang and rang.

"Come on, answer!" Nick growled at the piece of plastic in his hand.

Just when he thought it would go to messages, he heard Anna's breathless voice.

"Nick! I thought you were doing a photoshoot this morning. Sorry, I was just running in the door."

"I'm at the studio now."

She must have heard the anxiety in his voice.

"What's wrong?"

He cleared his throat, uneasy with what he had to tell her.

"You know I said it's a couples shoot, based on the story of Adam and Eve?"

"Yes?"

"Well, I'm supposed to be the serpent in the garden of Eden, trying to get the girl to eat the apple, or I'm pure evil or something, and the girl model is, well, Eve? Love and innocence? Right?"

"I think you'll find that Eve wasn't completely innocent … but carry on."

"Yeah, well, it's the *girl* they've booked…"

"You don't like her?"

"It's not that. I don't even know her, but … she's a *girl!*"

There was a long pause.

"You've lost me, Nick."

He sighed and started to run his fingers through his hair before he remembered that it had taken the stylist half an hour to make it look the way it did, the curls glistening as if wet.

"I'm supposed to seduce her. You know, make it look like I'm seducing her!"

"Oh. I … I don't know what to say. If that's the job you signed up for…"

"That's just it. I didn't realize it would be so … so … Christ, I don't even know what it'll be. It's this *girl!* She's thirteen! I'll feel like a flippin' paedo!"

He heard Anna's intake of breath.

"So young…"

"Yeah! They say she's really well known in the model world … Cee Cee, something."

Anna gasped.

"Wait! Not Cee Cee Eloy?"

"Yeah, that's it. Do you know her?"

Anna gave a pained laugh.

"Yes, she's pretty well known, but I didn't think she was that young. Mind you, Kate Moss was discovered when she was 14…"

Nick sat down heavily.

"I don't know what to do. They say if I walk off this set, I'll be finished. No one will book me again and I'll probably get my arse sued."

Anna's voice was stronger when she spoke again.

"You have the right to feel comfortable on set, Nick. So far, the only thing they've asked you to do is work with this girl. They haven't asked you to do anything inappropriate. Yet…"

"Fuckin' hell, Anna! The whole thing is inappropriate! She's *thirteen!*"

"I know," she sighed. "All I can advise is to go with your gut instinct. If you need to leave, then that's fine. I'll support you, whatever you decide."

"Thanks, luv."

Anna's voice dropped to a whisper.

"So, what are you wearing to seduce Eve?"

Nick laughed out loud.

"Not a lot."

"Oh, do tell!"

"A jockstrap that looks like a sock, and a dressing gown."

He could hear the smile in her voice when she spoke.

"Sounds sexy."

"It really isn't. It's a flesh-coloured sock and it's bloody uncomfortable."

"How can a sock be uncomfortable? You know what, never mind!" She sighed. "It's good to hear you laughing."

"Sorry I've been a miserable sod. I'll make it up to you."

"Oh, well … but you don't have to make anything up to me," she paused, and her voice dropped half an octave. "Actually, yeah, let's say you owe me—sounds fun!"

Nick smiled as he imagined all the ways he could 'owe' Anna, but then settled into a scowl as one of the runners knocked on the door and tapped her wristwatch.

"Gotta go," he sighed.

"Okay, call me later. Let me know if I need to start selling the house to pay lawyers' fees."

"Haha, will do."

"You know, I can't imagine a big perfume campaign would want to do anything that would reflect negatively on them. But seriously, Nick. Only do what you're comfortable with. We both know that photographs are around forever in the media. They'll always be there."

Only slightly reassured by her words, Nick went back to the set. It was several degrees warmer than the changing room with the studio lights already turned on.

Cee Cee glanced up from her phone as Nick sat on the next chair but one, leaving a space between them.

She chewed on a strand of hair and gave him a lopsided smile.

"It's kinda nice. No one's ever worried about that shit before," she said, as she took her game of Candy Crush to the next level. "Most guys are sleazy."

"Well, someone should worry about you," Nick said gruffly.

She gave him a smile that was older than her real age by many years.

"They wouldn't get very far in this industry if they tried. Did you say your name is Nick?"

"Yep, Nick Renshaw."

"Oh yeah, the guy Massimo recommended…"

He had?

"Well, Nick Renshaw, I might be able to work another ten years, but maybe not. I could be old news by the time I'm 16. Not everyone gets to have a career like Giselle or Naomi or Kate. Most of us are finished by our mid-twenties. My agent says I have to prepare to retire by the time I'm twenty."

Nick stared at her with sympathy and some understanding as her eyes focused on her phone.

"No one tells me what to do," she said. "I call the shots."

Nick felt the weight of her naivety in those words, meeting her adult gaze as she side-eyed him carefully.

"You seem kinda tense. Do you need something to take the edge off?"

"*What?!*"

Cee Cee shrugged.

"You just look mega stressed."

"No, I'm fine." He grimaced. "Thank you."

"Whatever. I saw you taking something earlier so I figured you were cool."

Nick frowned, cornered and on the defensive.

"It was ibuprofen. I've had surgery on my shoulder."

"Sure, whatever, man."

She popped a small blue pill into her mouth and sucked down some water from her bottle. At least four people saw her do it, but no one said a word.

Her name was called and she was escorted to the set for principal shots.

As she walked away, she swung around to face him, walking backwards on tiptoe, a huge smile on her face.

"Is it me, or is it weird that they picked the nicest guy in the biz to play the Devil?" and she laughed.

Nick was reeling from her admission, and uncomfortable that he'd been called on his use of painkillers. It was a good thing Anna didn't know. But they helped. He'd slept badly and his shoulder ached. He needed them. He definitely needed them.

I should stop.

Seeing this kid taking drugs on set and no one giving a damn, it gave him serious pause for thought.

This was such a weird situation: the thirteen year-old girl was acting like a thirty year-old, and Nick was adrift in a sea of shifting morals that he didn't understand. He just knew that the entire crew were eyeing him with a mixture of pity and impatience.

Part of him wanted to walk, but the part that refused to fail, fought for him to stay.

He decided to take Anna's advice—if he started feeling uncomfortable once the shoot started, he'd walk, and to hell with the consequences.

"Hey, Nick! How ya doin'? I'm Alan Schafhaus, the photographer. I hear you have some reservations about what we're doing here. I completely understand," and he held his hand over his heart, "but I promise you, I have nothing but respect for my models and want you to feel completely relaxed." And he laid his hand on Nick's shoulder. "We're all professionals here. You feel me?"

Taking a deep breath, Nick nodded and forced a smile.

"Sure."

"Great! Then let's get started!"

Like a conductor bringing the orchestra to a crescendo, Alan directed, organized and ordered.

Nick shrugged out of his robe, and immediately a woman ran up with a bottle of glycerin and rosewater, spraying him with a fine mist so his skin seemed to shine, his tattoos gleaming darkly. Another hairstylist darted forth, teasing Nick's curls into black coils that caught the light, snakelike, a diabolic and very masculine Medusa, a warrior.

When Nick caught sight of himself, it was with a shock at the strangeness and familiarity combined. He looked predatory; he looked as if he was about to steal someone's innocence. He thought back to the name the British Press had given him when he'd been accused of a series of affairs with his teammates' wives, all untrue: 'Nasty Nick'.

And maybe there was a tiny part of him that was looking forward to living up to that for once. As his mum used to say, 'You may as well be hung for a sheep as a lamb'. He'd already done the time for his supposed crimes…

Nick looked inside himself and found that there was more than the boredom and depression inside: there was a deep well of anger that injury had robbed him of one last year of rugby; one last year of being the man he was meant to be. Despite his charmed career, despite the years of success following the dark days of bad injuries, bad judgement and damn bad luck, there was a small flame of fury inside him, one that could be fanned into a roaring furnace, if given the chance.

Nick let a little of that anger seep through, suffusing his skin with heat, a glint in his eyes that warned you not to fuck with him, an imperious arrogance that said he found this whole process of modelling a lot vain and a little ridiculousness.

Despite the people surrounding him, arranging his hair, fixing his makeup, sprinkling his skin, he stood in isolation, tolerating but not participating.

Alan Schafhaus was filled with excitement. He sensed that this photoshoot was going to be epic. The weird angry vibe of the British model had the intense focus, the dangerous, predatory allure of a dark god, and Cee Cee's drugged up innocence would play perfectly against that. With the sixth sense of a man at the top of his profession, he knew that today would be great. He was almost salivating, desperate to let his camera get to work, but he played the conductor, his baton poised. And he had the perfect music to work by: *Danse Macarbre.*

Nick was spot-lit among shadows, a red filter turning the light eerie, and Cee Cee lay languidly, diffused yellow light giving a soft haze to her pretty, doll-like face.

Amazing, thought Alan, *that such emotional truth can be caught in the eyes of a child.*

Although in the eyes of the modelling world, Cee Cee was a seasoned professional, and Nick was the ingénu.

Intuitively, Alan Schafhaus knew that he couldn't rush this shoot. Gradually, he brought his principals closer together—a touch, a gaze, a lingering longing in the eyes.

In the end, there was nothing the least bit intimate about the poses Nick had to do with Cee Cee. Yes, she was close to him, their faces nearly touching, but it was more like a game of Twister, trying to put arms and legs in strange positions, flex his muscles, *and* show the expressions Alan wanted on his face.

He tried to be stoic, but the anger was there, and the photographer seemed to deliberately draw it out of him, making him repeat his poses time after time.

Over and over again, the poses were adjusted minutely. Over and over again, the lighting was altered, or Alan ripped his camera from the tripod and came in for a close-up, talking, commanding, ordering the whole time.

Cee Cee wrapped her long, coltish limbs around Nick; a leg around his hip, an arm around his neck—her wide-eyed innocence more apparent than real.

A wind machine blew her corn straight hair in a sheet of silk over Nick's shoulder and across his chest; her hands swept over his stomach and thigh. It certainly didn't feel like he was the seducer in this scene.

The camera loved the beautiful child-woman and the man-devil—and all the behind-the-scenes people felt the magic of what they were creating.

At the same time, it was all far more frenetic than the serene peace of Massimo's studio. Nick reached for his inner calm when his patience was all but gone after two hours of holding his body in unnatural positions as a simmering rage threatened to escape. But Cee Cee seemed to float above it all, connected but distant, never complaining.

Nick didn't know what she'd taken, but it was definitely working for her. He was almost jealous. Almost.

Finally, the shoot ended and Nick was handed a towel. He wasn't surprised to see that real sweat had replaced the glycerin and rosewater spray.

"Great shoot," said Alan, clasping Nick's shoulder. "The client is going to be blown away."

Nick nodded and stepped back, then remembering he was supposed to want a career in modelling, he added, "Thanks."

Cee Cee smiled at him languidly.

"Good working with you, Mr. Nice Guy. You didn't even try to cop a feel once." And she pointed a long, skinny finger at him. "I like you."

Nick watched her drift away, still high from whatever she'd taken.

A cloud of worry descended on him: *my child will never be abandoned like that.*

He and Anna had talked about children, some vague and distant point in the future when the time was right, but at that moment, Nick longed for his family—for Anna and their one-day child.

What the fuck am I doing here?

It was many months later when Nick first saw the results of the shoot with Cee Cee. He was shocked. The photographs for the perfume ad were far more erotic and intense than had seemed on set, with the photographer coming in close for several shots, catching Nick's expression of discontent and Cee Cee's youthful naivety, which was more apparent than real.

Leaping flames had been photoshopped in behind Nick, adding to the drama of the scene.

Nick winced: he seemed enormous next to the young model, hulking and dark, whereas she was ethereal and light; and it really did look like he was seducing her.

He wondered what Anna would think when she saw the pictures. What anyone else thought didn't matter, although he could almost guess the response from the British Press:

Naughty Nick and Teenage Nookie.

He heard the echo of Anna's words in his mind: _a photograph in the Press is forever._

Oh shit.

CHAPTER 14

"**G**OD, IT'S GOOD TO HEAR your voice!"

Nick had been in New York for three months, having only returned to London once for a brief visit.

Since his shoot with Cee Cee, he'd worked almost constantly on a range of small and medium-size campaigns. Things were beginning to work out for him, and he knew he had decisions to make.

He slumped on the bed in his tiny room, eyes closed and a smile on his face as he listened to Anna's voice. She sounded so close and he wished for the thousandth time that she was here in this room with him.

"Hey," she said happily. "How's your day been?"

He heard Brendan's voice in the background.

"Are you still working?"

"Just finishing up a few things over a bottle of wine. Oh, Brendan says hi and where did you get those boxer briefs in those photos you sent me?"

Nick laughed.

"Tell him I'll bring some back for him."

He heard a muffled disagreement in the background and Anna whisper-shouting, "I'm not telling him that!"

"What's all that about, luv?"

"Oh, just Brendan being Brendan."

"Do I want to know?"

"Definitely not!"

Nick laughed again, the lonely ache in his chest easing.

"Okay."

"So how'd your day go?"

Nick grinned into the phone.

"I got a new contract today—Miami Swim Week. Guess I'll be strutting my stuff on an actual catwalk. That'll be different."

He felt pleased with himself and was looking forward to trying something new. Plus, it felt like being a real model.

Anna's voice sounded a little shocked.

"Oh wow! An actual catwalk! That's awesome! Wait, what will you be wearing?"

Nick chuckled.

"I think the clue is in the name: swimwear. Apparently it's the biggest tradeshow for swimming stuff in the world. Well, that's what Adrienne said."

"Swimwear, huh? That sounds … hot. When is it?"

"In a couple of weeks, mid-July."

There was a long pause and Nick glanced at the phone, wondering if the call had been dropped.

"Anna?"

"Oh, yes, sorry. Wow, really? A catwalk in Miami! That's awesome."

"You think so?"

"Gosh, definitely."

Nick tucked his free hand behind his head and closed his eyes.

"Adrienne says there'll be a couple of hundred models there, mostly girls, I think. But yeah, it should be fun. Good exposure for me, lots of contacts, you know?"

Anna could imagine what sort of *exposure* would be involved only too well.

She missed him.

She missed him so much she ached with loneliness. Filling her days with work and more work and occasionally hanging out with Brendan wasn't the same as being with her soulmate.

And right now, he was so far away. She'd been tempted so many times to go to him, to take her work with her, but something always held her back—Nick's need to make it without her help. They'd fought about that—which meant that Anna had raised her voice and Nick had walked away. What she saw as giving support, he seemed to see as a weakness. It frustrated the hell out of her.

And she wished he'd tell her that he missed her, that he needed her: he never did.

But finally Anna's patience had run out—she missed him too much not to see him. So when he mentioned Miami, she had a brainwave...

"That sounds great. Really. Okay, wait ... um ... Nick, I could fly out for that, spend some time, what do you think?" Her voice was tentative. "I could see Mom for a few days then meet you in Miami. I don't want to get in the way of your work or anything..."

Nick was surprised by the lurch of happiness he felt. He thought he was getting used to being apart from Anna, but her offer opened the door on the loneliness he'd been trying to hide from himself.

"Really, you can take the time?" he asked cautiously. "I thought you were working on your book."

"I am…" She paused. "But it can wait. Send me the dates and I'll get a flight. I want to see you, Nick."

The longing in her voice travelled across the miles of ocean between them.

"Yes, God, yes!" Nick replied, his voice tightening from emotion. "That would be amazing."

Once again he heard some muffled discussion in the background.

"Brendan wants to come, too," Anna said, and Nick could hear the amusement in her voice. "He said … actually, you don't want to know what he said. Is it okay?"

"Yeah, why not. I hear the after-parties are something else."

There was another pause, then Anna gave a short laugh.

"I think he just fainted. Meh, he'll be fine."

"Do you want to tell him now or later that it's 85% women on the catwalk?"

Anna laughed softly and Nick felt his spirits soar.

"I think we'll let him find out for himself. Looks like I'll be seeing you in a couple of weeks!"

"I can't wait."

Anna replaced the phone, a goofy grin on her face. *I'm going to see Nick!* In all honesty, she thought he might say no, that he'd be too busy to spend time with her. But he hadn't.

"See, that wasn't so hard, was it?" Brendan said, squinting at her, his eyes vulnerable without the glasses he usually wore. "Miss I-must-give-him-his-independence. He's probably been pining for you as much as you've been pining for him."

Anna snorted and grabbed the muffin top hanging over her jeans.

"Do you call that pining?"

"I call that comfort eating, Dr. Scott. Time to get your little tush down to Nick's home gym and work off the flab." Suddenly Brendan's eyebrows shot up. "Oh wait! Are you up the duff?"

"Am I what?!"

"Pregnant, knocked up?"

Anna's cheeks blazed red.

"No!"

"You're not pregnant?"

"I've hardly had the chance, have I?" she replied tartly.

"So you're just carrying a little timber. Time to cut down on the full-fat caramel Frappuccinos. You'll get stretch marks before you're preggers."

"I haven't … I'm not that big…" she huffed.

Brendan narrowed his eyes at her.

"You told me you'd put on ten pounds since he went away, but I'm seeing at least twenty. Man up, Anna-banana—Miami is going to be full of skinny bitches with great tits. Get thee to the gym, woman, before your self-loathing writes its own autobiography."

"I really hate you," Anna muttered under her breath. "I told you that in confidence. You're breaking the BFF code."

Brendan gave her a megawatt smile.

"You don't hate me. Telling you the truth *is* the job of a BFF. So I'm telling you *and your love handles* to start planking like a carpenter at a home-build expo."

"Strongly dislike then," Anna griped as she went upstairs to change into her roomier yoga pants. "Really rather detest."

"Suck it up, buttercup!" he yelled after her. "I don't want you and your extra luggage making me look bad!"

God, she hated it when he was right.

Anna knew that she didn't want Nick to see her like this, especially since he'd be surrounded by beautiful girls a decade younger than herself. But not only that: even when he was injured, he'd never let himself go. Never.

Except for that one time before they'd gotten together and Trish said he'd started drinking.

It was hard to imagine because Nick was so fanatical about eating healthy and exercising every day.

God, every day!

She yanked on her favourite stretchy yoga pants and wrapped her hands around her new belly fat. She wished, she so wished it was the roundness that meant she was carrying his child. But it wasn't. And unless she and Nick found their way back to each other, it never would be.

With a grim determination, she tied her hair back and headed for the treadmill in the basement.

She had work to do.

After speed-walking for half-an-hour while Brendan lazed on Nick's weights bench shouting motivational quotes at her, Anna was pouring with sweat and having homicidal thoughts about her best friend.

"If you do that a hundred times a day, you'll be in shape for Miami," Brendan called to her.

"A hundred times a day?" she puffed. "Since when have there been fifty hours in a day?"

"I'm being motivational," he replied, flipping through a copy of *GQ*.

"You're being annoying. Go away."

"Don't get snappy. You're probably hungry. I'll fix you a nice green salad."

He swung his long legs off the bench and waltzed out of the door.

Anna sighed.

Nick worked out *every day*. How the hell did he do it?

She groaned and set the treadmill going again.

TWO WEEKS LATER and seven pounds lighter, Anna flew into JFK.

She saw her mother waiting for her, silver-grey hair carefully styled.

"Mom!"

Anna's mother hugged her tightly.

"Oh, honey! It's so good to see you!"

Anna studied her mother's face, noting the deeper wrinkles radiating from her eyes, grief engraved in the lines around her mouth.

The loss of her husband five years ago had been hard, desperately hard, but she'd managed to build a life for herself without him. The effort had taken its toll, but despite that, her mother's eyes were bright and clear, filled with happiness at seeing her daughter.

She squeezed Anna's hand and planted a lipstick kiss on her cheek, which she then rubbed off with her thumb.

Anna laughed.

"Oh my God! Are you going to spit on your handkerchief and wash my face, too?"

"Only if you eat ice cream the way you did when you were three years old."

They made their way to the luggage carousel and Anna hauled her huge suitcase down with a thud.

"My! You've packed a lot for a two-week vacation!"

"Oh God, I know! I was so indecisive so I just threw everything in."

Her mother eyed Anna's round cheeks and belly and hurtled to the wrong conclusion.

"Sweetheart, are you pregnant?"

Anna's face burned with embarrassment.

"Mom, no! I'm just carrying a little extra weight, is all."

"Are you sure? Because you know I'd love grandbabies."

"I know, Mom," Anna said, gritting her teeth. "You've mentioned that two or three times before." *Or maybe a hundred.*

"And when's the wedding happening? I can't believe that you've waited nearly five years already! What's the holdup?"

Anna burst into tears as her mother stared at her dumbfounded, then wrapped her arms around her again, cursing herself for speaking without thinking.

"Did you and Nick … break up?" she asked gently.

Anna sniffed and wiped her nose with a tissue.

"No, nothing like that. Oh God, Mom! It's just I feel like I'm the one whose life is on hold now. He's so far away and he's doing great. Of course he's doing great, he always does. I just feel fat and frumpy and *old*."

Her mother hugged her more tightly, then smoothed back her hair in the same reassuring and loving way that she'd been doing since Anna was a baby.

"That's such nonsense, honey," her mother said, wiping her thumbs across her daughter's wet cheeks. "You're young and beautiful, and I'm a silly old woman. Besides, you'll see Nick in a few days. I'm sure you can work it all out."

"I miss him so much."

"Of course you do, honey. That's natural. Long distance relationships are hard. When your father used to travel all the time with the team and you were so young, there were many, many times when it seemed too hard, but we survived, we pulled through.

Marriage, relationships take work. I think it's great that you're here, and like I said, I know you'll be fine."

"I hope so," Anna said. "I really hope so."

Her mother pressed her lips together but didn't say anything else except to comment on the horrendous New York traffic as they made their way to the parking lot.

"How's Brendan? I thought you said he was coming over, too?"

"Yes, but he's flying direct to Miami because he's taking some vacation time to see his parents first."

"Oh, really? I didn't think he got along with them?"

Anna made a face.

"He doesn't, but his mom has been sick so he thought he should visit with them. It's more his dad he doesn't get along with. Apparently his dad isn't happy having a 'queer' for a son. That's what Bren said."

Anna's mother looked sad.

"Children are so precious—it hurts my heart to think that lovely young man is treated in such a way."

"I know. He doesn't talk about it much," Anna sighed. "Only when he's had a few drinks. Anyway," she said, forcing a smile, "he sends his love and promises he'll take you salsa dancing next time you're in London."

"Oh my! I was rather hoping he'd forgotten that promise."

Anna laughed.

"No way! He's really looking forward to it. He calls you his 'American nana-banana'."

"Aw, how sweet. I think."

"He can be," Anna smiled. "He also mentioned shopping at Harrods, which is probably more your speed."

"Hey! I may be 63, but I can still move," her mother laughed.

"Yes, but you'd rather go shopping."

"How well you know me, daughter."

That evening, they enjoyed a quiet dinner at an Italian restaurant in Tarrytown, right by the Hudson River with a terrace that faced the setting sun.

It was peaceful and easy, and it reminded Anna how much she missed her mother. She reached across the table and squeezed her mom's hand.

"It's so good to see you."

"Oh, honey! It's such a wonderful treat to have you here." She paused. "So, do you want to talk about it?"

Anna hesitated, not sure what she wanted to say, or if she wanted to talk at all. But her mom had been through all the same issues with her dad when he retired from the NFL. Anna was a trained sports psychologist, but talking to another woman who'd experienced all the same feelings…

"I don't know what to tell you, Mom," she said, at last. "We were both looking forward to his retirement from rugby, we had so many plans." Her voice turned wistful. "We were going to get married, start a family. Nick was thinking about opening a gym near us and working with athletes from different disciplines. He said he didn't want to get into rugby coaching because he wanted to try new things…"

"But?"

"It's hard to explain. When the time came, he just didn't have enthusiasm for any of it. And when we looked into what it would cost to open a top class gym in London, the prices were crazy. He still might though. He was talking about going in with some of his old teammates, but I don't know. He doesn't seem that enthusiastic about it." She stared down at her plate. "Not even about marriage." Then she looked up at her mother. "How can I even think of starting a family with a man who just isn't there? And I don't mean physically, because even when he's in London, it's like he's somewhere else. I know he's been depressed and I know that I need to give him time to come to terms with the new normal. I hoped the modelling might give him that, and sometimes he seems to enjoy it, but I don't know. It's all feast and famine: one minute he's in demand and busy, working crazy long hours, and the next, nothing for weeks." She shook her head. "He needs ongoing goals to work towards—something long term. I thought that would be us, our family … but I guess it's not."

Her mother laid her hand over Anna's.

"Honey, I honestly believe he'll figure it out. Maybe he has to try several different things before he finds what fires his imagination. But it seems to me that in modelling he's picked another short-term career. I know that there are a few more silver foxes out there than there used to be, but it's the exception, not the rule."

Anna's eyes widened.

"I hadn't thought of it like that. Oh God! And I pushed him into doing this!"

"No, that's not what I meant," her mother chided gently. "You opened the door but he's the one who walked through it. In my opinion, all experience is useful in life; you never know where it might lead."

She leaned back in her chair and stared out of the window, her eyes half-closing against the light dancing on the river as the evening sun sank lower.

"Do you remember when you were a child and you wanted to try horse riding?"

"Sure! I pretty much hated it!"

Her mother laughed.

"Yes, you did, but you stuck with it for six months—you were so stubborn. And then you tried ballet…"

"Even worse!"

"And ice skating…"

"I wasn't too bad at that…"

"No, but you didn't stick with it either."

Anna's eyebrows drew together.

"What's your point, Mom?"

Her mother laughed gently.

"There's no harm in trying different things and admitting that they're not for you. Nick's whole life has been about rugby. Just give him the space to find what else he enjoys doing."

Anna's frown deepened.

"I am trying, Mom. It's just…"

"What is it, honey?"

"Sometimes I almost hate it that he's so good looking!"

Her mother gaped at her and Anna rushed on.

"There are *always* women staring at him, and men. Sometimes, it's like I'm invisible and they don't even see me. And now he's surrounded by all these incredibly beautiful and glamorous women, I feel like … I don't measure up. I know that's pretty shallow."

Her mother took a sip of water, her eyes taking in the tinge of desperation on Anna's face.

"Let me ask you something, sweetheart, and think carefully before you answer."

"Okaaaay."

"Think about one of these instances where you've felt invisible, when you've been ignored by other people…"

"Yes?"

"What did Nick do? Did he ignore you, too? Were you invisible to him? Did he see that you were annoyed and upset?"

Anna swallowed past the sudden burn of tears behind her eyes, and she shook her head.

"No, he always sees me. He always makes me feel loved."

Her mother gave a gentle smile.

"Well, doesn't that tell you what's important—the way *he* treats you? And besides, don't you think it's Nick that you should be saying all this to, not me?"

Anna considered her mother's words.

"Maybe. But I want him to come home because he wants me, not because my neediness has made him feel guilty."

"Is it neediness to tell your fiancé that you miss him?"

Anna paused.

"Yes, I think it could be. When we talk or Facetime, I have to bite my tongue to avoid saying anything that would make it sound like I was resenting him being away. I don't, not really. I want him to be happy, and if this is how he can find himself again, then I genuinely want it for him. I'm not denying that I find it hard and I get so lonely, but I want to support his choices, you know?"

"And do you trust him?"

Anna's answer was immediate.

"Yes!"

"Then there's your answer. He *sees* you, Anna. You're important to him. Give him time, but give him support," and she gave a slight laugh, shaking her head. "Do it your way, honey. You usually do— and it works out in the end. Go to Miami and show him that none of the pretty girls there bother you in the slightest. Show him that you support him whatever he wants to do."

Anna blinked back tears and took her mother's hand and squeezed it.

"How did you get to be so wise, Mom?"

"By living 63 years … and being married to a hot hunk of man for a blessed thirty-five of them."

And then they were both laughing and crying, and as they recklessly ordered a second bottle of wine, they agreed that men were a lot of trouble—but that some of them were even worth it.

CHAPTER 15

NICK STARED AT THE PHOTOGRAPHS in disbelief. Adrienne had sent him the Walmart campaign, his first gig in New York. And now … she'd warned him that he'd be disappointed. Nick didn't understand until he opened the email attachments.

He shook his head. What a friggin' joke.

In every single one of the photographs, his head had been swapped for another model's, a younger man with blond hair. They'd also photoshopped out his tattoos. Why the hell had they bothered to hire him if they didn't like anything about him? To be honest, when he'd first seen the images, he thought that they'd re-shot the campaign with another model, but when he looked closely, he recognized his crooked fingers, and the scar on the back of his ankle from tendon surgery.

The body was definitely Nick's, but only he would have known.

Well, him and Anna. It could be a coincidence, but he'd bet anything that it was the sleazy photographer taking his revenge on Nick for turning him down.

At least he'd still been paid for the job, but pride in his work had taken a hit.

Nick closed his laptop in disgust. The modelling business was a tough one to crack and he wasn't at all sure that he liked much of what he'd found.

Nick wasn't short of money exactly. He'd saved up during his four-and-a-half years with the Phoenixes, but he was only 34 and the money he'd earned had to last a long time, assuming he made three-score-and-ten as a minimum. He'd invested his testimonial windfall into his small property portfolio of two suburban houses in southeast London. The income from those was going towards keeping him in New York.

But a lot of the younger models that he met were right on the edge of struggling. Most worked two or three jobs, hoping to hit a well-paid modelling contract and be able to give up waiting on tables, courier work, dog walking, or other employment that allowed them a reasonable amount of flexibility to go to castings.

Most of them were broke.

If their agent decided it wasn't working for them in the US, they'd be shipped off to do a round of casting calls in Germany, say, and if that didn't work, on to London. And even though the agency bought the plane tickets, the money had to be paid back out of any work they found.

If they didn't find work, they were even more in debt and doubly screwed.

It was one of the reasons why they were all desperate to build up their social media presences—they wanted all the exposure they could get.

Nick, on the other hand, didn't have any intention of using social media: he'd been ripped apart by the British Press over the years, and he'd had his fill of it.

The week before he left for Miami, he spent time in the gym, putting in the hours of cardio, mostly running on a treadmill, to achieve the lean, ripped look that the swimwear company who'd booked him wanted—nothing too bulky.

He also shaved his chest and made an appointment for a fake tan and the inevitable manscaping that seemed to be a necessary part of the biz. Just nice and trimmed: bushes went out in the seventies, Adrienne said.

Nick shook his head—his life was certainly strange, although he'd found that he did enjoy mudpacks: really relaxing.

Following that, Adrienne gave him and two other models a rapid-fire lesson in how to walk on a catwalk—which apparently involved a lot more than just putting one foot in front of another.

"You can't just show up and walk like you normally would on the street: you don't want to look like an ape, rolling from hip to hip; and you don't want to be too feminine, either—women on the catwalk have one foot directly in front of the other; you need to be side by side, but without lurching. No, the male runway walk is somewhere in the middle. It needs to be elegant and confident; you need to command the room.

"Orion, don't look down—take long, steady strides; let your arms swing naturally by your side. Nick, don't make eye contact or interact with the audience unless the client asks you to. Look past the audience and focus on an imaginary point just beyond them. Keep your mouth natural. Don't smile unless the client wants that. Don't swing your arms that much!"

It all felt weird to Nick and seemed like the hardest command was to be natural. Suddenly, his arms felt bizarre, hanging at his sides, as if he didn't know what to do with them.

Adrienne watched them walk up and down the room again, frowning as they paused at the end for the room, pretending it was a catwalk. Nick felt like a right knob.

"Practise good posture," she called. "Walk tall with your body straight and your shoulders back. Bend your knees—not that much—try to relax. You don't want to look like a robot. More confidence, Orion. Nick: strong, purposeful, you're already naturally sexy."

But he practised because he wanted to look good; he wanted to succeed at whatever he tried. Even this.

NICK LANDED IN Miami mid-afternoon.

The air quivered with damp heat, and Nick immediately felt sweat break out across the small of his back. The light denim jacket that he'd worn in New York felt heavy in Florida's high summer.

Fortunately, his cab was air conditioned. The driver wove his way through a knot of concrete flyovers, nodding his head and tapping his hands to the rhythm of a Spanish-language radio station, until suddenly they were heading west along a high bridge with brilliant blue water on either side of them, leading to the impossibly white sands and decorative palm trees of South Beach.

They stopped outside a small hotel where Nick had reserved two rooms—one for him and Anna, and one for Brendan—near all the action but a little out of the way, too. It was only five floors and set on a quiet side street where you caught glimpses of the ocean, sparkling in the distance.

Nick collected his room key, pleased with the large, comfortable bed and pretty white bedroom. He ached with longing for Anna; the fact that she would be with him in two days made the need more intense.

His first job was to check in at the Convention Center where Swim Week as taking place, meet the client and see where he'd be working.

He changed into shorts and a muscle shirt, his feet happy to be in flip-flops. Grabbing his wallet, room key and sunglasses, Nick headed out into the sunshine, taking a moment to enjoy the warmth on his skin and the scent of salt in the humid air.

He felt hungry, not just for food, but for whatever adventures Miami would bring.

Nick strolled along Ocean Drive, enjoying the vibe that was so much more laidback than in New York. He paused to check out a Cuban restaurant, lured by the wonderful spicy smells drifting from the doorway. His stomach rumbled, and he had to step away before he weakened and went in to sample the *Frijoles negros* or *Papa Rellena*.

Before he'd tried modelling, he'd watched his diet, always eating healthily, but he'd never been hungry all the darn time. It was almost better not to get booked for a shoot so you could eat as much as you wanted. Not that he ever did, in case he got a job.

At times like this, modelling sucked.

On the plus side, no two-hundred-and-twenty pound Forward was going to try and rip his head off. Definitely a plus.

AFTER HIS MEETING with the client, Nick was left scratching his head, metaphorically speaking. There would be one catwalk event the day after Anna arrived, but for the rest of the time, Nick's job was to go to the parties he was told to attend and stand around chatting to people while wearing the client's swimwear. It wasn't quite what he'd expected, but he was happy to go with the flow.

At least he'd be able to eat something. It was amazing how much food had begun to obsess him. He was beginning to understand why appetite suppressants could be found in many models' medicine cabinets.

The other models booked by the client were friendly enough, a mixed bunch: mostly straight, a couple gay; Black, White, Hispanic, and everything in between. Long haired, short haired, shaved heads; with tats, with piercings, no body art. But the one thing they all had in common was their height of six foot plus and lean, ripped bodies. They were there to sell the fantasy.

He was surprised to find that several of them were shy. The New York models that he met had been mostly like Orion—quick to shout out their own merits. But here, the body confidant models, could also be quiet and very shy when you talked to them.

He spent the evening hanging out with them, just to be friendly, then headed back to his hotel room alone.

FOR THE NEXT two days, he went to the parties in the client's swimwear, and talked to people. He was photographed numerous times, and all the pictures made it into the British tabloids with descriptions of him partying hard and being seen with lots of different women—which was his job.

The only plus was that Anna was already in New York with her mother.

He called her as soon as the latest round of stories broke.

"I've already seen the pictures," she sighed. "They just make it all look so sleazy. I *hate* that they can make you look like such a manwhore. It's so unfair! *Nick's Nookie, Number Nine.* How do they have the balls to write this stuff?"

Nick didn't even have the energy to be angry.

"Bullshit sells newspapers. They've cropped all the photos and cut out the people who were standing next to me. They edit it so it looks like … well, you know."

Anna was silent. Nick didn't need to spell it out to her.

"I can't wait to see you," he said quietly.

"Me, too," she said, and Nick hated that her voice sounded so sad.

He'd promised himself that he wouldn't keep secrets from her anymore, but he couldn't tell her that he was hit on constantly at these parties. She didn't need to know that. Anna just needed to know that she was the only woman he was interested in.

THE LUNCHTIME PARTIES were more fun because they were more laidback, more like pool parties than work. The evening events were a little crazier, but he was only paid to be there until ten, so after that, the rest of the evening was his.

The next morning, Nick had a brief meeting with the client and other models about the catwalk show the next day.

He kept glancing at his watch, waiting for the moment Anna's flight from New York landed. Brendan's wouldn't be far behind, having left Heathrow the night before.

As soon as the meeting broke up, Nick strode along the street back to his hotel, waiting in the lobby for his Anna.

When he saw her stepping out of a taxi, he jogged across the small entrance, sweeping her into his arms and kissing her breathless.

"Hi!" she said, her smile lighting up Miami.

She was pressed against his chest, her curves and softness the antidote to everything that was wrong with the world.

He kissed her again and felt her melt into his arms.

"Hello! I'm here, too, if anyone cares!"

Brendan huffed with annoyance as Nick grinned at him, then leaned across the pile of luggage to shake hands.

"Sorry about that, Bren," he said with a grin. "I missed you, too."

"Huh, doesn't look like it. I didn't even get a kiss!"

Nick winked at him and helped carry the suitcases and bags to the check-in desk.

"Oh, Lord! I'm so ready for a quiet dinner and an early night," Anna yawned as they shuffled into the tiny elevator.

Nick gave her a chagrinned look.

"I'm sorry, luv. I'm supposed to have dinner with the other models tonight. But you can come, is that okay? I only just found out."

It was Brendan who nodded emphatically.

"Dinner with models? God, yes! What time?"

Nick glanced at him in amusement.

"Seven, mate. That enough time for you?"

"Ugh, I only have two hours to make myself beautiful? Well, I'll manage. Now, who should I channel? Brits, obviously: Eddie Redmayne or bad boy Alex Pettyfer?"

Anna smiled.

"I always think Eddie is quintessentially British, so.."

"Yes, you're right," said Brendan seriously. "Play to my strengths."

And he disappeared along the corridor with his two enormous suitcases.

Anna was laughing, but when Nick hung a 'Do Not Disturb' sign on the door and locked it, the smile was wiped from her face.

"That gives us one hour and 55 minutes," Nick said, his voice a low growl.

"What about the other five minutes?" Anna asked, wide-eyed.

"That's all you need to get ready. You're already beautiful," he said, tucking her dark hair behind her ears, before leaning down to kiss her.

THE WARM GLOW OF amazing sex with her beautiful fiancé lasted through the first course of dinner that evening with Nick's modelling colleagues.

And then the doubts began to creep back.

"So, you're not married?"

"Uh, no, but I'm engaged. To him," and she pointed across the table to Nick.

The model shrugged.

"Women don't care if they're married—they just want to say they've been with a model."

Anna's eyes widened and her mouth twisted with dislike as she eyed the twenty-something guy.

"Some women," she enunciated slowly and clearly.

He studied her, reading her response. She decided to change the subject quickly.

"How long have you been model— ?" she started to ask.

He turned away from her mid-sentence, completely ignoring her for the rest of the evening, and talking instead to the woman on his other side.

As soon as he'd worked out that she wasn't in the modelling business and wouldn't sleep with him, she was of no use to him.

The conversations were all about diets or exercise plans, even discussing the models they knew who used steroids, speed, or diet pills to get the shape they wanted.

After an hour of this, Anna found the intense conversations boring, and Nick seemed to be equally turned off. A couple of times, he'd tried to start a conversation about football or baseball or something … anything else.

Even so, the other models were fascinated by him. Maybe because he was British or because they were beginning to realize that he'd achieved things that they could only dream about.

Brendan, on the other hand, was having the time of his life. He was channeling his inner Eddie Redmayne by wearing a white shirt, tweed bow tie and matching cardigan with skinny jeans. The gay models were lapping it up and Anna knew that he would have his choice of men to take back to his room.

But after a while, he noticed that no one was talking to her and squeezed his chair in between hers and the model who'd ignored her most of the evening.

"How's it going, Annie?" he asked, slinging his arm around her shoulders, his voice slightly slurred with tiredness and alcohol.

"Great," she said in a sarcastic voice that made Brendan snort. "I'm having like the best time ev-er."

"Aw, your poor little, puddin'," he said, pinching her cheek. "Not your scene, darling?"

Anna blushed, very aware of the extra thirteen pounds that she hadn't been able to lose since Nick had been away. She'd spent a lot of lonely evenings with just a box of candy for company, and at first thought that when her pants felt a little tight that her jeans must have shrunk in the wash. When she realized that *Cadbury's Roses* and *Thornton's Selection* were not her friends, and because Brendan told her to, she stopped, then began working out. Seven pounds had gone quite quickly, but that extra flab stayed resolutely around her stomach, leaving it soft and white like uncooked dough.

It didn't help that in the last half-hour several long, lean and stunning female models had drifted over to their table.

She took another few sips of her cocktail, knowing that it wasn't the best idea she'd ever had, but already feeling *looser* than usual.

"Tell Auntie Brendan all about it," he said encouragingly, jogging her elbow so that she ended up taking a bigger slurp than she'd intended.

She wiped her hand over her mouth and shook her head.

"It's not like I'm a dog. I mean, no one has ever yelled at me in the street, 'Put a leash on that and you could take it for a walk!' But I'm average. I'm not like one of *those* girls," and she pointed to the gaggle of gangly models, "girls who are totally gorgeous and always going on about the quarter of an inch of fat that just *maybe* is sitting on their perfect butt, or their stomachs that are flatter than an ironing board, with legs that go on for miles, and tiny, itsy bitsy waists, and cheekbones that they could probably file their nails on. But I'm not a double-bagger either. I'm average."

Brendan stared at her.

"Am I really hearing this, Miss Pity Party? You of the super-stud fiancé and flourishing self-help author and broadcaster? Maybe you should read your own book."

"Yes, but that's it!" Anna frowned, only vaguely aware that she was slurring her words. "Nick isn't average. He's 6' and 180 pounds of pure muscle, washboard abs and a hard chest, biceps that really do bulge when he moves his arms, and his legs are long and muscled.

And oh my God! His butt is totally perfect. I'm sure I could bounce a quarter off it, but he won't let me try. He scowled and got all moody when I suggested it."

Brendan's eyes widened as he tried not to laugh, but Anna was on a drunken roll.

"He has the body of a Greek god, with the old fashioned manners of an English gentleman, who really does open doors for me and carries the groceries, takes out the trash without being asked. He's also a real sweetheart and is kind to his mom and dad and sister, great with old people, kids and animals, and amazing in bed."

"Um, Annie, I think you might want to slow down the drinking," Brendan muttered, trying and failing to pry the cocktail glass from her hands.

"It's hard dating a model," she said, tears collecting in the corners of her eyes. "Everyone judges you and wonders, *What does he see in her?*"

Brendan shot a panicked gaze at Nick who turned to look just in time.

"I think she's wired and teary, I mean tired and weary, so you should probably get a taxi," Brendan stage-whispered so loudly that the whole table heard him.

"Come on, luv," Nick said with a smile, helping Anna to her feet. "Time for bed."

Anna collapsed into his arms, and the last thing she remembered was being lifted into the air, snuggling against his hard chest, the warmth of his body comforting her.

CHAPTER 16

A NNA SQUINTED AT THE BRIGHT LIGHT SEEPING from behind the heavy curtains and wondered who was thumping on the wall, but when she rolled onto her back, she realized that the pounding was in her head.

She sat up groaning, both from the appalling headache and from the humiliation of her behaviour the night before.

She grabbed the glass of water on the bedside table with shaky hands, and drank it down gratefully, even happier to find that Nick had left her two ibuprofen to kick-start the healing process.

She was so furious that she'd wasted their first night together by getting drunk. Oh, she'd had such plans!

At that moment, the hotel door opened and Nick walked into the room. He was shirtless and sweat glistened on his tanned skin, making the tattoos seem to shimmer and coil around his body.

A t-shirt dangled from one hand and he wore running shoes on his feet. He looked amazing. He looked perfect.

And Anna felt frazzled and a lot less than perfect.

Nick gave her a sympathetic smile and sat down next to her. He smelled of sweat and the sea, and she saw salt drying on his calves and thighs.

"Why are you with me?" she blurted out.

Nick cocked his head on one side as if he didn't understand the question. Then he frowned, his honey-coloured eyes narrowing as he gazed at her.

He could have asked her why she was asking, or gotten annoyed that her self-esteem kept questioning his commitment, but he didn't.

"Because I love you," he said, his voice deep and serious. "Because each morning I wake up and remember that you're wearing my ring and that I'm a lucky bastard, and each night I go to sleep knowing that I've met the woman I want to spend the rest of my life with." He paused. "Is that what you wanted to know?"

Anna nodded, dumbstruck. Nick wasn't the most effusive of people, but sometimes…

"Yes, that's … fine," she said weakly.

Nick dropped a soft kiss onto her lips, stood up and gave her a wink as he kicked off his running shoes, dropped his shorts and sauntered butt naked into the bathroom.

Anna didn't stop smiling for the rest of the day.

She and Brendan sat at the back of the exhibition hall where the *Mr. XCess* menswear designers were showing their collection.

As the lights dimmed and Janelle Monae's music blared out, Anna clutched Brendan's hand.

The first man strutting along the catwalk looked as if he'd just strolled in from the surf, his blond hair long and naturally highlighted.

"Oh God, I want to count his abs," sighed Brendan. "With my tongue!"

"Behave!" Anna laughed.

"I *am* behaving," Brendan said huffily. "I haven't thrown myself at the stage, have I?"

"Not yet," Anna muttered under her breath.

Next up, two gorgeous men strode along the catwalk, their stunning bodies gleaming—one like polished ebony; the other lighter skinned, a gorgeous caramel colour.

Then three slimmer male models danced onto the stage, and Brendan wasn't the only one who was on his feet, dancing along.

Then a man with blond dreadlocks sauntered onto the stage and Brendan grabbed Anna's hand again.

"Do you think he's gay?"

"I have no idea. Why don't you ask him?"

Brendan nodded so fast, Anna was worried he'd sprain his neck.

Then her heart lurched and started to gallop as Nick strode onto the stage. Brendan squealed and had to stuff his fists in his mouth to stop shrieking. Anna could hardly draw a breath.

Nick swung his arms lightly, his gaze somewhere in the middle distance. He walked confidently to the end of the catwalk, struck a pose, turned on his heel, and headed back, high-fiving the model who followed him out.

"Oh, Annie! He's a real model!" Brendan whispered loudly.

This time it was Anna who nodded crazily. She was so proud of him; so proud that his work and commitment had paid off.

She couldn't stop smiling.

Not even when two women sitting on her other side commented on what a great body he had and how much they loved the ink decorating his body, and then sighed, murmuring how much they wished he was wearing Speedos instead of boardshorts.

Twice more, Nick strode along the catwalk, dark and intense, and then on his very final run when he was joined by all the other models and the designer, he threw a huge smile at the audience, who were clapping and waving.

Anna stood up and cheered with everyone else, happy he was happy, so proud of him.

And later that evening, when a twenty-something model with legs up to her armpits flirted outrageously with Nick and wrapped her arms around his neck as she sat on his knee at an after-party, Anna just raised her eyebrows and swapped an amused look with Brendan as Nick carefully set the woman back on her feet.

The post-catwalk party was the stuff legends are made of. Nick was paid to stand around shirtless, wearing only swimwear and flip flops, while champagne flowed and stunningly beautiful women sauntered around the pool in tiny bikinis or beach wraps, showcasing their peachy asses and round, perfect breasts.

White fairy lights were strung across gazebos, and the sun sank in a cauldron of red and orange, the sky catching fire to backlight the whole scene spectacularly.

Brendan was in heaven, attending his first ever luau, drinking cocktails decorated with a mountain of fresh pineapple, cherries, and paper umbrellas, then dancing to Hawaiian-themed tunes and doing his best impression of *An Englishman in New York*.

The entertainment ranged from Hawaiian melodies being played on a ukulele to a rock band, to a henna artist, tarot card reader, tattoo artist and illusionist, all adding to the noise, colour and sense of heady abandonment.

In the darker corners, cut lines of cocaine were snorted and joints were passed around. Pills were swapped and swallowed, and those flying high danced like there was no one watching.

Anna wasn't as shocked as Nick had been. While athletes could rarely get away with getting high, it was common in the fringes of the entertainment world. Because of her famous father, she'd been to her share of showbiz parties.

Of course, Anna couldn't completely get over being ordinary-looking among all the beautiful examples of humanity, but there were enough average-Joes—designers, clients, buyers, business people—so she didn't feel completely outclassed.

Nick was paid to mingle, and he was also networking, meeting people and making sure they remembered him for future work, but he kept an eye on where Anna was, sending her a private smile or a wink that made her skin hot just thinking about being with him later, in private, with no eyes on them.

She sipped her cocktail and gazed around, observing the colourful mass of humanity. It was so different from the rugged world of rugby that Nick had inhabited successfully for so long, and yet, against the odds, he also fit in here.

Although she wanted him home in London, if his career meant a permanent move back to New York, she'd do it in a heartbeat. It also meant that her mom was a short drive away instead of a seven-hour flight.

As long as they were together, they'd work it out.

She hoped.

Nick found it hard to concentrate at this final party when Anna was nearby, looking stunning in a pale blue dress that seemed to float over her curves, sweet and innocent compared to those blood red lips that had taunted him all evening. Every time she sipped her drink, sucking the cocktail through a straw, Nick felt his groin tighten impatiently. His iron will had never been tested more as he stood around making small talk with people he'd probably never see again.

Two hours later, he was off the clock.

Brendan had already disappeared, so Nick pulled on a t-shirt, grabbed Anna and jumped in the first taxi they could find.

She laughed happily.

"Are we in a hurry?"

His answer was short and gruff.

"Yes."

A smile curved her lips and she leaned against him as the taxi rushed through the night.

Once they reached their hotel room, Nick wanted to feel everything. He wanted to be with his fiancée again.

The need inside him was volcanic and urgent.

"We have all night," she whispered, wrapping her arms around his neck and trailing her tongue up the broad column of his neck.

Nick's answer was to slide her dress up her thighs and over her head, then toss her onto the bed so she gasped with surprise.

His heavy cock pressed against her and this time they both groaned.

Fast, furious love-making led to slow, soft words as the night crept around them, until finally, finally they were at peace.

CHAPTER 17

AFTER THE WONDERFUL WEEK IN Miami, the house in London seemed even emptier than usual. Anna was feeling unsettled, and loneliness clung to her, wrapping her in a cloak of depression.

Nick had seemed so contented, so keen to do well at this new career. Anna was happy for him. But she had to admit that a tiny part of her was disappointed, too—she'd hoped that he'd tell her he was ready to come home. He hadn't, and she wasn't going to beg. She'd promised herself years ago that she'd never beg another man for anything. Ever. But if he'd have asked her to move back to New York, she would have gone without a second thought.

Great. The self-help author who can't help herself.

Sighing, she stared at the length of her to-do list—it didn't seem to be getting any shorter. When she heard the front door open, she'd never been happier for Brendan's distraction.

"What?" he stared at her suspiciously when she met him with a beaming smile. "You're being weird."

"I'm just happy to see you, Brendan, honey-pie."

"Are you on drugs?"

Anna shot him a glare then sank back in her chair.

"Can't I just be happy to see you?"

Brendan dumped his laptop on the kitchen table and shrugged out of his jacket.

"I've told you before, you're not my type and I'm not going to have sex with you. Workplace harassment!"

"Ha ha, very funny. Oh wait, I'm not laughing."

Brendan smirked at her.

"Now tell Auntie Brenda what's really got you all menopausal?"

"I'm thirty-seven!"

"My cousin went through the menopause at 29. Tick tock, Dr. Scott."

Anna felt her heart contract and tears form in her eyes.

Brendan was by her side immediately.

"Oh, crappy-crap! I'm so sorry. I'm not usually so insensitive."

Anna let out a noise that was halfway between a cry and a snort.

"Yes, you are."

"Yes, I am, but not about something that matters. I was hoping Nick would have knocked you up when you were in Miami. I'd assumed all those moony looks led to lots of sexing. I can't wait to be Auntie Brenda for real."

Anna gave a small smile.

"There, that's much better," he said. "My Anna-banana should always have a smile on her face."

"Ugh, I'm a mess. Sorry, Bren. I just miss him."

"And yet again, you're telling the wrong man."

Anna pressed her lips together.

"I told you: I'm not going to guilt him into coming home."

"And I told *you*," Brendan enunciated clearly. "Men are simple creatures and need to have everything spelled out to them in foot high letters with the blood of a vestal virgin or an Arsenal supporter. He doesn't know that you miss him *unless you tell him*."

They stared at each other across the kitchen table until Brendan cracked his knuckles and leaned over to the coffee machine.

"You know what you need?"

Anna scowled.

"I'm really kind of afraid that you're going to tell me."

"Very funny, Ms. Laugh-Your-Arse-Off. You need a night out. Glam yourself up, put on some slap, comb your hair at least twice, and wear your push-up bra. Those pancakes of yours need all the help they can get."

"You ... that's ... ugh!"

Brendan shrugged.

"Speaking as one girl to another."

Anna drew a breath.

"So your great plan to cheer me up is to dress me like a..."

"...tart."

"I was going to say hooker, but okay, as we're in Britain, like a tart ... and what? Go pull some guy?! Go and cheat on Nick?"

Brendan rolled his eyes.

"You're talking out of your arse, and there's so much hot air, you must have windburn."

"Brendan! That's gross!"

He ignored her.

"What you need is a night on the town. Something to make you remember that there is life beyond sex-god Nick Renshaw." He raised a hand as she started to argue. "All I'm saying is go out and have some fun. Take a break, do something different. You do remember how to party like a single girl?"

Anna looked down.

"I'm not single."

Brendan raised an eyebrow.

"Anna, you're sitting around watching life pass you by because all you're doing is waiting for Nick while he gets on with his life."

Anna felt the sting of his words and it hurt.

"That's not true! I'm a professional working woman. I have my next book to complete and I still have my self-help column. I'm *busy*. I have deadlines!"

Brendan leaned back in his chair, studying her closely.

"It's not a crime to be broody, Anna. And for the record, I think you'd make a great mommy."

Anna swallowed. Sometimes Brendan's insight was scary. She didn't know whether to kick his ass or kick her own.

Brendan didn't push his point. Instead, he picked up his phone and sent a quick text message to someone, poured two cups of coffee for Anna and himself, and smiled as he got an almost immediate response to his message.

"Good, that's sorted. You're having dinner and drinks with Jason tonight."

Anna gaped at him.

"I'm *what?*"

"Jason Oduba is picking you up at eight. Look fabulous and thank me tomorrow."

"What? I can't!"

"Don't even try to argue with me, Anna. Call it research if you have to—you said you needed to interview him."

"Interview, yes; dinner, no."

"So mix a little work and pleasure. Jason's hot."

Anna argued for fifteen minutes, but Brendan was adamant: a night out with Nick's fun-loving friend and former teammate was just what the doctor needed.

FOR NICK, DISILLUSIONMENT had set in.

The colourful memories from Miami were fading already, and he was back in the grey grind of New York: castings every day; more people saying no than yes; back to being told he was too fit, too tattooed, too muscled, too big, too small, too white, too British—whatever the reasons were this week.

Since his success at Miami Swim Week, he'd had no further work, not even a sniff of something, and he missed Anna more than ever. Hell, he missed Brendan. At least he knew that Anna had a good friend looking after her in London and that she wasn't lonely.

Nick frowned.

Taking care of Anna was *his* job—and he couldn't do it from New York.

He also knew that he needed a goal, something to work towards, and that was rare in modeling: most work came in out of the blue with no warning, or maybe 48 hours to get yourself to a studio or location, or even on a flight somewhere.

It did mean that he was careful to keep in shape at all times, although that was nothing new, and he'd struck up a friendship with another Brit, Rick Roberts, who'd recently opened up a gym in Manhattan and was pulling in some very nice business.

Roberts was a fellow Yorkshireman and also from a sporting background, but dour and monosyllabic.

Nevertheless, the two men became friends. And it was also

one of the best equipped gyms that Nick had ever been in. It had Pilates machines, air bikes, functional equipment, prowlers, farmers walks, atlas stones, chains, plus a café bar, steam room, sauna, juice cleansing bar, swimming pool, in-house nutritionist, physio and a team of masseuses, plus all the usual classes and several well-known celebrity personal trainers.

It was something he might consider doing himself one day if he could get the financial backing. Possibly. Maybe. Or maybe not. He didn't know, and that frustrated the hell out of him.

All Nick's uncertainties came flooding back. Had it been the right decision to come to New York or was he wasting his time here? When it was fresh and challenging, he'd enjoyed it, but since Miami, it seemed more of a grind than fulfilling. And he couldn't stay apart from Anna forever.

What the hell am I doing here?

He had no idea that his entire life was about to change again.

It was a Wednesday afternoon when Adrienne called Nick's phone to inform him that a new client had booked him for a studio shoot the following day.

"I don't know the photographer," she admitted, "but they asked for you by name."

"Yeah? How did they hear about me?"

There was a pause before Adrienne spoke and he heard the click of her keyboard in the background.

"Honestly, I'm not sure. I don't think they said. Does it matter?"

"Not really, just wondering. What's the job?"

"A couples shoot—another romance book cover. I know, I know! You said that you didn't want to do anymore of those, but I gotta tell ya, Nick, this is the first bite you've had in a while. You should think very hard before turning it down."

Nick scowled. If it had been with Golden again, that wouldn't have been so bad.

"Who is it?" he asked grumpily.

"I'll tell you what I was told: it's for an up and coming author. Underwear, no nudity. Okay with you?"

Nick still had regrets about the steamy shoot he'd done with Cee Cee, even though the photographs had been beautiful.

"Nick? You there?" Adrienne huffed on the other end of the line.

"Yeah, okay I'll do it. No nudity, right?"

"Yes, and I made sure that's in the contract—I know how you feel about it. Be at the studio 2.30PM."

"Got it."

"They're flying in from the UK. I'll messenger the details over to you tonight."

Nick did his usual careful preparations: limited his food and water intake, shaved his chest and made sure that his beard was neat and tidy. Although he'd shave it off if they wanted him to, but he wasn't cutting his hair for anyone. Well, he might cut it for Anna, but after years of keeping it short, he was enjoying seeing how long he could wear it—maybe even Aquaman long. Maybe.

The following day, Nick turned up at the Greenwich Village studio at the appointed time, but the moment that he walked up the stairs, there was a weird vibe in the room, a tension that was unusual.

The photographer shook hands but seemed to have trouble meeting Nick's eyes, and kept glancing at his watch as if they were running late, although Nick had arrived a few minutes early.

He'd seen nerves and tension on other shoots where there were too many shots needed and not enough time, and everyone was under pressure; or the frenetic energy backstage at the Miami swimwear catwalk where dozens of models vied for space, elbowing each other by accident as they dropped their clothes and changed on the spot. But this was different.

For a start, the photographer was British so he knew that this was *the* Nick Renshaw, and he was jittery, although Nick didn't think it was drugs but nerves. Which didn't make sense. And when Nick asked him about the shoot, the photographer was evasive. It all added up to Nick becoming increasingly skeptical about what the shoot would be used for other than the romance novel he'd been told about.

As there was no one else in the room, he asked about the female model he'd be working with and was told that the model and author were the same person. Apparently, she was doing her makeup and would be on set soon. Once again, no name given.

It was strange that there was no stylist or makeup artist, and Nick's costume, if you could call it that, was a pair of very skimpy Speedos, what his Samoan friend, Fetu, would have described as 'budgie smugglers'. He wasn't offered a robe.

"These?" Nick asked in disbelief, holding up the glittery gold briefs on one finger.

The photographer gave a fake smile.

"Part of the story. All very tasteful, mate."

I'm not your mate, Nick thought, eyeing the photographer in a way that made the other man step back.

It seemed obvious to Nick that the 'no nudity' clause was just a blind, and even though he wouldn't actually be naked, clever angles on the day or photoshopping after the fact would make it seem as though he was nude.

"What's the name of the model?" he asked casually. "Or should I say author? So I can look at her covers and see the style she likes."

"Oh, she's really new," said the photographer with a sleazy smile that didn't meet his eyes. "This is her first book. But trust me, this is going to be *huge*."

Was this woman famous? Was that the reason for all the secrecy? Nick tried to remember if there was any clause about public disclosure in his contract. He didn't think so, but he couldn't be sure.

There was definitely something unsaid going on, some hidden agenda, but Nick had no idea what it could be. His gut told him the set up was wrong. So instead of changing into the ridiculous Speedos, he waited, pretending to read emails on his phone.

"Get changed whenever you like," the photographer said encouragingly.

"Yeah," Nick replied, without looking up. "What did you say your name was? Mate?"

"Ah, um, Roy."

"You got a surname, Roy?"

The man paused before answering, licking his lips nervously.

"Greenside."

Nick searched for the name, his eyebrows drawing together as he read the man's online profile.

"You work for the Red Tops?" he asked, frowning as he glanced up, using the colloquial name given to the British tabloid newspapers.

These were journalists who'd tormented him and printed lies when his and Anna's unorthodox relationship had first been revealed.

His bad feeling deepened.

"Man's gotta make a living, mate. You know that," the photographer said defensively.

Nick didn't reply, continuing to scroll through Roy Greenside's online pictures.

One image jumped out at him and Nick's bad feeling twisted his gut.

"You've photographed Molly McKinney—several times."

The man licked his lips nervously again, his eyes darting to a small room off to the side.

"Once or twice. But that's all a long time ago, Nick. Water under the bridge, right, mate?"

Nick stared at him hard-eyed.

Nick had made his peace with Kenny, but there was no way he'd forgive Molly or…

"Yeah, water under the bridge," said a laughing female voice.

The hairs on the back of Nick's neck stood up and he turned slowly to face the woman he despised most in the whole world.

"You."

Molly McKinney was walking towards him, strutting from the changing room wearing a ton of makeup and a barely-there string bikini.

"Hello, Nicky."

Nick waited for her head to start rotating or a swarm of locusts dive-bomb the studio.

"Surprised to see me?" she asked, gazing up at him from between her false eyelashes. "You weren't very nice to me at your testimonial, but I forgive you."

Nick didn't answer. He simply picked up his bag and started to leave.

"You can't go!" Roy shouted after him, picking up his camera and snapping away, catching the furious expression on Nick's face.

"The fuck I can't," Nick growled.

Molly laughed again, thoroughly enjoying being in the spotlight, and inching closer to Nick so Roy could get them both in the same shot.

"Stay and have some fun, Nicky," she grinned at the camera. "You're being paid well enough."

"That's right," said Roy. "You can't leave or you'll be in breach of contract."

"Fuck the contract!" Nick snarled.

"Aw, don't tell me you're still upset about our little misunderstanding? I thought you'd be over all that by now."

Nick stared at her incredulously.

"You cheated on me with a teammate when I was injured, the guy I'd asked to be Best Man at our wedding; when I finished with you, I even let you keep the sodding ring which you flogged on eBay; when I started seeing Anna, you began a vendetta that cost her career; and you lied to the Press about everything. Did I leave anything out?"

Molly gripped his arm and gave him a hard look, her false nails sinking into his flesh.

"You signed the contract, Nicky. The money has already been transferred to your account. If you leave, my publishers will sue you."

He shook her hand off, staring down at her coldly.

"You think I give a shit about that? I don't. Let them sue me—but I'll be damned if I pose for a book cover with you! If there ever was a book in the first place."

She put one hand on her hip and struck a pose, making her fake breasts jiggle oddly.

"Oh, there's a book alright," she smirked. "*Naughty Nick: My Life with the Real Nick Renshaw* by Molly McKinney. It's going to be a bestseller."

Nick's icy rage continued to grow. He knew that if he didn't leave now, they'd all regret it.

"Is this the person you want to be, Mol?" he said, biting out each word. "You want to be remembered for being a cheat and a liar? And just for the record, you never did know anything about me."

Her eyes sparked with malice.

"Oh no? A little bird told me that you've been partying it up on tramadol … or was it diazepam?" Her gaze narrowed. "I wonder what *Dr. Anna Scott* would think about that. She's been very vocal about the misuse of prescription painkillers in sport, hasn't she?"

Nick shook his head, disturbed at the level of sleuthing Molly had being doing.

"I had career-ending surgery for a torn rotator cuff. Christ, you're unbelievable."

"Ooh, Nicky! Hit a sore spot, did I? You thought no one knew. Well, let me tell you this, Mr. Big Shot, there are *always* people watching. And anyway, I'm not the one trying to make it as a professional model," she laughed coldly. "Your agent told us you were available any day this week or next. Not having too much luck, are you? And where's dear little Anna? Home alone with all your old teammates to keep her company?"

Nick's voice grew stone cold as he leaned toward her, his eyes dangerously dark.

"You're the one who'd know all about that, wouldn't you, Molly? I spoke to Kenny at my testimonial. He told me everything, how you'd come onto him when I was laid up after surgery, and then he apologized for making the biggest mistake of his life. Yeah, that's what he said. And he dumped your cheating arse, didn't he?"

He turned and left the room.

As he strode past, the photographer got in his face, continuing to take shot after shot.

A younger Nick would have grabbed the man's camera and slammed it against the wall, shattering the lens. A more hot-headed Nick would have punched the sleazy photographer, the consequences be damned. And a less mindful Nick would have told Molly that she was a sour-faced cunt and the worst lay he'd ever had.

But Nick was older and wiser now, and knew that confrontation was exactly what they wanted.

Nick pushed past them both as Molly screamed obscenities at him.

"You'll be sorry for the way you've treated me, Nicky!" she yelled. "You're so fucking finished! A has-been! I hate you!"

With grim satisfaction, Nick slammed the studio door behind him and jogged down the stairs.

Out on the streets of Manhattan, he stood breathing deeply, his hands shaking and his heart pounding from the strain of reining in his fury.

Think, he told himself. *You need to think.*

He pulled out his phone and called Adrienne.

"Nick? You're supposed to be at a shoot. What's going on?"

"It was a set up," he snarled into the phone as he stared up at the pale blue sky. "Fuckers set me up."

CHAPTER 18

Nick went straight to Adrienne's office, cutting through the busy Manhattan streets easily. Seeing the cloud of anger surrounding him, people stepped out of his way, half afraid.

Nick knew that he'd been foolish to give Molly and Roy any reaction: showing his anger had given them exactly what they wanted. But only a robot could have stayed stony-faced when confronted by their lies and deception.

He wanted to call Anna but he knew that she was interviewing Jason Oduba about his retirement from rugby, his new job as an assistant coach at Bath RFU, and plans for the future—all material for her new book on how professional athletes transitioned to ordinary, regular lives. Since Nick's retirement, her research and motivation had taken a more personal turn.

Yeah, and right now that could redefine irony.

Once he reached the Midtown agency, Shonda showed him into Adrienne's office, giving him a sympathetic look, the kind that a vet uses when telling you bad news about your furry friend.

"Nick, have a seat. Tell me in your own words exactly what happened."

Nick explained everything: his engagement to Molly, finding her fucking his former friend, the court case, meeting Anna, Molly's revenge—everything in nauseating detail—images that he'd long tried to block.

He didn't mention her accusation about being addicted to tramadol, but secretly promised himself that he'd ease back or even stop.

Adrienne listened to it all, recording the conversation on her phone and occasionally taking notes.

When he admitted that he'd lost his temper and tossed around a few f-bombs, she winced, sighed, and carefully laid her pen on her desk.

"Nick, it's like this: you walked off set from a photoshoot that you'd already been paid for. Did you touch either of them? Because if you did, you could be looking at a charge of assault, too."

"I had to push past the photographer because he was stopping me from leaving the room."

"And it's your word against theirs—and you've just told me that you were previously found guilty of assault against the woman. You see what I'm saying? Even if they don't take that route, I wouldn't be surprised if the publishers sue you for the cost of delay, studio hire, Ms. McKinney's and Mr. Greenside's time, the cost of their flights and hotels, some sort of damages or reparation. You'll definitely be sued for the return of your fee."

She leaned back and rubbed her temples.

"Your reputation is in shit city right now. I know the way these types operate—and no one will want to work with a model who causes trouble or someone caught up in a scandal. Bookings will be non-existent and if you'd had any work lined up, it would already have been cancelled. Word gets around in this town."

"So what do I do? Let them fuck me over? Let Molly win *again?*"

She sucked her teeth, tapping her pen on the desk.

"You've got two choices: keep quiet, pay up, and hope it all blows over."

Nick shook his head.

"They want the scandal—they don't want it to blow over. What's the other choice?"

"Go on the offensive. Get a Press interview lined up and give them your side first. That's almost always the side that people remember. Do you know any reporters in the UK who'd be more likely to side with you? This Greenside guy sounds like a real scumbag. Who's he pissed off in the past?"

A germ of an idea took root in Nick's mind.

"There's a TV reporter that's always been fair to me," he said reflectively. "Jasmine Khan. I've given her two exclusives. I could ask her."

"So she owes you?"

"I suppose so. Sort of."

"Good. And she's a woman, too. Even better. Call her now. Set up a phone interview today, then get your ass back to London for another exclusive."

"London?"

Adrienne gave him a grim look.

"Nick, even when you've put a positive spin on this, you're finished in New York. Maybe in six months I can get you more work, but right now, you'll be industry poison. Clients won't be associated with scandal," and she gave him a knowing look. "Not the kind that you'd want to work for, anyways." She shrugged. "And it might be the best idea to get out of town in case there's a warrant for your arrest. Unlikely, but don't take the chance. Act first, act fast."

Nick left Adrienne's office reeling. It definitely wasn't how he'd expected this day to go.

He jogged back to his cheap room, threw all his clothes in his bags, binned what he couldn't pack, and checked out.

He had no idea if Molly would try to get him arrested, but given her history, he wouldn't put it past her.

Flagging down the first yellow cab he saw, he headed for JFK, contacting Jasmine's office. For once, luck was with him: she was still at work and he gave his interview from the back of the taxi, leaving nothing out.

She was delighted with her scoop, and agreed to film another interview as soon as he landed back in London.

His second piece of luck was finding a flight leaving for Heathrow in just over an hour. Nick bought his ticket then sweated his way through the security line, making boarding by a cosy five minutes.

He still hadn't had time to phone Anna, so he sent her a text as he settled into his economy seat.

> *On my way home.*
> *Molly tried to screw with me again.*
> *Jasmine Khan has the story.*
> *I'll see you tomorrow.*
> *Love you x*

Anna had enjoyed her dinner with Jason more than she'd expected. He'd kept the flirting to a minimum and had been surprisingly insightful about what the end of his playing career meant to him, and why he'd decided to stay with the sport and become an assistant coach. He hoped that one day he'd eventually graduate to being manager.

The only part of the night that she hadn't enjoyed was when they'd arrived at *The Ivy* and a lone paparazzo had gotten pictures of them walking into the restaurant with Jason's arm around her shoulders.

Jason hugged everyone, but she knew that wasn't how it would look in the newspapers. She could imagine the headlines. She was so used to being cast as an anti-heroine that she was almost past caring.

Anna was just wrapping up her post-dinner interview with Jason when she picked up Nick's text. Her heart catapulted in her chest and she felt alternatively icy cold and boiling hot.

She dropped her head in her hands, her pulse still galloping.

"Shit! Are you alright?"

Jason's meaty arm was slung around her and his worried face peered into hers.

"I'm fine, I'm fine," she mumbled.

"Are you in the family way?" he asked, his voice concerned.

"What?"

"In the club?"

"What club?"

Jason rolled his eyes.

"Bloody hell, doc! Are you pregnant?"

Irritation helped restore her equilibrium.

"No! Why does everyone keep asking me that?" Then she sighed. "Don't answer—my muffin top, I know, I know."

Jason gave her a sheepish grin.

"Aw, no, you're not that fat. You just looked like you were about to faint. You sure you're alright?"

"Yes, no, I don't know. Look at this!" and she handed her phone to Jason.

His expression darkened.

"What's that stupid bitch done now?"

"I don't know!"

"Well, give him a bell," Jason said encouragingly.

Anna had been in London long enough to know that Jason was telling her to call Nick. She followed his advice but was sent straight to voicemail.

"He's not answering. He must have caught a flight already. I'm sorry, Jason. I have to call Jasmine right now."

"Yeah, no worries, luv. Tell your old man to phone me when he's back. Bastard owes me a pint. Come on, I'll drive you home."

THREE STORIES BROKE while Nick was halfway across the Atlantic.

Molly and Roy had lost no time in giving their side of the sordid non-story. But Jasmine Khan, with an eye on her career and a genuine liking and respect for Nick, had managed to get her exclusive interview with him out first:

When Ex's Turn Evil—Nick Renshaw's Stalker Nightmare!
"I feel sorry for my ex," says rugby's Mr. Nice Guy.

Nick had told Jasmine everything, including swearing at his ex- and at Roy Greenside, and that he regretted his loss of temper. Adrienne had done her part and returned the modelling fee in full, including her fifteen per cent.

Molly and Roy hit back with a far more lurid version of the story, in which Nick had terrorized them and threatened them with physical violence. The photographs of Nick's angry face were cited as 'evidence'.

Nasty Nick in Photoshoot Frenzy
"He's violent and unpredictable—I genuinely thought he'd hit me again."

There were photographs of Molly looking tearful, her eyeliner artfully smudged. But the fact that they'd flown out to New York and booked Nick for a shoot without revealing their identities played against them, and most people seemed to think they were in the wrong.

Unfortunately, that didn't stop Adrienne's agency and Nick being sued by Molly's publisher—they would be asking for damages in excess of a hundred-thousand pounds. The writ was being couriered to Nick's house and Adrienne's offices.

This wasn't a problem that would go away overnight. So far there was no mention of Molly's accusations of drug abuse, but Nick knew her—she hadn't forgotten. She had her reasons for saving that salacious piece of gossip. It was probably in her damn book.

The woman clung to publicity the way Spanx clung to an Oscar nominee's backside.

The third story wouldn't have warranted much interest if it hadn't been for the first two, but the pap who'd snapped Anna and Jason together was making the most of a minor windfall, and one of the seedier tabloids had picked it up.

Naughty Nick's Fiancée Enjoys Intimate Dinner with Ex-teammate

And one newspaper had put all the stories together: one-plus-one-plus-one, making four…

Renshaw Races to Save Relationship

Journalists were camped outside Anna's front door within ten minutes of Jasmine's story hitting the internet.

But this time, Anna was prepared. She'd already used the two hour head-start to adopt a siege mentality and turn their home into a fortress. Despite the lateness of the hour, she'd phoned Brendan for backup and moral support. Next, she called Nick's former rugby agent Mark Lipman for legal help and because he was someone she trusted. Even though Mark was now in his seventies and had been retired for three years, he knew his way around a scandal or two.

Third, she packed a suitcase and booked two hotel rooms under Brendan's name. And finally, she'd asked Jason to meet Nick at Heathrow in the morning. It would be a good way to squelch the embers of speculation regarding story number three.

Anna had learned from her years of being in the Press's spotlight: she wasn't going to be a victim ever again.

She'd toyed with the idea of using a car service to collect Nick from the airport, but she wasn't sure if he would check his phone before making a run through the terminal building. He might not look out for a driver holding up his name on an iPad, but he wouldn't miss a 6' 6" former teammate.

Jason wasn't the calmest guy ever, and tended to get into more fights and 'situations' than any other player, but he was also a good friend—and right now, Anna thought Nick needed that the most.

Brendan arrived at her house breathless with excitement and dragging an enormous suitcase, laptop and shoulder bag.

"We're going to a hotel, not witness protection," Anna said, eyeing his bulging bags.

"You'll be laughing on the other side of your sweet little tush if you get papped wearing old jeans and a sweatshirt, whilst I am the epitome of glamour, Little Miss Know-it All," he sniped back.

Anna shook her head. Only Brendan could make her smile at a time like this.

While he carried their combined luggage out to the Range Rover, Anna drew all the curtains in the house, double-checked that every door and window was locked, threw half a pint of milk down the kitchen sink and said goodbye to her home. It was upsetting not to know how long she'd be away, but she hoped it would only be a couple of weeks.

She'd learned the hard way that toughing it out didn't work with the paparazzi. Hiding until they'd gotten bored or a more recent story hit the headlines worked much better. Or, as Brendan always said, "Don't feed the beast."

NICK WASN'T PARTICULARLY well known in New York, but in London, he was *someone*. Unfortunately, most people with even a kissing cousin to fame would tell you that the two worst places for getting papped are LAX and pretty much anywhere in London, but especially Heathrow airport.

The Press had gone crazy over the latest 'Naughty Nick' scandal, and he arrived back to over thirty photographers, journalists and two news crews waiting for a quote.

But, like Anna, he'd learned how to deal with reporters, so he wore his sunglasses, kept a smile on his face, and simply told them that he was happy to be home and looking forward to seeing his fiancée.

When he spotted Jason Oduba in the crowd, his smile widened. Jason hugged the crap out of him, damn near lifting him off his feet.

"Welcome home, shorty," laughed Jason.

"You tosser! It's good to see you!"

So the only pictures that the papparazzi took were of two friends looking happy to see each other.

Stop the press.

CHAPTER

19

For ten days, Anna and Nick were engulfed by the media storm, the wave of lies from Molly and Roy Greenside battering at them. But this time, they were together, and that made all the difference.

Anna and Nick would have preferred to be in their own home, but they both knew that the best defence was to be seen out together looking happy, looking like a couple in love.

Brendan arranged for them to be seen having lunch at *The Palomar*, walking the red carpet at a charity film premiere in Leicester Square, and entering *Annabel's* nightclub in Mayfair. They stayed for ten minutes then left by the backdoor.

But just when it seemed the storm was abating, fresh accusations emerged.

The Rugby Rocket in Addiction Shock
Renshaw in Rehab

"Oh my God! Look at the lies these assholes are printing now!" Anna raged, waving a pile of tabloid newspapers. "You can't let this go, Nick. You need to put out a statement refuting it all. How dare they write this crap about you!"

Nick's heart sank as he turned his eyes to the newspapers that Anna slapped down onto the tiny table provided by the hotel.

He read the headlines without comment, then turned to the main part of the story.

Nick Renshaw has an addiction to prescription painkillers, says a source close to the former England Rugby Ace. It's rumoured that the addiction began after career-ending surgery to a torn rotator cuff in his shoulder. Friends of the star are concerned for his health, and suggest that his sudden return from New York where he had been developing a successful modelling career shows that his addiction is spiraling.

Figures supplied by the NHS report that one in eleven patients has been prescribed a potentially addictive drug in the last year. TV star and presenter of 'Britain's Got Talent', Ant McPartlin, recently completed rehab for his addiction to prescription painkillers and a conviction for drink driving.

The Priory is a well-known celebrity rehab centre, but offered a 'no comment' about whether Nick Renshaw has been a client when approached by our award-winning journalist...

Nick tossed the paper aside without finishing. The web of half-truths and downright lies seemed damning, but what killed him was Anna's certainty that it was all made up.

He looked into her dark eyes, blazing with fury on his behalf, and he swallowed the lump in his throat.

"I've been taking tramadol," he said bluntly. "Pretty much every day since my shoulder surgery."

Anna's mouth dropped open.

"But … but that was over a year ago?"

"Yeah."

She took a shaky breath and sat opposite him heavily.

"Nick, are you saying … is this *true?*" and she pointed a trembling finger at the newspapers.

Nick pushed his hands through his uncombed tangle of hair.

"I'm not an addict," he said defensively. "My shoulder has taken a long time to heal. I still get pain … I've been cutting down recently."

Anna seemed close to tears.

"You never said. I didn't know. I thought the pain was manageable. But Nick, tramadol is an opioid, it's addictive."

He grimaced but didn't answer.

"How much do you take?"

"One pill, sometimes two."

Anna swallowed.

"So, between 25mg and 50mg?"

"Yeah."

"That's … not so bad. We can deal with that." She closed her eyes. "God, I'm so sorry!"

Nick blinked.

"Why are you sorry? It's me that … it's not your fault."

Her eyes glistened and she scrubbed at her face impatiently.

"Jesus, I'm a trained sports psychologist and I didn't even notice my own fiancé was taking tramadol every day! I've been so sure that you were doing better, that you weren't depressed anymore. God, I've missed you so much, so much every long, pointless day, and I didn't say anything because I thought you were doing better without me, when all this time you've been struggling. So many times I wanted to beg you to come home, but I didn't. I wouldn't! Oh my God! I'm supposed to be the one who's a professional communicator! I couldn't help you! I couldn't help myself! It's all a lie!"

Nick's throat burned as he listened to her bitterness and hurt, her shame and disappointment. She'd missed him, she'd wanted him to come home. But she'd never told him how she felt. And he'd never asked.

He grabbed her arms and pulled her into his lap.

"Anna, my Anna, I'm sorry. I've let you down. I've let myself down. New York was so hard without you. I missed you every day and I should have told you, but I needed to do it on my own. I've fucked this up so badly."

Anna's shoulders shook as she fought her tears.

"I love you," she gulped. "So much. Let me help you. I can help you."

Nick nodded wordlessly, and held her trembling body against his.

The next few days were tough for Nick and Anna. A giant wedge of doubt stood between them, and building back the trust was hard.

Anna put together a plan to help end Nick's reliance on tramadol gradually, and he promised he'd see the surgeon who performed the operation to check that there were no underlying issues.

She also emptied the medicine cabinet of all painkillers.

Molly got her tits out for page three of *The Sun* and told everyone who'd listen about her new book. Unfortunately for Nick, all the recent publicity had been a godsend to her publishers and they were rushing the book into publication the following month. It looked like it would be a bestseller after all.

More seriously, the publishers were suing both Adrienne's agency and Nick personally for £175,000—each.

"Can they do that?" Brendan asked incredulously. "Well, of course they can, they have. But do they have any chance of winning? At all?"

After nearly two weeks of being front page news, Anna and Nick were finally sitting at their kitchen table together for the first time in too long, trying to piece together a strategy with wily old Mark Lipman.

Their story had been knocked off the front pages by speculation that Meghan Markle was pregnant. Anna had some sympathy for her—she'd probably just been eating too many afternoon cream teas with the Queen at Windsor Castle and now everyone thought she was … what was the expression? Up the duff.

Mark Lipman's voice came over the speakerphone.

"They do have a case because you walked out of a job that you'd been paid for. The fact that you've paid the money back is neither here nor there. Even though it was all underhand, there was nothing illegal about what they did."

"Bastards," Nick muttered under his breath.

"Agreed," sighed Mark, as Anna reached across and held Nick's hand. "But they do have a case since costs were incurred with flights, hotel bills, studio hire, other expenses, having to schedule a re-shoot etc. etc. But I doubt that would come to more than, say, £25,000 or £30,000. They're also trying to put a figure on lost sales because of the delay but that's a more tenuous claim. What I find remarkable is that a publisher would pay out for all of those expenses in the first place. These people keep a tight rein on their budgets—how can they afford to fund a photoshoot in the States? It doesn't add up." He sighed. "And don't forget, Ms. Catalano's agency is in the firing line, too. She could quite rightly sue you for her costs as well as loss of reputation."

"Bloody hell!" Nick put his head in his hands. "Is there anything we can do?"

There was a short silence while Anna exchanged a worried look with Brendan.

Anna knew that he had invested in property, but Nick had very little in the way of liquid assets, and if he ended up having to pay out hundreds of thousands of pounds, they could end up losing their home.

"Well," said Mark, at last, his voice thoughtful, "you could counter sue: the legal terminology is 'intentional infliction of emotional distress'. You'd have a low to reasonable chance of a positive outcome since most of the four key criteria are met: did Molly and Roy Greenside act intentionally or recklessly—yes; was their conduct extreme and outrageous—probably not; were their actions the cause of the distress—yes; did the plaintiff, you Nick, suffer severe emotional distress due to defendant's conduct?"

Nick nodded, cutting a glance at Anna.

Mark's voice cut in again.

"The 'severe' part is more of a stretch and it's possible, likely even, that a judge would dismiss it. But it might just make the publishers reconsider their position since any sort of litigation is expensive, and the indication that you'll fight them will definitely give them pause for thought. But let me ask you this: do you really want to drag everything through another court case which will give them more publicity for their damned book?"

Anna frowned.

"Can we stop the book being published?"

"Unlikely, not impossible. My advice would be not to bother. We already know it'll be a carefully constructed web of half-truths. The more you fight it, the more grist you give to their mill of lies." Mark cleared his throat. "Kenny Johnson contacted me last week. Molly had approached him to be part of the story—he turned her down. He wanted you to know that."

Anna and Brendan both turned to stare at Nick, waiting for his reaction.

"I'm not letting that lying bitch win this," he said, his voice flat.

"Then counter sue," Mark repeated. "Best case scenario, they drop the whole thing and you can do the same. You really don't want to go back in a court, Nick. That b— witch will rake up every bit of dirt she can find."

"And the worst case scenario?" Anna said quietly.

There was a long pause.

"They win their case; you lose yours; you pay costs for both. But I don't think it'll come to that. If I did, I'd advise you to pay up now. Look, I'll set up a meeting with the legal team I've used in cases like this. Listen to what they have to say; let them advise you." He cleared his throat. "I suggest you liquidate some assets now if you want to fight this case—you don't want this hanging over you, possibly for years. You'll need the money, son."

Later that night after Brendan had gone to his own home, Nick and Anna were in bed together. Nick stretched out, his large frame taking up more room than Anna was used to. While he'd been away, she'd been sleeping in the starfish position. Now she was draped across him, her head resting on his chest, listening to the steady beating of his heart, feeling reassured by the deep rhythm.

There was so much to say, but she didn't want to break this moment of stillness, a few stolen seconds of peace in the whirlwind of the last few days.

"What are you thinking about?" she asked after several minutes had passed, her voice soft and thoughtful.

"I'll have to sell the houses in Lewisham."

Anna sighed.

"Both of them?"

"I'm going to need the money," he said stiffly.

Anna craned her neck to look up at him.

"Honey, there's no guarantee the case will get to court."

Nick grimaced.

"You know that Molly is a vindictive bitch—I just didn't realise what a nutter she is, too. She'll want the publicity alright."

"True, but the publisher won't want to fight a court case—they're too unpredictable. Right now, they're going along with this for the publicity. But I seriously doubt that they'll want to be taken to court. Once you counter sue, that will make them sit up and consider their assets. They'll settle for costs, which will only be a few thousand. Hell, they'll have made more than that in advance sales of their awful book," and she huffed with annoyance.

"Maybe," Nick said grimly, "but you heard Mark: worst case scenario, this could ruin me."

A cold seam of ice penetrated Anna's veins, and she sat upright in bed.

"We're in this together, Nick. Whatever happens, it happens to both of us. To *us*. You're not alone in this."

"Yeah, well, it's me she's suing," he growled, turning on his side. "Not you."

He flicked off the light switch and the room plunged into darkness.

Tears pricked Anna's eyes, but she refused to let them fall.

She curled her body around his, resting her hand on his hip. But he didn't move, didn't respond, and eventually, he fell asleep.

Anna laid awake, fear burrowing deep inside.

CHAPTER 20

NICK READ THE EMAIL FROM HIS OLD TEAMMATE again. It was almost too good to be true, and would certainly be the answer to his immediate problems: it would get him out of London, and also pay him enough money that he wouldn't have to sell either of the properties in Lewisham, at least not immediately. It bought him time.

Although it meant leaving Anna again.

Nick rubbed his forehead. But she'd understand—he knew that she'd been worried about the money for the court case, as well.

The relief he felt at the opportunity to earn some money was overwhelming.

He'd tell her the good news when she came home.

IN ANOTHER PART of London, Anna was reeling. Both meetings she'd had that day had knocked her sideways.

Brendan was bouncing up and down with excitement.

"Oh my God! This is huge! Immense! Vast! This is just what we've been waiting for, Annie! And if you want to do any features on gorgeous gay men in London ... well, naturally, you couldn't do better than me!" He flung his arms around her and squeezed tightly. "This is so exciting!" Then he leaned back and examined her face. "Wait, am I the only one excited here?"

"No, no, really," she said weakly. "I am excited."

Brendan wasn't convinced and raised his eyebrow questioningly.

"Uh-huh. You look like you just realized that you're wearing someone else's week-old knickers and the Vicar's Shih Tzu peed in your herbal tea. *What* is going on with you?"

Anna choked on a giggle and then started to laugh. And once she started, she couldn't stop. Soon she was howling and snorting, her eyes watering and her mascara running, and Brendan's eyebrows had shot up so high, they seemed as though they were trying to crawl off his forehead altogether.

"Oh my God, you're on drugs," he gasped, passing her a paper napkin so she could wipe her streaming eyes.

People were turning to stare at them in the Soho coffee shop.

Brendan turned around and snapped at the gawkers.

"Haven't you seen a woman wet herself laughing before?"

That set Anna off again, and even Brendan managed a reluctant grin.

"Do you mind telling me what we're laughing at?" he said, leaning forward and dropping his voice to a whisper that could be heard two tables away.

Anna wiped her eyes then blew her nose.

"Sorry, I'm sorry. It's just … wow, life, you know?"

Brendan narrowed his gaze at her.

"So you're not on drugs? Hmm, maybe you should be because you're acting schizo. And since when do you drink herbal tea, by the way?"

Anna sat up straight and attempted to smooth down her hair. Her laughing jag had left her feeling exhausted.

"I just thought I'd try something healthy," she said.

Brendan leaned back in his chair and pinned her with a determined stare.

"How long have we known each other?"

Anna was taken aback by the conversation's change of direction.

"Gosh, since I came to London."

"And would you say that we know each other well?"

Anna blinked, surprised by Brendan's sudden seriousness.

"Well, yes, I would."

Brendan folded his arms.

"So why are you lying to me?"

Anna winced.

"Bren…"

It was the hurt look on his face that unravelled her.

"Bren, I … I'm sorry. It's been a really weird couple of weeks."

His glare softened.

"I know. But you can talk to me, Annie. God, you *know* that. Why aren't we celebrating? You've been asked to be one of the anchors on the most-watched daytime show for women in Britain. *Loose Women*'s viewing figures are up 7% on last year. The audience spiked 13% when you were on the show before. Apart from anything else, it'll be a giant fuck-you to Mouldy McKinney. Wait, you're not going to turn this down, are you?"

"I'll have to think about it."

"No."

"Excuse me?"

"No, you don't have to think about it—you have to tell me what is going through your stubborn little noggin."

Anna sighed.

"Okay, but you can't tell anyone. Especially Nick."

Brendan's mouth dropped open.

"Are you having an affair?" he hissed.

"No! God, no! Why would you even … you know what, never mind. No, I'm not having an affair. I'm pregnant."

Brendan's mouth dropped open, then he stood up and screamed.

"I'M GOING TO BE AN AUNTIE!"

"Brendan!"

He swooped down and pulled her into his arms, hugging her tightly.

"My little Anna-banana has a bun in the oven! You're going to be a mommy! Oh my God! I'm so happy I could cry!"

And when he finally let Anna sink back into her seat, he really did have tears in his eyes.

Several people in the coffee shop clapped and offered their congratulations. Anna blushed, cringed and thanked them politely.

Finally, after taking a bow, Brendan returned to his chair, wiping a hand dramatically across his forehead.

"A little notice next time you want to drop a bombshell on me, please."

Anna smiled sarcastically.

"Next time I find out I'm pregnant and get offered a major TV show in the same day, I'll text you."

"Fun-ee. Now, what does the Mr. Ruggedly-Handsome-Rugby-Romeo say about all of this?"

Anna stared down at her cold herbal tea.

"I haven't told him yet."

Brendan nodded.

"Well, we've only just found out about *Loose Women*, but surely he knows you're … oh my God, he doesn't know *anything?*"

"I went to see my GP this morning," Anna sighed. "I'd been feeling tired and kind of nauseous in the mornings. And I'm off coffee, as you see … I suspected, well, hoped mostly, so I did a home test. I went to the doctor's today for a blood test, and yep, it's been confirmed."

Brendan cocked his head on one side.

"Question: why aren't you turning cartwheels when you've wanted to be preggers for ages; and why haven't you told Nick?"

"That's two questions," Anna muttered.

"I'm wait-ing!" Brendan sang impatiently.

"I *am* excited," she said quietly. "I was beginning to think that there was something wrong with me. But I guess in Miami…"

"I knew it!" Brendan said smugly. "I could sense those pheromones wafting in the air. I'm never wrong about these things. Well, I'm never wrong about anything."

Anna smiled sadly at her best friend.

"Yes, you were right. Again. And the reason I haven't told Nick is … well, he's been really preoccupied with the Molly situation and he's worried about money." She looked down. "I'm afraid … I'm afraid that he'll just see a baby as … as a burden."

Brendan shuffled his chair closer to hers and slung his arm around her shoulders.

"Annie, darling," he said gently, "you're talking so much horseshit, we have roses growing under the table."

"Bren!"

"I mean it," he said, his voice gentle but firm. "You love Nick. Nick loves you. You've both wanted a baby for a long time now. This is a *good* thing. It's wonderful. Interesting timing, but still wonderful."

Anna nodded slowly.

"Yes, it is. I already feel so much *love* for this baby. But I'm scared, too."

"Welcome to the world, Annie. I'm not saying it will be easy, but it will be amazing. Tell him."

Anna nodded again and gave Brendan a watery smile.

"I will. Thanks, Bren."

"Anytime, baby-mama."

"Don't call me that."

"I can't promise."

"Bren!"

"Boo! You're no fun."

"Yes, I am!"

"Not."

"Am."

"Not."

"Shut up, Bren."

"Shutting up."

"I love you."

"You too, baby-mama."

"Aaaaaaaaaagh!"

ANNA WAS SURPRISED and pleased to find that Nick was home when she arrived back after her two appointments. She was bubbling with excitement and couldn't wait to tell him her news. Their news.

Brendan's enthusiasm and sheer joy had been the confidence boost she'd needed.

Whatever their problems, she and Nick would work them out together.

"Hey, handsome!" she called out.

"I'm in the living room."

Nick was sprawled out on the sofa, one leg hanging off the end, his t-shirt riding up his body to show his lean stomach and ripped abs. Anna's mouth watered as her hormones went into overdrive.

She leaned down, kissing him softly on the lips, an invitation.

But he didn't take it.

He kissed her back quickly, smiled, and sat up.

Disappointed, Anna plopped down beside him, preparing herself to tell him her news—to the power of two.

But Nick had news, as well, and he jumped in first.

"I've had an email from Bernard," he began immediately, excitement rippling around the edges of his voice. "You know, he played Scrum-Half for the Phoenixes."

"Bernard Dubois? Yes, of course. How is he? Is he still playing?"

"Yep, same position."

"That's great! Nice that he got in touch." Anna paused when Nick didn't answer right away, confused by the expression on his face. "It is nice, isn't it?"

"Yeah, sure."

"Where's he playing now?"

"Carcassonne Cuirassiers, a team in the south of France. They're in Pro D2 which is a second division, but he says they've got potential. He's their Captain, also assistant coach."

Anna smiled, still a little thrown.

"Lucky him! I loved the south of France when we were there with Massimo. Is Bernard near Cannes?"

"Eh, I don't think so. He said he was only fifty miles from the border with Spain."

"Sounds great."

There was a longer pause, and Anna's eyes began to close as tiredness suddenly swept over her. She smiled to herself sleepily. *Nick was going to be blown away when she told him...*

"Nick, I have someth—"

"He's offered me a job."

Anna's head jolted up so fast she saw stars.

"Excuse me?"

"Bernard, he's offered me a job."

"But ... what sort of job?"

Nick's lips moved as if he was chewing on the answer.

"Full-back."

Anna blinked, not certain that she'd heard right.

"Rugby? He wants you to go back to playing rugby professionally?"

Nick lifted a shoulder, his answer coming slowly as if he was considering every word.

"They're in danger of dropping down a league. He says I could really help them. I'd have to go soon though, because the season has already started."

Anna fought to keep her expression neutral when inside she felt a tornado of emotions whirling around.

"And what did you say?"

Nick glanced away before meeting her eyes.

"I said I'd think about it."

The ground shifted under Anna's feet. All her hopes crashed, swept against the rocks of Nick's palpable excitement. She swallowed, unable to speak, nodded then stood up and walked into the kitchen.

He followed her immediately.

"Are you upset, luv? Because if you are..."

Anna hid her face from him as she made herself busy filling the coffee machine, then remembered that she didn't drink coffee anymore.

"No, no, I'm not upset," she lied. "Just surprised, is all."

Nick frowned and shoved his hands in his pockets.

"One more year. That's all I wanted before I got injured. Just one more bloody year!"

Anna swung around to face him.

"But you're retired! Isn't that what this whole past year has been about? Finding something other than rugby? Make a clean break—that's what you said! And after your last injury…"

"I know I can't play at the top level anymore—fitness would definitely be an issue—but this team is struggling. I know I could help them." He hesitated. "And what they'll pay me will help with legal fees. I wouldn't have to sell the Lewisham properties right away. It would give me a breathing space…"

Anna shook her head, confusion and disappointment making it hard to think. She looked away.

"It sounds like you've already made up your mind."

There was a very long pause. The silence physically hurt.

"No," said Nick slowly. "I haven't made up my mind—I'm still thinking about it. But … look at me, Anna…"

She struggled to meet his eyes. Those beautiful honey-coloured eyes; those eyes that she loved to lose herself in.

"The modelling thing has been interesting, but even that's not something I can do forever. I enjoy the photography side more, but rugby is … it's been my life for so long. I thought I was ready to give it up, but it's hard. One more year, just one."

Inside, Anna was dying a little more with each sentence, with each hurtful word that dropped from lips she'd kissed ten thousand times.

"But … your shoulder? Just because it's not a top class team doesn't mean to say that the rugby will be any easier. You know that."

Nick held her arms and rubbed them lightly.

"I need this, Anna."

She shrugged out of his grip.

"Then you'd better go."

"Anna…"

"No, seriously, Nick, if that's what you want, then go. I'd *never* stop you from doing something that you want to do."

Her voice was a dull monotone.

"You don't sound very happy about it."

Anna shook her head.

"Because I worry that you'll be injured again. And … you've only just gotten back from New York, and it's been so crazy … I was hoping we could have some time for us," she finished abruptly.

Nick tugged his hair back with both hands.

"You know I can't sit around on my arse all day doing nothing, just waiting for Molly to drag me through the courts again. I have to do something!"

"I know that!" she cried out, then more softly. "I understand, I do. But going back to playing rugby … okay, say you do that for a year, or maybe two or maybe three. Then what? You'll be right back here, at this point in time, wondering what's next. Don't you want to make those choices now? Don't you want to see what else is out there?" *Don't you want me?*

Nick's expression answered her questions, and Anna took a deep breath.

"Oh. I see. Your mind is made up. Fine. Fine. Go then."

"Come on, luv…"

"No, it's fine. You go. I'll stay here. Again."

"It's just a year, not even a year—ten months…"

"Sure, Nick."

"Fuckin' hell! I can't do this!" His anger and frustration exploded into a barrage of words. "Why can't you be pleased for me? I thought you would be! Jesus, we've had so much shit thrown at us I thought we deserved some good news! But you…"

He seized his anger and frustration, his bewilderment and disappointment, and bolted from the room.

He didn't ask where she'd been and she didn't tell him her news.

The words had turned to ash in her mouth.

Anna sat alone at the kitchen table for a long time. The clock ticked loudly in the silence as her world fell apart. She'd been so sure, *this time he'll stay*, but he was leaving again.

The words she'd been longing to tell him had died in her throat when she'd seen the excitement in his eyes. He *wanted* to go, he was *happy* to leave. *Again.* Just days ago she'd admitted how much she'd missed him in New York, how she'd been close to begging him to come home, and now it was if she'd never said a single word.

Anger and resentment joined the misery in her heart.

Why can't I be enough for you?

CHAPTER 21

"Y OU DIDN'T TELL HIM."

Brendan's voice was accusing.

Anna shrugged helplessly.

"How could I? You should have seen his face when he talked about the offer Bernard had made. He couldn't pack his bags fast enough."

"You have to tell him!"

Anna slammed her cup onto the table and herbal tea slopped over her hand.

"No," she said with steel in her voice. "No, I don't have to tell him. *When* he chooses to come home ... *if* he chooses to come home, then I'll tell him. Right now, I'm so angry with him, I—"

"Then *tell* him that! Don't let him leave with waves and smiles if that's not what you're feeling!"

Anna gave a cold laugh.

"And make him stay because he feels guilty? No. He has to choose to stay. I won't force that decision on him."

"When's he going?" Brendan asked gently.

Anna gave a hollow laugh.

"The beginning of next week."

Her anger seeped away and despair took its place.

"Oh God, Bren! I thought that after New York, things would be different, but they're not. He's still searching for something and it's not me." Her hands folded protectively around her flat belly. "It's not us."

A small whimper escaped her and Brendan raced around the table and pulled her into his arms.

"I know he needs to work, I know he needs goals, but I can't believe he's leaving me again," she cried.

"Damn it, Anna! *Tell him!*"

"No!" she yelled, her anger matching her resentment. "I won't!" She forced herself to calm her breathing, if not for her sake, then for the new life stirring inside her. "He has to choose. I won't make him do anything. He can go chasing as many castles in the sky as he likes—I will *not* be his ball and chain. I won't!"

Brendan glared at her in disbelief and irritation.

"Stop looking at me like that!" she snapped. "I'm tired of being the passive one in this relationship, sitting back while Nick 'finds himself'," and she used air quotes, her voice quivering with scorn. "I've done everything I'm supposed to: I've sat back and supported him, given him space, encouraged him in his choices, and it's never enough … because he doesn't want to be here. With me."

Brendan hugged her tightly, his own voice cracking with emotion.

"You're wrong, Anna. He *does* want to be with you. You can work from anywhere, pretty much. The filming for *Loose Women* is just two days a week. You can do your slot then spend the rest of the week in France. They've invented these incredible things called aeroplanes—so go with him. Don't let your stupid pride get in the way."

Her eyes narrowed with sudden fury and she pushed his arms away, standing up and striding over to the kettle before turning and facing him.

"Pride? *My* pride? Well, you know what, Brendan? Yes, I do have some pride left. Not much, but some. Enough to say that I won't go chasing after someone who doesn't want me."

Brendan tugged his hair in baffled annoyance.

"Of course he bloody well wants you! I've never seen a guy so in love with someone. I just wish someone would look at me one day with even *half* of what Nick feels for you!"

Anna sat down heavily, slumping onto the kitchen chair, feeling as if her body weighed a thousand pounds.

"I used to think that, but not anymore." She laid her head in her hands as the tears began. "Damn you, Nick Renshaw," she whispered. "Damn you."

NICK TOOK OUT his frustration on the treadmill, pounding the miles until sweat soaked his body and his muscles protested. What was supposed to be a good day, him telling Anna his exciting news, had descended into … he didn't even know how to describe it. But it had ended with him storming out and spending the night in the spare bedroom. The long silence of a lonely night had been spent tossing and turning, knowing that Anna was close by but out of reach.

Today hadn't been any better. He'd woken up alone, a headache threatening to split his skull, and the oppressive silence had just grown heavier.

He was so used to Anna understanding him, he didn't get why she stared at him like a stranger as he struggled to make one of the biggest decisions of his life.

He thought she'd be happy that he had a chance to play again. Yes, he understood that she was worried about further injuries, but this was more than that. He replayed the whole conversation in his mind, but it still didn't make sense.

He'd heard Brendan arrive before lunchtime, so hoped he could talk Anna around.

Damn it! Did she really think he was the kind of man who could sit and watch her work herself half to death while he fannyed around doing nothing? He'd earned his own money since he was sixteen years old. He would *not* be dependent on someone else.

And now was the worst possible time to be unemployed. Bloody Molly fucking things up again—would he *never* be free of that bitch?

Nick heard the front door slam and knew that Brendan had left for the day. He took a deep breath and jogged up the basement stairs.

But Anna wasn't in the kitchen.

Nick was surprised to find her with her feet up on the sofa and her eyes closed. He saw the dark rings under her eyes and wondered if she'd spent half the night tossing and turning, too.

"Anna," he said quietly.

She jerked, her eyes springing open, and he felt guilty for waking her when she looked so tired.

"Oh," she said, yawning. "I was just taking a nap."

He sat down next to her, placing her ankles on his lap and massaging her feet.

For a moment she relaxed, melting against him, but then remembered they were still arguing and she sat up suddenly.

"This isn't working," she said flatly.

Nick was confused.

"What isn't working?"

Anna shot him a scathing look.

"This. Us. *We're* not working."

Dread plunged splinters of pain through his heart.

"Anna, no. We're fine … we're just…"

"No, Nick," she said, her voice frosting. "We're not fine. How can we be fine when you've been away for over three months, home for a couple of weeks, and now planning to move to France for the next eight months. No, we are not fine."

Nick sucked in a shocked breath.

"Anna, you know why I…"

"Yes," she snapped. "You've explained it all very succinctly." And she turned her cold eyes to him. "Did you tell Bernard yes?"

Nick met her hard stare.

"Yeah. I had to."

Anna nodded curtly.

"Then I think you should go."

He looked at her cautiously.

"You do?"

"Yes. In fact, I think you should go right now. Why wait? You clearly don't want to be here."

Nick struggled to keep up. It wasn't easy, because he couldn't believe what he was hearing—and his despair, his utter frustration with what she was saying ignited his temper, which was then fuelled by fear.

"Jesus, Anna! Why do you think I do this? Why do you think I put myself through this, force my body to go on? It's not because I'm chasing some ghost of glory, which is what you seem to think. I do this, I put my body through this every day *for us! I do it for us!*"

Her eyes were hard as glass as she stared back.

"I don't believe you," she said, folding her arms across her chest. That was all she said.

Nick's heart pulsed painfully.

"You think I'd *lie* about this?"

She stared at him disdainfully, her own pain locked and hidden away.

"I think you've been lying to yourself ever since your testimonial at Twickenham. I don't think you know what you want, but it definitely isn't a wife … or a family."

Nick gripped the sides of his head as if the words she was saying physically hurt him to hear.

"I want that more than anything. Anna, please!"

She turned away, staring out of the window.

"It doesn't feel like it. I haven't felt like part of this relationship for a long time." Her shoulders stiffened. "I've done everything to support you and I've waited for you to come home." She turned around and stared at him, her gaze hardening again. "But you only came back when you absolutely had to. You never came back for us, for me."

Nick shook his head helplessly.

"That's not true. I've done everything for us! I know I've been different since my testimonial—I fucking know that! I had no idea that everything would be so hard. I've been trying and trying— trying to be the kind of man who deserves you! Someone with drive! Someone with purpose—not a has-been. Can't you see that?"

For a moment, he caught a tiny movement in her lips, but the softness disappeared and her mouth flattened.

"No, that's not what I see."

He tried to reach for her, to hold her, to convince her with his touch, but she stood up and stepped away from him.

"I'd prefer it if you slept in the spare room again tonight."

Then she swept out of the room, and Nick had nothing.

He felt frozen, the panic and fear turning to a creeping cold that numbed him. How could he have got this so wrong? Had he misread everything? The look in her eyes when she told him that she didn't believe him, it had been the most intense mental pain he'd ever experienced.

He stared down at his hands, surprised to find that they were shaking.

They'd never argued like this. Not even when things were at their worst five years ago—she'd never looked at him with such remoteness in her eyes.

He'd seen the barriers going up, and it drove him crazy to realize that he'd made her do it; each brick made from another thoughtless, stupid thing that he'd said or done. He'd glimpsed the pain in her eyes before they'd cooled and hardened, and it damn near broke him: he'd done everything for her, but all she'd seen was his selfishness, him leaving her again and again. And he didn't know how to explain anymore that it was *because* of her he pushed himself so hard.

Anger began to burn inside him. He knew he wasn't good with words, but she had to listen to him, she had to hear him.

And Nick was not a man who gave up when he really wanted something.

He ran up the stairs and opened their bedroom door, letting it slam against the wall.

She lay on their bed with her back toward him, her spine stiff.

"Come with me," he said.

CHAPTER 22

Anna's brain tripped over itself trying to understand what Nick was saying to her.

He walked around the bed and picked up her unresponsive hands, holding them in his.

"Come with me. You're right. We've done the apart thing long enough. You're always saying you can work anywhere, so come with me! It'll be an adventure. Brendan can fly out once a week or whatever. We'll rent a house. Please, Anna," he said, his voice breaking. "Please. Come with me."

She pulled her hands from his and sat up slowly.

Nick's heart lurched when he saw that she was crying.

"Why?" she said, her voice raw. "What's the point?"

"Anna … I fucking love you. That's the point. That's why I want you to come with me." He rubbed his forehead. "I know … I think I know … I think I understand, but don't you see that I've been doing all of this for you, for us? How can I be a husband, a father one day, when I don't know what the fuck I'm doing? God, you work so hard, and I'm at home sitting on my arse. I'm trying, Anna! Believe me, I'm trying. Maybe I'm saying it all wrong, maybe I'm doing it all wrong. Fuck, I don't know what I'm doing, but without you, it doesn't mean anything. You, you're everything. And maybe I don't say it enough, but I want to deserve you and I know I don't. Everything I do, Anna, every breath I breathe, it's for you."

Anna swallowed, her heavy eyes meeting his.

She saw the pain and confusion. She saw the frustration and desperation. And she saw the truth: he loved her.

Was it really that simple?

He loves me.

"I've been such an idiot," she said to herself, her voice fading.

Nick frowned, uncertain of her meaning.

She scowled at him, her dark eyes flashing with fire.

"You maybe couldn have said all that a couple of months ago, or maybe six, or maybe twelve? You wait till *now* to tell me all this?"

Nick's expression faltered.

"I thought you knew," he said softly.

Anna sighed, a sound of exasperation.

"Nick," she said gently, cupping his cheek. "I'm not a mind-reader. I only know if you *tell me*."

He blinked and gave a tentative smile, closing his eyes and leaning into her hand.

"I'm not very bright, Anna. Too many knocks on the head."

She wrapped her arms around him and pulled him against her so his head was resting over her heart.

"It's true," she said, a smile in her voice. "For a smart guy you can be awful dumb. And I think it's catching, because I've definitely been suffering from the same brand of dumbness lately."

"Are we okay?" he asked softly.

"No," she sighed, "but I think we will be."

He sat up, drawing her with him, so they were both propped against the headboard.

"Will you come with me? To France?"

Anna rolled the idea around in her head. Brendan had suggested it, but she'd been so pig-headed, so certain that Nick didn't want her. So certain, and so wrong.

Nick's hopeful expression fell at her continuing silence.

"Actually," she said slowly, "I have something to tell you, as well. I was going to tell you yesterday when I came home but…"

She shrugged.

Nick swallowed, steeling himself for bad news.

"Two pieces of news," she said tentatively.

Nick wished she'd hurry up. He was having palpitations waiting for the axe to fall.

"I had a meeting with Isabel Buxton yesterday, the senior producer on *Loose Women*. And she offered me a job."

Nick had expected something else and now he was even more off balance.

"Doing what? Research?"

"Not exactly. She wants me to be one of the presenters, one of the anchors."

Nick felt as though his heart had stopped beating. *This was it. She was leaving him for something better.*

"Congratulations," he said, his voice hoarse. "You deserve it."

"Thank you," she said carefully, aware that his endorsement was hardly heart-felt. "I haven't said yes yet."

Nick looked down at his hands, those hands that were bent and gnarled from more breaks and sprains than he could count.

"But you will," he said, his voice empty.

Anna didn't reply immediately.

"It's two days of filming each week in West London. Two consecutive days. For the other five days a week I can be … anywhere I like."

A kernel of hope sprouted in Nick's barren heart.

"Where do you want to be?" he murmured, holding his breath.

"With you," she said simply. "If you want me."

Relief rushed through him like cool water on a blistering day, but Anna held up her hand as he started to reach for her.

"I have two pieces of news, remember? And the second one pretty much trumps everything else."

He looked up at her expectantly, his whiskey-coloured eyes wide and trusting.

Anna took her courage in her hands and met his gaze.

"I'm pregnant."

Nick stared. Doubted. And finally, finally, the meaning sank in.

A thousand words roared in his head, all were hopelessly inadequate, none of them could express how he felt.

He took her face gently between his broken, battered hands and kissed her softly, sweetly: her mouth, her cheeks, her forehead, the tip of her nose, making her giggle. And then he leaned down and gently kissed her belly.

Happy tears filled Anna's eyes and she stroked his unruly hair.

"Are you okay with this?" she whispered.

His head moved against her stomach in a tiny nod, but he didn't speak.

"Truly?"

When he looked up at her, tears glistened in his eyes.

"We made a baby?"

"Yes, we did."

Nick closed his eyes, and Anna watched the most glorious smile spread across his beautiful face.

"We made a baby," he sighed, resting his head on her belly again. "Hey, junior, it's your dad here. It's nice to meet you. Well, I won't meet you for a while…"

He frowned, glancing up at Anna.

"When's he due?"

" 'He' might be a 'she'."

"Okay. When's she due?"

"April 26th."

He leaned down again, still speaking to her belly.

"Okay, so we won't actually meet until April, but that's cool. I'm not sure if you're Little Nick or Little Anna, but don't worry about it. I'll just call you Mini Me."

Anna laughed as Nick grinned up at her.

"Hmm, okay," she smiled. "We might need to discuss that."

But Nick had a distant, dreamy look on his face, his happiness so obvious that Anna couldn't help the burst of joy that she felt through every part of her body.

"Kiss me, Nick," she whispered.

He sat up slowly.

"Is it okay to … you know?"

Anna laughed gently.

"It's very okay. In fact it's required."

Nick grinned back.

"Well, in that case…" and his warm, soft lips came down on hers, his beard brushing against her skin.

She reached up, tugging on his shoulders so he was hovering above her.

"And Nick?"

"Yes, luv?"

"I love you, too. I never stopped loving you. Never."

His expression became serious.

"Without you, I…"

His throat clogged and he couldn't go on.

Anna tugged gently on a lock of his hair.

"Nick, don't you get it? We're stronger together."

He nodded, still unable to speak.

Anna smiled, pressing a kiss to his lips.

"And yes, I'll come to France."

CHAPTER 23

Anna's announcement that she'd be following Nick to France sent Brendan into a frenzy.

"Oh my God, Annie! I have only *one month* to get all my outfits for *La Belle France!* How could you do this to me?"

She stared at him in amusement.

"Um, excuse me! Were you or were you not the person who told me, just two days ago, that I should go with him?"

Brendan waved her excuse away.

"That's not the point!"

"It kind of is."

He rounded on her with a fierce look.

"Nick, he of the butt cheeks that you want to bounce quarters off, is going to play rugby with a team of studly men, *French men*, who are God's gift to other men, and I have *nothing* to wear. Now, this may seem like a tiny dilemma to you, baby-mama…"

"I told you not to call me that!"

"…but to me, this is a life-defining moment!"

And he swept his laptop into his shoulder bag then announced that he was taking the rest of the week off to shop.

"But we have work to do!" Anna protested feebly.

"So do I!" he called over his shoulder. "And looking gorgeous is my top priority!"

Anna sighed as she heard the front door slam.

She loved Brendan, but sometimes he was just so … so … so Brendan.

Nick was leaving in two days. He'd been hitting the home gym hard and trying to build up some of the bulk that he'd lost while he'd been modelling.

Anna had been busy, too.

The French season had already started so Nick needed to leave immediately. For the first month, he'd be living in a house that the club rented near the training ground, together with three other teammates. In the meantime, Anna was looking at websites with rental properties in and around Carcassonne with a spare bedroom for Brendan and space for her to have a home office.

The club's relocation team were really helpful and had sent her details of a couple of houses that could work. They'd also promised to get her signed up with a local doctor as well as an obstetrician at the newly built hospital, *Carcassonne Centre Hospitalier*, which apparently had an excellent maternity wing.

They'd also agreed to pay for two flights a month for her and Brendan to travel to France, and Nick would be allowed to fly back to London on weekends when he didn't have a game. Privately, Anna thought that having the occasional weekend to explore the south of France would be fun.

They were definitely a considerate club to work for, considerate of family life; either that or they were so desperate to secure Nick that they'd have offered pretty much anything he asked for. But as far as Anna was concerned, that just meant they had good taste.

She was still worried about Nick getting injured again, and more than a little anxious about the possibility of having her baby in a country where she didn't speak the language, and far preferred the plan where she'd be back in London. She also knew that babies came when they were ready, and it would be sensible to be monitored in both countries.

Because their English was quite limited, so communication wasn't always easy, the people at the club were offering to arrange free French lessons for her and Nick.

Thank goodness for Brendan who was fluent in more than flirting.

When Anna told her mother the news—both parts—there was stunned silence followed by a happy squeal.

"Imgoingtobeagrandmotheratlast!"

Or words to that effect since Anna wasn't entirely sure what she'd said because she'd had to yank the phone away from her ear.

Then her mom promised to fly over as often as she could, including for the last month of Anna's pregnancy.

So Anna changed the search parameters on the house in France again: now she was going to need four bedrooms.

Nick's parents were equally pleased, and his mother insisted on speaking to Anna, and then promptly bursting into tears, crying and thanking Anna for making her son so happy.

Trish was bouncing, too, promising lots of shopping trips for baby clothes and maternity clothes, and planning to come to Carcassonne to "meet some French hunks".

"Not if Brendan gets there first," Anna mumbled to herself.

The only thing that stopped Anna's happiness from being complete was the ongoing threat of a court case.

So far, Molly's publishers hadn't backed down, but Mark assured her that it was just a matter of time.

Anna desperately hoped that he was right.

"My dear, they're after publicity more than money. Although the free publicity certainly has a monetary value. But they won't want to deal with a court case—especially being counter-sued, because they have a chance of losing that. They'll withdraw the writ at the most opportune time for them."

"But the book's coming out next week!" Anna groaned.

"Exactly. There'll be an initial burst of interest, then when sales start to flag, they'll have a second bite of the publicity cherry by magnanimously settling the claim out of court. Mark my words!"

And he laughed at his own joke.

Anna was dreading publication of the book. Nick refused to discuss it. He said that he'd wasted enough time on "that woman" and wasn't going to give "her bloody awful book" a single thought.

If only it was that easy.

NICK LEFT FOR France, excited about playing rugby again, and at the same time torturing himself by having to leave Anna behind "in her condition".

She reminded him that she was pregnant not ill, but he still gave her a long list of instructions on what to eat, how often to rest, what sort of exercise was regarded as safe during the first trimester, with a level of detail that surprised Anna, then started to annoy her.

In the days before he left, he watched her like a hawk, cooking only the healthiest meals and confiscating *all* her candy, cookies and cakes that she kept for emergencies.

"They're not healthy," he said severely, tossing the cake and cookies out for the birds, and throwing the candy in the trash. "Too much processed sugar isn't good for you."

Anna smiled sweetly and thanked him for being so caring, then slunk off to her office where she had a box of *Milk Tray* hidden in her desk under lock and key: emergency rations.

When she told Brendan two days later, he sighed and fanned himself.

"A hot daddy—it's the stuff dreams are made of. I'd call him 'daddy' any day of the week."

Anna shrugged and ate another chocolate. By now, there weren't many left, but at least this time no one would criticize her muffin top.

"Anna! What are you doing?" Brendan bellowed, grabbing the box of chocolates and holding them against his chest, a horrified look on his face.

"Bren! Give me my candy! NOW!"

"Sorry, muffin top, no can do. I have strict instructions from your baby-daddy. I have to make sure that you don't self-medicate on chocolate the way you did last time he went away. You may be eating for two, but in Nick's absence, I'm in charge of your dietary, um, issues."

Anna glared at him, her nostrils flaring.

"Give Me My Candy NOW."

"Um, Annie, you're scaring me a little," Brendan whined, rolling his desk chair away from her outstretched grabby hands as far as he could. "I can't! I promised Nick!"

Anna growled at him.

Brendan jumped to his feet and ran into the back yard, the box of *Milk Tray* still in his hands.

"Don't make me do it!" he screeched, holding the box above his head, threatening to shake the chocolates onto the small garden.

When Anna launched herself at him, he yelped, flung a chocolate at her face, dropped the box and ran.

Anna smiled to herself as she strolled back inside, her precious cargo clutched tightly in her hands. *No one* was keeping her from her candy.

CHAPTER 24

B ERNARD WAS AT THE AIRPORT to meet Nick.
"It is good to see you, *mon ami*," he said, shaking hands then embracing Nick and kissing him on both cheeks. "You look fit, a little skinny, maybe. But we will feed you up. You are too busy being a super model to eat well, perhaps?"

Nick laughed and punched Bernard lightly on the arm. Starving himself before a shoot had been his least favourite part of the whole modelling scene.

"It's good to see you, too, you bugger!"

"And how is the very beautiful and serene Anna? I hear that congratulations are in order. Let us hope that the child looks like her, or if the poor creature has to look like you, I pray he has his mother's brains."

Nick grinned.

"You sound jealous, mate."

"Not at all. I am very happily single."

Nick frowned.

"I thought you were back with Madeleine?"

Bernard and his wife seemed to have an on-and-off relationship, and she lived in Paris with their four year-old son.

"*Mais oui*, I am very happily single and married to Madeleine."

Nick shook his head. Some things just didn't translate.

On the drive from the airport, they discussed the club and all the players: who showed potential, who needed training, who lacked confidence, and who needed to be tried in a different position on the team.

"We have a very young team and a very old team," Bernard explained. "The old ones have experience, like us, *n'est-ce pas*? But the young ones need support, they need to be led. I think, Nick, that you should captain the team."

Nick raised his eyebrows.

"But you're Captain?"

"I'm trying to be assistant coach and the captain and a team player. It's not working so well for us. I want to move into coaching, so this will make sense."

"You don't want me to settle in first, see how they all play?"

Bernard shrugged, a gesture that could mean yes or no.

"They play tonight against Biarritz Olympique—you will learn all you need."

Nick narrowed his eyes at Bernard.

"So, basically, you're throwing me in at the deep-end and any changes will make me look like the bad guy. Thanks, buddy!"

Bernard laughed as Nick shook his head, conceding that he'd been set up.

"Any particular problems that I should know about?"

Bernard sucked his teeth.

"The team has problems, yes, but I think you will see for yourself very soon."

"A heads up would be nice," Nick said wryly.

Bernard smiled.

"You are a strategist, my friend. This will work well."

Nick hoped that Bernard was right. There was so much riding on it.

It took just over an hour to drive from the airport to the ancient town of Carcassonne.

Nick's first view of his new home was the famous fortress, a medieval citadel that sat atop a rocky outcrop, surrounded by lush green fields.

The town below *La Cité* was filled with limewashed houses with red terracotta roof tiles, so pretty that it looked like a film set.

"Yes, we are very lucky," Bernard nodded, seeing the expression on Nick's face. "The stadium is very historic, too. It is one of the oldest in France, built in 1899, and is near the castle. You will see tonight. But first, I'll take you to the team house."

Here we go again. New teammates.

Nick was hoping that this would go well. It was strange the way the nerves of being the new guy never went away.

Bernard followed the river along the valley, then pulled up outside a large whitewashed villa, surrounded by a crumbling stone wall with olive trees shading a Mediterranean garden, and with a number of older Renaults parked outside.

Bernard shrugged, indicating the villa.

"It's quite new, only 100 years old. It's been renovated, so you have Wifi. I know you will be eager to speak with *la belle* Anna."

Nick climbed out of the car, stretching his back and neck, hearing the creaks and cracks as his joints realigned.

Bernard smiled at him sympathetically.

"We are no longer young, *mon ami.*"

Whilst Nick agreed, he didn't necessarily need to hear that on his first day in France. And this was the second time Bernard had alluded to his age.

"How much longer do you think you'll go on playing?" Nick asked.

Bernard gave a Gallic shrug and shoved his hands in his pockets.

"How long can I continue? I don't know. This is my last season, perhaps one more. We will see."

Which was probably the only answer he could give. Then he gave Nick a long stare.

"This is why I need to be successful as assistant coach."

Bernard clapped his hands to dispel the serious conversation.

"Come, I will show you to your room."

The front door wasn't locked and Bernard led him into a cool spacious hallway with a narrow staircase at the end. He helped Nick carry his bags and guitar case up to a plain white bedroom that contained a large wooden bed, with pale blue curtains framing a small window with cream shutters. An ancient wardrobe in dark wood stood in one corner, a small set of drawers next to it, and a comfortable looking leather chair that belonged in a previous century's gentlemen's club. Best of all, there was a tiny *en suite* bathroom, newly tiled.

Nick peered out of the window and saw three large men, clearly rugby players, lounging in the weed-filled garden next to a new-looking swimming pool.

Two of them ganged up on the largest, who seemed to be fast asleep, and tipped him into the pool, sunbed and all.

He splashed around shouting and swearing in a mixture of French and English while the two men standing at the side laughed loudly.

Bernard watched with a patient, amused look on his face.

"They are like children, no? Come, you will meet your new teammates."

Nick followed Bernard back down the stairs and out to the poolside, where the big guy was climbing out of the pool and dripping onto the hot concrete.

"Ça va? Say hello to Nick—he'll be joining us as our new Fullback."

"G'day, Nick," said the blond guy with a thick Australian accent. "I'm Russ. I thought you'd retired, mate. Have you decided to go around again?"

Nick just smiled.

"You know what it's like."

They all understood what he meant, and seemed friendly as they shook hands.

Nick settled back against the heavy oak headboard and picked up his phone. He'd been longing to call Anna since he'd arrived, but knew that she'd been recording today. When they finally managed to connect, he had only twenty minutes before he had to head out to the stadium.

His teammates had left a couple of hours earlier, and Bernard had arranged for a taxi to collect Nick later.

"Nick! I've been thinking about you all day!"

He sank back against the soft pillows, his eyes closing with pleasure.

"How are you feeling? You're not too tired, are you? Are you eating properly?"

He heard her soft laugh and felt a corresponding smile tug at his lips.

"I'm fine! Stop worrying! And the filming went well. I wasn't as nervous as I thought I'd be. It was fun. And oh my God, they all fell in love with Brendan!"

Nick grinned.

"That doesn't surprise me. He's a smooth git."

"So, how was your day? Have you met your new teammates yet?"

"Some of them, yeah, the lads in the house. I'm going to the stadium tonight, so I'll meet the rest after. Bernard wants me to see them play first." He cleared his throat. "He wants me to be Captain."

"Oh wow! Really? So soon? I guess I'm not that surprised because, well, you're you."

Nick chuckled quietly.

"Well, it was a surprise to me, but Bernard wants me to make the changes the team need. I'm okay with that. I'm not here to be popular."

"They'll love you, babe," she said softly. "Of course they will."

"Doesn't matter if they do or they don't—but I do need their respect."

Anna laughed gently.

"Nick, you've led England to winning two World Cups! *Of course* they'll respect you!"

Nick wasn't so sure. The rivalry between England and France was always sharp and sometimes bitter.

"So, tell me about the guys you'll be living with. Any hotties for Brendan?"

Nick groaned.

"Don't ask me that! Russell is Australian and Inoke is from Fiji, so at least there's two people on the team who speak English. That'll make it easier. And there's Grégoire who's just moved down from near Paris for this season, so he's living in the house with us, too. I haven't heard him speak English yet, except to say 'hello'. They seem like a good bunch. I guess I'll let you know."

They talked for a little longer and then Nick had to rush to get his taxi.

"I love you," Anna whispered.

"Love you more."

As Nick stepped out of the taxi, he stared up at the entrance to the stadium. The fans were scattered in small groups and the place was less than a quarter full.

A team official escorted him to the locker room, and the hairs on the back of his neck stood up. He closed his eyes as memories flooded back: so many games, so many training sessions. God, he'd missed this.

He was introduced to the rest of the team who were warming up for the game. Bernard spoke in English, but the coach's speech was in French. Nick instantly regretted not paying attention during his French lessons at school.

As the team ran out to the field, Nick took his place lineside by the coach. He was excited to see his new team play. He'd been told to expect differences, but as the game progressed he saw massive problems: the ref wasn't on the ball; the players were slower and less skilled but big and dirty. He saw blatant illegal and borderline dangerous tackles that the ref wasn't picking up. The rest of the game was all over the place with loose balls and illegal forward passes. It was messy and undisciplined

Nick had his work cut out.

As Grégoire, his new teammate, drove through the wide arch of the stadium's entrance the next morning, Nick felt the familiar rush of adrenaline, the excitement of walking into his world and being part of it again.

The stadium had been modernised several times, but still reflected the hundred plus years of history, the many, many games that had been played here—the victories, the losses, the defeats and disappointments. And, most likely, career-ending injuries.

He banished that thought. Today would be a good day.

As they arrived at their training session, they were all quiet, no doubt thinking about the shambles of the game the night before and the team's humiliating defeat in front of a home crowd. Only Inoke seemed happy to chat to Nick. The Fijian had a sunny personality that seemed to go with his surprisingly high-pitched voice, even if it didn't fit his massive frame.

"You played with Fetuao Tui, hey, Nick?"

"Yep, good bloke. Very fast for a big bugger."

Inoke giggled.

"No hurry, no worry. But the man runs like a goat is nibbling his nuts!"

Nick laughed, but then he couldn't get the image out of his head.

He liked Inoke—he lifted people's spirits. Nick had seen him out on the field the night before, calling encouragement. Players like him could be more of an asset to the team than a player with greater talent but fewer people skills.

Like Laurent.

He'd spotted the Winger, seen his pace and ball-handling skills; but the man wasn't a good team player and came across as something of a bully, bad-mouthing other players when they made a mistake, swearing at the referee and at fans.

Players like him were trouble. And Nick would be keeping a close eye on him.

Nick's first team meeting was held in a small room next to the main office. Bernard came out and shook his hand, grinning broadly before kissing him on both cheeks—again—and pulling him into a tight hug.

"Your official welcome, *mon ami*."

"Thanks," Nick smiled, raising his eyebrows.

He was introduced to the small management team and the head coach, Pière Gabon, a friendly man in his late sixties who didn't speak a word of English. Then he met the senior players group who were there to back up the Captain.

Bernard told them first of his plans to hand over the captaincy to Nick.

There were surprised murmurings, but nothing negative. Instead, they seemed pleased and intrigued that he'd joined them.

Finally, Nick was introduced to the rest of the team. He already knew Grégoire, Inoke and Russell, but the others were faces on a field. Of course, he'd done his homework and studied their form so he had a working knowledge of their strengths and weaknesses, all the information that a Captain needed at his fingertips.

Nick was watching Laurent's face when the captaincy news was announced. The man scowled and muttered something in French that Nick was pretty sure he wouldn't like.

But there was time for him to get to know Laurent: Nick suspected that the other player wouldn't enjoy the experience.

He gave his welcoming speech while Bernard translated it, watching the faces of the men he was expected to lead. He'd given the Captain's speech many times when he'd played at the Phoenixes, but there he'd known all the players well, having come up through the ranks with them. Here, he was an unknown quantity.

The players listened politely, several showing interest, but only Laurent continued to ignore him.

At the end of his speech, Nick moved among them, shaking the hands of each, finding some small, positive thing to say to each of them about the game the night before.

There was an unpleasant moment when it looked as though Laurent wouldn't shake his hand, but Bernard snapped something at him in rapid French, and the man curled his lip, briefly gripping Nick's hand.

Nick frowned. He didn't like the attitude or the fact that he could smell alcohol on the man's breath. Good thing he had a remedy for that.

They all headed to the locker room and changed into their training kit. Nick pulled on the new colours for the first time, wishing he could take a tramadol to ease the ever-present ache in his shoulder, then led them off on laps around the field. Lap after lap after lap, until the team started to complain. Nick kept the laps going until Laurent pulled off to the side of the field and threw up.

Nick jogged toward him with Bernard following.

"Never turn up to another training session stinking of alcohol," he said coldly, Bernard translating briskly. "Never ignore another Captain's speech, and never mouth-off at the referee or the fans again. You can change, or you can change teams. I don't tolerate arseholes. Are we clear?"

"*Comprends?*" Bernard demanded.

Laurent nodded sulkily, wiping spittle from his mouth.

Bernard smiled at Nick.

"He understands."

CHAPTER 25

B RENDAN GASPED AGAIN AND Anna glared at him.

"Stop it!"

"I didn't say anything," he huffed.

"You keep … making noises!" Anna snapped, irritated and on edge.

"Well, pardon me for breathing, Ms. Bad-tempered-bun-in-the-oven."

Anna slumped in her chair.

"I'm being a bitch. I'm sorry, I can't help it. It's just … *that wretched book!*"

Molly had published her kiss-and-tell-all story—*Naughty Nick: My Life with the Real Nick Renshaw,* and it was already a huge hit in the UK, quickly topping the charts in both hardback and e-book.

She was also appearing on several chat shows, coyly telling people that she and Nick had been a hot item and desperately in love, but if they wanted to know the details, they'd have to read the book.

Reviews were terrible, but that didn't stop the sales. Everyone seemed to want to know if 'Nice-guy Nick' had feet of clay.

Anna felt her blood pressure shoot up every time someone asked her about it. The bitch even had the nerve to send them a copy of the book via her lawyers. The book that Brendan was reading right now.

"Knowledge is power," he informed her when she tried to toss the book in the trash where it belonged.

So Anna was refusing to read it, but suffering by watching Brendan read it instead. She'd made him hide the cover with a paper bag, but Anna still felt anger thrum through her veins. A blowup of the cover seemed to be in every bookshop and, annoyingly, it kept popping up on her Amazon feed when she went to look at baby buggies or washable diapers. The photograph showed a slightly startled Nick with his arms around Molly. It had been taken at their engagement party. Anna *hated* that picture.

Her gaze snapped back to Brendan who was sniggering at something. And every now and then he'd gasp, shake his head, laugh or roll his eyes. It was driving her nuts, but she couldn't make herself leave the room either.

Of course, the book had been mentioned on *Loose Women* since it was a topical news and chat show. Anna had been pre-warned by the longest serving anchor, Ruth, that the producers wanted her to address it. She was forced to respond to a question about it in front of the live studio audience while the show was being filmed.

So when Ruth asked Anna if she'd read the book, she simply smiled and said, "I rarely read fiction."

That had gotten her a big laugh and a round of applause, but inside it hurt. It hurt to think that the venomous bitch was getting away with telling lies about Nick and about Anna, too. Not only getting away with it, but making money from it. There was no justice.

Brendan gasped again and Anna lost it.

"What? What!" she snarled, stalking around the kitchen table and grabbing the book from Brendan's hands.

"Oooh, I don't think you should read that page!" he squeaked, cringing away from her.

Nick was a sex machine. We did it three or four times a day, sometimes more. My legs were always open, so was my mouth. He couldn't get enough of me.

"God, Mol! You're the most beautiful thing I've ever seen. I'm going to cum all over your tits."

He wasn't allowed to have sex before a match but we did it all the time anyway. He said that being full of man-juice made him a better player. We did it at half-time all the time, too.

Anna screamed and threw the book across the room, narrowly missing Brendan who had ducked behind his chair and was holding the toaster over his head for protection.

"I hate her!" Anna yelled. "I hate her so much! And her writing doesn't even make sense!"

And she burst into tears, sinking into her chair and sobbing on the kitchen table.

Brendan emerged slowly, checking it was safe before he pulled his chair next to Anna and propped an arm around her shoulders.

"She's not worth crying about," he said, stroking her hair gently. "She's just a withered old tart, with more cosmetic enhancements than a makeup counter at Harrods."

Anna wailed and Brendan cringed as the piercing noise sliced through his left ear. He'd never known her to be so emotional. If it 1

"You're welcome."

CHAPTER 26

Nick was frustrated with the team, but he'd fallen in love with Carcassonne. He'd thought that the south of France would be sleepy and the pace of life slow. In some ways that was true, but there was another side to it.

The people and colours were vibrant. Conversations in rapid French exploded all around him. Many of the townspeople seemed to know who he was and came out of bars and cafés to shake his hand. Several took selfies.

At first, he thought it was to do with being part of the Cuirassiers, but Bernard had laughed and told him that Massimo's calendar with Nick on the cover had been the biggest selling one since the charity project had started. In fact, they'd had to reprint three times. It was one of the reasons that the Cuirassiers had been so accommodating when they offered him a contract.

"It is your famous derrière, *mon ami*," Bernard explained, nodding philosophically and slapping Nick on his shoulder.

That information had left Nick feeling bemused: even in a rugby-loving town, he was better known for the calendar shoot he'd done than having led two national teams to win the World Cup. In the end, he'd shrugged his shoulders and smiled for as many selfies as his fans wanted.

He'd been told that a small brasserie in the town plaza, *Chez Felix*, was one of the club's sponsors. It was a family run business with great coffee and beef served on the bloody side. That took some getting used to, but the warmth of his welcome helped him overlook the small detail.

It seemed as though the Cuirassiers were a community club, with half the town involved in one way or another.

He couldn't wait to visit the amazing farmers' markets with Anna, held twice a week in the town square. He'd gone on his first Sunday and loved the stunning displays of fresh food: huge, ripe tomatoes, melons, peaches, apples that gleamed in the sun, plums, damsons, and a kaleidoscope of coloured vegetables that he couldn't identify. Traditional folk tunes played by local musicians rang out on every corner. Nick loved it already; he hoped that Anna would, too.

He was surprised when his phone rang with a Paris area code.

"Hello? *Bonjour?*"

"Monsieur Nick Renshaw?"

"Yes, I mean *oui?*"

"I'm Miriam Duchat, personal assistant to Hugo Compain," she paused as if waiting for the significance of this name to sink in, but Nick was none the wiser.

"Yes?" said Nick.

There was a soft huff at the other end of the line.

"Hugo is the editor for *Vogues Hommes International*. He would be interested in arranging a photo shoot with you."

"Oh right, thanks," said Nick, surprised. "But I'm not really modelling anymore."

There was a shocked intake of breath.

"But he wants you!"

"Um, well, that's good to hear, but I have a full-time job and it's difficult for me to get away."

"He would be prepared to send the photographer to London," the woman said sharply.

"Eh, I'm not in London very often. I live in Carcassonne now."

"*C'est vrai?* Truly, you are in France?"

"Yep. I'm playing for the Cuirassiers."

The woman's voice rose an octave.

"But that is very exciting news! Adrienne said you were retired!"

"I was, but…"

"Hugo is a huge rugby fan. I know he will want this shoot. We can send the photographer to Carcassonne, or we will fly you to Paris."

Nick was taken aback.

"Well, I guess that would be okay. It would have to fit around practices and games."

He could hear furious typing at the other end.

"Send me your schedule and we will set this up. Your agent is still Adrienne Catalano in New York?"

Nick hadn't talked to Adrienne in a while, but if he had an agent at all, she was it.

"Yes, that's right," he said.

"We'll be in touch. *Au revoir.*"

And she was gone. Nick stared at his phone. He'd assumed that his modelling days were over, but now it seemed his two worlds were about to collide. And if he knew anything at all about rugby players, he was about to have the piss ripped out of him.

Who did she say the shoot was for?

He soon found out because just ten minutes later Adrienne was lighting up his phone with text after text, which meant one or more of several possibilities:

a) She was excited

b) There was money in the deal

c) She'd taken too many happy pills

d) All of the above.

When he read her texts, he began to understand what the big deal was. Even Nick had heard of *Vogue*, although he hadn't been aware that twice a year a men's international version was published. He was now, and when he read what they were prepared to pay him for one day's work, it was a no-brainer. Every penny he earned was going into the anti-Molly fighting fund.

His phone rang again, and since Adrienne was calling him this time, he felt obliged to answer.

He made his way through the market crowd and found a small coffee shop where old men were smoking the foul-smelling Gitanes and arguing about the government.

"Nick, baby! You are the luckiest s.o.b. on the planet. Are you shitting me? *Vogues Hommes* wants you for the cover!"

He ordered an espresso and a glass of water, then sat enjoying the noise and colour of Carcassonne.

"I'm guessing that's a pretty big deal then?"

He could almost hear her rolling her eyes four thousand miles away.

"Yes, Nick," she said firmly. "It is a *very* big deal. It's the kind of deal that models wait for their whole lives. Tell me I'm setting this up for you, Nick!"

So he agreed. One more photoshoot.

The following day, Adrienne called him back.

"I've checked your calendar with the Club, and the shoot is scheduled for four weeks from Thursday—be in Paris by lunchtime. And Nick?"

"Yes?"

"Enjoy it, baby. This could open a lot of doors for you."

It was probably a good thing that Adrienne couldn't see the indifference on Nick's face. Anna was his first priority and rugby the next. There wasn't room for much else. But the Cuirassiers publicity department had turned cartwheels when they found out that he was wanted for a *Vogue* shoot. They'd immediately sent out a press release and were fielding calls from reporters across France and even in the UK. Nick was happy to let them deal with that—he had other things on his mind.

He'd been thinking about the deal that Molly's lawyers had offered. Fifty thousand was a lot less than they'd originally asked for and it meant that Adrienne's agency wouldn't be affected either, but Nick was still torn—he didn't see why Molly should get anything else from him.

He hated that she could still get to him like this, that he had to think about her at all. And he hated that it affected Anna, too. She said she'd support his decision, whatever he decided.

If he paid the money, it would all be over much sooner, he knew that.

He pulled out his phone and called his lawyers.

"This is Nick Renshaw. I want you to pass on a message to Molly McKinney: tell her, no deal. And I'll see her in court."

He ended the call, wondering if he'd just lit the fuse that was going to blow his life apart.

CHAPTER

27

As Anna and Brendan walked down the steps from their small plane, a wave of heat washed over them.

"Bliss!" Brendan sighed, slipping his Aviators over his eyes.

Anna had to agree. The warm air felt wonderful after the cold snap that London had been experiencing. And the tiny airport of Perpignan was in stark contrast to the concrete wasteland of Heathrow in other ways, too.

Instead of rows of Victorian terrace houses and grey apartment buildings, they'd flown over pale green fields, burned almost golden by the long French summer, and the rocky coastline where low hills and ancient stone villages brushed up against the deep blue of the Mediterranean.

Brendan walked through Immigration, simply flashing his British passport. He was a citizen of Europe for now, although not for much longer once Britain pulled out of the EU. It took a little longer for Anna to reach the arrivals hall.

Nick and Brendan were standing together, smiling and laughing. She paused, watching them both, happy that the two most important men in her life were friends, happy to be in France, happy to be reuniting with her fiancée. *And with the father of my child*, she whispered to herself.

Nick glanced across and saw her, his smile widening.

He strode across the small arrivals hall and wrapped his strong arms around her, pulling her against his chest. He smelled of cinnamon and spice, sunshine and Nick. He smelled wonderful. He smelled like home.

They stood together, not talking, not thinking, just being.

Then he cupped her face in his large, rough hands, and kissed her lips softly.

Anna sighed against him, losing herself in the kiss, until…

"Hello! I am here, too, you know! And no one has given me a welcome snog!"

"Shut up, Brendan," Nick and Anna said together, then burst out laughing.

"Well, that's nice," he grouched. "I come all this way, carry her ladyship's luggage, and all I get is a manly handshake."

Nick slung his arm around Brendan's shoulder and kissed him on the cheek.

"That's hardly a snog," Brendan complained, but he seemed mollified.

The hour's drive to Carcassonne passed quickly, as each of them swapped news, commented on the small villages and towns that they passed, the gentle curves of the hills and the sudden, stark rocky outcrops.

In the distance, the Pyrenees soared toward the clouds, a natural barrier between France and Spain, just a few miles to the south.

Anna rested her left hand on Nick's thigh and he glanced across to smile at her.

"No feeling up the driver unless I can play, too," Brendan sang from the backseat.

"Then you'll have to find your own driver," Anna sang back.

"Ooh! That sounds fun," said Brendan, perking up. "I need to renew my license."

Anna groaned. She was too tired to play word games with him.

"I think you'll like it here," Nick said quietly.

Anna already loved it.

ANNA AND BRENDAN'S first night in Carcassone was full of fun and laughter, good food and friendship, and memories that she'd treasure forever.

She still remembered the hurt she'd felt when Nick first told her about Bernard's offer, but now it was clear that it had been the right move for Nick ... the right move for their relationship. Doubts lingered, but they were more distant now, more insubstantial and shadowy.

Nick's housemates had arranged a barbeque in their honour, but it wasn't a case of just throwing some steaks on the grill, but a banquet eaten outdoors.

A buffet table had been dragged outside and was laden with delicious fresh fruits, amazing salads, a variety of cold meats and several different cheeses, all pungent. The smell of freshly baked bread from a local *boulangerie* made her mouth water and her stomach rumbled loudly.

Inoke, the Fijian Prop, a very large man with a surprisingly high voice, had contributed a dish of *Kokoda* from his native country, a tuna-like fish marinated in freshly squeezed lemon juice and left to cook for several hours. It was delicious and Anna was ravenous.

She was touched by the effort that they'd all gone to, and it was good to see how relaxed Nick felt around them. She'd wondered if they might be more reserved since he was their Captain, but no, they were friends and teammates.

Brendan was rather restrained around them at first, waiting to see how well they'd accept him, but after the first hour and the first round of drinks, he fit in perfectly, especially as he could hold two conversations at the same time: one in English, and one in French.

A carafe of local wine was passed around again and Nick waved away a small glass which Anna cast longing looks at as she sipped her Perrier water.

As the sun sank slowly, the stone wall behind them radiated heat that it had absorbed during the day, and crickets, *Sauterelles*, chirped loudly in the warm night air.

Anna felt sleepy and satiated as she leaned against Nick, his fingers brushing up and down her bare arm, her head on his shoulder.

She was even happier when Nick's teammates promised that they'd give Brendan a great night on the town, leaving the house empty for Nick and Anna to have some alone time.

Brendan was in seventh heaven at the prospect of a night out with three hot rugby players, and when they scooped him up, he went willingly.

The moment they were alone, Nick's lips fastened on Anna's, and she found that she was suddenly wide awake and not at all tired. He picked her up honeymoon style, his lips moving to her neck as he trod the narrow stairs to the small white room, where they made love, bathed in the moon's mellow light.

THE NEXT DAY, Nick and Anna went house-hunting.

With the club's help, Anna had found two possible properties for them to look at with a view to renting for the rest of the season. Much as she genuinely liked his new teammates, sharing a small house with so many people wasn't going to work long term, although Brendan mentioned that he was thoroughly enjoying the scenery around the swimming pool.

He seemed to have hit it off with Grégoire, in particular.

"Is Grég gay?" Anna asked, gazing out of the window as Nick drove past rolling fields and vineyards groaning with heavy fruit, some already harvested.

Nick thought for a moment.

"Dunno. He's never mentioned any girlfriends and he doesn't seem that interested in women when I've been out with all the lads. Maybe?"

Anna smiled.

"I think Brendan has a little crush on him."

Nick's eyes widened comically.

"Woah! Brendan is gay?!"

Anna laughed and playfully slapped Nick's arm. He pretended to pout.

"I thought Bren had a crush on me!"

"Oh babe, he adores you completely—don't be jealous."

Nick smirked and shot her a quick smile.

"There must be gay rugby players," she said thoughtfully. "But I can't think of any. Have you ever played with gay teammates?"

Nick's eyes followed the winding road, but he nodded slowly.

"Yeah, thinking back, there were a couple of guys who came out after their playing careers had finished. But there are a few more these days. Gareth Thomas is the guy who comes to mind. He came out in 2009 and then played for two more years—he was capped for Wales a hundred times. Great guy, a Winger."

Anna nodded.

"Oh, right. That was before I came to the UK, but I remember hearing his name. That must have been pretty brave of him."

Nick nodded.

"Yeah, there've been a few before—an Australian player came out in the nineties. It's more accepted now, I think." He sighed. "I know there's this stereotype of the rugby thug, but if you're a good player, a good team member, that's all that matters. And when Gareth came out, his teammates supported him all the way—that's what a team is: we're there for each other. Family."

Anna understood. She knew how hard it had been for Nick, playing for the Finchley Phoenixes for four years, then losing his rugby family so abruptly. She could also see how much it meant to him to be part of a team again.

And she worried what would happen when Nick's season with the Cuirassiers was up.

Nick pulled into the tiny courtyard of an old farmhouse, looking doubtfully at the GPS display, but this was definitely the place.

The stone walls were crumbling in places and the paint on the wooden shutters was peeling. An air of abandonment and sadness hung over the old building.

Anna fished in her purse for a giant iron key that the realtor had given her. It was heavy and pitted with rust, but she strode forward, determined to be positive.

The substantial wooden door swung open with a theatrical groan and Anna half expected Lurch to come lumbering along the hallway.

Cobwebs bloomed in the half-light, and she ducked down, flinching when some caught in her hair. She got as far as the kitchen, shrieked, and crashed into Nick as she turned and ran.

"What's wrong?" he snapped, grabbing her arms.

"Beetles!" she squeaked, shaking free, and shot out through the front door.

Nick peered into the kitchen and saw that the floor was shiny, dark, and moving. As he flicked on the light switch, thousands of black beetles scuttled across the worn linoleum.

Nick shuddered and followed Anna.

She was pale when he climbed back in the car, and had even closed the windows.

"That was…"

"…like a horror film, Nick said.

Anna nodded.

"Let's get the heck out of here!"

Nick couldn't agree more.

At the second house, Anna made Nick enter first. But this one was completely different—a *fin de siècle* villa painted primrose yellow with white shutters and a red tiled roof. Sunshine poured in through the wide windows, and the floral curtains stirred in the breeze when Anna flung the French doors open in the backyard. Well, it was more of a tiny patio, a small sun trap, but it had some sturdy looking garden furniture and a real grapevine scaling the sunny wall.

Anna's optimism came flooding back, and she ran into every room, crossing her fingers that she wouldn't find anything that would rule it out. Especially any creepy-crawlies.

But the villa was as serene as it was beautiful and her spirits soared.

"I love it!" she said as she came flying down the stairs into Nick's arms. "It's perfect."

Nick smiled, his eyes creasing with happiness.

It felt like everything was finally coming together.

THE NEXT MORNING, Nick and the guys left for an early training session, with the hope that they'd be finished by lunchtime.

Even though it was October, the little walled garden radiated warmth, and Anna sat under the shade of a large awning, drinking tea and feeling pleasantly worn out from a long night of love-making with Nick.

They'd agreed terms with the villa's owner, and would be able to have the keys the following week. It had all been so easy, so civilized, the deal agreed on a handshake. The owner was a fan of the Cuirsassiers. Nick's name was good enough for him.

The sun's gentle rays seeped into her body, and Anna felt a deep sense of peace. After the hectic months they'd had, it was incredibly welcome.

Suddenly, Brendan screeched in her ear.

"Ann-ie! Wake up!"

"Oh my God, Brendan! What?!" she yelped, her heart jumping.

"Ooh, sorry, baby-mama! I was overcome with excitement."

He flopped down on the sunbed next to her.

"Guess what?"

"No," said Anna grumpily.

"Ann-ie! Go on, guess!"

"Nope."

"Spoilsport!"

"Child."

"Grumpy granny knickers!"

She raised an eyebrow.

"Do you have some news to tell me, Bren?"

"Ooh yes! I'm so glad you asked!" His voice dropped to an excited whisper. "I slept with Grégoire!"

Anna sat up, now fully awake.

"Really?"

"I wouldn't make up something like that!" he said huffily, then caught her expression. "Okay, so I totally would! But I'm telling you the truth! I slept with Grégoire—and it was wonderful. I'm in love!"

Anna smiled.

"Aw, that's great, Bren! I'm really happy for you."

Brendan blinked and stared at her.

"That's it? You're *happy* for me?"

"Well, yes. Um, very happy."

Brendan leapt to his feet and started pacing up and down.

"I don't think you understand. He's incredible! He's sweet and kind and funny, and a total hottie hunk. His schlong is at least a foot long—I'm feeling it all the way to my toes."

"Bren! Ew! TMI!"

He turned his face towards her, his expression earnest.

"It's love. I've never felt anything like this before."

"Honey, you've known him for five minutes, so let's not get ahead of ourselves."

Brendan scowled.

"What difference does that make? You were attracted to Nick the first time you saw him, before you even knew who he was. Five minutes or five years, Grégoire is *the one*."

Anna wanted to hope for the best. Seeing Brendan happy would be wonderful. But he did have a tendency to exaggerate. A lot.

"And how does Grégoire feel?" she asked carefully.

Brendan beamed.

"He says he's never met anyone like me before."

Anna was pretty certain that was true.

She told Nick the news as soon as he returned from training. He didn't seem excited.

"Why are you pulling that face?"

Nick sighed and sat down next to her.

"Because the team is struggling and I need Grég to have his head in the game, not thinking about whether he's going to get some tonight."

Anna bristled immediately.

"And would you say that if he'd met a new woman?"

"Yes. Especially a woman," and he raised an eyebrow.

"I'm sorry," she said. "I shouldn't have said that."

Nick shrugged.

"You're not wrong. Once word gets out, it'll be harder for Grég. The team will be okay about it—mostly—but opposing teams will use anything to get under your skin."

Anna winced knowing that Nick was right. She knew the psychology of gamesmanship all too well, but she also remembered some of the vile things players on other teams had said to Nick when they were both mired in scandal.

"Poor guy," she said sympathetically.

"Yeah, and if Bren does his usual disappearing act after dating him for a week, I'll send Grég to you."

"Gee, thanks!"

"Well, you are a trained sports psychologist, luv. Besides, you're good at pep talks for the broken-hearted."

Anna sighed and nodded.

"Oh dear."

BUT THEY WERE both wrong: for the rest of the visit, Brendan and Grégoire were inseparable. Brendan met him from training and they went off together exploring the towns and villages around Carcassonne; they ate together every night, and shared a bed, too.

Brendan glowed with happiness, spending hours telling Anna how wonderful his new lover was when Grégoire had to go to training or an away-game.

Interestingly, Nick reported that Grégoire was playing better than ever: far from not having his head in the game, happiness gave him confidence, and that was winning the Cuirassiers points.

His teammates were a little surprised when Grégoire came out to them but, on the whole, they accepted him, delighted with their unexpected winning streak.

Anna smiled and listened to Brendan extolling Grégoire's virtues: his handsome face, his sexy body, his enormous penis (as Brendan insisted on telling her repeatedly). She was waiting for the other shoe to drop. But two weeks later, by the end of their visit, they were still going strong.

When they were back in London, Anna was aware that Brendan texted and emailed Grégoire, and even went so far as to announce that Grégoire was his #officialboyfriend.

Brendan was happy.

NICK WAS BECOMING more and more irritated with Laurent's attitude. On a good day, Laurent was a strong player, but he wasn't a *team* player. He seemed to have a particular beef with Grégoire ever since he'd learned that the younger man was gay.

When Nick discussed the problem with Bernard, he pulled a face and shrugged his shoulders.

"He's from Paris, he hates everyone the same: *les provinciaux*; men like Grég, *un crevette discret*; younger players; southerners; northerners..." he glanced at Nick with a weary smile on his face. "He hates *les Anglais* most of all."

"Thank for the pep talk, buddy," Nick said, raising his eyebrows. "But I'm serious—he's causing trouble."

Bernard sighed.

"I know this, but he is talented. Give him another kick in his *derrière*—see if that works."

Being Captain to a team of players who disliked each other intensely was bloody hard work.

It was two days before Nick's *Vogue* photoshoot in Paris. Laurent was being a dick about it, but since he was a dick about everything, Nick ignored him. But the muttered words and sneering looks were tiresome. If Nick's French was more fluent, he'd probably have been more annoyed, but since Laurent made a point of refusing to speak or understand English, Nick had to do everything in French, with Bernard's help.

But during this particular training session, it was Grégoire who bore the brunt of Laurent's jibes and disparaging comments. The man was a bully, and because Nick wasn't the kind of man he could bully, he was picking on Grégoire.

Nick had had enough: Laurent had been warned to change and he hadn't—now he had to pay the price.

They were running through realistic game-plays—the guys who played on the left wing versus the guys who played on the right.

Grégoire had the ball and just as he passed it, Laurent came in with a late tackle and took him off his feet.

Grégoire hadn't seen Laurent coming—he'd been completely blindsided, and lay on the ground, winded. Laurent stood above him, smirking as the Coach blew the whistle.

"*Follasse sportif!*" Laurent sneered.

Nick wasn't sure what Laurent had said, but from the look on Grégoire's face, it was nothing pleasant.

"Laurent! *Ici!*" Nick yelled. "Get over here!"

At first the man pretended not to hear, but he couldn't ignore Nick's angry bellow echoing across the field a second time.

"Laurent! *Maintenant! Vas-y-en!* NOW!"

The man scowled at Nick then smirked at Grégoire.

"*Il kiffe ton mec!*"

Grégoire scrambled to his feet, still struggling to breathe, anger and hatred on his face. Nick saw immediately that Grégoire had lost control, but he was too late to stop him lunging at a surprised Laurent and punching him in the face. Laurent tripped and landed on his backside.

"*Putain!*" Fuck!

Grégoire was on him in a second, and he got in several good punches before Laurent headbutted him in the face. The skin on Grégoire's forehead split, blood pouring everywhere.

Nick and Bernard yelled at them to stop, but the two men were long past listening to reason. Nick sprinted across the field and yanked Laurent backwards by his collar, dragging him bodily off Grégoire. Laurent howled and elbowed Nick in the face. He felt his cheekbone explode with pain and blood gushed from his nose and down his chin. His eyes were watering so badly he could hardly see, but he didn't let go of Laurent who was thrashing around, drumming his heels in the dirt.

Bernard had wrapped his meaty arms around Grégoire, stopping him from throwing himself at Laurent again, and the rest of the team ran forward, keeping the two players apart.

Finally, order was restored, and the two men glared at each other, Grégoire shaking his head like an angry bull, flecks of blood flying from his face.

"*Merde!*" *Shit!*

The elderly medic limped onto the field, studied Grégoire forehead, Nick's cheek, and Laurent's broken nose, threw his hands in the air and summoned them all to the locker room.

Nick was pretty certain that he'd have a black eye. The medic handed Nick a bag of ice to help take the swelling down.

The relief was immediate.

He sat on the physio table, holding the ice to his throbbing face, and swore softly in French and English.

At least his language skills were improving.

"WHAT DID LAURENT say to Grég to make him throw a punch?"

Later that evening, Nick Facetimed Anna. That always made him feel better.

"He'd been saying stuff to him ever since he heard Grég was gay: little digs when no one else could hear. But he deliberately didn't throw the ball to him in the last game. I noticed that, too, and had a word with Laurent. He denied it, but I told him not to let it happen again."

Anna frowned.

"It sounds like Grég had been dealing well enough. What set him off this time?"

Nick gave a pained grin.

"*Il kiffe ton mec*—basically Laurent told Grég that I fancied Brendan, but in a really insulting way, uh, little pouf, something like that."

Anna gasped.

"What an asshole!"

"Yeah, it was the last straw for Grég." Nick sighed. "He'll be fined and suspended because he threw the first punch, but I'll make sure Laurent gets worse. I won't have bullying on my team."

Nick's voice was grim.

"I know that you have to discipline both of them, but is there any chance they could talk it out, as well?" Anna suggested. "Maybe handle that side of it?"

"The way he's feeling right now, I've got a good idea how Grég would like to handle it," Nick said wryly, gingerly touching his swollen cheek.

At the end of the line, Anna laughed gently.

"Ah yes, rugby logic."

Nick grunted.

"They'll both miss playing in at least one game, but they'll still have to come to the away-game against Grenobles. That's a five-hour ride on the team bus, so…"

"Ah, captive audience," said Anna.

Nick grinned.

"Something like that."

The following day, both Grégoire and Laurent were suspended from the next game and fined a weeks' wages each. Laurent was also told that he was on his final warning—one more fuck up and he was out. The gravity of the situation seemed to have finally sunk in, because he apologized to Grégoire as instructed without a single sarcastic comment.

Grégoire gritted his teeth and shook the man's hand.

But it left Nick two players short from his starting line-up with an important away-game coming up in ten days. At least it would give two of the first team squad members a chance to be in the starting line-up, and two other players from the second team were promoted up to the bench.

Nick had a spectacular black eye, but at least the swelling on his cheek had gone down after icing it carefully. Which meant that the *Vogue* photoshoot would have to be cancelled.

He emailed Adrienne with the news and waited for her to light up his phone.

CHAPTER 28

NICK WAS WRONG. AGAIN.

When Adrienne had called him back, not at all happy, he'd assumed that was the end of his modelling career, for now, at least. But an hour later, she phoned him again, considerably more positive because the photographer wanted to go ahead with the shoot: Nick was to show up as expected.

"Who the hell wants to photograph someone with a black eye?" Nick exclaimed to Anna when they spoke that evening.

"I have no idea," she said calmly. "Maybe it makes a change from all the pretty-boy Mr. Perfects they usually have on the cover of *Vogue*."

Nick's laugh was wry.

"Are you saying I'm a bit of rough?"

"Hmm, now there's a loaded question! How do you want me to answer, babe?"

THE NEXT DAY, Nick caught a flight to Paris. He was met at *Charles de Gaulle* airport by a limo service and whisked past the *Arc de Triomphe*, past the *Tour Eiffel*, and through the bustling streets of Paris. No one tried to peer through the tinted windows, but Nick still felt like a celebrity.

He pushed a button to lower the window a crack, and immediately sneezed as a bus belching diesel accelerated into the lane next to him, making his eyes water. He rolled the window up hastily and leaned back in the leather seat, willing the pain away. A tramadol would feel pretty good about now, but he'd almost managed to give them up. Unless he'd been hammered on the pitch, then all bets were off. But he was trying.

With red, watering eyes, Nick saw that the driver had turned into a nondescript street and stopped outside a building that looked like a warehouse.

The driver opened Nick's door and smoothly pocketed the €10 tip with a sleight of hand a magician could be proud of.

Nick stared up at the brick building and felt that first tingle of excitement that he had before a game, the same mix of nerves that he'd had before Massimo's shoot, but not since.

He'd spent so much time resenting the interruption to working with his team, that he'd forgotten that there were many things about doing a photoshoot that he enjoyed, especially if he could learn from the photographer, too.

He was just about to ring the buzzer when the front door opened, and from then on, Nick learned that things were done differently on a *Vogue* shoot.

A man who could have been Brendan's French twin ushered Nick inside, introducing him in perfect if heavily accented English to the team: hairdresser, makeup artist and manicurist, senior stylist and her two assistants, one of whom was a trained tailor, lighting engineer, art director, and finally the photographer, Henri Cassavell, who was the king of the show, greeting Nick regally and seemed fascinated by his damaged face.

The photographer was a vigorous man in his late sixties, with deeply tanned skin and a face like a ploughed field. His hair stuck up in odd tufts like cotton balls, and his eyebrows were thick and grey, perching over his nose expectantly.

But his dark eyes were clear and penetrating, and he examined Nick minutely, then nodded briskly.

"*Bon!* Let's get to work!"

He clapped his hands and all the assistants who'd been holding their breath flew into action.

Nick was hustled away, given water and strong coffee, as the senior stylist conferred with Monsieur Cassavell.

Several suits in different tones of charcoal were brought out, inspected and dismissed, until the correct shade was found. Then the same process with suits in navy blue.

Seven crisp white shirts were rejected before one in fine Egyptian cotton was selected. One of the assistants hung it up and used a steamer to take out the creases.

Four pairs of gleaming Tom Ford shoes in Nick's size were brought out, displayed in their shoe boxes, emerging from swathes of white tissue paper.

He lost count of the number of ties that were presented to

the senior stylist, before three were chosen to show to Monsieur Cassavell.

Nick was offered a robe and changed quickly while discussions in rapid French took place all around him. He was pleased that he understood most of what was said. He also managed to take some behind-the-scenes shots, earning a curious look from the photographer.

Nick wondered if he'd committed some sort of *Vogue* sin, but the man merely came over to examine Nick's camera and ask some questions.

"What sort of camera have you got? Oh I see you're using a 50 ml lens. How do you find it?"

"I like using it for close-up shots and behind the scenes and interiors, especially when there's low lighting. Is that alright? Do you mind if I take a few pictures? While you're not shooting, of course."

"That's fine. Are you interested in being a photographer?"

Nick shook his head.

"I just like taking pictures, but who knows?"

Monsieur Cassavell smiled and slapped Nick on the shoulder. It felt like the ice had been broken.

Often, models were treated like mere content, literally clotheshorses on which to hang designer outfits; Nick was much happier when he was treated as a person.

But then it was all business again.

The makeup artist insisted on shaving his chest again even though Nick had done it the day before, inspecting his skin minutely before massaging in some oil that smelled sharply of citrus.

Then twenty minutes of combing and trimming his beard was followed by makeup sponged onto his face, neck, chest and the backs of his hands. The manicurist tutted and fussed over his bent fingers, trimming the nails, then polishing them to a glass-like sheen.

There was a long conversation between the makeup artist who looked despairingly at Nick's battered face, and the photographer who seemed to want to emphasize the damage. In the end, the slight blackness under his left eye wasn't covered up with foundation—if anything, it was emphasized.

It all seemed bizarre to Nick, but Monsieur Cassavell was pleased.

Eyeliner, lip-gloss, mascara and powder were applied, and then the hair stylist gripped his hair between her hands, moulding and pulling, combing and gelling into tousled perfection.

When Nick slid on the underwear, shirt and suit that had been prepared for him, for the first time in his life he had clothes-envy. Everything fit him perfectly, but even then, the tailor made minute adjustments, slightly altering the hang of the jacket across his broad shoulders.

God, it felt good, and he even though he wasn't vain, he loved the way it looked.

"How much would this suit cost?" Nick asked.

"This item," said the tailor, "is a Trader Blu suit in Batavia Twill. This Armani retails at a little under €3,000."

Nick swallowed—that was his monthly wage at Carcassonne.

With a swooping sensation, Nick realised that all these outfits, even the ones that had been discarded, had been ordered specially for this shoot. He'd always known that his athletic body-type couldn't be easily accommodated by off-the-peg clothes. It was humbling and oddly exhilarating.

As Nick's transformation was completed, Henri Cassavell talked to him in depth about his vision for the shoot—to show the work behind the creation of a rugby star, his words. He wanted to see the bent fingers, the defined muscles, the scar through Nick's eyebrow, the evidence of surgery on his shoulder, elbow, Achilles tendons as the body beneath the suit was revealed, and, of course, his black eye.

The set had been dressed with a background of heavy silk cascading to the floor behind a formal drawing room chair; the lighting was stark, giving the room a monochrome effect.

The photographer was intense but focussed, totally in command of his material—Nick.

He photographed every part of him, even asking him to remove his shoes and socks, exposing vulnerability, as he put it, in Nick's bare feet.

"Nick, more intense. No, intense, not angry … that's it. Raise your left shoulder, dip your chin, yes, good. That's it! Hold it! Don't move!"

And the camera shutter rattled like a machine gun.

"Good, extend you right leg, more relaxed, don't look at the camera, look past the camera. Down a little, move your chin to the right."

Nick was almost waiting for him to say, 'Rub your stomach and pat your head'.

"Now look directly at the camera, yes, good. That's it! That's it! That's the look! Hold it, don't move! Yes, that's what I want! You're strong, you're powerful! Show me strong! Show me you're undefeated! You're a warrior, a winner! Yes, yes, that look! Those eyes! That's it! That's what I need! Hold it!"

The photographer was slightly reserved, but polite and gracious to everyone—he was captain of his ship, and Nick could respect that.

Nick moved, posed, focussed, followed and found himself intrigued by the work, the psychology that went into the shoot. He listened to everything he was told, completely intent on doing the best job he could.

Three hours flew by, and Nick was surprised and a little disappointed when they were finally done. It had been a fascinating experience and he'd learned so much. Even though he was still pretty much a novice, no one had made him feel ignorant, and God, the clothes were fantastic! He wondered if he'd be allowed to keep them. It seemed unlikely, and he sighed as he pulled on his jeans and t-shirt.

The senior stylist noticed the glances he'd been casting at the suit, and gave a small smile.

"Monsieur Nick, would you do us the honour of keeping this suit?" she asked.

Nick's grin was wide.

"Really? It's okay?"

"It has been altered for you—we couldn't sell it," she shrugged.

"Heck, yeah! I thought you'd never ask," Nick joked as she passed him the suit in a carrier.

Nick was delighted. He'd never been able to keep any of the clothes from a shoot before.

Henri Cassavell shook his hand fervently.

"It has been a pleasure, *mon ami*. We will make a beautiful cover for *Vogue Hommes International*, yes?"

Nick blinked.

"The cover?"

The photographer laughed, highly amused.

"*Mais oui!* No one told you this?"

Nick gave the photographer an apologetic smile.

"Uh, yeah sorry. I forgot."

"It will be a great cover, Nick Renshaw. The camera loves you … and your black eye," and he laughed. "And we French love our rugby heroes. We love the cut of a good suit even more," and he smiled broadly.

CHAPTER 29

As Nick boarded his flight back to Carcassonne, the whole day in Paris seemed surreal.

The only sign that he'd modelled for a *Vogue* photoshoot was the gel in his hair and the suit-carrier in the overhead locker.

Now he was back to the day job of captaining a rugby team who were still struggling.

Yes, they'd started to win a few games, but the team was inconsistent and still suffering from the odour of bullying.

The idea of talking it all out definitely had merit, and Nick was going to use the long bus ride to their next game to force the team to bond, once and for all.

The team boarded the coach for the five hour drive to Grenobles. It was an important game, but one they'd be playing without two key members, since Grégoire and Laurent were both suspended. Their punishment was to sit line-side but not be permitted to play. For an athlete, to be fit and ready and have to sit on the side-lines was torture. But they both knew that they'd earned it.

At the front of the bus sat the physios, Bernard and Nick. But at the back, Nick could hear Laurent mouthing off.

Banter was one thing, but the guy just didn't let up and he didn't learn. When Nick twisted around to see what was going on, he could see Grégoire's face changing, growing angrier as the needling went on and on.

He was well aware that rugby lads liked to joke around and that some of the horseplay could be rough, but this was divisive and bad for team morale.

Nick stood up to make his way to the back of the bus and Laurent smirked at him, raising one eyebrow, a direct challenge to Nick's authority.

"Laurent, you're bang out of order!"

He was so angry that he'd spoken in English, even though he'd picked up a fair bit of French over the last few months, but his meaning had definitely communicated itself.

"*Monsieur Captiaine Passif*," Laurent said slyly to his crony, implying that Nick was the bottom in a gay relationship, the passive partner.

It was Grégoire who hit breaking point first.

"Enough! This is boring me now! Yes I'm gay! You all know that. If any of you have a problem with that, with me, say it now to my face."

He turned to Laurent slowly.

"We are all grown men here, so if you have a problem with me or how I play, say it! Do I smell? No! I smell great!"

He sniffed his armpits as several of the players laughed.

"Definitely not that. Is it my haircut? My awesome fashion sense?" and he winked at a few players. "Or perhaps it is the fact that I am the only gay player in this team!"

The bus fell silent.

"Shall we have a conversation? We do not have to speak only with loud grunts and burps, we can hold down intelligent conversations— the mindless violence happens on the pitch; we are civilized off the pitch."

Laurent turned his head to gaze out of the window.

Grégoire frowned, his eyes darkening with anger.

"Fuck it! You know what? Let's get all the crazy fucking questions you want to ask out of the way today; all those questions that you don't have the balls to ask me one-on-one. This is your chance to ask me anything. Maybe then I can just concentrate on my job—I like the banter as much as any of you, but sometimes it goes too far and I need a break from the yap, yap, yap in my ears, like a small Jack Russell nipping at my ankles. Everyone has a breaking point and I'm not far from knocking one of you out, and that is something I most definitely will regret. We are a team, aren't we? In this together? Even if sometimes we piss each other off, or we don't always agree. Right, Laurent?"

Laurent shook his head, but he was listening, and Grégoire's voice grew louder.

"That is the truth—we get over it for the sake of the team, because *that's what teams do!*"

He looked at the rest of the players challengingly.

"You have fifteen minutes, boys, so go for it! Ask me anything you want. Go on! I know you're curious. Ask me!"

He lifted his chin and stared down at his teammates.

Russ broke the silence.

"Grég, mate, do you swing both ways, because my girlfriend

316 | STUART REARDON & JANE HARVEY-BERRICK

thinks you're a good looking bastard and I want to know if I should be worried?"

Grégoire burst out laughing.

"She's too beautiful for you, *mon ami*, that is true! But no—I only like guys. Although it depends on the guy." And he shot a dark look at Laurent. "I have high standards."

The team fired question after question, their curiosity given free rein.

"Are you a giver or a taker, Grég?" asked Inoke, a big smile on his face.

"Both," Grégoire answered evenly, "but you're not my type either. Sorry, Noakes."

Inoke pretended to look disappointed and Grégoire threw a wink at him.

"Have you always liked guys?" Maurice asked, a small frown creasing his forehead.

Grégoire matched his expression, thinking about his response.

"I always knew I liked guys," he said quietly, "but I never thought it was right."

His answer was sobering and it made some of the team think a little more, finally figuring out that being a gay athlete wasn't easy.

"What is your type then?" Raul asked curiously.

"You're safe, don't worry, Raul. You're too hairy for my taste. We would call you '*ourson*' a baby bear! But to put your mind at rest, my type is … Brendan."

"Is he your boyfriend?" Raul asked, throwing a quick look at Nick.

"Yes, Bren is my boyfriend. I hope you will make him welcome again next time he visits."

Grégoire worked through the questions one after another, sometimes answering seriously, sometimes with funny comments or anecdotes, making the lads laugh, and everyone except Laurent took part. Even the players who'd sided with the older player before had noticeably abandoned him.

Nick went back to his seat, feeling more relaxed. He noticed that Laurent still didn't seem impressed, but Laurent was never impressed by anything.

Grégoire had found the perfect answer to the constant banter. His Q&A session had broken down barriers, and the other members of the team had got all the questions off their chests.

By the end of the bus journey, Grégoire's sexuality had lost much of the curiosity factor and they'd moved on to talking about the team they'd be taking on the following day.

Nick gave a wry smile: if only all situations could be solved with a 15 minute question time.

Bernard nudged him.

"That was interesting. Let's hope it has a long-term effect.

Nick nodded.

"Yeah, I hope so. Good on Grég for that—no fear at all, just like on the pitch. He's really impressed me today. I always admired him, he's a strong player and a character in the team. It'll be interesting to see how Laurent responds, now he's lost his audience."

Bernard clapped him on the back.

"Yes, very educational."

The following day, the Cuirassiers were in high spirits and Nick couldn't help thinking that clearing the air had been nothing but positive. Laurent and Grégoire sat side by side as the team played without them. They didn't speak to each other once, but Grégoire didn't seem to notice, jumping up and down and encouraging the team.

They played better than ever before, and scraped a win against Grenobles. Only four points, but a win was a win.

As the season progressed and the days grew shorter and colder with snow visible on the distant mountains, more wins followed—and Laurent kept his mouth shut. His playing was mature and his experience showed, but he was still not part of the team. Bernard and the management were talking about trading him. Only Nick was still willing to give him the benefit of the doubt. It was hard to explain why, but he understood the older man's frustration at playing in what was probably his last season and in a second league team.

He just didn't have to be a dickhead about it.

Bernard was smiling when Nick entered the tiny, cramped office of the management team.

"Nick, good game today. Please, sit."

Nick shook hands with the Coach, Manager and Chief Executive. He'd been called into this meeting immediately after the last game, and he expected it was to do with Laurent's future. He still wasn't sure how he felt about that: Laurent had played well and his experience could be a great benefit to the team; but Grégoire was improving game by game, his confidence increasing, letting his skills show. Plus, he was a team player.

If it came to a choice, he'd take Grégoire.

"So, Nick, we asked you here today to discuss your future with the Cuirassiers."

Nick was surprised. This wasn't what he was expecting.

"Since you've joined us, we have started winning games and the fans are coming back. We think the second half of this season could go really well for us."

Bernard nodded at Nick encouragingly.

"We would like to offer you a two-year contract to continue here as Captain."

Nick leaned back in his chair, feeling the quiet satisfaction of being part of the team, a pride in the fact that he was doing his job well.

He already knew the answer he was going to give them.

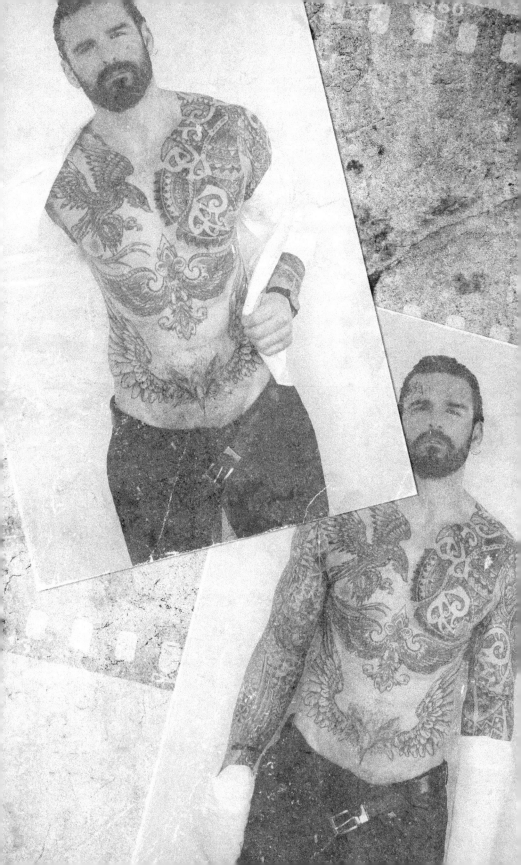

CHAPTER 30

THE INDIAN SUMMER OF SEPTEMBER had long since fled London, followed by a brief Fall where thick fog hung along the Thames, then quickly turned to hard frosts and car windscreens that had to be scraped every morning.

Anna's belly was just beginning to show, and she was torn between feeling fat and frumpy, and proud of the signs of new life growing inside her.

Filming with *Loose Women* was going well, and she'd gotten into a routine of working at the West London studio on Tuesdays and Wednesdays to film four shows, then driving to Heathrow with Brendan immediately after filming and flying back on Monday.

Nick had moved into their rented villa, a mile from Carcassonne, and was enjoying some peace and the change of pace from living with three other men. And maybe, being a decade older than them and the Captain, he needed his own space. He said he'd been playing his guitar again, too.

The villa had four large bedrooms, two reception rooms, one of which made a fine home office, and it was only a thirty minute drive from the beach. It was also less than an hour from a very popular ski resort in the winter. Nick was a little grumpy about that since his contract with the Cuirassiers didn't allow him to participate in anything deemed dangerous. Which seeing the number of injuries he'd already gotten from rugby seemed rather bizarre. But that's the way it was: no skiing for Nick. Brendan however, had already given his seal of approval and promised Anna that his backside was "sensational in salopettes."

Trisha had been out to visit twice, and had even persuaded Nick's parents to travel across once, although they'd preferred to take the Eurostar train from London and spend 12 hours travelling, rather than fly.

And Anna's mother was planning to join them for Christmas, which would be spent partly in London and partly in Carcassonne, with a couple of nights in Paris to go shopping, at Brendan's insistence.

Unfortunately, the court case with Molly's publishers was on-going, and Nick had been forced to travel back to London twice to meet with his lawyers who, despite everything Mark Lipman had said, were now preparing to defend the action in court.

It was stressful at a time when everything else was going well.

But at least the book had dropped out of the bestseller charts and had gone on to become a byword in bad writing. Brendan told Anna that it had been nominated for the *London Literary Review's* 'Bad Sex in Fiction Award' which had gained the book even more notoriety since it was published as an autobiography, not fiction.

Anna didn't care. She just wanted the whole wretched fiasco to be over with.

Besides, she had other things on her mind—their baby was coming into the world, and she wanted everything to be perfect. As much as it could be. But having two court cases hanging over them put a damper on everything. Nick was refusing to back down, too, and was proceeding with the tenuous 'intentional infliction of emotional distress' case against Molly and Roy Greenside.

He'd only agree to drop the charges if Molly's publishers did the same: right now, they were locked in stalemate.

Anna paced their kitchen in Hampstead, sipping warm water this morning in an attempt to offset the queasiness in her stomach. Morning sickness hadn't bothered her for a few weeks now, but today was special for all sorts of reasons, so maybe this was just nerves: Nick was coming home, and they were going to find out the sex of their baby.

Not that they had a preference, only the same hopes as every new parent that their child would be healthy.

She heard a taxi pull up outside and hurried to the front of house in time to hear a key being inserted into the lock, then Nick was walking through the front door, a beanie pulled low over his head and a huge smile on his face.

Anna rushed into his waiting arms, relishing again his warmth and strength, soaking up the sensation of security.

When she lifted her head from his chest, he caught her lips in a quick kiss.

"Are you ready?" he asked.

Anna laughed.

"You've just walked through the door! Don't you want to get a coffee first?"

Nick shook his head.

"Nope. I want to get going. I can't wait to find out if it's Little

Nick or Little Anna you're carrying in there," and he touched her swollen belly reverently.

"Okay, but I have to pee first," and she pulled a face.

A couple of minutes later, she'd picked up her coat and purse and climbed into the Rover. Nick was already running the engine, sending warm air from the vents to heat it.

The hospital was just over a mile from their house, which hadn't been in Anna's mind when they'd bought their home, but it was turning out to be very useful, too. On some of the nicer days, she'd walked there for her appointments, especially as parking was usually horrendous.

Forty minutes later, Anna was wearing an ugly hospital gown and Nick was bouncing lightly on his toes, radiating happiness and a laidback excitement. He kept catching her eye and winking. His certainty that everything would be fine calmed her. He seemed full of energy despite an early start and two flights, with a tedious stopover in Paris.

She watched as he read the posters on the walls of the maternity waiting room, his nose wrinkling at some of the photographs.

He was different now, calmer, happier, and the depression that had dogged him since his testimonial had lifted.

He was different physically, too, having rebuilt the muscle he'd lost when he'd been in New York. His shoulders were heavier and his thighs even thicker. Anna had to look away—her pregnancy hormones were yelling at her to jump him right now.

At that point, the technician arrived, saving Anna from embarrassing herself.

"The gel will feel a little cool," he warned.

Anna jerked when the liquid was squirted across her lower abdomen. Nick leaned over the technician's shoulder as the sonogram wand was pressed firmly into the sticky goo, his eyes intent, flipping between Anna, and the confusing black-and-white images on the computer screen.

The technician frowned, adjusted the wand, and gave them a quick smile.

"I'm just going to get one of the doctors. I won't be a minute."

Anna's stomach lurched.

"Is something wrong?"

"I'll be right back."

Sudden terror squeezed her heart and she turned terrified eyes to Nick. He looked worried but was trying to hide it. He reached out to hold her hand.

"It's alright, luv," he said.

The words should have been reassuring, but as the seconds ticked past, Anna felt like crying.

Please God, please don't let there be anything wrong with our baby…

Finally, the technician returned with a doctor.

"Hello, I'm Dr. Subarashi. I'm just going to take a look."

"Okay," Anna whispered, gripping Nick's hand even more tightly.

The doctor pressed the wand over her belly again, a small frown as he concentrated on the computer screen, studying different angles.

"Well, I think we have a little surprise here," he said at last, smiling encouragingly.

"A good surprise?" Anna asked, her voice husky with emotion.

"I'll just let you listen to the heartbeats and you'll see for yourselves."

He turned up the volume, and Anna heard an underwater wooshing sound. No, *two* wooshing sounds.

Nick stared at the monitor, his eyebrows shooting up.

"Is that … is that *two* babies?"

The doctor smiled at them.

"Yes, there are two foetuses and they both appear healthy."

Anna seemed speechless so Nick fumbled on.

"But, there was only one baby at seven weeks. She had the scan."

The doctor smiled gently.

"Sometimes it happens that one of the babies hides behind the other during an early scan and doesn't appear until later. But I can assure you, that you have two healthy babies in there."

"Bloody hell!"

Nick's knees buckled and he sat heavily in the plastic chair. He was still holding Anna's hands.

"Twins!"

"Congratulations," said the doctor, looking from one to the other.

Finally, Nick found his voice again.

"Can you tell if they're boys or girls?"

"I thought you might ask that. As they're slightly smaller than a single baby, it's a little hard to tell, but I'd say at this point that it seems likely that you're carrying twin girls, Ms. Scott."

The doctor gave them yet another packet of information and advice that Anna could barely take in, then they were left alone.

Nick's face was almost comical, beaming one minute, then seeming disbelieving the next.

"Wow, we're having twins."

"I know," Anna said weakly. "I was worried enough about one, but *two!*"

"We'll be fine," Nick said confidently. "You'll be amazing, I know you will. Now do we tell my mum first or yours."

Anna smiled her first real smile.

"Let's get to the car and tell them together."

But when they got to the car, Nick leaned across the central console, kissing her hungrily. Anna's hormones had been jumpstarted and her hands were all over him, tugging at his zipper, as she traced the outline of a thick erection in his jeans.

The windows misted up, and with a groan, Nick grabbed her wrists and held them tightly.

"I'm loving your way of celebrating," he coughed out, "but we're in the car park of the Royal Free hospital and a little old man just gave me a thumbs up."

Anna's face turned crimson as she peered out of the window, seeing the shuffling gait of an elderly man with a walking stick retreating into the distance.

"He didn't!"

"Swear to God," Nick laughed. "Come on, let's go home."

"What about telling our mothers?"

"Later," he said, slotting her seatbelt into place and reversing quickly.

TELLING THEIR MOTHERS together had been fun—crazy, what with all the shrieking and yelling, but fun.

That had been after Nick had taken Anna to bed and shaken the bedframe so hard that a picture had fallen off the wall.

"I'll fix it later," Nick muttered, still catching his breath.

Anna was limp, lying on her side with her thighs pressed together—even her skin seemed in shock with the thoroughness of Nick's love-making.

"Well," she gasped, "that's one way to celebrate," and she rolled onto her back.

Nick was leaning on his elbow, smiling down at her.

"You look awful smug," she commented.

He grinned.

"Yeah, we're having twins. I guess I have super-strength sperm."

Anna rolled her eyes.

"Yes, that must be it." She paused. "Do you have any twins in your family?"

He shook his head.

"Not that I know of. You?"

"I don't think so. I'll ask Mom."

Nick stretched out on the bed and Anna snuggled against him, using his arm for a pillow.

"It is pretty cool," he said in a low, thoughtful voice. "Wow, two girls. That is definitely not what I expected when I landed at Heathrow today."

Anna bit her lip.

"Good surprise? You're not disappointed that you won't have a Little Nick running around?"

He shook his head.

"No, not even possible to be disappointed." He smiled. "I don't know how to explain it, but as soon as I saw the images, it became real." He rubbed the centre of his chest with his free hand. "And … I just felt this incredible … love. My child, my children. And when I thought … when the technician went away, God, the thoughts that were running through my head. But then the doctor said twins! I can hardly believe it. But I just feel so…" He shrugged. "It's intense."

Any final hesitation that Anna had felt dissipated for good. Nick was fully on board with this. He'd told her how he felt, that he already loved his unborn daughters.

"You're going to be such a great, daddy," she said softly.

"I'm going to try."

"I know, and you'll be amazing."

"We'll have to think about names," he said with a smile. "I've always liked the name Ruby."

"Oh, that's sweet! I like that. What about Beth? Do you like that name?"

Nick nodded, but he had a distant, thoughtful look on his face.

"I suppose we should set a date. I dunno, shall we get married now?"

Anna didn't know whether to kiss him or slap him. Instead, she pulled herself up in bed and glared at him.

"That has to be the *least* romantic suggestion ever."

Nick smiled up at her, the slight salt and pepper in his beard not at all detracting from his youthful appearance.

"I don't know what you mean, luv. That was heartfelt, that was!"

Anna flopped down on the bed again. If he'd asked her six months ago whether she wanted to get married, she'd have jumped at it, but right now, she had other priorities.

"No, let's wait until the babies are born, then go somewhere sunny and relaxing—a family vacation. We could rent a big villa and invite my mom and your parents, Trish, Brendan and any of the guys you want to invite. I think we've got enough going on without planning a wedding, too."

Nick squinted at her.

"You sure? We could do it quick and quiet at a Registry Office. What about Marylebone Town Hall?"

Anna scowled.

"No way! I'm only getting married once, so I want it to be somewhere lovely, not a Registry Office!"

Nick grinned.

"Marylebone is famous. Paul McCartney married Linda there."

"I don't care! I want somewhere with sunshine!"

Nick shrugged.

"Fair enough. We'll do it next year. When I'm not playing."

Anna's breath hitched.

"Not playing?"

Nick nodded.

"The Cuirassiers offered me a two year contract—I turned them down."

Anna swallowed.

"Really? You've decided? I mean, you're sure this is what you want? You love playing there!"

Nick rolled on his side to face her.

"Yes, I like playing for them and the season is going well."

"But ... you don't want to stay?"

And the words she didn't say hung in the air: *while you can; while you're fit enough.*

Nick smiled, his eyes warm and sincere.

"I know I'm not the sharpest pencil in the box," he began, earning Anna's frown, "but everything I want is right here. I'm sorry it's taken so long to work that out."

He held her hand and kissed it, then kissed her belly, his new favourite resting place for his lips.

"But ... you love playing again! And the Cuirassiers have offered you another two years…"

Nick was shaking his head the whole time.

"No, I'm not losing a minute more of watching our kids grow up than I have to." He sighed. "That minute when the technician buggered off to find a doctor, that was the longest minute of my life. Nothing else mattered but that the babies were healthy. Not that we knew it was two of 'em then. All I wanted to know was that the baby was okay and that you were okay. Winning didn't matter, rugby didn't matter. What matters is what we have here. I don't have the fire for it anymore. Here, with you and our babies, that's where I want to be."

Gently, he ran his forefinger under Anna's eyes, feeling the wetness of tears.

"You're it for me, Anna."

CHAPTER 31

THE CAMPAIGN THAT NICK HAD SHOT with Cee Cee was timed to release just before Christmas, and suddenly the adverts for the top-end perfume were everywhere.

Predictably, his teammates plastered the locker room with the pictures torn out of magazines and newspapers, and Nick had to endure comments about the darkly erotic images and Cee Cee's extreme youth.

It brought back all the feelings of unease and increased them a hundred per cent. Nick didn't think the images looked like him, and his eyes seemed to blaze with fury.

The perfume soared in popularity leading up to the holiday season, but the pictures only reminded Nick of the frustration he'd felt being in New York, and his disgust at the dual standards of the modelling industry.

Cee Cee sent him a text message with smiley emojis and a lot of dollar signs. He hoped she was happy.

He was just pulling another graffitied photocopy of the ad off his locker, one that had given him horns and a tail, when Nick heard his phone ringing. He almost missed Mark Lipman's call as he stood dripping in the locker room at the Cuirassiers stadium having just finished a gruelling training session.

He flicked his hair out of his eyes, grabbed a towel with one hand and his ringing phone with the other.

"Nick! I've got something you're going to want to see—I'm emailing it to you now. I'll stay on the line while you read it."

Nick wrapped the towel around his waist, ignoring the drops of water that trickled down his chest and back.

He opened the email and read it through while Mark was on speakerphone.

"Who's Renata de Luca?" Nick asked.

"She's the editor who worked on Molly's book. And this email from her proves that they knew that you'd say no to a photoshoot with Molly and so deliberately misrepresented who they were. Your contract stipulated a romance novel cover shoot, correct?"

"That's what I was told, yes."

Nick could hear the excitement in Mark's voice.

"Yes! Exactly! My dear boy, this is the break we need! Because in law, any false statement made to induce a party to enter into a contract (even if it's not a term of the contract) may still give rise to rights and remedies. This leads us to examine the characteristics of an actionable representation, the differing types of misrepresentation, that is to say, misrepresentation, misleading or deceptive conduct. *Prima facie*, Nick, you have a very good case here for fraudulent misrepresentation."

Nick was listening hard, a spark of hope inside him, but Mark's legal language was difficult to understand.

Mark hurried on.

"If the judge agrees with you that the misrepresentation is fraudulent, you can recover damages for deceit in respect of the fraud, and the contract is voidable in equity and at common law."

Nick felt the tension of expectation fill his body, the type of positive energy that enabled him to sprint the length of a rugby field and score an impossible try.

"So this email proves that Molly's publishers lied in the contract? We can force them to drop the case?"

Mark laughed happily.

"Better than that, my dear boy! Your lawyers will draft a letter saying that you're taking the publishers to court for deceit in respect of fraud. Forget the contract, that's gone. And what's more, if this goes public, you can sue the publishers for defamation, *and* reiterate that you'll be suing them for infliction of emotional distress, to whit: 'If settlement is not reached we will execute our right, against your client, to seek damages for intentional infliction of emotional distress'. QED."

Nick was breathing hard as if he'd just been running, his phone clamped to his ear.

He'd won. He could finally get rid of Molly for good.

"One question, Mark: how did we get hold of this email?"

There was a long pause.

"I thought you might ask that. Yes, it's a good point. And I'm not at liberty to give full disclosure. But I will say this: it turns out that having daughters whose friends intern at a wide variety of companies, including publishers of somewhat dubious celebrity memoirs, and said friends remember that you were kind to them when they were invited to the Members Room at a certain rugby club that shall remain nameless … well, let's just say that they feel more loyalty to you than to a certain media whore who may or may have not called her 'a tea girl with ugly shoes and a fat arse'. I speculate, of course."

Nick laughed grimly.

"That sounds like Molly."

"So," said Mark, "the email has been handed over to the lawyers on both sides as part of the discovery process, and Molly's team are seeking settlement. You could choose to sue. How do you want to proceed?"

Nick ran his free hand over his face, tugging on his damp beard. Ahead, the road divided, and there were two paths he could take. A part of him wanted to punish Molly for her lies and deceit; part of him wanted revenge, wanted her to suffer the way she'd made Anna and himself suffer. But if he'd learned anything at all in his 35 years on the planet, it was this: hating Molly hadn't brought him happiness. The love he felt for Anna and their unborn children eclipsed all the negative emotions associated with his ex-.

And now he had the power to crush her completely, he found that forgetting her and moving on with his own life was more than enough for him.

"Tell the lawyers to send the letter, but to accept an offer of costs. That's all."

Mark sucked in a surprised breath.

"No reparations? You're sure, Nick?"

There was a short pause.

"Yes, I'm sure. I just want it to be over and done with. But also tell the lawyers to make it known that if Molly goes to the Press with any part of this, I will sue them. The chance of losing any of her own money should keep her quiet."

"It's your decision, Nick. But for the record, I think you're making the right choice." Mark's voice was quiet. "I'm proud of you, son."

Nick smiled to himself.

"One more thing: could you email me the address of a certain friend of your daughter, so I can thank her?"

Mark laughed.

"Unfortunately, I don't think that would be a good idea in case word got out. But I can tell you that a certain young lady happens to have a birthday coming up next month, so perhaps you could send her a little something to help her celebrate?"

Nick grinned.

"Thanks, Mark. For everything."

"You are very welcome, my boy. Send my regards to your dear fiancée for me. I hope to have supper with you next time you're both in London."

The call ended and Nick inhaled deeply, feeling lighter than he had in a long time. And the first person he wanted to share that with was Anna.

Of course it was, because he was desperately in love with her—and man enough to admit it.

"SO LET ME GET this right," Brendan said, waving his third glass of champagne at Anna. "It's slam dunk and Fuck You, Mouldy McKinney! You ain't taking *us* to court for breach of contract, we're taking *you* to court for deceit in respect of the fraud; fuck the contract because that's gone, baby. And if this shit goes public and you taint Nick as an arsehole, he'll do you for defamation; *and* just to tidy this up nicely … here you go … you've caused us so much stress because of this shit, he's suing you for infliction of emotional distress. Kiss my delectable derrière, bitch! Mwah! Hasta la vista! Bon voyage and Goodnight Vienna!"

Anna giggled over her orange juice as Brendan held forth in the middle of the fashionable Soho House in Covent Garden, thoroughly enjoying himself.

When Nick had phoned with the news, Brendan had immediately insisted that they glam themselves up and go out to celebrate. Anna had resisted at first, feeling tired and with swelling ankles at the end of a long day, but it had been the right thing to do. The two potential court cases had been hanging over them since the summer; being free of that burden was definitely something to celebrate. Of course, it would have been better if Nick was there with them.

"You're enjoying this, aren't you, Bren?" she asked teasingly.

"You bet your sweet little baby bump I am!"

Anna smiled.

"Well, Nick only threatened the 'infliction of emotional distress' because attack was our best form of defence, but now the whole thing can just go away," and she waved her hand as if the court cases were wafting through the air.

Brendan pouted.

"We're not going to sue her even a little bit?"

Anna shook her head.

"No. You know Nick prefers the laidback approach, and now he knows we don't have to go to court, he's come over all Zen and is willing to let it go. I wouldn't say he's quite at the forgive and forget stage, but it's the right thing for him." She gave a small smile. "It's the right thing for us. Just thinking about that woman raises my blood pressure at least ten points and I really don't need that kind of stress, especially now."

Brendan sighed theatrically.

"Spoilsport."

Anna winked at him and raised her alcohol-free drink in a silent toast.

At that moment, Jason Oduba strode back from the bathroom, his 6' 6" frame cutting a swathe through the minor celebrities and those enjoying drinking without being approached for selfies: Soho House was for members only and very exclusive. Anna had her membership as a perk of working for *Loose Women*, although she rarely took advantage of it.

Jason had somehow miraculously appeared at the club half-an-hour after she'd arrived with Brendan, and Anna suspected that Nick had sent him to act as a babysitter.

The huge rugby player glanced at Brendan, still waving his champagne glass, and gave a tight smile.

"Time to make a move, buddy. Nick gave me strict instructions to make sure Anna gets home at a reasonable time."

Brendan blinked at him owlishly.

"We only got here three dinks … I mean three drinks ago. She's not going to turn into a pumpkin—well, not for another four months. The night is young and so am I!"

Jason leaned down and whispered something to Brendan that made him sit up straight, seeming a lot less tipsy than he had a few seconds earlier.

"Yes, right, gotcha. Anna-banana, it's time for mums-to-be to go home for an early night and a cup of Ovaltine."

Anna waved them off even as she yawned and rubbed her temples, willing away the persistent headache that had plagued her for two days.

"Oval— what? Aw, thanks for caring, guys, but I'm okay for a few minutes. One more drink and then we call it a night?" She yawned again. "God, I used to be able to work all day and party all night. Not anymore."

"That's because you're cooking a couple of buns in your woman-oven," said Brendan in a hushed voice that probably reached the other side of the room.

Anna wrinkled her nose.

"You know, I never thought how gross that sounded, a bun in the oven, until you talked about my 'woman-oven', Bren."

He giggled nervously, batting his eyelashes at Jason.

"Ooh, the Dark Destroyer wants to go. Come on, Annie! Mush! Mush!"

"I'm not a sled dog, Bren!"

But then Anna saw why they'd been trying to hurry her along—Molly McKinney and entourage—one bored-looking 19 year-old soccer player, a rising star on the Tottenham Hotspurs team—had just walked into the bar.

Brendan raised his eyebrows and stared belligerently.

"Is she babysitting him?"

Anna's heart started to gallop. Of all the bars in all the world, why did she have to run into the one person she truly detested? She wasn't yet as sanguine about the bitch as Nick. She wasn't sure she ever could be.

Anger in its purest form shot through her, making her almost dizzy with rage.

Molly saw them, paused dramatically, then stalked toward them on five inch heels, her body in danger of toppling over from the enormous, inflated boobs glued to her thin frame.

Brendan lifted his chin to speak, but Anna reached for his hand, warning him not to. It would be too horrible if they got sued for slander just when both the court cases were in the past. And she had no doubt that Molly was capable of such a low act.

Molly ignored Brendan, glanced at Jason standing protectively behind, then glared down at Anna.

"Oh, look who's lowering the tone. If they're letting just anyone in here now, I'll have to cancel my membership."

Anna sighed. Nick said he wanted to leave his ex- in the past, but like the proverbial bad penny, she kept on showing up.

"I have nothing to say to you, Molly. There's nothing here for you. Please leave."

Molly seemed surprised by Anna's calm tone, irritated even, if the narrowing of her eyes was anything to go by.

"Life is like a box of chocolates—it doesn't last long if you're fat. And you've been piling on the pounds," she said nastily. "Is that why Nicky went to play in France? To get away from your fat arse?"

Anna just stared, an incredulous expression on her face.

"Oh my God, Mouldy McKinney, your wit precedes you," quipped Brendan. "Is there any point to you? At all? Anything? No, I thought not."

Anna's anger lessened a notch as a small, amused smile threatened to break free. Brendan was right—there was no point to Molly. She lived her life on a carousel of stage-managed drama that was as pointless as it was useless.

"I never knew what Nicky saw in you," Molly continued viciously, "but then again he's away more than he's home, isn't he? He's probably just tired of you and too nice to tell you to your face."

Anna cocked her head on one side looking at Molly, studying her heavily made-up face and unhappy mouth.

"Don't you get tired of it?" Anna asked, genuinely interested to know the answer. "Don't you get tired of being so bitter?"

Molly's eyes widened.

"You're a man-stealer, a liar and a home-wrecker!" she screeched.

Anna's blood pressure began to rise again, and her determination not to engage was lost in a surge of anger.

"That's complete bullshit. We both know the truth, but you keep spouting this crap as if you actually believe it! Nick caught you with his best friend, actually saw you both bent over the couch, fucking. You're a liar and a cheat, and yet you play the victim card over and over. You had the love of a good man and you threw it away by screwing his best friend. And then you were stupid enough to get caught."

Anna's voice was exasperated, but Molly pointed a long, accusing fingernail at Anna.

"He would have come back to me, I know he would. But there you were, pretending to be his friend, pretending to be his psychiatrist..."

"Psychologist."

"What-the-fuck-ever! He would have come back!"

Anna gave a brittle, disbelieving laugh.

"No, he wouldn't. Not ever. Not in a million years."

Molly's face creased with anger.

"You're a slut! And American! I know that you were shagging your teacher at university. You come over here and pinch our men..."

Anna gaped.

"Are you for real? This isn't a reality TV show. Do you believe half the bullshit coming out of your mouth?" She turned to Brendan and Jason. "I've had enough of her brand of crazy—let's just leave."

"And another thing," Molly shrieked. "Who did you pay off to make my publishers lose their balls?"

Anna shook her head and gave Molly a pitying smile.

"The case was fraudulent and you knew that," she said softly.

"Nick was paid to be on the cover of my book! He broke the contract! He..."

Anna's attempts to stay calm failed and her voice became heated.

"Nick would never have knowingly have agreed to do a photoshoot with you. God, are you completely delusional?" As she wrestled to keep herself in check, her voice turned icy cold. "Wait, don't answer that—obviously you live in a fantasy world of self-deception. So I'll spell it out for you."

"Ooh, this'll be good," Brendan whispered as Anna rose to her feet, facing Molly, her eyes flashing with restrained fury.

"First," she bit out, "you're a cheat, and Nick despises cheats; second, you're a liar—see first point; third, he calls you his 'worst mistake'; fourth, he never wants to see your lying, manipulative, bony ass again; fifth, leave us the fuck alone!"

"You're not even attractive!" Molly yelled. "I don't know what he sees in you!"

"Nick loves me," Anna said firmly, crossing her arms in front of her, "and one of the reasons is because I'm not a raving bitch."

"You tell her, Annie!" Brendan cheered.

Jason stepped in front of Anna as Molly started to raise her hand.

"Don't even think about it," he growled. "Why don't you sod off and take your toy boy with you?"

"Fuck the lot of you!" Molly yelled, frustrated that the conversation hadn't gone her way. "This isn't over!"

That was one of the worst things Molly could have said to Anna: she so badly wanted this bitch to stay in the past.

She felt a wave of dizziness overcome her and she sank back to the couch she'd been sitting on. Her headache became a pounding fist in her head. She was fighting to breathe evenly. Anna squeezed her eyes shut, afraid that she was about to faint.

"Annie, are you okay? You've gone as white as a sheet," Brendan gasped, grabbing her hand.

Anna couldn't speak, willing the dizziness away.

"Anna?" Jason crouched down in front of her, his kind face worried. "Get her some water!" he shouted at the surprised bartender.

Anna felt the cold glass pushed into her hand and she took a small sip. Her hands were shaking so badly, Jason held the glass to stop it from slipping. Her pulse was racing, her heart hammering against her ribs, and a thin sheen of sweat coated her entire body.

"I … I don't feel so good," she whispered. "Will you take me home, please?"

Jason glanced at a distressed-looking Brendan.

"I think we should take her straight to the hospital, mate."

Brendan nodded briskly.

"Yes, I agree."

"I'll go get me car," Jason shouted over his shoulder as he rushed off.

"Huh, and they call *me* a drama queen," said Molly, her hands on her hips and an unimpressed scowl on her pretty face.

"You stupid trout-pout trollop!" snapped Brendan, still holding Anna's hand, dabbing at her damp forehead with a paper napkin. "Has the Botox gone to your head? You've caused her enough stress for a lifetime—and she's pregnant!"

Molly's mouth opened and shut like a landed fish, her expression baffled, her forehead trying to wrinkle in thought. As Brendan's words sank in, she blinked rapidly, her eyes darting around at the people who'd been watching the slanging match.

"Is she alright?" she asked softly.

"Do I look like a bloody doctor?" Brendan shouted impatiently, on the verge of hysteria. "Of course she's not alright!"

But before Molly could speak again, Jason returned, scooped Anna into his beefy arms, and hurried from the room with Brendan hot on his heels, speed-dialling the Royal Free Hospital.

CHAPTER 32

"*M*ON AMI, YOUR PHONE IS GIVING me a headache!"
Nick was standing at the bar talking to Inoke and turned to
see Bernard waving his phone at him.

After their most recent home-win, they'd all gone to *Chez Felix*
for a meal. It was part of Nick's relentless team-building activities.
Laurent had come and was miserable as usual, insisting on sitting
and drinking alone, but at least he'd come. He and Grégoire avoided
each other as much as they could and were coolly polite to each other
when they couldn't, but that was an improvement from fist fights
during a training session.

"Brendan is calling you," said Bernard, handing the vibrating
phone to Nick.

At the mention of Brendan's name, Grégoire glanced up, a half-
hopeful look on his face.

"Hi, Bren. Did you have a good … what? When? What happened?" He listened intently. "Which hospital?"

He felt the blood drain from his face and he gripped the bar with his free hand. He was falling off a cliff, the ground was roaring up towards him…

He realised that Brendan was still talking.

"Yeah, I'm still here. I'll get there as soon as I can … no, I don't care. Tell her I'll be there. Bren, I … just … thank you."

He ended the call and turned on his heel, his head thrumming with the news.

Anna, my Anna.

She was ill, and he was in another fucking country, a thousand miles away, hours away. *Stupid! Stupid! Stupid!*

"Nick?"

Bernard took a pace towards him, his forehead creased with concern.

"Is everything okay."

"Anna's in hospital. I need to go."

Bernard looked stunned for a long moment, then snapped into action.

"I will drive you to the airport."

Several of Nick's teammates mumbled their sympathies, but he hardly heard them, nodding curtly.

Nick jumped into Bernard's passenger seat as his friend revved the engine. They screeched out of the car park and were soon racing along the road to the airport.

His clumsy fingers flew over his phone as he booked the first flight he could, which meant changing at Paris.

"Shit! I can get as far as Paris, but there's no connecting Heathrow flight until the morning!"

He grimaced, his frustration, his desperation painfully clear.

"What about you fly to Paris then take the train, the Eurostar?"
Bernard asked. "That could work."

Nick felt a cold numbness seeping through him. If he lost Anna,
he would lose himself. He couldn't lose her. He couldn't.

All the bullshit of the last year, everything he'd put her through
… why weren't they together right now? Why was he in France when
she needed him in London?

How could I be so fucking selfish?

He forced himself to concentrate on checking the times of the
train and how many minutes he'd have to make the connection: it
was tight, very tight. But if luck was on his side…

He bought the ticket anyway, sending up a quick prayer to the
universe.

With nothing more to do than watch the night-time countryside
slip past, he phoned his mum.

She answered on the first ring.

"Hello, luv! This is a nice surprise! How are you?"

"It's Anna," he said gruffly, his throat tightening as he said the
words. "She's been taken to hospital. I don't know—it looks serious.
I'm on my way to London now."

There was a stunned silence.

"Oh Nick! Oh, I'm so sorry! What can we do?"

"I don't know … I don't think there's anything … she's in the
best place. I just need to get there."

He felt so fucking helpless.

"Have you told her mother?"

Nick nodded, even though his mother couldn't see him.

"Brendan called her. She's getting the first flight out of JFK.
Look, will you tell Dad and Trish for me?"

"Yes, of course, luv. Try not to worry. Well, that's silly, I know you will until you've seen her. Just look after yourself. Give our love to Anna, and tell her to look after my grandbabies!"

His mother's voice was so soothing, he was glad he'd called her. Not that she could do anything.

Nick felt helpless. All his strength, all the hours he'd spent in the gym building that strength was pointless, useless. It couldn't help Anna. It couldn't save her. He couldn't do anything.

Nick leaned back in the car, pressing the heels of his hands against his eyes as the miles passed by far too slowly.

At the airport, Bernard quickly explained Nick's frazzled appearance and lack of luggage. The airline employees changed from faintly hostile to accommodating and helpful in a second, and Nick began his slow journey back to London.

Anna was frightened. It had all happened so quickly: one moment she was celebrating with Brendan and Jason, and then suddenly she was in Accident & Emergency at the Royal Free Hospital in Hampstead.

She clamped her hands around her stomach as she tried to steady her breathing, tears running down her face.

Jason carried her to a hard, plastic chair and made her look at him.

"You've got this, doc. You're going to be fine, yeah?"

Brendan was gripping her shoulder almost painfully, his breathing as ragged as hers.

Anna nodded weakly.

There were so many people in A&E and the waiting area was

crowded. Jason pushed to the front and demanded someone check on Anna.

"I need some help here! She's pregnant with twins and really dizzy—she can hardly stand!"

A triage nurse bustled forward, her presence immediately reassuring.

"Okay, let's get some details here. Any spotting?"

"No," Anna whispered.

"Okay, that's a good start," and she took Anna's pulse, giving nothing away in her expression.

Anna was taken by wheelchair to a curtained bed in the Medical Assessment Unit as the nurse took her details. And then they waited, all the while her hands clasped around her belly as she whispered to her babies, begging them not to leave her, begging them to be alright.

Finally, another nurse took Anna's blood pressure and although it was very high, reassured Anna that she seemed to be out of immediate danger. A third nurse took a urine sample to see if there was too much protein in it—apparently that was bad. The second nurse came back with the equipment for a sonogram and left it there without a word.

And finally, over an hour after they'd first walked through the door, they saw a doctor, who walked into the curtained area studying a set of notes.

"My babies? They're okay?"

The doctor smiled, introduced herself and sat beside Anna while Jason and Brendan stood.

"Let's take a look, shall we, Ms. Scott?"

Squelchy gel was squirted over her and Anna held her breath, holding Brendan's hand in a death grip as the wand was pressed against her stomach. Immediately, the dual heartbeats sounded through the tiny booth.

Tears of relief leaked from Anna's eyes and Brendan was red-eyed, too. Jason pulled out a tiny gold cross he wore around his neck and kissed it.

"You'll be pleased to know that everything looks good in there. I'll need to give you an exam just to be thorough."

"What's wrong with me?" Anna asked. "I wondered … are you checking for pre-eclampsia?"

The doctor smiled kindly.

"Do you have some medical training?"

"Yes, but I haven't practised in a while."

"Well, I'd have to agree with your assessment. The symptoms for pre-eclampsia can look very dramatic, and of course although many cases are mild—such as yours—the condition can lead to serious complications for both mother and baby if it's not monitored and treated."

"I've been to all my pre-natal checks," Anna said defensively.

"Well, now we're aware of the condition, we can treat it," the doctor continued soothingly. "Being an older mother, and having twins, that can increase your chances of risk for pre-eclampsia.

Anna gritted her teeth.

"Are they IVF babies?"

Anna shook her head.

"We'll start you on a low dose of aspirin and take it from there."

"My babies, you're sure they're okay?" Anna asked, still needing reassurance.

The doctor nodded, her calmness helping Anna.

"There are no signs of distress. We'll need to admit you overnight to monitor you, just to make sure. But everything seems fine."

"You're sure? You're absolutely sure?"

Anna was getting herself all worked up, but Brendan held her hand, helping her to calm down. She wished it was Nick holding her hand.

Brendan seemed to read her mind.

"He'll be here soon, Annie. He's on his way."

It took four hours for them to find a bed for Anna. Four long, wearying hours where she lay on a narrow gurney in MAU, and Brendan and Jason tried to get comfortable sitting on hard hospital chairs as the minutes ticked by slowly.

Eventually, Anna was admitted into a ward with five other women, including an elderly lady who clearly suffered from dementia and cried out at frequent intervals. Even though it was night and they were supposed to be resting, alarms were going off and nurses were walking in and out, talking loudly.

Finally, Anna was moved to a single room, and exhausted and still afraid, she fell asleep.

Brendan and Jason tiptoed from the room.

ANNA WAS RESTING or trying to. The hospital bed was hard and she couldn't get comfortable, but the following morning she was feeling much better.

"You're thinking too hard, Annie," Brendan said, his voice gently critical. "You're supposed to be resting."

She sighed and rolled onto her back. She'd been advised to lie on her left side to take the pressure or restriction off certain veins that contributed to her elevated blood pressure.

She was so happy to see Brendan, freshly shaved and smelling divine.

"Have I told you lately that I love you?" Anna smiled.

"Yes, but a boy can never hear it enough," he announced, nodding his head.

He reached out and squeezed Anna's hand as Jason appeared. He grinned at the scene in front of him.

"Aw, you two are cute. Nick will be jealous!"

Brendan smiled at him sweetly.

"Actually, I heard one of the nurse's speculating on which of us was the daddy, or wondering if we were both daddies and Anna was our baby-mama donor."

Jason laughed loudly and smooched his lips at Brendan who looked faintly horrified.

"Give us a kiss then!"

"No! I might get straight cooties!" and he shuddered.

Jason pulled a face.

"It's 'cos I'm black, innit?"

"Because you're disgustingly hetero. It might be catching. Oh alright then, I'll try anything once."

Jason leaned down and laid a smacker on Brendan just as one of the nurses walked in. She smiled to herself, then took Anna's blood pressure for the millionth time.

Brendan fanned his face as Jason winked at the nurse.

Anna was enjoying the double-act; she wasn't enjoying being in hospital.

"Look, you guys," she said when the nurse had gone, "It's really sweet that you're here, but honestly, I'm fine. They're keeping me in for a few more hours until the obstetrician does the rounds. I'm not going anywhere," and she sighed again. "I think you should go home."

Brendan looked indignant.

"What kind of BFF abandons you in your hour of need? Anyway," he said, his feathers still slightly ruffled from Jason's kiss, "I'm rather enjoying being a knight in shining armour."

Jason nodded.

"I like the way your boy thinks, doc. He's alright."

Which was high praise from the big man. The tips of Brendan's ears turned pink.

"Jason is staying until it's time to pick up Nick, and I'm not going anywhere. We made a blood oath—without the icky blood."

Anna's eyes began to tear up again.

"Does he know about the pre-eclampsia? Have you told him?"

"Of course, Anna-banana! I called him last night after you were admitted. What kind of P.A. would I be if I hadn't done that?"

Anna forced a smile.

"How was he?"

"Relieved that you're okay and that the little currant buns are holding their own. He sends his love."

"Thank you," she sniffed.

"Oh my God, here come the waterworks again!" sighed Brendan.

Anna half-laughed, half-sobbed.

"I hate you, Bren!"

"It's her hormones," Brendan confided to Jason as if she wasn't there. "Just watch out when Nick gets here—he won't stand a chance. She'll be climbing him like an indoor gym. Mind you," he said with a side-eye at Jason, "I've often thought of doing the same thing."

NICK ARRIVED AT the hospital tense and irritable, his eyes burning with tiredness.

Brendan's call when Anna had been admitted had gone a long

way to taking the edge off his fear, but he wouldn't be completely reassured until he saw her, until he held her in his arms.

When he finally found her room, Brendan was asleep in the chair next to her bed, and Anna was watching him with a gentle smile on her face.

She saw Nick immediately and her lips trembled.

"I'm here, babe. I'm here."

Nick didn't know how to hold her, afraid of damaging her somehow, but Anna held out her arms to him and he sank into an awkward half-crouch, burying his face in her neck, breathing her in and trying to ignore the scent of hospital all around him.

They held each other for a long time until Nick's back was groaning. When he finally stood up, massaging his tight muscles, Brendan had slipped out of the room. Neither of them heard him go.

He slumped into Brendan's chair gratefully, still holding Anna's hand.

"How are you?"

"Embarrassed mostly," she said with a wry smile. "They'll definitely remember me at Soho House—I know how to make an exit."

Nick didn't feel up to laughing about it—he was still worried as hell.

"What are the doctors saying?"

"That I can go home today, but I have to rest with my feet up and try to avoid getting stressed." She gave a tired laugh. "It's kind of ironic that I was celebrating not being stressed when all this happened."

"I'll fucking kill Molly!" Nick growled, his eyes hard.

"She did me a favour," Anna said softly.

"What?!" Nick's voice was too loud for the small room.

"Seriously. I could have gone on for weeks thinking that everything I was feeling was normal."

Nick frowned.

"You didn't tell me you were feeling bad."

Anna grimaced.

"Well, that's the point: pregnancy is a long list of feeling crappy. My hormones are all over the place and I have the weirdest emotions. I started crying when I saw an eggplant in the grocery store because they described it as an aubergine. I felt so sorry for it!"

Nick blinked.

"Um?"

"I know! It makes no sense, but I'm trying to explain to you. And then you get swollen ankles and feet. I said goodbye to pre-pregnancy shoes a month ago. You get gas, headaches and a weird craving for *Reese's Pieces* melted onto toast."

She didn't mention the haemorrhoids that were beginning to bother her, the constipation, heartburn, drooling at night, let alone the urgent and often need to pee.

"There's all this stuff that happens to your body, so I would have just gone on thinking that I was fine, but seeing Molly got me here and now they can keep monitoring me. And I'm not going to think about her for another second."

"But she…"

"I mean it, Nick! I never want to hear that woman's name again."

Nick gave in reluctantly.

"Okay." He paused. "You're really okay? You and the babies, you're all okay?"

"We're fine."

A different, older doctor arrived with the junior medic who had pulled the late shift, doing their rounds of the patients who'd come in during the night.

"Good morning, Anna. How are you feeling now?"

"Much better. A little tired. This is my fiancée, Nick."

The doctor smiled at him then focussed on Anna.

"Well, the good news is that the level of protein in your urine has dropped, and your blood pressure has also levelled off. Now, Anna, you have to take things a lot slower. You're an older mother," Anna winced at the reminder, "and you're carrying twins. Both of these factors increase your chance of having pre-eclampsia, but by having regular check-ups, avoiding processed food and caffeine, and taking plenty of rest, you'll be fine. If you have any nausea, changes in vision, or shortness of breath, come back immediately."

From the look on Nick's face, Anna knew that she'd have a hard job of convincing him that she was going to be alright. When he'd walked in the door, he'd been carrying the weight of the world on his shoulders.

But despite the suffocating coddling that she knew would be his way of coping, she'd never felt more loved.

Anna was recovering from shock and fear, but Nick still felt his heart racing when he thought that something could have happened to her and the babies, something that could still happen, and something that was beyond his control. When he thought about losing her, his chest tightened and adrenaline crackled inside him. But there was no one to fight, no way of defending her.

He tried to be laidback for her sake, but inside, he was crumbling.

Every time he looked at her, his heart jolted painfully, reminding him of what he could have lost. The shadowy memories of his sudden flight from Carcassonne would stay with him for a long time. He was afraid to let her out of his sight.

Even when Anna was allowed to go home later that day, he almost had a panic attack leaving the room she was in, and had to check and re-check that she was okay. He'd insisted on buying a blood pressure monitor on the way back from the hospital, and took a reading every hour. He knew that he was starting to annoy her, but he couldn't seem to stop.

"Nick, I'm going to take a bath," said Anna, watching him pace the room.

"Right! I'll run it for you!"

He heard her voice calling after him that she was perfectly capable of running her own bath, but he was already turning on the taps.

Then he turned and caught his reflection in the mirror.

Calm down. She's fine. The babies are fine. The doctors wouldn't have let her home if she wasn't okay.

He sucked in a breath, catching the faint scent of Anna's perfume in the bathroom. It was so normal. It helped, but he still felt that prickle of anxiety under his skin.

When the bath was half full, he poured in a capful of Anna's favourite bubble bath, and watched the foam rise around the sides of the tub.

He hated feeling weak, and seeing Anna in a hospital bed had brought back memories, bad memories, of another time when he'd been weak, when he hadn't been in control.

How do I handle this? How do I push the fear away?

Nick jogged down the stairs to tell Anna that her bath was ready. He had to force himself to watch her climb unsteadily to her feet and take the stairs slowly, as if each step was exhausting. He wanted to carry her up the stairs, but the last twenty-four hours had taught him to act casual, to be calm. To be 'Zen', as Anna put it.

It was bloody hard.

His heartrate slowed minutely as she lay back in the warm water with a sigh, her warm, brown eyes catching his, and she reached out a foamy hand to him.

"There's three of us in this tub—think we can fit in a fourth?"

He grinned at her, his eyes lighting as he stepped out of his clothes in a few seconds and sank into the warm water gratefully.

Anna scooted forward so he could sit behind her and stretch out his long legs either side of her.

Her damp hair tickled his chest as she leaned back and closed her eyes.

"What's going through your head?" she murmured. "I can hear your thoughts crashing around from here."

Where do I start?

Nick couldn't sort out one thought from all the noise in his head.

Anna carried on speaking.

"They'll be doing scans every four weeks from now on to make sure everything is okay, and I'll have antenatal check-ups every two weeks. I'm going to be fine. If I thought telling you to stop worrying would help, I would. But time will tell." She paused. "You know that there's a good chance I'll need a caesarean. It's not a hundred per cent, but it's a possibility that we need to prepare for."

Nick swallowed, but didn't voice his fears. He stroked her hair back and leaned forward to kiss her temple.

Anna smiled.

"Well, they haven't decided yet, but if that happens, I'm going to have a hard time lifting the babies after they're born. I'd like my mom to stay a while. Is that okay?"

Nick closed his eyes.

Looking after Anna was *his* job. He hated that having Anna's mother take over was necessary.

"Yes, of course, luv," he said. "Whatever you want."

"Thank you. I'm so glad she'll be here tomorrow. I can't wait to see her." Anna was silent for a moment. "I was scared. Really scared."

"I know," he said his voice low. "So was I. But everything's going to be fine now."

And he hoped that the more he said it, the more he'd believe it.

CHAPTER 33

NICK HAD TEN DAYS OFF—TEN precious days to celebrate Christmas and enjoy being in London with Anna and his family.

The doctors had sent her home but advised bed rest, advice that Nick was taking very seriously and refusing to let Anna lift anything heavier than a cup of tea.

He lay in bed, listening to the central heating as it ticked over early on Christmas morning. He'd been awake for hours, watching Anna sleep, seeing her profile emerge from the fading night.

She'd been breathing deeply and evenly, and watching her grounded him. Terror of the unknown had made him feel like he was drifting again, untethered, but Anna was his anchor, keeping him safe while the stormy seas of his fears battered him. He breathed with her, one breath at a time, rationalizing his panic into something manageable.

Instead, he began to tick off the tasks that still needed to be done. They'd already started stockpiling twice as much of everything for the babies via the joys of online shopping, and he'd bought a deluxe baby buggy for two—the Formula One of strollers with extra wide wheels so he could take the twins out for a run with him.

He'd painted one of the spare bedrooms in neutral colours because Anna had insisted that pre-programming the girls with all things pink was not happening on her watch. Nick didn't mind—his babies could be anything they wanted to be.

In the room down the hall, he heard the door open as Anna's mother padded down the stairs.

Nick slid quietly out of bed, pulled on sweatpants, socks and a long-sleeved t-shirt and went down to the kitchen to join her in an early morning cup of tea.

Despite his months in America and France, he still preferred tea first thing in the morning.

He found Susie fiddling with the coffee machine.

"Good morning, Nick," she said brightly. "I hope I didn't wake you?"

"No, I've been awake for a couple of hours," he admitted with a shrug of his shoulders.

She smiled at him sympathetically.

"My advice to you is to get all the sleep you can now!" and she laughed. "I don't think Anna slept through the night until she was three."

Nick grimaced and Susie patted his hand sympathetically.

"Now, why don't you tell me what's keeping you awake?"

He pressed his lips together and turned to fill the kettle.

"I haven't slept much since she came home from the hospital."

Anna's mother reached across the table and squeezed his hand.

"Oh, Nick."

She fixed herself a cup of coffee and sighed as she sipped at the dark brew.

"Did Anna tell you that I had pre-eclampsia when I was carrying her?"

Nick's eyes widened.

"No!"

"It sounds terrifying, and of course if it's untreated it can be serious, but now Anna is being closely monitored, she'll be fine." She glanced at him over her coffee cup. "Coddling her isn't what she needs right now."

He pulled a face.

"Is that what I'm doing?"

Susie gave a soft smile.

"Perhaps just a little. My daughter is a smart cookie. Now she knows she has to slow down and rest completely, she'll do what she needs to do." She sipped her coffee. "Have you two decided how you're going to manage the travelling and living arrangements for the next few months?"

Nick nodded.

"Anna mustn't travel to France—I'll come back as often as I can and…"

Susie sighed.

"I asked if *you two* have decided."

Nick paused.

"The doctor said she needs bed rest."

"Yes, but just for a few weeks until they've got her blood pressure under control. Then she can ease back into a gentler version of her life." She glanced at him over the rim of her coffee cup. "Let Anna set the pace."

"Did she say something to you?"

"I'm simply suggesting that you should discuss it together," Susie answered diplomatically. "Ask her what *she* wants, and what she feels she can cope with. Spending time with you in the south of France might be exactly what she needs, away from the hustle and bustle of city life. Just think about it." She smiled. "Oh, and Nick? Merry Christmas!"

He grinned at her.

"Merry Christmas, Susie."

Brendan arrived two hours later with a gust of cold air and infectious laugh.

"The party can start now! Nana-banana, you look beautiful!" and he swept Anna's mother into a hug, followed by Anna and Nick, then he marched into the living room and dumped a huge pile of gift-wrapped parcels under the little Christmas tree.

"God, I need sherry!"

Anna raised her eyebrows from where she was resting on the sofa.

"Sherry? Really?"

"It's retro—I only drink it at Christmas." He smiled wistfully. "Grég gave it to me—he said it was so English that it reminded him of me."

"You could have invited him, Bren," Anna said gently.

Brendan shook his head.

"No, he's seeing his family and…" he gave her a hopeful smile. "He's telling them about me."

"Oh wow! That's great!" Anna clapped her hands. "Wait, are you worried?"

Brendan shrugged a shoulder.

"Not really. They know he's gay and they're okay with that." He gave a light laugh. "They'll probably be more shocked that I'm English."

He made himself comfortable and produced a bottle of dry

sherry from his shoulder bag, then proceeded to share it with Susie, until they were both giggly.

Shortly after that, Nick's parents and sister arrived. It was only the second time that the parents had met, but thankfully everyone got along well, laughing at Brendan's outrageous antics and his version of the Queen's annual Christmas address to the nation.

Nick looked around at his family, everyone he loved in the same room, and felt that sliver of peace expand inside him.

Later that afternoon, when he'd insisted on carrying Anna up to bed so she could take a nap, he wrapped the duvet around her protectively.

"Don't go yet," she said. "I love having everyone here, but I need a little alone time with you," and she reached up to massage away the lines of worry from his forehead. "It's going to be okay."

Nick closed his eyes as he stretched out beside her, carefully surrounding her with his large body.

"I know. It's just…"

She stroked his hair, her touch soothing.

"You have to try not to worry, Nick. We have a lot of weeks to get through yet. You'll make yourself ill if you carry on like this. The doctors will keep a close eye on me. And I promise I'll be sensible."

That drew a small smile from him.

"I know, luv. I can't help it. When I got Brendan's call…" His voice faltered. "I want to be here with you. I don't want to go back to Carcassonne. I'll break my contract and…"

Anna grasped his hand.

"Nick, no. You've worked so hard and the team is starting to win now. You have a good chance of making it through the Cup Final. I don't want you to give that up."

He propped himself on his elbow to meet her gaze.

"You and the babies are more important than any game of rugby.

I want to be here. I don't want to make the same mistake again."

"Honey, you can't watch me 24/7."

Nick looked as if he wanted to argue.

"It wouldn't be good for either one of us," Anna said gently. "Yes, I'm going to rest as much as the doctors want me to; I'm going to listen to my body because I want to take good care of our babies. But, Nick, I *will* be going back to work … ssh, let me finish. It won't be full-time and I'll take every precaution, but doing nothing isn't an option. You know me too well to think that it could be."

Nick sighed and lay back on the pillow.

"I don't know what I'm doing."

"Neither of us do. It's uncharted territory, but we'll work it out. I have a check-up next week and then the doctor can help us put together a plan that works for both of us, okay?"

Nick closed his eyes and nodded.

"Okay."

IN THE WEEKS and months that followed, Nick measured time by the progress of the Cuirassiers up the league table, and by the progress of Anna's growing belly.

Reluctantly, he'd agreed to go back to France and captain his team, but his heart was still in London. They'd both realised that too much travelling wasn't going to work for Anna, so this time it was Nick who was spending his days off catching flights. Sometimes Grégoire came with him, staying with Brendan at his flat in Hoxton.

Anna was pleased to see her friend so happy and crossed her fingers that it wouldn't end badly. She'd become very fond of Grég, too.

Nick made as many of Anna's hospital appointments as he could, and each subsequent scan showed two healthy babies developing at a good rate. The obstetrician had recommended that Anna have a caesarean, and somewhat reluctantly, she'd agreed. The date was 15th April, and Nick felt a measure of relief in knowing exactly when his girls would be born.

He was with Anna in London when *Vogues Hommes International* was published, and Nick had to admit that the cover was a great shot. He was wearing a suit, but his shirt was open, showing just a hint of ink, and he was staring right at the camera, focused and intense, his blackened eye obvious.

"You look hot, dangerously hot … or hotly dangerous," Brendan insisted, scanning other photographs from the shoot that had been used on an inside spread.

Then he glanced up at his boyfriend and said something in rapid French that made Grégoire blush.

"Laurent will be jealous of Capitaine Nick," he said, in heavily accented English, making them all laugh.

"It's pretty cool having a fiancé who's a model," Anna teased him. "Although when it comes to getting makeup tips, you're quite a disappointment."

Nick squinted at her with a chagrined look.

"Yeah, yeah. But I really enjoyed working with Henri. He was a great bloke."

He dug the balls of his thumbs into the arches of Anna's poor, swollen feet, and she groaned appreciatively.

His dick was equally appreciative but he figured he'd probably better not think that way too much. Anna was very selective about love-making these days, and it was all entirely on her terms. But damn, she was sexy, all round and full of his babies.

There were only a couple of positions that were comfortable for her, but it all depended on how much her back was aching or how sore her breasts were.

"Have you thought anymore about what you're going to do with all those behind-the-scenes photos that you've taken?" she asked curiously. "I think the website portfolio is a great idea."

Nick nodded slowly. He wasn't very confident that anyone else would want to see his snaps from Massimo's studio, Manhattan, Miami and more. But it wasn't just Anna who had encouraged him—Brendan and Grégoire were also saying that he should display his work. Doing that online seemed the safest bet—not too personal.

Once again, Nick was locker room fodder for his teammates, but this time, Nick sensed an undercurrent of admiration that amused him. The French players took their designer clothing seriously. And, after all, it was *Vogue*.

He was inundated with offers, and even accepted one or two of them. He did a fun and flirty photoshoot with *IconEzine*, stripping from a dark suit to his briefs, in a series of photographs that gave the publishers one of their best-selling issues to date.

Finding that he could pick and choose was liberating, and the Cuirassiers were happy to support his growing celebrity for their small club.

Brendan spent as much time as possible with his boyfriend, more than he did with 'the old married couple' as he'd taken to calling Nick and Anna. He promised that he'd be in London with her when Nick couldn't, but Anna knew that Brendan missed Grégoire horribly when they weren't together.

It made her heart happy to see the growing love between them. But time ticked past faster and faster, and the date for her c-section was approaching.

SUSIE FLEW INTO Heathrow during Anna's 31st week, and the two women spent the time buying baby clothes and toys, and long afternoons chatting as Anna felt less and less like going out. She was happy to have her mother there, and it gave Brendan a few precious weeks to spend with Grégoire.

Two days before the c-section was scheduled, Nick arrived home excited and full of energy. Maybe even a little nervous.

Anna felt too uncomfortable to be scared—she just wanted her babies *out*.

They rested on the bed together, Nick stroking her enormous stomach as a wave of heat left Anna feeling hot and sweaty.

"It's going to be okay, isn't it?" she said softly.

"Yeah, and I'll talk to Beth and Ruby beforehand so they know the drill," he teased. Then he leaned down and spoke directly to her stomach. "No playing around until after the birth—your mum's nervous."

Anna laughed and tugged a lock of his unruly hair.

"I'm glad you're here," she said quietly.

He looked up, his honey-coloured eyes full of love.

"There's nowhere else I want to be."

On the morning of Anna's surgery, she lay on the sofa pale and tired, with her swollen feet on a cushion, She'd been uncomfortable for the last few nights and was very ready to birth the babies.

Nick walked into the room carrying her hospital bag with her overnight toiletries and all the extras that they'd told her to bring.

"We have plenty of time. I'll just put the bags in the car."

"Thank you," she said, her voice dragging in tiredness.

Nick leaned down to kiss her hair.

"We're in this together—me, you and the twins, family."

"Then you deliver them," she said grumpily.

"I can't believe how fast it's gone," said Nick, shaking his head and ignoring her bad mood. "Today we'll meet our girls. I'm going be a dad. Me! It's still not sunk in yet."

"Yeah, well you've got a couple of hours before it gets very real," she said huffily, as her stomach rumbled.

Thankfully, she didn't even feel hungry, which was just as well since she wasn't allowed to eat. She could have water up until two hours before the surgery—that was all.

Just as she was about to ask, Nick brought her a glass of warm water and another antacid tablet, prescribed to reduce stomach acids that could make her feel sick. She chewed it unenthusiastically.

"How are you feeling now?"

She rolled her eyes.

"Like a walrus!"

"Aw, no. You've hardly got any moustache at all."

She glared at him beadily.

"Not a good day to joke about it," she said tightly.

Nick kept his mouth shut. He'd been doing that a lot lately.

Anna's mom walked into the room, a slightly hesitant smile on her face.

"Ready to go?"

"Oh God, so ready!" Anna groaned, accepting Nick's help to haul herself off the sofa.

It was a short drive to hospital, so they were checked in a little early. Anna was ushered into a small room and reminded that she had to remove all her jewellery. Reluctantly, she removed her engagement ring and gave it to Nick for safe keeping. She hated taking it off.

"Don't worry," said Nick, seeming to read her mind. "You'll get it back in a few hours."

Arriving early was supposed to give Anna time to relax in her room, but she just became more and more nervous.

"It's going to be fine, babe," he said soothingly and risking getting his head bitten off again. "The doctors have done this a million times before."

"Yeah, well, I haven't!" she snorted. "God, I'm sorry. I'm just anxious that's all. The twins are, too. I can feel them."

She rubbed her enormous belly tentatively.

Both Nick and Anna changed into the ugly theatre gowns and hats. At least Nick got to wear pants and little booties with his outfit—Anna was naked under the paper thin robe.

He held Anna's hand as the doctor came in to explain the procedure, reminding them it was all routine, and that they were next on the list.

Anna gulped and squeezed Nick's hand with a vice-like grip.

"I'll be here the whole time. Don't worry, you're going to do fine."

The team of nurses came for her and she smiled bravely at Nick as he winked and followed her into the operating room.

"Hello again, Anna," said the midwife. "Hop up on here."

"I can't hop much—it's more like hauling a bag of dough. A really heavy bag."

The midwife smiled.

"Well, not for much longer. Hello, Nick."

He smiled, standing out of the way, but feeling his heartrate kick up.

"The operating table is tilted slightly sideways," said the midwife. "That's so the weight of your womb doesn't press on anything that sends blood to your lungs. Now, we'll just check that you're not anaemic…"

There were several last minute checks, and Anna's anxiety began to climb. She squeezed Nick's hand nervously.

"You're going to be fine," he said soothingly, love shining in his eyes. "We'll be meeting our girls soon."

"Ruby and Beth," she breathed.

"Yep, and they'll be beautiful, just like their mum."

Anna didn't feel very beautiful as she was given her epidural and a catheter was inserted into her bladder.

Then, while Nick looked the other way, she was cleaned with antiseptic and shaved.

Nick leaned down and murmured in her ear.

"I've always wanted to see you with a Brazilian."

She snorted and laughed.

"I don't think they've done that. Although, I'm not sure. I can't feel anything down there."

A cuff was placed on her arm to monitor her blood pressure, and electrodes were stuck on her chest to check her heartrate. Nick was glad they hadn't done that for him—his heart was racing, although looking at him, you'd never know it.

Finally, a screen was erected across Anna's chest so neither of them could see the operation.

"You can ask for this to be lowered as the babies are born," the midwife said reassuringly.

The anaesthetist nodded, and the surgeon peered over her glasses at Anna.

"I'm going to start now," she said clearly. "You'll hear some slurping sounds as the amniotic fluid is suctioned out, and you might feel some pressure and tugging on your belly when we bring out your babies."

Anna smiled bravely, not taking her eyes off Nick.

He squeezed her hand as the surgeon began.

He watched her eyes but he could see that the epidural was working and she was feeling no pain.

"I'm taking the lower baby first," the surgeon said quietly.

Nick kept his eyes on Anna. She blinked rapidly, her forehead creasing.

"You're doing great," he whispered. "You're doing great."

Nick thought he'd be anxious, but now it was finally happening, he was more excited than anything else. And besides there was oxygen in the room if he needed it.

Part of his mind was in the moment with Anna, almost feeling what she felt, but another part of him was trying to get his head around the idea that soon, very soon, he'd be a father, someone's dad. Two tiny babies—that was a massive responsibility. Two tiny beings to protect, to look after, to watch grow. He was excited for every minute of that.

Anna squeezed his hand tightly as if asking what he was thinking.

And then, miracle number one was born, and a tiny, purple baby with a squashed, screwed up face was wrapped in a blanket and placed into Nick's arms. He bent down and showed the little girl to Anna, and she reached up a trembling finger to the baby's silky cheek, almost afraid to touch her.

"Oh my God!" she cried, as tears trickled down her face. "Oh my God! Hello, Ruby," she whispered. "Oh, Nick! She's perfect! She has your eyes!"

Nick nodded, his chest crushed with the love for this small being.

"Hello, Ruby. Daddy's here. Welcome to my team."

Anna giggled, hearing Nick's baby-voice for the first time.

Ruby mewed like a cat as he cupped her tiny body against his chest. Then a smiling nurse wrapped the tiny baby in a special blanket as Anna whimpered.

"Where are you taking her?"

"She needs warmth now," said the midwife kindly, "and I need to do her Agpar score. C-section babies are always a little colder. She'll be fine. Don't worry."

Nick felt as though he'd be worried for the next 18 years—probably for the rest of his life.

Suddenly, a fast bleep of alarm sounded and all the medical staff started to hustle. Nick was pushed out of the way.

"What's wrong? What's happening?"

But his words were lost in a rush of jargon.

"Nick!"

Anna's voice was filled with fear. Nick squeezed her shoulder, giving her his strength.

"It'll be okay."

His words were soothing, but his throat was tightening with the same fear.

Something was wrong.

The monitors screamed until the surgeon yelled for them to be turned down as she frowned and scowled, and Anna felt a strange tugging sensation in her belly.

An oxygen mask was placed over her mouth, and she breathed deeply, but her frightened eyes were glued to Nick.

Nick felt his body start to panic, but he needed to hold it together for Anna.

What's happening? What's going on?

And the surgeon spoke, her voice relaxing.

"There she is!" she said. "Oh, my apologies, little one. It seems we have a boy."

"What?"

Nick and Anna spoke together, but the doctor hadn't lied. A tiny baby boy with a scrunched up face was place in Nick's arms.

"Oh!" Anna gasped.

Nick stared down at the child, thinking that he had Anna's nose and chin—and he definitely had a tiny, miniature penis.

A son. I have a daughter and a son. This is perfect. My babies are perfect. How did I get to be so lucky?

"I can't call you 'Beth', little man," he said, thinking of the names that he and Anna had picked out months ago. He smiled down at Anna. "What do you think about calling him Phoenix?"

She laughed and smiled and cried.

"I think that would be perfect!"

Little Phoenix was taken away for his own tests, but the midwife assured them that everything was fine.

Anna had the placenta removed and then got her stitches before she was cleaned up and taken to recovery. When she was finally allowed back to her room, she found Nick and Susie holding the babies, their twins.

Susie was as shocked as they'd been when she found that she had a granddaughter and a grandson when she'd been expecting two girls.

"You were right about the gender-neutral clothes," she smiled at her exhausted daughter. "You did good, honey."

Anna drifted off to sleep as Nick stared with wonder at the little humans he'd helped create.

His parents had planned to come but had been prevented by a bout of flu. They coughed and spluttered their happiness when he called them, and Trisha promised to visit soon.

Nick was mesmerized by the twin's little fingers and tiny toes, counting every perfect eyelash fanning round cheeks. Love, a tidal wave of love washed over him. It was terrifying but wonderful, too, but when tears trickled down his cheeks, Susie just smiled to herself.

Ruby and Phoenix—two little miracles born of the complicated lives and simple, easy love of Nick and Anna.

After everything they'd been through, after the long road they'd travelled, finally, he'd found peace. He felt blessed. And Captain of a new team.

THREE DAYS AFTER leaving hospital, Anna and Nick were at home with their new family. The doorbell rang for the fifth time that morning. Nick opened the front door and Anna heard a short conversation before he returned with an enormous bunch of colourful flowers, so vast that Nick was completely hidden behind them.

"My! That is a darn big bunch of flowers! Who are they from?"

Nick searched through the foliage and finally located a small card clipped to the outer packaging.

"It says, 'Congrats. Molly'."

Anna looked up at Nick, surprise and confusion on her face.

"Really? You think they're really from her."

Nick nodded. He'd omitted the fact that the card also said, 'To Nicky and Anne'.

"Yeah, they're from her. Molly doesn't do discreet."

Silence.

"I guess not." Anna hesitated, wondering how to frame her question. "Do you think it's over now? Her vendetta?"

Nick lifted one shoulder.

"Hard to say for sure, but yeah, I do."

Anna gave a small smile.

"They're nice flowers."

Nick pulled a face.

"Okay, they're ostentatious and kind of ugly, but it was a nice gesture."

Nick nodded.

"I feel kind of sorry for her," Anna went on. "I have everything she ever wanted: babies, a TV career, a writing career…" she smiled at Nick. "And I have you." She paused. "Okay, maybe not everything—I don't have her Double-Ds, although since Ruby and Phoenix have arrived my boobs are enormous even if they feel more like udders."

Nick winced.

"But yes, I have what she wants and she seems so … bitter."

Nick shook his head.

"Molly always wanted more: bigger house, better car, bigger tits, designer clothes. But it didn't make her happy, not really. Because she was competing with an idea that wasn't real."

"That's very philosophical of you. Very Zen."

"Ha, maybe. But even if we'd stayed together, she wouldn't be happy. She'd want Kim Kardashian's money and her arse, and I still think she'd be envious of everyone who had more than she did. You're right—she's not happy—but it's nothing to do with me. She's nothing to do with me, or you, or us: not anymore."

Anna smiled down at the sleeping twins and at the beautiful man whose love had helped her bring them into the world.

Yes, she had everything she wanted, and she knew how incredibly lucky that made her.

CHAPTER 34

AGAINST ALL THE ODDS, THE CUIRASSIERS had made it to the final. The team that was in danger of being relegated at the beginning of the season had dominated their last 13 games of the year, storming to tremendous victories.

They were in the top half of the league table, but their dominant performance had led to this moment.

Nick wiped sweat from his eyes as it trickled through his hair, matting it to his scalp, and his shirt was stuck to his chest. He squinted up at the relentless blue sky, the late May sun burning down on the back of his neck.

The fans were fully behind the Cuirassiers at last, and the old stadium was full to bursting point.

The fans were going wild, very vocal, singing the Carcassonne team song, the sound echoing around the stadium. The opposing fans duelled with them, yelling out their own song, the notes clashing together tunelessly.

Nick was in the moment, feeling the crowd, feeling the energy. As his last game, he wanted to show it all on the field. He'd had a great game up to this point and knew it was the best season the club had had in twenty years. His club, his team.

Seventy minutes into the game, both teams were running low on energy—now, it was about who wanted it most.

Commentator 1:
It's a been a rough, tough bruising encounter today between Carcassonne and Limoux. There's just ten minutes left to play and Carcassonne are really taking charge of this game. Captain Nick Renshaw and Winger Grégoire Dupont have been dominating figures, and have contributed to the impressive rise to success that Carcassonne are having this season—definitely a favourite to win today.

Commentator 2:
Yes, Louis. It seems incredible that this is the same team that was staring at relegation at the beginning of the season, with loss after loss. All credit to the Captain for pulling the team around. But let's get back to the action.

Commentator 1:
I couldn't agree more, Marcel. The ball goes wide to Laurent Le Clerc. He side-steps one, hands off another ... he breaks with just the Fullback to beat. Grégoire Dupont is supporting. Laurent dummys the ball and gets tackled by the Fullback. Ouf! Grégoire doesn't look too happy about it—Laurent missed a great opportunity to pass the ball. The opposing fans are cheering. As play goes on, they're both having words. What a game this is shaping up to be!

Nick raced over, stepping between Laurent and Grégoire, pushing them apart.

"Pack it in, you two! We still have the ball. Let's go!"

Nick tried to get his head back in the game, but having to keep one eye on these two idiots was wearing—they were always at each other throats. Usually, Laurent started it, and today was no exception. He should have passed the ball, everyone knew it.

Commentator 1

This is the last five minutes of the game—the teams are locked in at twelve-all! It could go either way. It's the last tackle. Limoux are on the attack. They hoist a huge kick out wide, and the Limoux players are chasing hard, but Renshaw out jumps them! He catches the ball clean and is on the ground. He breaks one tackle, hands-off Grimaldi. He looks tired. His legs are heavy. But look at that concentration in his face! He wants this! He's earned this! The crowd are on their feet! They're chanting his nickname, La Flèche, La Flèche! *The arrow!*

Commentator 2

Yes, he looks tired now, but he knows he has to keep going! He's going down the wing, it's a foot race between La Flèche *and the Limoux's Winger and Fullback. They look like they're going to catch him but former Captain and assistant coach Bernard Dubois is in support. He's open, he's calling to his teammate. Renshaw whips a long pass across to Bernard. He catches the pass, runs along to the sticks with one hand in the air! He dives! He scores!*

Commentator 1

The stadium has erupted! The fans are on their feet! Monsieur Le Referee is looking at his watch, he lifts his whistle! It's all over! Carcassonne win! Who would have predicted that just six months ago! What an achievement! What a story! One for the record books.

Nick laughed with relief, clapping and cheering as Bernard was lifted onto Russ and Grégoire's shoulders, carried around the stadium, the conquering hero.

As Nick stared upward at the streamers falling onto the field, the drums, the trumpets, the singing, the fans, he smiled. The French sure knew how to celebrate a championship winning team.

A group of fans invaded the pitch, hugging the players, crying and singing and cheering. It was utter, beautiful mayhem.

Bernard hugged Nick tightly, thanking him over and over for coming to France and helping him turn the team around. Nick hugged him back, understanding Bernard's mixed emotions as the two men celebrated their last ever game together, their last ever game as professional athletes, their last playing for this team or any team.

But this time, Nick wasn't sad. He was glad it was all over. His body was tired and he could feel the heavy weight of exhaustion in his legs. His shoulder ached and his Achilles tendon had never been the same. His body wasn't as fast, his explosive pace was more limited. He'd never feared injury when he was younger. But despite all of this, his heart was light and he saw a new and different future before him—a father and a husband, his new team.

It had been a magical season and he was proud of what he'd achieved. But for him, the magic had gone, the passion wasn't burning inside him anymore. It was a strange feeling.

The players started throwing their shirts into the crowd, a tradition at Carcassonne for the last home-game of the season.

Nick gave his shirt to a youngster who attended every game, week in, week out, rain or shine, a future Carcassonne player in the making for sure.

"*Je vous remercie!*" said the kid, overawed that the English Captain had given him the prized shirt.

"No worries, little man," said Nick.

Nick glanced over and saw Grégoire giving his shirt to Brendan. Then he bent over and whipped off his shorts, too, handing them over to his red-faced boyfriend who seemed lost for words.

Nick paused, and looked again. He'd never known Brendan not to have a sassy comeback, but his smile lit up the Stand.

Just then, Grégoire dropped to one knee.

"No way!" Nick whispered to himself, watching the action across the field.

But yes, Grégoire was asking Brendan to marry him right there on the side of the field.

The crowd and Grégoire's teammates were watching with excitement. Brendan covered his mouth with his hand, and paused as if he was in shock.

Then Nick saw him throw both hands up in the air and let out a huge shriek.

"Yes! YES! YES! Yes, I'll marry you!"

Brendan jumped over the low barrier, making his own private pitch invasion and threw himself at Grégoire as they both kissed. The crowd yelled and Nick cheered himself hoarse, happy for them both.

Damn! What a way to end a final—definitely one for the record books.

Nick jogged over to congratulate both of them.

"Alright, put him down, Grég," he laughed. "Congratulations, guys. Bren, you'd better go and call Anna because she's already mad at missing today, and when she finds out that Grég proposed, too…"

"Oh my God! Where's my phone? I need to call my little Anna-banana! I need to talk wedding suits to someone who'll understand."

Brendan laid another smacker on his fiancé, then jumped back over the barrier before the security lost their patience.

Then he turned and yelled at Grégoire.

"Future husband? What about those lucky Speedos?"

Grégoire laughed and smiled as he yelled back.

"I'll give you these later if you play your cards right!"

Brendan held his hands over his chest in the shape of a heart and mouthed silently, I love you.

THAT EVENING, NICK celebrated the win with his teammates, but he knew that for him the game was truly over. He wasn't injured, he was still fit, but he knew the sport had lost its spark for him, even with the success they'd had as a club, the great fans, living in a beautiful country. He was the Captain and he'd been playing great all season. There was nothing wrong, but it didn't feel right, not without Anna.

Nick sighed as he looked around at his celebrating teammates. It wasn't where he wanted to be. He wanted to be at home with Anna and the babies. He wanted to smell their amazing milky baby-smell; he wanted to watch as she fed them, held them, changed them, watched them sleep.

He knew that he'd been searching for something this sport couldn't give him anymore, but at least now he knew what it was that he'd been trying to find: peace, a purpose. In one way, he was captain of a new team: Anna, Ruby and Phoenix. Huh, maybe vice-captain—Anna was the one in charge.

He hadn't spoken to any of his teammates except Bernard. Nick knew that his friend didn't really understand. Bernard had chosen to continue his career in rugby even after he would no longer run onto the field as a player. And from the outside everything in Nick's life looked great: Captain of a successful French side, winners. And all in his first season—from a rugby perspective it couldn't have gone any better.

But inside, he knew that he'd lost his passion for the sport he'd loved for so long.

But that was okay.

Because he knew where he was supposed to be.

The whole of Carcassonne had gone crazy. There was a full weekend celebrating, an amazing festival with music in the main square, and a topless bus took the team around the town with the trophy on display.

The Mayor congratulated the team, presenting Nick with a plaque that said:

Nick Renshaw
La Flèche
Son of Carcassonne

And the dates of his victory.

It was a great end to Nick's career.

But the part he was looking forward to the most?

Going back to London to be with Anna and the twins.

CHAPTER 35

Fourteen months later…

THE SCORCHING JULY SUN SOAKED INTO them as Brendan, Susie Scott, Nick, Anna, and their extended family arrived at the small airport.

Anna and her mother were each carrying a twin, for now sleeping soundly, exhausted by a day of travelling. Brendan and Nick pulled their luggage off the carousel at baggage reclaim, with Brendan high on pure relief that his suitcase was there and that his wedding outfit hadn't been lost.

Nick listened to the description of Brendan's suit, shirt, thread count, cut and tailoring with a small smile on his face as they piled their luggage onto an airport trolley, then finally found where their rental car waited for them, an eight-seater minibus, child seats included.

"Oh God, I love weddings," Brendan chattered. "I'm just not sure I'll enjoy this one. I mean I will, obviously, and the Best Man's speech will be awesome," and he shot a bright look at Nick. "I just want to get to the part where I start enjoying it."

Nick and Anna exchanged an amused look. After fifteen months of guarding the twins and watching them grow into healthy, chubby babies, they'd finally begun to relax into parenthood. The home routine was run like clockwork—although perhaps a little less so when Nick was left in charge—and Anna's mother had been an enormous help, moving in for the first, difficult weeks, then staying to enjoy her grandchildren.

Nick's parents made the journey from Yorkshire at least once a month, and Trish sometimes came with them, as often as she could be pried away from her new boyfriend, a single father who'd accidentally rammed into her with his shopping cart at the supermarket.

Nick had enjoyed his final weeks of playing rugby for the Cuirassiers, even more so when they won the Championship Cup beating every other team across the whole of France in their league.

But Nick had been very ready to be a fulltime dad back in London, and occasionally a part-time model. Offers were still coming in, but he was far more choosy about which projects he said yes to, only working with photographers that he liked and admired—and didn't take him from home for too long.

He'd also published his behind-the-scenes portfolio on his new website to a positive response, and was considering how he might take that interest further.

Besides, being a father was wonderful, better than he'd ever dreamed, but also tougher and more exhausting. He and Anna were both very ready for a holiday.

The Greek island of Santorini basked in the afternoon sun, the air vibrating with heat. The landscape was rugged, with jagged, towering cliffs, and small villages clinging to the steep mountainsides, the whitewashed square houses glittering like sugar cubes.

The beaches were stark and beautiful, made from black sand, the remains of an ancient volcanic event thousands of years earlier, with the deepest blue Aegean sea sparkling all around them.

Nick felt a deep sense of peace as he drove slowly across the beautiful island, even Brendan's incessant nervous chatter was soothing, and he smiled as Anna's laughter pealed out.

The twins were already seasoned travellers with trips to the south of France, Yorkshire, and twice to New York. Although he'd learned early that every extra pair of hands was a huge help.

He'd also learned that they could both be soothed when he played them his guitar, especially Ruby, the feistier of the two twins. It became a standing joke the amount of luggage they seemed to take everywhere.

Nick pointed the car north, driving past sun-blasted fields, formal rows of vines, stunted in size but abundant in grapes, steadily climbing higher, until he reached the elegant white façade of the *Hotel Grace*, perched overlooking the ancient volcanic basin, the caldera.

Brendan was out of the car in a second, bouncing with excitement.

"Oh my God! It's even better than in the brochure! I can't wait! I wonder if Grég is here yet. Has anyone seen him?"

But the first person they saw was Bernard, strolling toward them in shorts, loose shirt and flip flops.

"*Mes amis!* It's good to see you. I have missed these little rascals!"

And he scooped Ruby into a hug, making her squirm and cry with indignation.

"Back to your mama," he said, hastily handing her to Anna.

"Where is everyone?" Brendan asked.

"By 'everyone' he means Grég," Anna said drily.

"Ah, the boys took him into the town to celebrate," Bernard smiled. "I offered to wait here for you. Besides," he said, "I prefer the solitude."

"Didn't Madeleine come with you?" Anna asked, referring to Bernard's infrequently seen wife.

"She's in the spa," he said with a wave of his hand.

"And Rémy?"

Bernard sighed.

"He is with his grandmother in Sèvres."

Nick didn't comment. He knew that Bernard's marriage was rocky and that if he wanted to see his son, he had to travel to Paris. Madeleine had originally followed Bernard to London when he went to play for the Finchley Phoenixes, living there for three years until she became pregnant and insisted on moving back to Paris. She refused to uproot her life again to live in Carcassonne. She'd visited once in all the time that Nick had been with the Cuirassiers.

Nick thanked his lucky stars that Anna was different.

Carefully, he unhooked his sleeping son from the minivan's childseat and placed a kiss on his damp forehead. Out of the two of them, Phoenix was the quiet twin. His sister was always awake first, first to cry with hunger, first to grow bored, first to need attention. Phoenix would sit with a smile on his face and dribble on his chin, happily playing with his bare toes, as if they were a great mystery.

Feeling the intense heat on the back of his neck, Nick grabbed a tiny, white sunhat and pulled it over Phoenix's head, watching the small frown smooth out again, his sleep uninterrupted.

A porter stepped forward with a luggage cart, and loaded up all their bags as they checked in.

The hotel was full of rugby players, their families or significant others, including Russell and his very glamorous girlfriend Natascha;

most of the Cuirassiers; Grég's parents, brother and sister-in-law; and Inoke who was flying solo. Even Jason Oduba had flown out for the ceremony, bringing his new fiancée with him. He and Brendan had bonded at the hospital when Anna had first been taken ill.

All of the hotel's twenty-one rooms were full of wedding guests, including a beautiful villa that stood a little away from the main hotel. Brendan and Grégoire had splashed out and taken that for themselves.

"The Honeymoon Suite?" Anna commented, as they were shown to their rooms.

Nick grinned at her.

"Pretty nice, hey?"

Stunning was a better word. The wide balcony gave them a view down the steep mountainside to the deepest blue sea beyond. The white curtains fluttered in the breeze, making the heat bearable.

"Oh my God! Look! We have a little plunge pool!" Anna sighed. "That's it. I'm moving from London with the twins."

"What about me?" Nick laughed.

"You can come if you promise to change all the diapers."

"I thought I did that anyway," he muttered into his beard.

Anna pretended not to hear.

Then they heard a small commotion outside as a bus full of half-drunk rugby players pulled up in the hotel's courtyard entrance.

"I think the boys are back," Anna remarked. "You want to go say hi? I'm going to nap with the babies."

Nick looked torn, and Anna smiled at him.

"We'll be here when you get back. Say hi to Grég for me—and keep an eye on Brendan."

Nick smiled, kissed her on the cheek, then placed a gentle kiss on each of the twins before heading out.

Two minutes later, just as Anna was drifting to sleep, drugged and drowsy with heat, there was a soft tap on the door, and her mom stuck her head inside.

"You can go with Nick if you like. I'm always happy to watch these little ones. They do the cutest things."

"Thanks, Mom, but I'm fine to lay here and do nothing. Want to join me doing nothing?"

"There's nothing I'd like better than doing nothing with you."

The two women stretched out on the balcony's sunbeds, shaded by a wide umbrella, glasses of water sweating on a small table.

Anna closed her eyes again, a small smile on her lips.

"Happy, honey?" her mom asked.

Anna's smile deepened.

"Yes. Completely."

"Nick seems happy, too. Calmer. He's a good father."

Anna opened her eyes and beamed at her mother.

"Yes, he is. He's much more laidback than me. I'll probably be the one who has to say 'don't eat dirt', and 'no dating until you're twenty', that sort of thing."

Her mother laughed.

"Yes, probably." She paused. "You're good together. You make a great team. I'm happy for you."

Anna smiled.

"That reminds me of something I said to Nick once: we're stronger together. I know life isn't always straightforward, but being apart didn't work for us." Then she looked at her mother. "What about you? Are you happy?"

Her mother's smile faded a little.

"I'm content, yes. Seeing you and Nick together is wonderful, and spending time with these precious ones…"

"But you miss Dad."

Anna finished the sentence for her.

"I always will, honey. But that's the sign of a great love. We had 35 wonderful years together. I don't regret a single day of them." She sighed. "But I wish he could have met Ruby and Phoenix."

Anna squeezed her hand.

"I know, Mom. I know."

THAT NIGHT, THE whole wedding party dined together, then lazed around the stunning infinity pool, watching the sun sink into the Aegean, the waters turning a darker blue and finally black, as lights twinkled in the villages below.

Grég was tossed in the pool fully dressed by Nick and Bernard, ignoring Brendan's scandalized shriek about the designer linen pants he was wearing, then most of the guys jumped in, too, and Anna sat with her feet dangling in the water, smiling at their antics.

As evening turned to night, the guests drifted away in ones and twos, until only a few of the hard-core drinkers were left behind.

Susie had retired to her room and the twins were sleeping soundly in their cots, so Nick and Anna took advantage of the rare reign of peace and made love in silence, the sounds of muffled laughter from outside floating upward in the warm air.

CHAPTER

36

Anna felt Nick's warm lips on her bare neck.

"You look beautiful."

Her cheeks turned pink. A compliment from her man could still make her blush.

She touched her hair self-consciously. The hairdresser organised by Brendan had arrived early, and had effortlessly sculpted Anna's shoulder-length hair into an elegant chignon, a set of tiny, white flowers woven into the design.

Her dress was knee-length, a foamy sea-green cluster of tulle floating around her legs, and a sweetheart neckline of lace.

Her bouquet was resting on a damp cloth in the bathroom.

She lifted her eyes to Nick, the breath catching in her throat as she took in the easy elegance of his navy three-piece suit, crisp white shirt and dark neck tie.

His shoes were polished to a high gloss and his long hair was tied back, showing his sharp cheekbones and beautiful smile.

"You look very spiffy, Mr. Renshaw!" Anna said. "You could be a model."

Nick winked at her.

"We are a spiffy couple, Dr. Scott. Ready to go to a wedding?"

A loud wail interrupted them.

"Oops, Ruby sounds annoyed. I'd better go rescue Mom."

Anna hurried to the adjoining room where a slightly frazzled Susie was trying to convince Ruby to wear her little ballet slippers that matched the adorable white dress with the lacy hem.

Phoenix was wearing navy blue shorts with a white short-sleeved shirt and bow tie. He was staring with puzzlement at the little blue shoes on his feet.

Ruby was still yelling her head off so Anna picked her up to calm her.

"Mom, let her go barefoot. She hates wearing shoes when she's hot."

"Barefoot, really?"

"Trust me, it's better than her screaming all through the ceremony."

"Well, if you think so…"

"Can you pop them in your purse in case she changes her mind?"

Anna's mother smiled.

"It's a good thing my purse is the size of Texas! You were never this much trouble!"

Anna shrugged and gave her mother a grin.

"Mom, she got your clotheshorse gene—you only have yourself to blame. You sure you'll be okay twin-wrangling?"

"Of course, but if it gets too much for them, I'll take them to the pool for a swim instead."

With everyone organised, Anna retrieved her bouquet of tiny

red roses and white gypsophilia, and headed to the villa where the wedding ceremony was taking place: Brendan's wedding to Grégoire—the unexpected but much anticipated match between the English drama queen and the French athlete, a man of exotic good looks and few words.

Anna was happy for them. One day she and Nick would get married, but today was not the day.

Muscular and dapper rugby hunks in designer suits lined the chairs, protected from the fierce sun by a gauzy canopy, decorated with small sprigs of local wildflowers.

Nick and Anna waved at Grég's family, whom they'd met the night before, and scanned the rows of familiar faces, friends and teammates. But two chairs at the front were empty, and Anna's heart sank. She looked at Nick and he shook his head sadly.

They left Susie with the twins, and went inside the villa to find Brendan.

As soon as he saw them, he raced forwards, biting his lip.

He looked slender and handsome, dressed in a close-fitting reddish-maroon suit, with white shirt and white silk tie, a tiny corsage of miniature red roses pinned to his lapel.

"Annie, did they come?"

The half-hopeful look on Brendan's face was enough to break Anna's heart.

She exchanged a look with Nick, whose stern expression said so much.

"No, honey," she said gently. "They didn't."

At that moment, Anna hated Brendan's parents. He'd given them so many chances, offered countless olive branches, but his mother had never once stood up to her overbearing husband, or stood up for Brendan. Their neglected son had bought them two first class tickets to Santorini, and had reserved a luxurious room at the boutique hotel, but the empty seats outside were a testament to their callousness.

They hadn't come to his wedding. They hadn't even sent a message.

Brendan's hopeful expression crumbled and his lips quivered.

Anna reached out and held his hands tightly.

"Don't, Bren. This is *your* day—yours and Grégoire's. Don't let your parents spoil this, too."

He nodded and tried to force a smile.

"I know. I'm being an idiot. I just thought … I thought, hell, a free holiday. I thought they'd come for that … or maybe sit at the back and heckle."

He tried to laugh.

"Bren…"

"I'm fine, Annie. Honestly. I didn't really expect them to come," and he swiped at the tell-tale moisture under his eyes. "I just … I really, really hoped. But I'm stupid like that." His voice dropped. "They'll never accept me, will they? I'm just the queer son that they're ashamed of and…"

"Bren, stop," Anna said firmly. "I mean it. Now listen to me. You are loved by so many people. Honey, don't you get it? You *do* have family that love you and they're all here today. My mom has all but adopted you and Grég—you're the sons she never had: family."

Brendan blinked furiously, but Anna was on a roll.

"Do you think for one moment that Nick and I would entrust our precious babies to just anyone? There's a reason that you're they're godfather. We know that if anything happened to us," and she swallowed, "that you'd take care of them. That's how much you mean to us, Bren." She cupped Brendan's cheek with her hand. "And Grég loves you, he adores you and would do anything to make you happy. You guys have found a very precious love. Bren, honey, you are surrounded by love." Anna dabbed at her own tears. "We love you very, very much. You are wonderful and amazing, Brendan Massey. You are a very special man. I'm so happy I met you."

Brendan accepted her warm hug, laying his head on her shoulder.

"Baby-mama, stop!" he teased, sounding husky and still tearful.

"Don't call me that."

"Not even on my wedding day?"

"Especially not today."

Brendan stood up straight, pasting on a smile.

"You're right. I know I'm very lucky. I have you guys and I have Grég. I'm blessed and…"

Nick interrupted, stepping forward, laying his hand on Brendan's shoulder.

"Grég's the lucky one—lucky he found you. I saw what he was like before you guys met: he was a loner, trying to fit in with the team but not sure how they'd react when they found out he was gay. But since he's been with you, he's come out of his shell and I've seen him improve as a player with every game. You've given him the confidence to be who he is."

Brendan's eyes were wide.

"You … you really think so?"

"I know so," and Nick turned his intense gaze on Anna. "And when you find someone who does that for you, you never let them go."

Anna squeezed his hand as Nick continued.

"You're my friend, Bren, my brother; you're family, like Anna said." Then he grinned. "But don't make me say it all now—I'm saving the good stuff for the Best Man's Speech."

Then he pulled Brendan into a hug and whispered something that Anna couldn't catch.

"Oh my God, don't make me cry *before* the service," Brendan moaned. "Even waterproof mascara isn't fool-proof."

Nick laughed and thumped him on the back.

"Come on then, buddy. Time to go and find your groom."

As they left the room, the melodious vocals of French crooner Charles Trénet began to sing about '*le chanson d'amour*', a song of love.

"I know it's a bit naff," Brendan hissed out of the side of his mouth to Anna, "but it's Grég's mum's favourite song. And he said he'd give me a blowjob tonight if I played it. I've chosen something much cooler to play us out at the end."

Anna got a fit of the giggles and struggled to compose herself, Nick just shook his head in amusement.

They walked up the aisle of chairs, all three of them hand in hand. Ahead stood Grégoire, tall and proud, a huge smile on his face when he saw Brendan. His suit was cream with a pale blue shirt and white neck tie. Nick and Anna could well have been invisible—his eyes were for Brendan only.

When they reached the officiant, Anna kissed Brendan on the cheek and took the empty seat reserved for her; Nick shook hands with Brendan and Grégoire, then stood to one side.

The three men were magnificent together, tall and handsome: Brendan in his reddish-maroon suit, Grégoire in cream and Nick in blue—the colours representing both the French flag, *La Tricolore*, and the flag of the United Kingdom.

The officiant spoke heavily-accented English in a deep, sonorous voice, talking of love and commitment, responsibility and obligation, kindness and compassion.

When he called for the rings, Nick pulled them out of his pocket and laid them on a velvet cushion. Then he sat down next to Anna and held her hand.

At the end of the service, Anna smiled as Adam Lambert's *Time For Miracles* played out the happy couple.

It was a good day, and Anna hoped with all her heart that Brendan was happy and not thinking about his absent parents.

The dinner was magnificent and champagne flowed freely.

"You alright, luv?" Nick asked at the end of the meal as he took in her distant expression.

"Yes, just thinking, you know? I'm going to miss him so much."

Nick put his arm around her.

"I know, but you'll see him every couple of weeks."

Brendan was going to live in Carcassonne with Grégoire in the same house that Nick and Anna had rented. He'd promised that he'd keep working for her, but Anna was realistic—there'd come a time when he wouldn't want to leave his husband every two weeks to travel to London. God, she understood what that was like, but it would be very hard to give up her best friend, even to a man as wonderful as Grég.

She smiled a little sadly.

"Everything has changed so much in the last couple of years. It's hard to believe it sometimes."

Nick nodded.

"I know. It's been crazy at times. But I think we've found a balance, don't you?"

Anna agreed, resting her head on his shoulder.

"Don't get too comfy," he said. "I've got to go and give my Best Man's speech yet."

She laughed lightly as she sat up straight, and Nick tapped a spoon against his wine glass to get everyone's attention.

He stood up, drawing every eye to him, and gave a broad smile.

"It's that time, ladies and gentlemen: the speeches!"

A ragged cheer went up that showed more than a few of the guests had been enjoying the champagne.

"Before I start, I would just like to say how handsome Brendan and Grégoire look today…"

Cheers rang out again in agreement, as well as some more ribald comments. Grégoire and Brendan smiled at each other, then looked over at Nick who was conferring with a member of the hotel's staff. Behind him, a projector screen was being rolled down.

"Perfect timing," he said, as the staff member handed him a remote control. "But … neither of these two handsome devils started out that way…"

Brendan looked horrified, but Grégoire just laughed.

Nick had done his research and put together a montage of school and childhood pictures. Grégoire's parents had cooperated in sending Nick dozens of photos to choose from, showing a skinny boy with freckles, gaps in his teeth, followed by teenage pictures showing braces, bad haircuts, and the time he'd dyed his dark hair blonde, and wore spray-on jeans bleached white.

Grégoire laughed and cringed, and called out to his parents and traitorous brother.

There were fewer pictures of Brendan because his parents hadn't replied to Anna's requests for photographs. Despite her repeated attempts, all her messages and calls had been ignored.

She'd still managed to find some images by having access to the private part of his Facebook pages and stealing his phone when he wasn't looking. She'd even emailed his old schools, explaining the problem, and had been sent two pictures of a cheeky six year old with huge NHS spectacles, and then a picture of a cool teenager going through an emo phase.

Brendan looked scandalized and pointed an accusing finger at Anna.

"That's it! I'm telling Nick about your secret stash of chocolate. Bottom left drawer of her desk!"

Anna laughed but realized she needed to find a new hiding place as Nick raised an eyebrow.

"Well," said Nick, "let's just say Grég and Bren, you aren't looking the best there, buddies!"

He flipped the screen, showing more funny photos one after another. Brendan had his head in his hands, covering his face with embarrassment as he peeked through his fingers. Grégoire was laughing and couldn't seem to believe that Nick had dug out so many dodgy pictures: he was clapping, laughing and teasing Brendan, encouraging him to relax and enjoy it. The crowd loved it.

"I'm sorry, Bren," Nick called. "I'm only playing! I love you, you know that."

Then he flipped to a new set of photographs showing pictures of the night Brendan and Grégoire had first met.

"These are the handsome devils we know today," and he flipped through dozens of photographs that silently documented their best moments, the beginning of their love affair.

Brendan smiled and squeezed Grégoire's hand as they both looked at the screen and the memories came flooding back.

Nick spoke again, his expression more serious.

"I'm so happy you both found each other. Life, love, they have a funny way of guiding two souls together," and he glanced over and winked at Anna, smiling as she blew him a kiss. "Life is truly what you make it, guys, the memories, the moments, the good times, the bad times—treasure it all."

There were murmurs of agreement.

"Bren, I'm very proud of you. You've always gone above and beyond for Anna, as well as me and the kids. There's a reason that we picked you to be their Godfather—and it's not just because we know you'll buy them awesome presents on their birthdays…"

Brendan laughed as he wiped his eyes, and Grégoire put his arm around his new husband's shoulders.

"Life hasn't always been easy for you, but you've never let anything hold you back. You're such a fun-loving guy to be around, selfless and loyal, too. I love you like a brother and you deserve all the happiness in the world. I'm proud that you chose me to be your Best Man today."

He exchanged a look with Brendan, something important passing between the two men—a look that spoke of love and trust and lifelong friendship.

Nick cleared his throat as the emotion of the day affected him.

"Can we all raise a glass!"

All the guests lifted their champagne glasses as Nick led the toast.

"To Bren and Grég! Be yourselves, be amazing. Long life, health and happiness! Cheers!"

EPILOGUE

Anna

WHAT MORE CAN I say about Nick?
He's had two amazing careers where he's climbed to the top of his profession—rugby and now modelling.

It took him a little while to understand where he fit into the domain of top models, the possibilities and the limitations. It was a strange new world, but found his way in the end, because he's strong, so strong.

And now he's become interested in photography, I wouldn't be surprised if he makes a success of that, too.

My model boyfriend! Just thinking about it makes me smile. I found it so intimidating at first, the way he was surrounded by beautiful young women all day long, but he was never interested in them, he never made me doubt him. Not ever. It was myself that I doubted. I had to have a long hard look at myself—my inside self—and try to find out why I felt such fear and doubt. It wasn't much fun analysing myself like that, but I think I'm stronger for it, too.

He still gets hit on all the time—by men and women—but that's not his fault, and now it makes me smile.

Nick, my own personal male model. He doesn't always get it right and he's far from perfect, like me, but he's mine and I love him with everything in me, body and soul, head and heart.

I love his kindness, his caring, his incredible energy and drive. I love seeing him explode into action, his enthusiasm pushing past every hurdle. I love his quiet moments, seeing the introspection, the depth of his thoughts, the vulnerability, and the resolution that comes from knowing himself. I love the way he plays with our babies, takes care of them, and teaches them.

And as the years roll by, we'll watch our children grow, and each laughter line, each wrinkle and each grey hair will be part of the story of us, and I will welcome every one of them.

I let him go because I loved him. I wanted him to live the biggest life he could. I wanted him to feel the possibilities as he soared to new heights, but he always had a home to come back to. I left the door wide open, letting him know he is loved. He is loved.

And he came home.

My beautiful man.

My lover.

My Nick.

THE END

NOTE FROM THE AUTHORS

In the story, Nick suffers from an addiction to tramadol, a painkiller commonly supplied after surgery or for chronic pain. Although aspects of *Model Boyfriend* are based on Stuart's life, he has a very strong anti-drug stance, and has never been addicted to painkillers.

It's a serious problem affecting many athletes as they try to recover from injury, and we felt it was important to include this in the story.

On a happier note, we gave Brendan and Grégoire their dream wedding on the beautiful Greek island of Santorini, with all their friends and family (well, most of them).

But in real life, same-sex marriages aren't legal in Greece. We hope that one day they will be.

Jane & Stu <3

REVIEWS

We really hope that you enjoyed Nick and Anna's story, Brendan and Grégoire's, too.

Reviews are lovely and important to us because they help other people to make an informed decision before buying this book.

So we'd really appreciate if you took a few seconds to do just that by clicking this link on Amazon.

Thank you!

Jane & Stu

If you would like to read more of our writing and our forthcoming collaboration set in New York *Gym Vs Chocolate*, please sign up to our newsletters.

ACKNOWLEDGEMENTS

To Kirsten Olsen, our wonderful editor, advisor, friend, sounding board, all around Super Woman, who also became a femme fatale in the story, trying to seduce Nick. All the best jobs ;)

To Golden Czermak for graciously agreeing to a cameo role in this book, and for sharing some insider info ;)

To Lisa Ashmore for legal advice on Nick's court cases

To Elisa Wang for letting us shamelessly use her name—and create her alter ego Ning Yu! Also Denise Catalano, Shonda Riffe Smith and Natascha Luchetti—yes, you're in there, ladies!

To Michelle Abascal-Monroy who generously organised our blog tour

To Tonya Allen, beta reader and travel buddy.

To the Reardonites and Jane's Travelers for their love and loyalty

To Sheena Lumsden for behind the scenes support

To all the bloggers who give up their time for their passion of reading and reviewing books—thank you for your support

To our readers—you have great taste ;) You rock!

MORE ABOUT STUART

Stuart is a retired England International Rugby League player who's career spanned 16 years as a professional playing for several top League clubs, including in France. He has had several major injuries that nearly ended his career just as in *Undefeated*, the amazing collaboration with Jane, where we first meet Nick and Anna.

Currently he is a Personal Trainer living in Cheshire, and has an online fitness program: *Fear Nothing Fitness*.

Contact Stuart at:
Instagram_
Facebook
Twitter
Pinterest
YouTube
Tumblr
Website
Goodreads

Sign up for Stuart's newsletter here -->_https://goo.gl/rBzpF1

MORE ABOUT JHB

I enjoy watching surfers at my local beach, and weaving stories of romance in the modern world, with all its trials and tribulations.

It's been the best fun working with Stu on this story. More than fun, fascinating and enlightening, too.

And I really love to hear from readers, so all my contacts are below. Please do drop me a line.

Instagram
Facebook
Twitter
Pinterest
Website
Goodreads
YouTube

Sign up for Jane's newsletter here --> http://eepurl.com/-B3zn
Join my facebook reader group, Jane's Travelers

MORE BOOKS

Stuart Reardon & Jane Harvey-Berrick
An ordinary man ... an extraordinary life
Undefeated (Undefeated series #1)
Model Boyfriend (Undefeated series #2)
Touch My Soul (Novella)
Gym Vs Chocolate (coming soon)

Jane Harvey-Berrick
Series Titles

The Traveling Series
All the fun of the fair ... and two worlds collide
The Traveling Man (Traveling series #1)
The Traveling Woman (Traveling series #2)
Roustabout (Traveling series #3)
Carnival (Traveling series #4)
The Traveling Series Box Set (Traveling series #1-4)

The Education Series
An epic love story spanning the years, through war zones and more...
The Education of Sebastian (Education series #1)
The Education of Caroline (Education series #2)
The Education of Sebastian & Caroline (combined edition, books 1 & 2)
Semper Fi: The Education of Caroline (Education series #3)

The Rhythm Series
Blood, sweat, tears and dance
Slave to the Rhythm (Rhythm series #1)
Luka (Rhythm series #2)

The EOD Series
Blood, bombs and heartbreak
Tick Tock (EOD series #1 – coming soon)
Bombshell (EOD series #2 – coming soon)

Printed in the USA
CPSIA information can be obtained
at www.ICGtesting.com
LVHW010006170924
791271LV00024B/156